Planet Lara

TEMPEST

ELIZA GORDON

S·G·A
BOOKS

e Number Two—Lara must contend with the reappearance of
Ramirez, a fugitive Clarke Innovations has been shielding all
years. Jacinta unveils disturbing secrets that reshape the history
s been fed about her late mother's past—and how much that past
atens to derail their cumulative future.

When overwhelming stress sends Lara to the bottom of the whisky
:tle, Finan gently reminds her that slipping into old habits won't fix
hat's broken. As she tries to pull herself together, a tragedy strikes
nat brings her and Finan close again, but with a series of cryptic clues
arriving on the island, the mystery of Dea Vitae, and its sought-after
treasure, deepens, with menacing consequences.

Lara and Finan must work with investigators, and a few unsavory
players, to dismantle the sinister machinations of Dea Vitae before it
destroys their blossoming romance—and the sanctity of Thalia Island
herself.

The Welcome to Planet Lara series is written like an episodic
drama. Books One and Two end in **CLIFF-HANGERS** (with
storylines resolved in Book Three).

Please note that *Planet Lara: Tempest* includes medical scenes
involving reproductive complications that some readers might
find triggering.

∾

**Coming soon to audio from
Dreamscape Media!**

PLANET

will ta
Jacint
these
Lara
thre

b
w

PLANET LARA: TEMPEST

BOOK TWO IN THE WELCOME TO PLANET SERIES

ALTHOUGH the Dea Vitae cult has been evicted from Thalia Island, Lara Clarke and her grandfather's eco-utopia are still in peril. Rupert's ongoing lymphoma treatment in Vancouver deposits Lara at Thalia's helm—with no idea how to navigate the rough waters. And though Finan is back from the mainland after two tense weeks of silence, the sting of his unscheduled departure lingers.

Beyond the grind of running her own "planet"—while privately grieving the loss of her beloved grandfather and worrying if the cancer

ADVANCE PRAISE FOR
Planet Lara
TEMPEST

"I loved it. This is the best of the Eliza books. And that's saying a lot."

JEANINE LIPP, AUTHOR

"*Planet Lara* is the **MUST-READ** series of 2021. Taking the best of women's fiction and romantic suspense to create something wholly unique: **Enviromance.** Shove whatever book you're currently reading back onto your to-be-read pile and pick this up **NOW**!"

KATIE READS, BOOK BLOGGER

"A brilliant, fast-paced, and witty sequel to *Welcome to Planet Lara* ... *Tempest* is a sequel that endures the hype of the first and leaves you on a heart-racing cliff-hanger that will have you craving the final novel."

KATRIN B.

"*Tempest* gripped my heart and didn't let go ... Full of amazingly developed characters and plots, you'll be left wanting more ... Eliza is writing a story that's well thought-out and full of just enough swoon and suspense to still be believable. Five stars!"

DEB H.

"Extinction is the rule. Survival is the exception."

CARL SAGAN

"There are some things you learn best in calm, and some in storm."

WILLA CATHER

"On my world, it means hope."

KAL EL, SUPERMAN

First edition August 2021

Cover design by Bailey Designs Books

Ebook ISBN-13: 978-1-989908-05-1
Paperback ISBN-13: 978-1-989908-06-8

www.sgabooks.com
www.elizagordon.com | www.jennsommersby.com

ALSO BY ELIZA GORDON

Planet Lara Series:

Welcome to Planet Lara (Book One)

The Revelation Cove Series:

Must Love Otters (Book One)

Hollie Porter Builds a Raft (Book Two)

Love Just Clicks (Standalone, Book Three)

Standalone novels:

Dear Dwayne, With Love

I Love You, Luke Piewalker

TO MY DEAR READERS ...

First: This book ends on a **huge** cliff-hanger.

I know! I'm a jerk! I'm *sorry*. I love them. I can't HELP IT. My books play out like movies or serial dramas in my head. And I have to stitch together all the plot threads, though not in a single book. If I were to do that, the book would be 300,000+ words, and that's just silly for a romance/suspense/mystery/whatever the hell these books are.

Just pretend you're watching your favorite show on Netflix and having to wait for the next season to pop up, only you won't have to wait, like, a YEAR, because Book Three is headed your way in December 2021. It's like waiting for season two of *The Witcher*—how much longer must I be patient before My Darling Henry graces my screen again in those leather pants? Surely, he needs another bath by now. I volunteer as tribute!

Second: *Planet Lara: Tempest* includes medical scenes involving reproductive complications that some readers might find triggering.

I'm not a huge fan of trigger warnings because it's basically like giving away the plot, but I also don't want my darling readers to be blindsided and thus hurt when they get to this part. Hang in there. I've got you.

xo,
  Eliza

ONE

THE VISITOR

Jacinta Ramirez—my dead mother's friend, the woman in the photo wrapped around Cordelia in the open door of her plane— sets the weighty rock with the smudged black letters warning of trouble on the beach on the breakfast bar. I've moved around to the other side to put the counter, and Finan's weird present, between us. But then Jacinta raises both arms and I realize the knife I've just slid from its spot in the butcher block is a little overkill.

"What happened to your hand?" I ask. Her right arm stops at the wrist, at the joint, the skin tucked over the blunt end.

She smiles. "Every choice comes with a cost. Can we dispense with the theatrics?" She nods at my raised weapon.

"You're not going to hurt me?"

Jacinta rests her forearms on the bar and pulls her long, black ponytail over her shoulder, an eyebrow lifted.

She *was* just sitting in the chair, waiting. She *did* turn on a light rather than shove a lethal weapon between my ribs.

"Fine." I put the knife away. "How did you get in?"

Jacinta twists and looks around the cabin. "I like what you've done with the place. I watched them finish building it. I wondered if you'd make it over here."

1

"Over where?"

"To Archibald's island."

How did she finish watching them build it?

She points at the opened present. "I'm guessing those aren't glass slippers?"

"Not quite."

"He's a good man. At least what I've seen, what Rupert has told me." She leans forward far enough to peek into the box. "Strange taste in presents. Your mom hated pickles."

I chuckle, the jar blurred through my wet eyes. "I am so fucking tired right now."

"Yes, it has been a long night for you."

I look up, silver streaks in her black hair visible under the pendant lights hanging over the breakfast bar. She's just as beautiful as she was in the photograph, albeit older.

"Do you have anything to drink?"

"Uhh, yes. I can make tea, or—" I check the fridge. Two bottles of Finan's favorite beer. My heart squeezes. "There's fresh orange juice—"

"Something harder. Like I said, I thought we might ... talk."

I open the freezer and retrieve the vodka I stole from the Tipping Point that fateful night just two weeks ago—has it already been two weeks since Kelly Lockhart barfed the sensational details of my mother's misdeeds to the whole of Thalia Island?

Yes, Lara, it has, which is why she and her cheap mascara and icky boy toy are in an RCMP transport making their way to Jail Town.

I set the frosted bottle on the counter between us, followed by two glasses. "I don't much like Russians, but I will drink their country's identity," Jacinta Ramirez says. She pours and downs her first shot with a loud sigh and a shiver. I sip mine—I am weary from the long night, and too many unanswered questions litter the floor already.

She helps herself to a refill but doesn't throw it all down her throat. "I will answer the easy stuff first. I've told you my name. I am from Mexico City, the third of eight children. What is left of my family is beholden to the Sinaloa Cartel that runs roughshod over our country. I am not going to fill your head with clichés about Mexico or her people—our shared neighbor does a good enough job with that." She sips. "Your mother was my best friend, my business partner, and my lover. She was the most amazing and frustrating human I've ever known or ever will know." Another sip, her eyes sparkling in the light. "I have been living on Thalia Island for over a year"—she throws her thumb over her shoulder—"in the woods."

"And you know Rupert."

Her laugh startles me. "Of course, Lara Jo. How do you think I got to be here, in this beautiful place?"

No one other than my mother or grandfather has ever called me Lara Jo. I'm not sure if I should be angry or warmed by her use of it.

Humboldt barks from the porch. It echoes like the roar of a giant. "I'll get him," Jacinta says. As she opens the screen, Humboldt slides through and wags his butt like he does for Finan. Guessing they've met before ...

Thanks for the heads-up, slobber dog.

Jacinta crouches and scrubs his head and ears with her one hand; he whimpers and whines and bathes her face with his tongue. She then says something to him in Spanish, and he flops onto his back and shows her his belly.

"Oh, come on, Humboldt, a little self-respect."

Jacinta pats his chest and rejoins me at the bar. "The next most obvious question is how the hell did I get on to your island."

"Probably a good place to start."

"There's a bunker here. Your grandfather built it years ago. Rupert gave me the keys and made some upgrades."

"And you've been here a year. Without anyone knowing."

"I'm good at hiding."

"Obviously." I sip the vodka, unappreciative of the burn in my throat. "I don't understand why."

"Because there are people in the world who want me dead. Rupert, thankfully, is not one of those people. He offered me sanctuary, and I took it."

"People ..."

"Mostly my brothers. Two of them have moved up the ranks in the Sinaloa Cartel. We had a disagreement." She shrugs and lifts her handless arm.

"A disagreement."

"A person can learn to live with one hand. Living without a head is much harder." She grins and finishes her drink, pouring a third. "But I don't want to talk about my family squabbles. I'm retired from all that now, living the good life," she says, lifting her glass. "Please tell me how Rupert is doing. I haven't talked to him in a few days."

In a few days. So they're talking on the regular. She's been *on this fucking island* and he didn't tell me?

"He's sick. The treatment sucks." I press my fingers into my tired, burning eyes. I need to take off my makeup—my face is sticky and gross. "Jacinta, why are you *here*, in my house, tonight?"

"I thought you could use some moral support. After the showdown at the town hall and Finan leaving—"

"How do you *know* about all this?"

A sly smirk edges across her face as she reaches into the Velcro'd pocket of her cargo pants. From it, she pulls out a smartphone with a bigger screen than my iPhone's. She sets it on the counter, swipes it open, and then holds it up.

Nine small black-and-white boxes consume the rectangular face of the device. "Surveillance?"

"Do you honestly think Archibald Clarke would leave his precious island unprotected?"

My thoughts race—there's been surveillance this whole time? Did Rupert know? Did he *lie* to me about it? Why would he do that? Is there anything on this the RCMP could use?

"Why now? Why are you here *now*?" I flatten my hands on the counter, close my eyes, and take a deep breath. "None of this makes any sense."

"It does. And it will. Again, we don't have to unpack everything tonight. I just wanted to let you know that I'm here, and I've got you covered."

I snort and take a drink. "Mm-hmm, I've heard that before."

4

"Your mom used to say that we should never let the sun go down on our anger—read it in a book she loved as a kid. Seems the sun not only went down on your anger but the source of it got on a boat and skipped town."

"I am not talking about Finan with you." Humboldt plants himself next to me, his droopy eyes and lolling tongue asking for a cookie.

"Your dog seems to like him," Jacinta says behind me as I yank free a Greenie from Humboldt's treat drawer. "That accounts for something."

"Like I'd let an animal pick my boyfriends."

"Animals have better instincts than humans."

I slam the drawer closed. "OK, well, this has been fun, but I am really, *really* tired, and unless you have something super interesting to share with me tonight, I'm wondering why our little reunion couldn't have waited one more night, considering I don't even remember meeting you, like, ever."

Jacinta polishes off the vodka in her glass and slides it away, screwing the cap back on the near-empty bottle. "I promised your mother I would look after you. Since I couldn't do that when you were young, I am going to make amends by being available to you for whatever you might need—"

"As long as it involves staying hidden on Thalia Island."

"Yes."

"And monitoring with your little magical cameras I didn't even know existed."

"The cameras aren't mine. They're Archibald's, or now yours, I suppose. I simply live in the space they feed into. I will take you to the bunker when you're ready. It's impossible to find if you don't know where you're going."

"Again, this doesn't make any sense ..."

"It will." She smiles. "I'm glad you got rid of those horrible people."

I nudge the rock on the counter. "Thanks for the tip about the beach that night, although knocking on the door would've worked too."

5

"And ruin the intrigue?" She flaps her hand at me.

"Wait—did you know about them before? That they were here?"

"No. I knew Kelly Lockhart was not good for Thalia, but their involvement with the cult was a terrible surprise."

"And you found out from—"

"Rupert."

"Of course." When he's done with cancer, I'm going to kick his posh British ass.

She pulls her ponytail over her shoulder.

"The photo of you and my mom in the plane …"

"Cessna 208 Caravan. Her second love, after you, before me." Jacinta smiles.

"Did she die in that plane? My grandfather looked for her. Like—you're not here to drop some big reveal that she's actually alive."

Jacinta's expression darkens. "She died, Lara. I'm sorry I can't bring a happier ending to that story."

"I don't even *know* the story. I know she had a plane. She flew around the world taking incredible photographs, she allegedly flew drugs for bad guys and opened some schools and clinics, and then she died. We had a memorial service, planted a tree, and installed a bronze plaque, after which I was expected to move on and forget about her." The box where I keep all these emotions tightly bound tears at the seams. "Honestly, I can't do this tonight."

Jacinta rounds the bar, and before I can protest, she envelops me with her strong body. Over her shoulder, Humboldt watches, half his green, bone-shaped cookie hanging from his jaw.

She pushes back and stares at my exhausted face. "You are her spitting image, you know." A lone tear runs down Jacinta's cheek. It dawns on me—I'm not the only one in pain over Cordelia Clarke's absence. "She loved you very much."

My throat is too tight to speak, so I step out of her reach.

Jacinta wipes her face with her sleeve and clears her throat, that wide smile returning. "There is much more to say, but this is a good start." She turns, pauses to kiss Humboldt's head, and then moves toward the corner chair where a heavy, dark-green flannel shirt rests over the back. I hadn't even noticed it. "One night, when you're a bit more settled, I will show you the bunker. Safer to move around when the island is asleep."

I open my mouth to protest but then realize I will have nothing else going on at night, now that Finan is off the island. Plus, I have questions. *A lot* of questions.

"Oh—can I get a few rolls of toilet paper?" Jacinta says. "With Rupert away, my stores are a little low and I've cleaned out his cabin's supply."

Such a mundane request but it's so out of place in this intense moment, I laugh. A quick trip to the hall closet and I return with a sealed eight-pack of two-ply.

Jacinta tucks it under her arm. "And I promise, too, soon we'll talk about that thumb drive."

My heart hammers again. The thumb drive. The password-protected folder labeled *JR*.

"How—"

"Good night, Lara Jo." The door whooshes closed behind her. I rush to open it again, to yell after her to give me the password, but she's been swallowed by the dark.

TWO

LOTS TO DO

Thursday ~ Fifteen days later

For the first week following Jacinta Ramirez's mysterious arrival, I race home from work at five thirty on the dot, hoping to see her sitting on my porch or again hiding inside my cabin.

By the end of the second week with nary a hint of her, I've run the gamut of worrying that she was eaten in the woods to contemplating perhaps I imagined the whole thing, dreamed it in an alcohol-induced haze, and maybe she was nothing but a spectre—a ghost from my mother's past—come to wreak havoc on my present and future.

But do ghosts need toilet paper?

Why did she show up *now*, drop a few truths, and then—poof!—without at least a follow-up? I'd gladly take another rock with a charcoal-scratched note on it.

I called Rupert the day after Jacinta's appearance, but he was out of it. Instead I talked to Sergeant Wes Singh, a longtime friend of Grandfather and Number Two—and the guy who broke the Dea Vitae case wide open here on Thalia—who seems to be at Rupert's West End townhouse more than he's not. Wes said the prior day's round of whatever chemo or antibody treatment they'd given Rupert was tearing apart his guts. When he wasn't in the bathroom, he was sedated. Anything important on my side of the Georgia Strait had to wait.

Not even Humboldt has been any help. I send him into the field once we pull in every night, hoping he'll pick up a scent and lead me to her bunker. Alas, Humboldt is a bullmastiff, not a bloodhound, and this is not a Disney movie. The only thing he's concerned with after a long day of inspired farting in my office is dinner.

He's even starting to get a little chubby now that he's not running around the fields with Finan. And he figured out after the first few days that sitting by town hall's front doors whining to go out brings no remedy. Though it's a poor second choice, the council chambers offers plush carpet and lots of room to spread his slobber wherever he wants. Like right now as I wait for those who remain on Thalia Island to saunter in, fresh coffees and warm pastries in hand, thanks to Tommy's Diner.

People are friendly enough—the ones who *really* didn't like me no longer live here—but those who *are* here are uneasy about the empty residences in their small neighborhood and the abridged town council looking after their needs. To make the meetings feel more intimate, therein reminding the settlers that we are still working toward a singular mission, Tommy and Catrina and I forgo the mics and our seats on the dais and instead stand on the first level in the gallery while people find seats. A few cold glances still brush past—the parents in the room haven't forgiven me for those horrifying slideshow photos while their kids were in attendance—but Catrina promises that, too, shall pass. Eventually.

She said the same thing about Finan's anger, and yet fifteen days in, he's still off the island. I can count his attempts to get in touch on two fingers, and the hundred texts I've started can't be read if I delete them before sending. If he stays gone another week, I will have Clarke Innovations HR send him a formal warning that he's in jeopardy of losing his position here.

Hey, it's just business. If I'm in charge of keeping the island on track, I don't have time for Mr. Rowleigh's shenanigans.

With Rupert temporarily out of commission, and Kelly, her Prince Charming-knockoff Hunter, and Stanley the shepherd and Tipping Point manager permanently gone, it's up to Catrina, Tommy, and me to run the meetings. No one has any idea where Ainsley Kerr—a.k.a. Iona MacChruim, the purported grad student who is actually the duplicitous head of the local Dea Vitae cult—is, but the regular updates from Wes, plus the new addition of Clarke Innovations security on the island, proves that the law isn't done looking for her or uncovering the damage she's caused. If anything, her woes are in their infancy, especially now that Dea Vitae is a headliner on worldwide news.

Come to find out, Interpol, Scotland Yard, the FBI—they're all *very* interested in the activities of this tiny Scottish lass and her industrious minions. It's made Wes Singh a bit of a local hero, depending on which channel you're tuned in to, but I warned him during a private call the other day—be careful. That tide changes very quickly. The public is fickle. We want Thalia Island famous for her earth-friendly innovation and community, not because a bunch of law-averting perverts tried to poison everyone and take over.

And I'm absolutely *dying* to know if he is aware of the bunker surveillance system, but I can't exactly ask, just in case it was a hallucination.

I'm going to guess no one *does* know about it since Clarke Innovations' beefy head of security, Len Emmerich, and his team have been busy over the past week installing well-disguised surveillance cameras in strategic locations around the island. No memo or email was issued; no public opinion was gathered. The cameras are going in, and if you don't like it, ferry's that way.

Catrina raises her arm next to me, the signal that we're ready to start. The crowd of forty-odd residents quiets quickly. In seeing how few of us are here, it is still shocking that so many were involved with Dea Vitae—and that they were so adept at hiding any trace. While some vehemently denied membership even as they packed their things under CI security supervision, their presence on Cordelia Beach that night sealed their fates. As Sergeant Singh reassured me the next day,

I need to let the RCMP do their work. These people are no longer my problem.

Except they are. Their homes, now empty, need cleaning and resetting in preparation for a new wave of settlers that will soon assimilate. The second group we'd been expecting was paused, awaiting further and deeper investigation by Clarke Innovations and associated police agencies. Disgruntled would-be residents who've sold homes and given up apartment leases to move here have been vocal on social media, which is not helping matters. And yes, lawsuits have already been filed.

I pinch the bridge of my nose against the headache that just won't leave.

Catrina offers an update on what we've been cleared to share by the Serious Crimes Team. She invites Joey, the senior-most agritech who's been standing in for Finan, to come down and update everyone on the rebuild progress at vertical farm B, how anyone who wants to help with early harvesting of our summer crops is more than welcome, "now that Ainsley is gone." He hazards a quick glance my way—Joey knows that Ainsley is in trouble and won't be coming back, but until *I* get to know Joey a little better, less is more. Whatever he wants to know about Ainsley, he can get from the news. I have no idea how much these folks bonded around late-night campfires and shared blunts.

I hate that I have to suspect everyone of everything. I thought being on Thalia would take that away. *Oh, naive Lara, you're so cute,* shoulder devil whispers.

Especially now that I've learned my mother's life partner, likely a fugitive of some stripe, has been living in a tech-filled hobbit hole right under my nose.

Before Joey returns to his seat, I inform the residents that we are interviewing a new biotech lead to take Ainsley's place, a young man named Benny Ackerman (yes, the Cannabis Cowboy I met at the Fairmont lounge in my Before Thalia life, though I don't offer this detail), and that if he makes it past the next round of interviews and the security clearance, we'll be bringing him and his young family onto the island to meet everyone. It was all Eugenia's idea—I begged my darling philosophizing bartender to come live here, too, since she sort of saved my life that night after Connor dumped me and I lost my loft —but she has a full life in Vancouver. It's enough that we keep in touch via social media, and I always appreciate the bites of Eugenia wisdom that randomly show up via text message.

So I called Benny and offered him a job a few days after the blitzkrieg, and he was so excited about the possibility of overseeing actual farms again, he had to take a minute to compose himself.

Plus, having someone on the island who knows how to make a killer mojito does not sound terrible.

Tommy updates folks on the Tipping Point general store, including the limited hours it'll be open for restocking our personal supplies "until we can get someone in to run it full time." I've been dealing with inventory, shipments, and special orders, even manning the till, but there's so much to handle in my actual job, we can't keep the store open ten hours a day right now. We still have maintenance crews on the island, but almost a dozen of them were escorted away that calamitous night. And as many of the remaining residents have their own jobs, it's not like I have an abundant labor pool from which to draw. Far from ideal.

Questions arise about future residents, the new doctor's schedule, if we're going to recruit a dentist to the island, and about when music lessons will resume at the school (one of the Cordelia Beach weirdos was a musician teaching the island's kids—I know—*shudder*). I answer what I can, deferring to Catrina and Tommy since people seem more inclined to listen to them.

Before we adjourn, however, I do raise my hand to introduce the last topic on our agenda. "It will be necessary for us to fill the vacated spots on council." A few people sit straighter on the padded bench seats. "The three of us agree that it would be best for all of TI's residents to decide who those folks are, as this is still a democracy." I smile warmly, hoping the ice in the room will thaw a little. "If you're interested in participating in our civic process, it does, of course, come with a small salary. We would like to move on this as quickly as possible."

A woman in the third row—Thalia Island's wealthiest resident, renowned author Alice Corwin, married to Professor Corwin who follows the missus around as if led by an invisible leash—raises her hand. "How many seats need filling? Kelly, Stanley, and Ainsley are gone, so that's three. And poor Rupert ... what about Finan Rowleigh? Is he returning?"

Catrina and I lock eyes for a beat. "Finan will rejoin us soon. His sister's twins are still in the NICU, so he's been in Vancouver as a support to his family."

"When it rains, it pours," Mrs. Corwin says, a kind smile on her face. Everyone loves Finan—no one wants him gone.

"Will you be maintaining your position, Lara?" Her kind smile dissolves.

"I will. I am still the project administrator, ready to move on from the missteps of the past few weeks so we can get back on track toward fulfilling Grandfather's mission." I look away before she can ask another question. "As soon as we adjourn, I will send out an email via Lutris detailing the role and responsibilities of council members. Those of you interested, please state your intent. If we have more than three potential candidates, we will coordinate a mini election, if you will, to allow residents to choose who will fill the seats. Ideally, we'd like to have everything settled within a week—with summer officially here, there is much to be done, not the least of which includes approving the next round of settlers."

"Shouldn't we wait to hold council elections until after the new settlers arrive?" Mrs. Corwin asks.

"Ideally, yes, but since it's just the three of us right now, we could really use your help. We could consider making the appointments interim, say, lasting for six months? That way it wouldn't be a tremendous burden for those who are already juggling jobs."

Several heads bob in agreement. "Excellent. OK, can I have a show of hands that this arrangement is agreeable?"

Mrs. Corwin is the first to raise hers, nudging her husband in the side, his glasses teetering on the end of his wide nose, his head bent over his phone. He looks up and raises his hand; most of the other residents do, too, including the kids. If children didn't give me hives, I'd think it was cute.

"Then it's settled. Thank you very much for coming today, and watch for Lara's email to follow shortly," Catrina says, adjourning the meeting. As residents stand, stretch, chat, and file out, Tommy kisses his wife's cheek once and dismisses himself to return to the diner for the coming lunch rush. I join her in tidying council chambers, grabbing the vacuum out of the hall storage cupboard since one of the kids decided their Danish would be better off in a million pieces on the floor. By the time I get to the spot to clean it, Humboldt has managed it for me.

"Have you heard from Finan?" Catrina asks, breaking the silence as she stacks dirty coffee mugs in a gray bin to take back to the diner for washing.

"No. But you have, clearly, if you know about his sister's babies."

"I called to check on him. His mother and I have become Facebook friends over the last year."

I nod. I don't want to care ... but I do. "His sister's babies are sick?"

"Preemies. That's not uncommon with multiples, but their lungs are a little underdeveloped, so they're still at BC Children's."

"If he wanted to talk to me, he would've made the effort. Feels a bit convenient that his sister just happened to go into labor the night everything fell apart." The words sound as harsh coming out of my mouth as they did in my brain.

I turn on the vacuum to pick up what Humboldt didn't inhale. Out of the corner of my eye, I can see Catrina is done cleaning, now waiting at the end of a row, the dish bin balanced along the bench back.

Sigh.

I turn off the vacuum and give her a tight smile.

"Call him, Lara."

"Maybe. You at the clinic today?"

"You'd think that four dozen people would be able to live without a doctor for a single day," she says, hoisting the bin. "I'll be back this afternoon—hoping we can get those council seats filled without a fuss."

I restart the vacuum as she heads up the stairs, coffee mugs *tinking* in the bin. Though chambers doesn't need it, I keep vacuuming, every level, under the padded benches, the benches themselves, the stairways, the dais, under the council desks, until my baby-blue silk blouse is drenched, rivulets running from under my bra down my stomach, my face dewy with exertion. Humboldt ambles up the three short steps to the elevated council members' area and sits, a long string of drool hanging from his chin, his mopey eyes staring at me, tail thumping against the floor.

He needs to potty.

I yank the cord from the wall and quickly wrap it up. "Come on, Big Dog," I say. He bounds down the stairs ahead of me, out of chambers, his long nails (which I don't know how to trim) clicking on the hallway's hardwood floor as I slide the vacuum back into the closet. I let him out front, he plods to the side of the building into the drought-resistant tall fescue where he knows he is to do his business, and then, not a fan of the rain, he hurries back under the covered porch area, happy to shake off right near me.

"Humboldt, seriously?" I wipe the muck off my black skinny pants, annoyed that once again, this beast has sullied my otherwise very cute outfit.

"You know he's a baby about the rain."

I freeze mid brush of my pant leg, but only for a second before looking up at the person towering over me. "Then I guess that makes him more of a princess than I am," I say. "Come, Humboldt." I turn and walk back into the building with my beast without holding the door for the newcomer.

Last I checked, Finan Rowleigh knows how doors work.

THREE

ICEBERG, RIGHT AHEAD

Humboldt knows the drill. We do our business, then we get a treat. I try to drag him down the hall toward the kitchen where he would *usually* be snorting and pawing at his snack drawer; instead, he's hopping and whining at the glass, his tail whipping like he's preparing meringue for the queen.

"You're a traitor," I mumble, releasing his collar, though I doubt he hears me over his pitiful fussing. I retreat to my office just as Finan enters the building and crouches to be smothered in frothy, excited kisses from the world's worst dog.

I close my office door behind me, but I'm not petty enough to lock it. And when Finan passes by with Humboldt at his heels, my heart pounds so hard, my hands go cold.

Fine. Ignore me. Probably for the best, anyway.

I nudge my computer awake and open Lutris. I have work to do. Like write and send an email about the council vacancies. Shaky hands flattened on the desktop, I close my eyes and breathe deeply for a few seconds to get myself together. I cannot allow Finan Rowleigh to have this kind of power over me. We're colleagues. Coworkers. Nothing more.

Liar.

Shut up.

My office door opens without even a warning knock. Humboldt pushes past, a soup bone hanging from his mouth. "Ew, are you kidding me? He's going to get that everywhere!"

Finan steps in and quickly rolls up the small area rug where Humboldt prefers to eat his treats. "I'll wash the floor when he's done."

"Whatever."

"May I sit?"

"Finan, I have a lot to do. Are you here to stay or to clean out your office?"

He perches on the couch edge—not quite committing to staying, but not leaving either. "I'm back."

"Great. I'm sure you have a million things to handle. Joey's been filling in for you, so head out to farm B and get up to speed."

"I've stayed in touch with Joey. I'm up to speed."

"Good. We also had a town hall meeting this morning, and we're going to fill the vacant council seats. That's what I'm doing right now, so if you'll get to work—"

"Stop. Please. Can we press pause for a second?"

I turn in my chair, arms crossed like they're battle armor to protect me—to protect my heart underneath. "It's fine, Finan. You made yourself perfectly clear the last time we spoke. I'm not some insecure prom queen who needs reassurance that you still think she's pretty. We have a ton to do, so if you'd kindly get to it, I can cancel my request for HR to start looking for your replacement."

His face hardens. "My replacement?"

"As the project administrator for Thalia Island, I have taken on the jobs of four different people in the last two weeks. I didn't know if you were coming back, since you've not communicated that intent to me, so yes, I've emailed Human Resources." I cross my fingers under my elbow so he won't see that I'm lying.

"Is this how it's going to be from now on?" Finan's jaw clenches.

"How else do you want it, Finan? I don't want to give you any further opportunity to be disappointed in or disgusted by me." The sting from the night of my ill-advised slideshow wherein I exposed Kelly and her band of idiots rushes back; it takes everything I have to keep my emotions in check. I don't want him to know how much I regret it, how embarrassed I am, how, in hindsight, I know what I did was stupid and wrong.

"I was hoping we'd be able to talk about it."

"And that's why you took off with nothing but a note and a pickle plate left on my porch? That's why you didn't call or text me, even though you were able to stay in touch with Joey? Doesn't sound like you were much interested in talking."

"This is bigger than a text conversation."

"So silence is better?"

He stares down at his boots and runs a hand through his hair, over his beard. Both are longer than usual. He doesn't look himself.

"Catrina told me about your sister's babies. I hope they're OK."

His head bobs once. "A boy and a girl. Rowan and Ivy. They're doing great. Just tiny," he says, and then abruptly stands. "I'll be in my office for the next hour answering emails. When I head out to the farm, I can take Humboldt with me."

I look over at my dog, enamored with his icky, sticky soup bone. "I'm sure he'd love that."

Finan leaves my office without another word, clicking the door closed behind him.

And my heart crumbles into a thousand icy chunks at my feet.

FOUR

DOCTOR, IT HURTS WHEN I DO THIS

W ith the council email sent and my turncoat dog occupied, I grab my laptop and head to the diner for a working lunch. I need a change of scenery for an hour or so—every time the main door opens, I freeze, listening for Humboldt's nails on the wood floor and Finan's heavy, booted steps.

Not great for concentration.

Tommy's is quiet, and I have my choice of booths to enjoy a Thai peanut chicken salad with mixed greens without anyone needing anything. I angle my laptop away from the main counter and instead of poring over emails and my to-do list, I cue up my favorite medical drama that I'm behind on, thanks to the unforeseen disasters that have rocked my world over the last three months.

Rude.

When the waitress slides my plate and sweating glass of Diet Coke onto the table, I thank her, plug in my earbuds, and prepare to get lost in the on-screen drama of a certain fictional Seattle hospital.

Three bites in, Mrs. Corwin has a different idea about how I will be spending my lunch hour.

I tab away from my show and remove my earbuds. "Hello, Mrs. Corwin."

"Lara." She slides into the booth without invitation and folds her well-manicured but veiny hands in front of her on the table. "As you know, I was a longtime friend of Archibald's. Living here was something we joked about at charity fundraisers and golden-shovel events for his innumerable environmental projects."

"Yes. He was fond of you too." I have no idea if my grandfather was fond of Mrs. Corwin.

"In light of the goings-on of the past few weeks, I can see just how much you are in over your head, especially without darling Rupert here."

I fold my laptop closed and sit straighter.

"Please don't misunderstand, Lara. I've known your family for a very long time. I remember when Rupert first started working for Archibald—*that* is how old I am. And believe me when I say that I have no ill will toward you after the stunt you pulled—Kelly Lockhart was awful, and I'm relieved she and her ilk are gone from the island."

"As am I."

"Though I do not agree with your methods, I understand how someone like you would think such a display was necessary."

"Someone like me?"

Mrs. Corwin leans closer and flattens one hand on the tabletop, stopping short of making physical contact. "I want to help. Put me on council. Allow me to use my many years of philanthropic maneuvering to lighten your hefty administrative load. I want to make Thalia Island work the way Archibald envisioned." Her eyes and voice soften. "I want to *help*."

"Thank you, Mrs. Corwin." I swallow hard, biting back what I *really* want to say.

Think of Thalia Island, Lara.

"I would very much appreciate having someone on council who has the same ideals and vision for my grandfather's mission as I do."

She sits back, resuming her stern face. "I have already replied to the email via Lutris. I look forward to you and Catrina and Tommy confirming my place by dinner this evening. While I understand it is important to the mission to include residents from all walks of life, we need people of experience and action on council, people with know-how and an established foundation. Kombucha recipes and drum circles are all fine and dandy, but we'll have time for that later—when we're sure we can feed ourselves."

Mrs. Corwin raps her knuckles on the wood tabletop. "Now, we have much to do, including the drafting of a bill of rights for island residents. Do you have that?"

"We have a Code of Conduct—"

"That's different from what I'm referencing, dear." She pulls a small leather notebook from the inside pocket of her bright-red Columbia rain slicker. "Secondly, I will seek to establish a series of guilds and activities for the residents to join, to foster a greater sense of community. As it is, you are assigning community-based tasks via the Lutris system, but there is no sense of togetherness, especially after recent events."

Not loving that she's harping about *recent events*, as if they aren't fresh in my mind. "It is our hope to eventually get everyone—"

"Not eventually, Lara. *Now*. If you want Thalia Island to thrive, you have to put in the work." Mrs. Corwin slides out of the booth before I can respond. She then points at my half-empty glass of soda on the table. "You should stop drinking that poison. You need to set a better example for the residents. I'll make a motion that we stop importing carbonated, artificially sweetened chemicals to the island. For the betterment of all."

She spins on the heel of her Merrell hiking boots and practically jogs out of the diner.

You can take away my loft apartment, my clothing allowance, my Town Car, my assistant, my private plane, and my housekeeper, but you are *not* taking away my Diet Coke, lady.

"Back off," I mumble as I pour in two fingers of Japanese whisky.

"Tell me you're not ruining good whisky by adding it to that."

I jump, quickly hiding my new flask under the table so I can secure the lid and throw it back in my bag. Embarrassment flames my face; the society smile scurries in to hide it.

"Dr. Stillson. How are you?" I ask, offering my hand for a shake.

Our new doctor—thirty-five, blondish curly hair, round tortoiseshell glasses over long-lashed eyes the color of the Salish Sea. There's a reason he's already had appointments with every eligible resident on the island: he's single, and according to Catrina and her hiked eyebrow, looking.

"Good. Busy. Hungry. What's that?" He points at my plate; I tell him. "What kind of dressing?"

"Uh, some sort of peanut vinaigrette? Light, not overwhelming."

"May I join you?"

"Of course."

He smiles and moves toward the counter to order. *Nice teeth. Nicer ass.*

My conscience clears her throat in my head. *Ahem …*

What?

What do you mean, what? Does the name Finan *ring a bell?*

It does. And is he here? No.

Whisky for lunch, and you're already looking for a new booty call.

Oh my god, it's SALAD. Go away.

Dr. Stillson returns and slides into the spot Mrs. Corwin recently vacated just as I tuck away my laptop and its fake doctors. "Catrina tells me you all are swamped now that you've lost half your town council."

"That would be a correct diagnosis." *Oh, Lara, gag.* Thankfully, he humors me with a grin. "How are things over at the clinic?"

"I never knew a generous handful of very healthy people could have so many questions."

"I'm sure it'll slow down. At least until the next group arrives. The residents were anxious after the salmonella situation, so they're thrilled you're here to help. Poor Catrina was run off her feet."

"She's an amazing practitioner. I'm lucky to work with her." His smile stretches all the way across his face. Genuine and warm.

"I agree. She's pretty great." *Like the mom I never had.* "You're all settled in and everything, then?"

"I am."

The young waitress with her brunette hair in two braids slides his lunch in front of him, lingering for a second so she, too, can partake of the handsome young doctor's attentions. She hurries away only to return with a glass of ice water.

"Fresh lemon. I know you like lemon," she says, her fair complexion betraying her.

"Thanks very much, Laramie."

She grins and hurries back behind the counter.

"Laramie. I did not know that was her name, and I've been here way longer than you," I admit quietly.

"It's a doctor thing. I try to learn names and faces right away. Makes it easier when they come to me for something they find embarrassing." He digs into his salad, moaning with the first bite. "God, this is good."

My naughty little mind sticks on that moan. "Mm-hmm. Yes. Tommy is a master."

"You've done a good thing here, Lara," he says around a mouthful of greens. "This place is amazing."

"It's not amazing because of me."

"Humble too."

"No, seriously. I'm still trying to get my sea legs."

"So far, it's terrific—and it'll only get better."

"Let's hope. Thank you."

"I was so happy when the Foundation offered me the job."

"And *we* are so happy you decided to take it, and show up early."

"I was a little worried when I saw the news about the food poisoning, but knowing what we know now"—he pauses to take a healthy swallow of his lemon water—"I can't believe it was intentional."

"Definitely not how I saw my first week playing out," I say, wishing I could take a sip from my soda but also not wanting the new doctor to think he needs to slip AA brochures into my town-hall mailbox. "Laramie? Can I get a water too?" My throat is suddenly sub-Saharan.

"I'm really looking forward to learning how to grow my own food. I had a spot in the community garden in Kitsilano, but people kept stealing my vegetables. The email from earlier said you'll be starting up the planting classes so we can get things going?"

"Uh, yes. We will. Soon. Very soon." I have no idea what he's talking about. What email?

Laramie slides my water onto the table just in time. I down half of it, then dab my lips with a cloth napkin. Afraid he will continue asking me about whatever planting classes he's just mentioned—or anything else from an email I didn't write and obviously haven't seen—I deflect and ask him about his life as a doctor, his family, his future plans.

He's in the middle of explaining how he'd love to be a hundred percent self-sufficient with his small plot of Thalia land when the bell above the diner door dings and a familiar face waltzes in.

Humboldt is the first to find me. He pauses for a second to sniff at the doctor's blue-scrub-clad leg under the table and then attempts to climb onto my bench, his front two legs propped on the cushioned bamboo seat. "Humboldt, down! You're a mess!"

Finan slides up next to the table and pulls Humboldt back onto all fours. "Sorry. We're just on our way to get lunch. Should've fed him first." He extends a hand. "Dr. Stillson, good to see you." The doctor shakes it. I cringe when he smiles; a piece of cilantro is wedged between his perfect front teeth.

"I wish you guys would call me Liam, at least when we're not in the office."

Finan looks at me. "Lara."

"Finan."

"Would you care to join us?" Dr. Stillson asks.

"You know, I'm about done here. Finan is welcome to my spot."

"No, thanks, Doc. I'm just grabbing a sandwich to go." He looks at me, his eyes hard. "Much to do before the sun sets. Enjoy the rest of your lunch." He waves and saunters toward the counter where Laramie has a brown paper sack ready to go. He pays quickly and as he passes our table again, he waves goodbye to Dr. Stillson, but not me.

"He seems like a good guy. Catrina says he has been a huge factor in getting the island up and running."

Deciding I don't care what Dr. Stillson—Liam—thinks, I pick up the spiked drink and finish it. "Finan's great. Thanks for joining me. I'll grab yours," I say, pointing to his unfinished plate. As I fish my wallet from my bag, I contemplate whether I should tell the doctor about the cilantro.

Nah.

I slide out of the booth, bag over my shoulder. "Let me know about those gardening classes," he says. "Maybe we could go together?"

"Nothing gets me more excited than perfect soil composition." I wink and hide my Finan-shaped annoyance behind a plastic smile and fake wave.

I stall my exit long enough to lean over the counter and ask Laramie to add our lunches to my tab and apologize for the Humboldt-shaped paw prints on the seat. "Also, one of those to go, please." I point to the glazed strawberry turnover in the Plexiglas case near the register.

As I rush down the block, I again chastise myself for the choice of open-toed power heels when the weather report is only a thumb swipe away. Shoving the turnover into my face helps.

A little.

FIVE

FAUX PAS

The email Dr. Stillson was referring to?

Written by Alice Corwin. Before she accosted me at the diner. Seems she's already got the gavel in her hand, and we haven't even assigned her a chair yet.

Fine. If a seventy-something multimillionaire wants to arrange quilting clubs and yoga circles and best practices for growing gargantuan gourds, one less thing for me to worry about. And since my secure phone has three missed calls on it by the time I'm safely ensconced in my office, I definitely have other things to worry about.

"Wes, hey, sorry, I was in a meeting. What's up?"

"Just wanted to let you know the RCMP will be on the west side of the island this week, combing again."

"Again? For what?" I shiver when I think of the two arm bones Humboldt delivered to Finan and me during our first visit to Cordelia Beach. Turns out, they belonged to the security guy—Derek Irving—hired by Clarke Innovations. He showed up for work once and then mysteriously disappeared.

"Looks like Kelly Lockhart is singing a different tune about what happened with Mr. Irving."

"Do I want to know?"

"Not yet. But we're coming back over to have another look. Just tell Finan and his crews so no one gets spooked."

"Thanks for the warning," I say. "Have you seen Rupert today?"

"Last night. He's sleeping a lot. The treatment takes so much out of him. I'll stop by after work. He doesn't like the new nurse."

"What happened to the cabana boy?"

"The agency said they can't fill every shift with hot twenty-some-things who look like Antonio Banderas," Wes says, chuckling. "And the one lately is a feisty Filipina momma who makes him use the bedpan. As you can imagine, our Rupert is *not* impressed."

Our Rupert. I love that he calls him that. "I should be there with him."

"You already know what he would do if you showed up," Wes says. I can hear the smile in his voice. "I'm taking pho over tonight. He PVR'd *Great British Bake Off* and in a weak moment, I promised I'd watch. I'll make sure he checks in."

"Thanks."

"Stay safe, kiddo," he says, and then disconnects.

I never thought I would miss Rupert. He was always so annoying and bossy when I was growing up. Since my mother was rarely around, I went through an agency's worth of nannies. Boarding schools quickly lost patience with me for anything long term, so Rupert was unofficially charged with my upbringing. My grandfather was a busy man with no time to look after a headstrong child, and the more Rupert tried to train the stubbornness out of me, the more willful I became.

Once I aged into my trust fund, I only had to see him once a year at the meeting wherein he would lecture me about wasteful spending, threatening to rein in my personal budget if I didn't straighten myself out. After a couple years of those threats, I saw they were toothless. I was Archibald Magnus Clarke I's granddaughter. No one was going to tell me how to live my life or how to spend his money.

I once went two whole years without having to talk to or see Rupert—our respective assistants dealt with whatever was related to keeping me out of trouble. When my grandfather insisted on a birthday fête for my twenty-eighth—I suspect he knew his mortal play was approaching its final act—Rupert and I had to reconnect over the party prep, albeit mostly via text and email and a few short, tense phone calls during which we argued about why I couldn't serve foie gras and Dom Pérignon. He insisted on a less extravagant budget and said we would use the saved money to send fresh drinking water to the Neskantaga First Nation in northern Ontario.

And then Grandpa Archie kicked the ethereal bucket, right there on stage at his big ribbon-cutting ceremony for the new environmentally conscious, self-sustaining, family-friendly high-rises Clarke Innovations is building in downtown Vancouver, and I unwittingly found myself handling the second oar in the boat alongside Rupert.

I would never tell him this, but I do love that jerk. He'd better not die.

My email pings with yet another delivery of resident problems, so I sniff away any hint of weakness, pop a couple breath mints, and steel myself for whatever carnage is yet to come.

What I would give to be sunbathing naked in Ibiza right now. Ohhhh, like three summers ago with that actor I'm not allowed to mention per his lawyer's trigger finger with the NDA but whose name starts with an H and ends with an -enry and he spends some of his movie-making time in a very tight blue costume emblazoned with a giant red S.

Mmmmm, delicious indeed.

A quick glance at the countdown clock on my computer's desktop is a sobering reminder that I have 322 days left of this carnival.

Ten more months of Rupert's Schedule A chores. Ten more months of worrying about solar arrays and phosphorus-extracting wastewater sanitation systems and failed HVAC pumps in vertical farms. Ten more months of pretending Finan is an ass and I'm better off without him.

Maybe Dea Vitae should've sacrificed me on Cordelia Beach instead of that poor raccoon.

What? Too soon?

∼

A knock on my office door sets my heart to racing. "Yes?" I brace for whoever it will be—including Finan.

It's one of his crew guys. Young, dreadlocked, reeking of pot and patchouli. "Hi, Ms. Clarke. Just brought the mail in from the ferry and there are some big boxes here for you?"

"Oh! Yes! Thank you …"

"Geordie."

"Right. Sorry. Geordie. I'm the worst with names." I slide my feet back into my heels, straighten my blazer, and follow Geordie out of my office into the mail area. A wheeled parcel cart supports four waist-high rectangular boxes. "Ah, so glad to see they shipped these correctly."

"What are they?"

"Artwork. My mother's photographs. From all over the world."

"Wasn't your mom, like, a—"

I flash him a deadly look.

"I'll just unload the mail," he says, unzipping the Canada Post bag.

"That's all there is?" I nod at the red-and-gray pouch he's clutching.

"Yeah. Since Kelly left, we get hardly anything. Makes the job so much faster."

Although Kelly Lockhart isn't the head honcho for Dea Vitae—that distinction has been assigned to the sweet, carrot-nurturing waif we knew as Ainsley Kerr—Kelly is high up in the organization, and the lead pathogen for our little infection, allegedly taking her orders on the sly from Ainsley/Iona. As such, Kelly *did* get a lot of mail—and the police seized all of it.

Wes quietly shared that the incoming Kelly-directed letters and packages were all Dea Vitae related, containing everything from cash to bad art of angry ocean deities to hallucinogenics to cell phones and videotapes with devotions recorded to Tiamat, the vengeful goddess of the salt sea. Apparently some people even sent hair—yes, pubic included—and vials of their blood meant for the sacrifice rituals. It's all evidence now, and I am *very glad* her dreck is no longer on my island.

I retreat to the kitchen for a box knife to open my deliveries. Upon returning, Geordie is gone.

Good. I don't have to explain myself, or my mother's lifestyle, to some kid who needs to use some of his marijuana budget for shampoo and deodorant.

I'm careful to unzip the packaging tape and slice the cardboard slowly. I have no idea which is which, so I pull the first cushioned canvas from its shell, pleased to see the corners have been protected with wooden triangular supports. I unfold the thin cotton wrap around the first canvas, holding my breath.

I exhale on a wide grin as the elephant's eye peeks out.

With the care of a surgeon, I uncover all four canvases, certain that when I'm done here, I will go order a dozen more. The elephants of Mali, a lioness and her three cubs from an endangered population of Asiatic lions in the Gir Forest of India, the critically endangered western lowland silverback from a trip to the Congo that almost got my mother killed, and a colony of endangered Galápagos penguins.

With the canvases gently leaned against the lobby walls, I stare at each one, willing the subjects to talk to me, to tell me what Cordelia Clarke was feeling on the days she took these photographs.

"Those are incredible."

A shiver runs through me at the sound of his voice. "She was very talented."

"You going to hang them in here?"

"That's the plan."

"You want some help?"

"I know how to use a hammer, thanks."

Finan sighs behind me. "I'll send one of my carpenters over. These need to be hung properly, as they would be in a gallery."

"Are you saying I'm incapable of hanging some pictures?"

"I'm not saying anything, Lara. I'm trying to help. Give your mother's art the respect it deserves." He backtracks to the main door to open it and let Humboldt in. "I have a meeting with the foreman about farm B in ten minutes. OK if we use the conference room?"

I lift a hand gesturing for him to help himself but refuse to make eye contact.

"I'll get Humboldt fresh water. Then I'll leave him with you, yeah?"

"He's my dog," I say, moving to clean up the packaging materials. "When can your carpenter be here?"

"I'll call him now."

"I don't want these left on the floor overnight for people to touch."

Finan pulls his phone from the pouch on his belt and dials. Someone answers, he makes his request, and disconnects. "Payton will be over in a half hour."

I still have my back to him. "Perfect. Thank you."

While I fold the thin cottony overwrap for reuse or recycling and tear free the mailing labels from the cardboard packaging, I feel Finan's eyes on me, but I'm not giving in. He was the one who left me, who left Thalia, after he promised he would never do such a thing.

After another pointed sigh, he walks away, his boots clomping down the wide hallway. Relief weakens my knees, my hands shaking.

I can't work in this environment, on edge about Finan Rowleigh appearing in the middle of something to fluster me. Even more infuriating? I've never let a guy get in my head, or my heart, the way I allowed Finan. I shared parts of myself no one has ever seen. Opened those steel gates and let him waltz right in and make himself comfortable.

He can go on about how I revealed my true character that night with the X-rated slideshow, but he's shown a bit of himself too—that he chickens out when the feces hit the fan. I did one stupid thing he didn't approve of, so what, now I'm supposed to grovel and apologize and beg him to decide I'm of high-enough moral fiber to meet his exacting standards?

"Fuck that," I mutter.

"Excuse me?"

I spin and am met with the surprised look of one of the residents—Gillian Peck, a young mom with two kids—her little one grasping on like a baby capuchin, the other staring curiously up at me. Gillian has her mail key poised just before the lock of their family's box.

"Yeah, fuck that," the older kid says, a jumble-toothed grin stretching across her face.

"Harmony! We don't use that language!"

"She said it first," Harmony says, brushing the end of her blond braid against her chin.

"Oh—oh, no—that's not what I said."

Gillian looks like she's about to melt me with her laser vision. "I am so sorry. Harmony, your mom is right. We don't use that language."

The young mother thrusts in her key, checks for mail, and then slams the little door closed. She grabs the girl by her presumably sticky hands and turns toward the door, pausing only to survey the leaned canvases. Her face softens for a beat as she scans from one to the next, lingering on the lioness with her babies. Her gaze then hardens again as she looks at me.

"If you want this place to work, you need to get your shit together." And then she yanks Harmony's arm to move her away from me and out of the building.

She's not wrong.

SIX

PLUS-ONE?

hankfully, the task of filling the empty council seats does not
turn dramatic, nor does it require an election. Mrs. Corwin gets
her spot without challenge, though not by dinner as she commanded
when she interrupted my lunch break. The other two vacant spots are
filled by Dr. Liam Stillson, per pressure from Catrina that he could
offer his reasoned, scientific voice, and Lucy-Frank Makamoose, a
gorgeous First Nations visual artist with a quiet demeanor and strong
ideas about environmental protectionism and reconciliation.

It's a good balance of age, brains, and cultural and socioeconomic
backgrounds. And our first full-council meeting is an absolute delight.
Though none of the original members say it out loud, it's clear we are
going to get so much more accomplished without Kelly's melodrama
or personal agenda slowing things down. While Finan and I continue
to sit at opposite sides of the table with only awkward glances shared
when our eyes meet, it's getting easier to see him around the building
without my heart threatening to skip town.

Because I miss him.

Since he's been back, I've written and deleted a new crop of a thousand texts and singularly finished an unhealthy volume of hard alco-

33

hol, hoping no one notices how barren the Tipping Point's liquor shelves have become.

Yes, I know. Slipping into Old Lara, Pre-Thalia Lara, pre-Finan Lara is not something I'm proud of. I've not seen Jacinta again, so that wound festers, though a few nights over the last month, I have come home to find a foil-covered casserole dish filled with the best enchiladas I've ever eaten; another night it was wildflowers in a glass milk bottle; a third, a leather-and-wood bracelet with my mother's initials carved into it.

She's here—she's just not showing herself to me. Nor is she sharing the password to that damn locked folder. What could it possibly contain that she doesn't want me to see yet? And why is she not returning to share more of our connected lives?

My days are slammed with work I'm still not very good at, which makes every decision feel like I've just sprinted up another sand dune that might give way under my feet. And every single day, someone indirectly reminds me that I'm not as qualified for this job as maybe I should be, except in the case of Mrs. Corwin who tells me so right to my face. I am not ashamed to admit that I have looked online for suites and apartments I might be able to afford on $30,000 a year, should I give up before my year on Thalia is finished and opt to slink away and take the allowance Grandfather's will offers. Such math always leads to the depressing reminder that instead of going to school and learning something I could later use to feed myself, I chose to test out cocktail recipes and mattresses from Mykonos to Côte d'Azur.

Lara the genius.

My former therapist would be so disappointed if she knew I was regularly self-medicating to put myself to sleep, alone in my cabin beside a smelly, oversized dog-child.

Please don't tell Rupert.

Thalia Island and her residents enjoy two solid weeks of (mostly) calamity-free bliss, something I was afraid to hope for after the horror show of my first weeks here. Apparently, when you have people working toward a singular mission, things get done! The demolition on vertical farm B is complete with every salvageable piece ready for reuse or upcycling, and as of yesterday, the first floor is framed in. Sergeant Wes Singh and his team have been on the western side of the island twice in the last fourteen days, literally combing Cordelia Beach for more clues in their investigation of who killed our security contractor, Derek Irving. Although I got a stern talking-to by one of Wes's superiors about how we should never have moved the bones and how we should have called the RCMP immediately, they are moving forward. I didn't screw anything up too badly, or if I did, Wes hasn't slapped my wrist over it.

Not a single resident has asked about the police presence, which means no one knows, or cares. And Rupert's PET scans are showing diminution in the areas of concern, plus he's awake for more hours of the day, a relief we all share on so many levels.

Even the gossip posse online seems to have grown bored with us in the absence of any new leaked videos or salacious tidbits. Where I used to take a sort of sick pleasure in seeing how many Google Alerts I received in a day—if they're talking about me, they haven't forgotten me—I'm glad there are juicier morsels out there for the vampires to sink their fangs into. At least for now. It's one thing for people to rip apart my hair or clothes or who I'm dating or if I need to lay off booze and pastries, but when it comes to Thalia, less gossip is definitely better.

Though I did take a moment to scroll through the feeds when news broke that my ex-boyfriend, actor Connor Mayson, and fellow small-screen thespian (and supposed fiancée) Suze Simmons had been dismissed not only from their respective talent agencies but from their roles on their (awful) TV show, *Super George*, stemming from their involvement in the "posh beach sex romp" and alleged ties to "Dea Vitae, a terrifying new end-times cult sweeping the globe."

Oopsie.

I won't ever say that Karma is a bitch because I happen to think she's *awesome*, and if she ever wants to hang out on my island, I'll make up the adorable spare room for her with my finest Egyptian cotton, high-thread-count sheets. I'll even draw her a bath and put the prosecco on ice before she arrives.

Big Dog rolls over and yawns. He's too big for his new dog bed. Auntie Catrina meant well, but clearly she didn't measure him before ordering. "Come on, let's go potty and get your dinner." I stand and stretch, my butt asleep from too many hours in front of the screen. Even though it's Canada Day—technically a holiday—we're at the tail end of a tertiary finalization of applications for the settlers who were supposed to have joined us in the days after the Dea Vitae raid. Of that pool this time around, only a handful were disqualified for refusing to confirm or deny affiliation with the cult.

Therefore, we have a new crop of humans arriving early next week, which means no rest for the wicked. Tonight's dinner-hour council meeting is to initiate the vetting process for the third wave of applicants, something we need to be quick about. We've already missed the population and productivity targets set forth by the Clarke Foundation for Q2, but given the special circumstances, the board is more concerned about the battles on the legal front than if I have enough bodies in the houses and school and if we're producing sufficient crop yield to consider exports in our second year.

As Rupert said, "Growing pains are expected." Doubt anyone envisaged a perverse cult infiltrating the island, but them's the breaks.

Summer in British Columbia means the sun hangs around long past happy hour; the sky will be bright until after nine o'clock. Our thriving bee population makes use of the extra daylight and the lovely warm temperatures, buzzing lazily about the courtyard while I wait for Humboldt to find a spot to empty his bladder.

"Hey, Lara. Coffee delivery. Two sugars, no milk." Dr. Stillson—Liam—hands me a compostable takeout cup from the diner. "I brought Canada Day cookies too." He hoists his right arm; a paper bag hangs around his wrist.

"Tommy makes the best cookies," I say. "Thanks for this. How did you know?"

"Because it's after six on a holiday Thursday, I know how damn tired I am, so caffeine and sugar it is." He sips from his own cup.

"Doesn't look very good for the town doctor to be pushing stimulants on our impressionable residents." I take off my lid to avoid burning my tongue.

"Impressionable. You?" he says.

Humboldt plods over, a stick twice his width gripped in his jaw. Every time he does this now, I'm grateful it's a stick and not an ulna.

He drops it at my feet. I pick it up and throw it back out into the tall grasses.

"Smart dog."

"*Spoiled* dog," I say. I omit the part about how he's also depressed because he hasn't been hanging out with Finan nearly as much as before.

"Meet you inside?"

I nod. As Liam walks away, his scent lingers—an earthy cologne, almost too flowery for my taste. I've never seen him clean-shaven, always that five o'clock shadow hanging around, and he almost looks like he belongs with the Hemsworth clan, maybe the brother who didn't quite make the cut for the magazine cover. Hot, yes, but not so much that mere mortals are afraid to talk to him.

And according to Catrina, the mere mortals of Thalia Island have *no* problem filling the good doctor's schedule with appointments, just for the opportunity to talk.

"Come on, Humboldt," I holler. If he digs another hole in that slow-growing fescue, I will never hear the end of it.

Reluctantly, he trots toward me, though when his pace increases and his tail motor revs, I know who's coming up behind me.

"Heyyyyyy, buddy," Finan says, kneeling. Humboldt even offers him his new stick. Ugh.

"I'm going to pour his dinner. Don't let him dig." I replace my coffee's lid and leave the courtyard before the words poised on Finan's lips have a chance to tumble out.

Inside the lobby, Dr. Stillson stands examining the photograph of the silverback. "These are incredible," he says reverently. "I can't help but stop and look every time I come in here."

"My mother was very talented."

"Indeed." He looks over at me, his coffee cup close to his chest. "What about you? Did the apple fall far from the tree?"

I chuckle. "Very far."

"How do you know? Have you tried anything? Photography, maybe?"

"I'm the only person I know who can take a blurry picture with an iPhone."

He smiles. "Something else, then."

I sip my coffee, eyes on the lowland gorilla staring back at me. He doesn't seem threatened. In fact, he's looking at my mother's lens like he wanted her there, like she was welcome. "On this trip, they stayed in a camp for two months, to get the gorillas to trust them. She was with a long-term research group out of the UK. Right before her visit was finished, the camp was attacked. One of the research fellows was killed, but my mother managed to hide until it was over."

"Jesus ..."

"Apparently it was pretty intense. Why she would go to the Congo ..."

"You weren't with her?"

"Oh god, no. Just one of her many stories she shared after she got home. I was maybe eight around this time?"

"Wow. So she was gone a lot."

I nod.

"These gorillas are endangered?"

"Critically."

"Your mother sounds like an amazing woman."

"She was."

The door opens behind us, and Finan and Humboldt saunter in. The dog still has his stick, which means the chewed shards will end up all over town hall. Whatever. My former housekeeper Vera would die of shock if she saw how proficient I've become with the vacuum and its extendable hose.

"Hey, Finan," Dr. Stillson says. Our lead engineer waves and continues past. "I suppose we should get in there."

"I suppose."

Stillson moves aside to allow space for me to step in beside him. "Seriously, though, you can't just work all the time. I see your car here when I walk to the clinic in the mornings, and I see it when I'm done for the day. Sometimes I even see it when I've popped by the pub for a beer." He walks very slowly down the hall toward the bustling conference room. "Alice Corwin has come up with that list of possible activities—"

"Community builders."

"Yes, those." He smiles. "Why not try a paint night or maybe pottery? I could be your plus-one."

Oh my god, is Dr. Stillson asking me *out*?

We've reached the threshold to the conference room. "Think about it."

"Maybe after the new settlers arrive. There's so much left to do."

"How about this—how about next week, at the welcome party, you save me a dance, and we can talk more about finding your artistic voice?"

"Are you two joining us, or are you having your own private meeting?" Alice Corwin crows from the head of the table. When she took over Kelly Lockhart's chair, I did not protest. Let the old biddy run the meetings so I can focus on how many minutes left before I can crawl under my feather duvet with a bottle of Suntory.

Dr. Stillson gestures for me to enter. I take my usual seat, my cheeks burning from being caught flirting in the doorway. And sure enough, when I look up, Finan's eyes are on me …

And they're sad.

It seems the lowland gorilla isn't the only thing who's critically endangered in here tonight.

SEVEN

SO MANY SECRETS

I wake Friday morning to the ringing of the secure burner phone plugged into its charger on my nightstand.

"Hullo ..." Humboldt lifts his head next to me and then drops it again, sighing as he returns to sleep.

"Lara, honestly, it's eight o'clock. Wake up." Rupert's voice sounds stronger than it has in a while.

"Why are you harassing me ... I don't have to be at the office until nine." I push up against my pillows. "Hey, you sound good."

"I awoke with a renewed vigor," he says. "A calm in the storm."

"That's so great to hear. What are the doctors saying?"

He rattles off something about white counts and a possible transfusion and a positive response to the last round of immunotherapy and that if all goes to plan, he will be back on Thalia in a month's time.

A month? That seems too soon. And yet so far away.

"Enough of the medical jargon as I know it's flying right over your head." He pauses to sip something on the other end. "Quick now, tell me what's on your agenda for today."

"Benny Ackerman and his family are arriving? I think that's it ..." I yawn, my brain socked in with sleep fog.

"Their place is ready?"

"Stanley's was the best for their needs. Why did a single guy need three bedrooms?"

"No longer our problem," Rupert says. "Do welcome Benny on my behalf and tell him I look forward to meeting in person. These bloody video screens make me appear vampiric."

I almost tease about if he's picked out his new hairpiece, but even for me, that's cold. Besides, I can always ask Wes next time we talk.

"Moving on"—he clicks his tongue, an annoying habit made even more annoying over the phone line—"ah, yes. Apologies. Scrolling through the list here. It looks as though they will be moving forward with charges against Kelly Lockhart for her involvement in the murder of Derek Irving. The same will be true for Ainsley—Iona—whenever they can find her, though she is in enough trouble that, if caught, she will never again see the light of day."

I sit straighter, the fog clearing. "Wait—are you serious? Kelly *killed* that guy?"

"Allegedly, she confessed. Only after they found a cell phone on that side of the island—her Thalia Island phone, no less. It was dead but once revived, it contained a video of unsavory goings-on involving our poor security man." Rupert sips again. "Apparently she's gone full unhinged at this point. Talks endlessly about the goddess Tiamat and end times. Wes is not supposed to be sharing this, so mum's the word."

"Rupert! I tracked her that day—her little mermaid avatar on the Lutris system—it showed her on the west side of the island. That was the first time she confronted me over getting into the resident files because I thought she was nowhere near town hall."

"Mr. Irving would've been dead long before that. But only a fool like Kelly would videotape torture on her *work phone* and then lose the damn thing."

"Oh my god ... I cannot believe those people were on our island, Rupert."

"Remember, tell no one. Not yet."

"Yes ... but it still gives me the creeps. That poor guy."

41

"Wes said the video is disturbing. Be glad we weren't the ones to find it."

"What if they come back?"

"They won't. Not with Mr. Emmerich and his muscled horde on the ground."

"There *are* a lot of muscles here, Rupert. I think you're going to like it," I tease. He clears his throat. "And hmmm, I wonder if we should've had surveillance from the beginning?" I smile and rest a hand on Humboldt's slumbering head, wishing I could mention the surveillance Jacinta allegedly has access to.

"Even a broken clock is right twice a day," he mutters. "The reason I'm phoning with this news so early is that I wanted you to hear it from me first, instead of Crown counsel or our lawyers. Not surprisingly, Kelly Lockhart is now suing Clarke Innovations, and we are, of course, countersuing, which means you will be subpoenaed to provide witness testimony for the civil action as the case moves through the system."

"*She* is suing *us*? For what?"

"Defamation and some such. She wants two billion dollars."

I laugh so loud, I scare the dog. "Oh my god, she *is* delusional. Why do I have to testify? We already gave our statements to the RCMP."

"You and Finan will both be summoned to appear. For what you witnessed on Cordelia Beach that night. Our lawyers will be busy shredding her case and character, so just do what they ask."

"I don't want to keep rehashing this nightmare."

"It's part of the process, Lara. You will sit at the table and answer the lawyers' questions, and then you and Finan go for cocktails. Have a night in the city."

Cocktails and a night in the city with Finan? Right.

The line is quiet.

"Are you still there?" he asks.

"Yes. Sorry. Any idea when this will happen?"

"I do not. As soon as I hear from our legal team, you will be the first person I call." Rupert speaks, rather tersely, to someone on his side; I wait until he's finished. "This new nurse is an abomination."

I smirk, thinking of Wes's earlier summation. "Let her do her job."

"I am *perfectly* capable of walking into the lavatory and urinating into the toilet like a grown man. Her disregard for my decency is appalling!"

The alarm on my other phone goes off. I silence it as Rupert gripes on about the quality of nursing care. And speaking of urinating, Humboldt stretches and eases himself off the bed, my cue to put on slippers and open the front door. On the porch, I am greeted with another present.

A woven bowl full of perfect little red cherry tomatoes, some still attached to the vine.

I look around the as-yet unplanted front field, which is going to need tilling again before it's of any use, but no one's there. Finan's truck across the way is gone. He must've gotten an early start.

"Did you hear what I said?" Rupert asks.

"What? Sorry. No—I'm just letting Humboldt out for a pee." I hug the bowl of tomatoes against me and go back into the house. "Rupert ... now that you're a little more lucid, we need to talk about Jacinta."

He sighs. "Is she well?"

"I think so. She hasn't been back since that initial night, at least not to talk. She keeps leaving me presents. Fresh tomatoes on my porch just now."

"She calls to check on me."

"That's nice, but since you're feeling better, I'm actually pretty goddamn mad that you didn't tell me she was here. Or that she was even alive. Or about the bunker or the *surveillance* she has access to— are the cops able to use any of that?"

"**No.** And please, do not mention any of this to Wes. I have not disclosed Jacinta's presence to you because her situation is ... complicated."

"Then *un*complicate it. Explain it to me."

The same background voice from earlier nags at Rupert. "Lara, I promise everything will become clearer, when it's safe for all parties involved. I have to get off the phone before Thumbelina tries to fasten another adult diaper on my person."

"I heard that, Mr. Bishop!" the voice behind him says.

"Rupert, come on—I need to know why she's here."

"Actually, you don't. Just be glad she is and know that she is looking out for you in a way I cannot. And Lara—don't tell anyone else."

"No one else knows?"

"Not even Finan. Not a word. Must go. Cheers, little cyclone." He disconnects. I'm still pissed, and confused, but he hasn't called me little cyclone in forever. Sort of like Jacinta calling me Lara Jo. Maybe he's worried about his treatment and it's softening him?

I scoop the tomatoes still attached to their very fresh vine and hold them against my nose. So fragrant. You cannot get this juicy earthiness from store-bought produce, something I am quickly becoming more snobbish about the longer I live on this island.

I pop one of the luscious globes into my mouth and groan. I eat half a dozen more before letting Big Dog in for his own breakfast and then pack the rest in a glass Snapware container for lunch.

If Jacinta Ramirez wants to hide on Thalia Island and bring me presents, I guess I'm just going to have to suffer through it.

EIGHT

FRESH MEAT

Benny Ackerman, his gorgeous partner Amalie, and their tiny baby Sativa (yes, after the strain of marijuana) stroll off the noon ferry with smiles wide enough to light the night sky. In Rupert's continued absence, I've commandeered his Tesla. The trunk has barely enough room for their hand-carried luggage, which includes an exceptional amount of baby gear.

Remind me to never have children.

The rest of their stuff is in our EV supply truck that just off-loaded and will meet us at their new place. I like this system better—having to ask Finan for use of his rig was not something I wanted to do today. We had just enough room in the weekly shipment from the mainland to load the Ackermans' household belongings, terrific as this means I don't have to coordinate a spot for them in the containers that will follow next week's round of settlers.

Honestly, this Dea Vitae chaos has been a logistical nightmare. The people arriving next week are a smaller group from the second-planned wave who made it through the extra background evaluations conducted after everything melted down. Since that second-wave group already had their stuff loaded into our containers before we discovered the cult's infestation, we had to go back in and unpack

45

their crap into storage units until the rejected parties are able to find alternate accommodations.

Like I said, a *nightmare*.

Right now, however, is the dawn of a new start for the Ackermans, and Thalia Island. Once we have Baby Sativa strapped in, I give the family a scenic tour while concurrently explaining ferry schedules, showing them town hall, Dr. Stillson's office, and the open Main Street businesses, the school-slash-community centre, and then the farms where Benny will be spending his days. Upon pulling up to the Ackermans' new residence, I'm glad to see the delivery guys are sweaty-faced and the small garage is stacked with boxes for Benny and Amalie to deal with.

Just as I turn off the car, the baby lets out an angry wail. "Perfect timing," Amalie says. "I'm about to burst." She grabs at her boobs; the right front of her shirt is damp.

Again, I repeat: Never let me have children.

"Then let's go in, shall we?" I say, glad for something to do other than talk about Amalie's breast milk. I lead the way.

"The guys had a key to bring in your stuff, but otherwise, these"—I dangle the house keys and then drop them in Benny's outstretched hand—"are yours. Come on in."

We slip off our shoes inside the door, and I pull on a pair of the blue surgical booties I keep in my bag (heels, hence no socks). "This is the Powerwall. The roof, as you know, is basically a giant solar panel. The manual to figure this all out is here." I move to the breakfast bar to grab the thick binder. "Anything you need for life on the island is within these pages. Oh, and this is the Lutris portal. Everyone on the island has one in their residence and/or office, and there's a down-loadable app for your phone." I tap the tablet screen, bringing it to life, and demonstrate its simplest features, though the baby's hungry howls dominate my attempts at conversation.

"Benny, take notes. I need to feed her." Amalie shuffles to the stair-case. "Thank you for everything, Lara. I can't wait to talk more!" As she disappears around the corner, the quiet mostly returns. My ears ring.

"Sorry. Sativa has killer lungs."

"She does. Congratulations again. She's beautiful."

Benny smiles, although to be fair, I don't think he's stopped smiling this whole time. "Lara, seriously, we cannot even begin to thank you for this opportunity. I am so fucking excited to be here." He laughs nervously. "Excuse my language. I'm just—you have no idea— that hotel was sucking the life out of me. And with the kid now, you know how expensive it is to live in Vancouver."

I nod, only because I had no idea how expensive it was to live in Vancouver until very recently.

"We are very happy to have you here. And tonight, you guys have to come to Tommy's Diner for dinner. Everyone is dying to welcome you—"

Before I can finish my sentence, Benny throws his arms around me in a bear hug and then quickly steps back. "Sorry. Sorry. I'm about to burst with happiness."

"The feeling's mutual, Benny."

I walk him through the rest of the house and then give him the requisite HR packet, as well as a Thalia Island cell phone and his own monster key chain.

"Should I get in touch with Finan today?"

A shiver always rushes through me when someone says his name out loud. I wish that would go away.

"If you want, just to check in? Council knows you're arriving. Maybe take today and the weekend to get settled, and then you can start bright and early Monday morning."

I again walk him through the Lutris tablet, showing him the town's general schedule, which includes the new settler arrivals on Tuesday and Wednesday and then a big welcome dinner Friday night. "You will shadow Finan and Joey for the first month or so, until you get to know the crews and where everything is. Never be afraid to ask questions—that's why everyone has a work phone." I tap his where it sits on the counter.

"Benny ... diaper bag!" Amalie yells from upstairs.

"Oh, that sounds desperate. I should let you help—if you need

47

anything, I'm always available via phone, text, or Lutris, and I'm pretty much always at town hall."

"Thank you again, Lara. Buy you a beer tonight?"

"Actually, the only thing I require is one of your mojitos."

He laughs and extends a hand. "It would be my honor."

"BENNY!"

I scurry to the front door and into my shoes before I have to see anything related to diaper bags or why Amalie might be in such urgent need for its contents. With a quick wave, I'm out the door.

As I slide behind the wheel of Rupert's car, Sativa's mighty screams echo in my ears as I check my phone for messages.

Two missed calls from Finan, followed by a text. My hands are instantly clammy as I swipe to read it.

Meet me at the medical clinic. Humboldt's injured.

NINE

MOMMA RACCOON 1, BIG DOG 0

While I don't always love living in a place so small that
everyone knows what I'm thinking even before I think it, I *do*
love that two minutes gets you from the residential area to pretty
much all the island's main services.

I screech into a spot in front of the doctor's office, right next to
Finan's silver truck. I pause for a second when I see blood smeared
across the driver's side door.

Inside the waiting room, a handful of people sit quietly. The young
mom from the other day is here, both of her kids in tow. The older
one—Harmony, I think?—has her hands over her ears, her eyes big
and tear-filled when she looks at me.

The howled yelp and scream from beyond the reception area
explains why.

"Lara, come on through," Catrina says, opening the door to grant
me entry into the hallway.

"What happened?" I ask, following her to the last room on the left.

"Seems Humboldt found a momma raccoon and her kits. Mom
went crazy, and Humboldt didn't know what was happening, so he
sort of just took the beating until she let go." Catrina pauses before

she opens the door. "There is a *lot* of blood. Ears are very vascular, and his is torn almost in half. Don't be alarmed."

I nod and she opens the door. Finan is practically lying on top of Humboldt who is wrapped in a beach towel while a gloved Dr. Stillson inspects the damage to my dog's ear and face.

"Oh god ..." I say, just in time for Catrina to shove a chair behind me. I collapse and she shoves my head between my knees.

"I warned her," she says and then rubs my back, advising me to take deep breaths, to be calm so Humboldt will be calm.

"I gave him a bit of sedative—I do have an animal kit here—but I don't think it's enough. He might be a bit overweight, but I didn't want to overdo it. Dogs have a different metabolism from people."

I sit back in the chair, my neck and underarms damp like I've just sprinted. "Can you fix him? Do I need to take him over to Vancouver?"

"I can stitch him up, if I can calm him," Dr. Stillson says just as Humboldt yowls.

"Lara, scoot closer so he can see you," Finan advises. "Maybe that will settle him."

I do what he says, trying not to notice the blood or the raw, exposed flesh. "Nope. Nope. Nope." I drop my head again.

The doctor and Catrina laugh, but Finan sighs. "Then come stand over here so he knows you're near."

"I *will*, Finan. Give me a second."

Dr. Stillson's phone rings on his hip. "Yeah ... hey, Lori, yeah, it looks like it's clean through. The right ear is torn, as is his lip. His face is scratched, and there's a decent gash on his neck. Yeah, eyes are OK, as far as I can tell." Humboldt fills the small room with a mighty howl.

I'm able to stand now, so without looking at the gore, I move and lower my face onto my dog's side, rubbing his rump, leaning over Finan with my eyes closed to whisper in Humboldt's ear. "You're OK, buddy. I'm here. We're gonna fix you up." His tail thumps against the padded exam table.

"No, we didn't get the raccoon, but she has new babies, so they let her be." The room fills with the sound of Big Dog's anxious panting and the buzz of the veterinarian's voice through Dr. Stillson's phone. "Sure. So, Benadryl to calm him down. Right … right, OK. If I send someone over to the mainland, can you have supplies ready for a pickup? I'll need anesthetic, a drip kit, pain medication, antibiotics, and definitely a rabies booster. I have suture kits, but if you have something better suited … yeah, he's a big boy. Hang on"— he pushes the phone aside—"Lara, how much do you think he weighs?"

"Easily 115 pounds," Finan answers.

Stillson returns to the call. "You can send a cone, but I very much doubt he'll wear it. Whatever you think is best." More talking on the other end. "Excellent. I'll have someone over in the next few hours. Email me the total, and we'll get you paid right away. Thank you so much, Lori. Give my love to Thea."

He hangs up.

"OK, so, who wants to take the boat over to Vancouver?"

Dr. Stillson did whatever math was necessary for the Benadryl dosage, and we managed to get Humboldt quiet enough to sleep on a pile of blankets in the exam room. I don't have a dog crate for him—do they even make those in Humboldt size?—so Catrina and the doc agree to keep him until I return from Vancouver.

Except I don't know how to drive a boat, hence why I am sitting in linen slacks, a bamboo-cotton blend blouse, and my favorite Alexander McQueen wedge sandals, my upper half wrapped in a borrowed flannel down coat that smells like the back of Finan's work truck. Since my seat on the passenger side in this vessel's cockpit spins away from the steering wheel, I pretend to take in the scenery rather than engage in small talk while Finan moves us out of the marina and into the strait.

It's a typical summer day in British Columbia, i.e., yesterday was hot but today it's cool and overcast, off-and-on rain, and brisk wind, making the water choppier than usual. My toes will freeze off before this day is over.

"One of these days, you'll wear those hiking boots," Finan says, eyes ahead as he slows us against the worsening chop.

"Not today," I say.

"Benny make it over all right?"

"He did. They're settled. That's where I was when you were looking for me."

"He seems very excited about getting to work. He's already texted and left me a voicemail."

"He's a good guy. Here's hoping he knows how to farm."

"Growing up in Alberta, I'm sure he'll be fine," Finan says. "His partner seem nice?"

I turn my chair. "Finan, are we really going to do this? Talk about bullshit?"

He snorts. "It's not bullshit. Benny is filling a significant hole in the crew. I was just hoping to get a more personal side of him, one that isn't facts lifted from an HR file."

"You can get your fill tonight at dinner." I spin away.

He's quiet for the duration.

~

The vet's office is in Burnaby, but because we don't have a car at Horseshoe Bay right now, Dr. Lori has a young, pink-haired tech waiting for us at the marina. She hands over a small cooler with some medications and then a duffel bag full of everything Dr. Stillson might need to fix up my dumb dog.

"There's some extra stuff in there, too, for next time," she says. Her scrubs have kittens on them.

"Let's hope there is no next time," I say, taking the cooler. "Please thank Dr. Lori again, and have her send the bill for all this right away. Plus the delivery fee. I'm so grateful."

"Good luck!" The tech waves goodbye and disappears into the parking lot as we head back to the moored boat. Finan secures the supplies in the cabin, unties, and takes us back out to sea.

About halfway across, the boat slows.

"What's happening? Are we out of charge?" I ask, spinning my seat to look over at the console. Nothing would be more perfect on a day like today than to get stranded in the middle of the Salish Sea with Finan Rowleigh.

But he's calmly leaned against the boat's side, one hand on the wheel, his eyes on me.

"We need to talk."

"Right now? Humboldt is bleeding to death all over the doctor's office. I think we can talk later."

"No. He is *not* bleeding to death. It's an ear laceration. An extra ten minutes isn't life or death. And I can't go on living like this, with you ignoring me all the time."

"You think we can work this out in ten minutes?" I say, snorting derisively.

"We can start."

"Fine. Start."

He lowers the throttle so we're barely puttering along. The water is still tipped with whitecaps, rocking us a little harder than we would be if we were moving faster, and the nippy wind whistles through the cockpit covering. I wrap his coat tighter around me, trying not to notice that I appreciate its scent.

"I am sorry for the way I handled things that night," he says. "There was *a lot* going on, and the slideshow sort of seemed ... excessive."

I look away—I can't hide the annoyance, and humiliation, on my face.

"I should not have left the way I did—"

"Well, at least we agree on *something*."

"But I needed to go help my sister and mom, so it worked out in the end."

"Very convenient."

"Lara, I am trying to communicate here. Can you stop being nasty for a second?"

Flames ignite in my eyes as I turn toward him, jumping to my feet, hanging on to the bar on the dash so I don't lose my balance in the rocking boat. "Fine—you hated what I did. You hated the slideshow. I *get it.* I am *sorry* you found it so offensive. I know I screwed up," I snap. "But *you* said you had my back. Is that what that means? You have my back until I do something you don't like, and then you bail?"

"I *do* have your back. I did then and—"

"You *left!* For two whole weeks! You left me to deal with the fallout of everything all by myself. How does that qualify as having my back?"

"I ... I don't know. You're right—it was shitty. Things were fucked up, what with the cops there to clean house and then those photos on the screen like that, with kids in the room—"

"She did it to me FIRST! Jesus, Finan, are you too soft to understand vengeance?"

"No. I'm not." He stands taller. "I know, in your world, the rules are different. People do mean shit to each other, which is repaid in kind. I know that ruining a person's reputation is like an everyday thing—"

"Don't you dare. I have *never* done anything like that before. I did what I did because Kelly has *ruined* my grandfather's legacy. She has *ruined* my mother's name, and mine right along with it. Have you seen what people online are saying? Did you see how we were trending for a week there, how they're now calling it Cult Island? Or how about Cartel Island?" I'm shaking with fury as I lift a finger and stab it in his direction, just shy of his chest. "Don't you *dare* preach at me about how the rules are different in my world because you know that's horseshit. People are terrible *everywhere.*"

Finan scrubs a hand through his hair. "When I saw the slideshow —that *that's* what you're capable of when someone crosses you—it freaked me out. I'm not saying what those people did on that beach was right. It was depraved and sick. All of it."

You have no fucking idea. Kelly tortured and murdered Derek Irving.

But I can't tell him that.

He swallows hard, rubbing at his beard. "But if you unleash that kind of vitriol on people who have wronged you, what did that say about us? What did that say about what you might do if anything ever went wrong between you and me? Would you organize intimate details of our time together in some twisted PowerPoint? Would you splatter our most secret moments all over the internet in some embittered brand of revenge?"

I'm so angry at my body right now for betraying me. I don't want tears—I want fury. I want laser beams to shoot out of my eyes and clenched fists that can crush stone and I want rockets in my feet so I can fly away from this person I thought I could trust.

But as I'm not a superhero, the first tear races down my windburned cheek, chased by a string of others. I clench my jaw to make sure Finan knows they are not tears of weakness but of defiance.

"That's what you think of me? You think I would do that to you? To us?"

He shakes his head and steps closer. All he has to do is reach out

...

I hop back into my seat and rotate away with a warning look.

"I made a mistake. I miscalculated," he says, his voice softer. "We were under a ton of stress and everything was happening so fast—the reality of the sabotage on the island was overwhelming, and then with my sister's babies and the complications there and Rupert being sick, and I knew I was falling in love with you, but it just felt too soon—"

"Nooooo. Stop." I again face him, even if it means he sees me ugly crying. "Don't you just throw that in there like it doesn't matter. Like it's an *excuse* for you abandoning me when I *needed* you. After you promised time and time again that you'd always have my back." My throat strains, my voice shrinking. "Because you *know* no one has before. I *trusted you*, Finan."

He looks away but when his eyes catch mine, it's his turn to grapple with tears. "I hope you will give me the chance to prove that I am sorry. I meant what I said, Lara. I—"

"Don't. Don't you tell me you love me because you think it will magically fix everything."

His sigh sounds defeated.

"You've been home for seventeen days, and you haven't made a move to talk."

"But I have! You're always busy or doing your damnedest to avoid me or mooning over Dr. Stillson."

"HA!" I sniff. My queendom for some Kleenex.

"I get it. He's handsome, he's smart, he's single—"

"Please stop talking. Can we go now? Your ten minutes are up."

"Lara ... I miss you. I miss what we were starting."

I hold my arm aloft and furiously tap at my wrist, as if indicating my invisible watch.

Finan's shoulders tighten as he moves back to the steering wheel. He throttles up and gets us to the Thalia Island marina in record time.

I watch the blustery water out the port side for the duration of the journey as my tears soak into the fabric of Finan's borrowed coat.

Maybe he will feel them later.

TEN

I'M FINE. EVERYTHING'S FINE.

U pon our return to Dr. Stillson's office with the veterinary supplies, the waiting room is cleared out. Catrina is behind the front desk, bent over a pile of paperwork. Her relieved smile greets us.

"That was quick!" she says, again opening the side door to let us into the back area. "Doc is in there reading to him from an internal medicine journal." She smiles. "Your dog apparently is very interested in the inner workings of the liver."

"Maybe because he wants to eat it," I say. "Washroom?"

Catrina points to a door in the opposite direction.

I tuck inside, my exposed toes still cold despite the cranked heat in Finan's truck during the brief ride in from the marina. The face looking back at me in the small mirror—mascara everywhere. Shameful. If Catrina asks, I will blame it on the windy conditions out on the water.

I tidy myself, moving faster when a renewed yelp echoes from down the hall. As I scurry into the exam room, Humboldt is lying on his side, panting, eyes worried. Dr. Stillson has a syringe in his hand, and Finan is again holding the beast down with the towel, albeit awkwardly given his height and the small room and the fact that Humboldt is on the floor rather than on the exam table.

"He's too anxious to try to lift him," Dr. Stillson explains. "I've just given him a tranquilizer. Once he's out, we can move him back to the table and I'll stitch him up. I'll give him the rabies booster too—any chance you have his past medical records?"

I shake my head no. "I will ask Rupert next time we talk."

"He'll need the booster, anyway. You never know with raccoons."

Within that short conversation, Humboldt's eyes have grown heavy, his breathing slowed. On a stainless steel exam cart, Catrina has opened the suture kit and a bunch of other stuff I don't know if I want to see used.

"Lara, you're white as a sheet again," Dr. Stillson says. "I can't have you passing out in here, so why don't you go wait out front and we'll get busy?"

"You sure?"

He nods.

"Finan?"

"I'm fine," he says, not looking up.

I slip out, a hand on the wall to manage the light-headedness, and ease myself into one of the waiting-room chairs. The shakiness is an unsavory recipe of stress, worry, hunger, queasiness from the blood ...

And sadness.

He said he loves me.

Does he mean it? Or was he just saying that to temper my anger?

I want to tell him how stupid I feel about that night, that I regret what I did. I want to tell him how much I miss having him in my bed, his huge body wrapped around me, the taste of him on my lips, the smell of him on my skin, how seeing him next to me means he's just a whisper away. As much as I am reluctant to admit it right now, Finan Rowleigh is still the last thing I think about before I fall asleep, and the first thing I think about when I wake up.

Well, almost. Usually the first thing I think about is where Humboldt is and if he's bouncing by the front door to go out for a wee.

But that's only because I really like my area rugs.

Maybe if I can get Finan alone in a quiet place, like, over for dinner or maybe coffee, we can sit and talk without the anger—and the embarrassment, which I'm still soaked in.

Because aligned with what he said, I, too, miss what we were starting. I've never felt about anyone the way I feel about Finan.

And as I rest my head in my hands to keep the tears at bay, I know that this dull ache in my chest is because I miss him.

Desperately.

The hall door opens, and he's there.

"Everything OK?" I ask, trying to hide the crack in my veneer.

"Dr. Stillson's got it under control. I need to get back to work." He moves through the waiting room without slowing.

"Finan …" He's opened the main clinic door but pauses long enough to look back at me. "Thank you. For your help today."

"Yup." Then he's gone, practically jogging to his truck, off to deal with whatever has sprung up in his absence.

"Guess I'll see you at dinner," I say to the quiet.

An hour later, Catrina comes out wearing her kind smile, two glass juice bottles in hand. "Apple is all we have," she says. Grateful, I take one as she sits in the adjacent chair. "All is well. The patient is stitched and hopped up on pain medication. Doc gave him the rabies shot and the first injection of antibiotics. There's a bottle of pills to finish the course—two weeks' worth. You'll wanna keep it in the fridge. You can hide it in a piece of cheese or sausage. Shouldn't be too hard."

"He eats everything," I say. "Thank you so much."

"Thank Liam. He did the hard parts. I just handed him stuff."

"Still …" I finish the juice like a starved five-year-old and recap the emptied bottle. "Guess I was thirsty."

"It's been a long day."

I nod and lean forward, hoping to keep the emotion hidden. Catrina rests a hand on my back. That's all it takes.

"Everything feels so much harder now, Catrina." She reaches

across to the square coffee table and grabs a box of tissues. Seems she's always giving me tissues. "I used to just live my life and party and go out and shop and travel and do whatever I wanted. And now, I've got this overwhelming job and I'm in charge of people's lives and I have a *dog* and Finan and I are fighting ..."

She rubs in circles and then leans her head against my shoulder.

"You're a grown-up now, Lara. This is real life. Before was ... something else."

I laugh through the tears. "Before I didn't have to feel anything. I didn't *think*—I just *did*. It was so much easier."

She sits up and nudges me. "But was it?"

"I need Rupert to get better so he can come home and help. I know that sounds selfish, but he always knows what to do."

She chuckles. "He does. And he'll be back as soon as he can. Until then, he's relying on you to steer the ship."

I turn in my chair so we're facing each other. "But that's the thing, Catrina—I have no IDEA how to steer a ship. Not figurative or literal. I couldn't even drive the boat over myself today. I had to spend that time feeling awkward and angry because Finan and I have the communication skills of chimpanzees."

She laughs out loud. "Love is hard."

I shake my head. "He said it. On the boat today. The L-word."

"I figured something was up, given the condition of your mascara when you walked in."

"I don't know what to do."

"How do *you* feel about him?"

I shrug. "I miss him. A lot."

"So, what are you waiting for? Are you playing hard to get? Because that can backfire very quickly."

I wrap my right hand over the still-cold toes of my left foot, my leg bent on the wooden chair. "He said that what I did that night, with the slideshow—it freaked him out that I'm capable of something so rotten."

"And ..."

"And he's right. I hate that he's right. I *hate* that I went through with it."

"Did you tell *him* that?"

"I don't know. I mean, I tried, but it was loud on the boat, and we were sort of yelling at each other …"

"You need to figure out what you want, Lara. If you want Finan, tell him. If you don't, cut him loose. And if you don't say or do anything, well, then the choice might no longer be yours to make."

A door from down the hall opens, followed by footsteps. Catrina leans close. "I don't have to remind you that a certain adorable physician is single and very interested in taking you out for adult beverages. Not that that helps you at all."

"Not at all," I say, a small smile squeaking through.

Speaking of adorable physicians, Dr. Stillson joins us in the waiting room. "You OK, Lara?"

I sit up and paste on a happy face. "How's my ferocious predator?"

"He will live to see another day. Hopefully not another raccoon den, but another day, for sure."

As I stand, I realize I'm still wearing Finan's coat. It is the weirdest outfit, made weirder by the feeling that I'm doing something wrong, talking to Dr. Stillson while wearing another man's coat.

This is very confusing.

Because Dr. Stillson *is* remarkably handsome and kind. He wiped an entire afternoon of human patients off his schedule to tend to my dog, for Pete's sake.

"So, I think he should probably hang out here for a few more hours. He's sleeping right now from the pain medicine and the leftover tranquilizer, but once he's awake and able to walk, he should be fine to go home."

"How can I ever thank you for this?"

"I'd take a cold beer and some good pub food," he says.

"I think that can be arranged."

We agree that they'll set up a small camera in the room with Humboldt so we can watch him from an app on Dr. Stillson's phone since we are apparently having dinner together? Is this what I just agreed to?

As Catrina is closing down her workstation for the day, I insist that they allow me to pay not only for the supplies from Dr. Lori but for their time and expertise as well. By the time the arm wrestling over cost is finished, Humboldt is into me for nearly $1500.

Way to go, Big Dog.

Catrina turns off the lights and locks the main door, her keys in hand. "You're coming to Benny's welcome dinner, yes?"

Shit. Right. Tommy's Diner. Not the pub.

"Yes. Yes, I am," I say. "I'll need to pop back to my office and freshen up."

"And find some socks?" she says, nodding at my open-toed shoes. "One of these days, you'll give in."

"Ha."

"I guess when Doc is removing your frostbitten toes ..."

"Maybe then."

"See you in a bit, sweetie. Bye, Doc!" she says, letting herself out the back door. Dr. Stillson is in his office, now on the phone. I'm sort of in limbo in the hallway, watching Humboldt sleep on a pile of blankets on the exam room floor, not sure if I should leave or ...

"Hey, sorry, just calling Dr. Lori to let her know how it went." The sharp scent of hand sanitizer wafts from his direction. "OK, I've got the camera set up there"—he points to a ball-shaped device suction-cupped to the metal cabinet above the sink—"so we can grab dinner, if you're up for it."

"Yes, but, um, actually, we're having the welcome-to-Thalia shindig at the diner for Benny, so everyone can meet him. He's taking over the spot vacated by Ainsley Kerr."

"Sure, that's cool. Dinner there, and then that beer across the way?"

Oh dear. "Sounds perfect."

He peeks past me to look in on Big Dog. "Don't worry. He'll be fine," Dr. Stillson says, resting his hand on my upper arm.

On the sleeve that belongs to another man.

"Thank you again," I say, pivoting toward the door. "Meet you at the diner in, like, half an hour?"

"Sounds perfect," he says, repeating my words.

As I slide in behind the wheel of Rupert's car, my heart beats so loud in my ears, it almost drowns out the alarm bells clanging in my head.

Almost.

ELEVEN

DEEP THOUGHTS

The diner is packed with crew members and residents alike. Benny is holding court, Amalie with baby Sativa in her arms tucked in a booth, looking on adoringly at her partner as he regales his new coworkers with sordid tales from the Alberta farm fields and, of course, Vancouver's chic downtown drunks.

My cheeks warm when the conversation pivots to his stories about the Fairmont, but upon our eyes meeting across the crowd, he winks once, as if to reassure me he has no plans of telling them about the many, many hours I spent decorating that bar.

I think Benny is so happy to be here with a good-paying gig on an island full of like-minded people that he wouldn't dare bite the hand that feeds him.

Speaking of hands, Dr. Stillson makes use of his as we move through the crowd to find a spot at the far end of the lunch counter— either his palm against my lower back or a soft grip of my upper arm (now shed of Finan's work coat, replaced by my own coordinating silk blazer). Tommy and his staff have prepared a delectable Mexican feast, spread down the rest of the bar in silver chafing dishes kept warm by tiny flame pots—and it seems once folks make it through the line, they're eating wherever they can find a clear foot of real estate.

64

"Any chance you'd want to go across the way and get something a little ... quieter?" Dr. Stillson asks against my ear.

I nod and hold up a finger. I squeeze through the sea of humans of various fragrances and states of cleanliness to stand on an overturned crate next to the booth where Amalie bounces the baby against her chest. It takes a second for the din to quiet, but once it does, I give a quick welcome-home speech for Benny and his family, remind everyone how grateful I am for their continued devotion to our mission (*"Always remind them about the mission, Lara,"* Rupert says in my head), and then invite any interested parties across to the Wandering Salamander for drinks and karaoke after they're done laying waste to Tommy's amazing buffet.

Quick applause, and then I'm officially off duty. As I navigate toward Dr. Stillson waiting by the door, I spot Finan sitting in the end booth with Joey, his head agritech, and Lucy-Frank Makamoose. He doesn't miss a beat in whatever he's saying, his eyes drifting past me like creek water over a mossy rock.

Ouch.

Upon reaching the doctor, I shove the sting into my box of neglected emotions and tape it closed.

"Shall we?" he says.

"After you." The bell above the door announces our departure, though I doubt anyone notices.

I hope at least one person does.

The quiet of the Salamander is a welcome salve to the chaos at Tommy's. I'm surprised to see Len Emmerich and a few of his guys around a big table in the corner, already three empty pitchers deep. Seems they got an early start on the Friday night festivities.

Len bobs his head in greeting when he sees me leaned against the bar, waiting to order much-needed libation.

The pub itself is owned by Clarke Innovations, managed by an island resident. And since the prior manager was one of Kelly's besties, he was marched off that night alongside his weirdo friends. Taking his place as of three weeks ago is an attractive, thirty-something woman named Dakota, handpicked by Rupert—she's apparently the daughter of a longtime friend, and after losing her own quirky, pop culture–inspired diner to a fire, she didn't have the heart or energy to start over.

She seems nice enough, though we've only talked a couple times when she's come in to town hall. Once she was having problems with the Powerwall at her residence; the other time she needed a maintenance crew member to help with moving kegs. Her arrival was quiet and without fanfare, unlike Benny's, but the crews have been stressed under the weight of Ainsley's sudden disappearance, so his arrival is like the calm after a storm. Plus I think everyone is just so happy to have a moment without a blazing fire, literal or figurative, that it's time to party.

When Dakota popped by my office about the kegs, she asked if I'd want to grab lunch sometime. "Of course," I said, because that's what polite administrators do. It hasn't happened yet—and upon seeing her, I realize I sort of forgot. I hope she's not lonely. I've been doing my drinking at home (*naughty, naughty*) and the island's been so tranquil lately, I feel bad she hasn't had more customers.

We'll make up for it tonight. With the town council seats filled, the online chatter about Dea Vitae diminishing, Benny's arrival, and the new settlers expected next week, the island hums with a pleasant energy I haven't felt before. Dare I think of it as hopeful, that we might be back on track, moving toward achieving Grandfather's vision for a modern, working utopia?

"Hey, Lara. Great to see you in here," Dakota says, returning to the bar after delivering another pitcher to Len and his gang.

"I'm so happy you're here to see!" I sound a little too head cheerleader. "Everything running OK?"

"Like a well-oiled machine," she says, smiling. Her eyes have a sad sparkle in them … I really need to invite her to lunch next week and make sure she's all right.

She nods at the doctor next to me. "Dr. Stillson. What can I get for you guys?"

"Any chance we can get dinner? Tommy's was a madhouse," he asks.

"Not hot food. They borrowed my grill master for the big to-do—but if you're cool with easy stuff, I have a cook-in-training who can do chips and salsa with fresh guac, or turkey sandwiches?"

"We'll take both," I say. "Doc, preferred drink?"

"Whatever your newest lager is," he says.

"I'll start with the same."

"You got it." Dakota nods and moves into action. Dr. Stillson's fingers on my elbow direct me toward a two-person high-top table in front of the unlit gas-powered fireplace. I slide onto my seat, sort of wishing the fireplace was on—my poor toes are still bare and *still cold.*

Upon sitting, I pull the Handi Wipes from my purse and wipe down the table and the table's edge. Stillson has his phone out, but I can feel him watching me. "Do you not trust the cleanliness here?"

"Neurotic habit I can't kick," I say, wadding the used cloths into a ball and setting them aside. "Also, recent bout of food poisoning, remember? Not looking for a repeat."

"Those wipes aren't exactly eco-friendly," he says.

"I won't tell if you won't."

He chuckles and holds up his phone. It's streaming video of my slumbering dog. "One less thing for you to worry about."

"Thank you. How long will he be out?"

"Long enough for you to have a beer and food, and maybe regale us with some impressive vocal stylings?" He nods toward the tiny stage against the eastern wall. A small, disco-style light ball hanging from the ceiling sits idle, waiting for its companion—the new karaoke machine—to wake up.

"I'm going to need a lot more than *a beer* to partake of that nonsense."

Dakota slides up next to us, dropping recycled cardboard, soy-ink printed coasters with the Wandering Salamander logo onto the table, followed by our foam-topped, amber-hued beverages. My mouth waters as though I haven't seen liquid refreshment in a month. "Food will be right up," she says, pausing to look at Stillson's phone. "Aw, is that your dog? I heard he got hurt."

"Tangled with a momma raccoon," the doctor says. "First time I've ever sutured a bullmastiff ear."

"And hopefully the last," Dakota says, taking the words right out of my mouth.

"Bring him next time you're in, Lara. My pittie girl died at fifteen last year. I miss having a pup," she says.

I wait until she's back behind the bar before lifting my glass and holding it so she can't see my lips. "I'm worried about her," I say.

Stillson looks over at the bar nonchalantly. "Why?"

"She seems lonely."

"Homesick, maybe?" Doc sips his beer. "Although who could ever be homesick with an unlimited supply of this." He takes another drink, heartier this time.

"Maybe. Apparently, her restaurant burned down. She's probably still reeling from that."

"That would be a shock to the system."

I think of the vertical farm B inferno and how scary that was—and I hadn't invested my life savings or hard work into its construction or operation. "*And* she lost her canine companion of fifteen years? I didn't even want a dog, but now that I've got one, I don't want to lose the big oaf."

Liam chuckles. "He is very slobbery."

I sip and dab my lipstick on a cloth napkin. "I need to hang out with Dakota. Let her know she's not alone. I wasn't great when I first got here."

"Did you leave lots of friends behind in Vancouver?"

How much does he know about my former life? "Not really. More just a significant lifestyle shift."

"It's definitely smaller and much, much slower. I do miss my friends, I will admit. Especially my best friend, Cole. We went through medical school together. He's a plastic surgeon now. Making the big bucks."

"That didn't appeal to you?"

"Nah," he says. "Family practice. My mom's a pediatrician, Dad's an internist. I always liked Mom's stories better."

"Nice. Family business, then."

"Sort of."

"No siblings?"

"Just me."

"Same," I say, "but I always wanted a little sister. Someone to boss around."

He points at me with his raised glass. "I can see that."

"Control freak." I raise a hand. "Probably stems from a lack of control pretty much my whole life?"

He nods. "What about your father?"

"No clue. The running joke is I sprouted in a field in the middle of Canada and my mother was flying overhead, saw me, landed, scooped me up, and named me after Superman's mother."

Dr. Stillson laughs loudly. "Are you serious? You're named after Superman's mother?"

"That's the rumor."

"OK, well, I see you in a whole new light now, Lara Clarke." He takes another long drink of his beer. "What do you think of this place? Are you like our sad bartender, lonely and pining for your field in the middle of Canada?"

"Thalia Island is a job. I'm here because my grandfather wanted me here. It's nice. I'm keeping busy and slowly making friends"—I gesture to him—"but I'm not one of those sorts who has a ton of close connections. Being who I am has made longtime friendships difficult, especially with women."

"Why do you think that is?"

"Beats me. You're the doctor." I know why, but I'm not getting into it with him. I hardly know this man.

He grins. "Well, it's definitely quieter here. Like I said, that's been the biggest adjustment for me, I think. Life was so chaotic and busy with med school and residency. Everything was like go, go, go for so many years, and then they spit us out into the real world where we have to, like, manage everything—patients, sure, but also the business side of things. Payroll and taxes and malpractice insurance and supplies and HR issues. Running an office is a pain in the ass. I just wanted to practice medicine, not spend endless hours bent over government paperwork."

"Ah, see, that's where you lucked out. Catrina is basically an administrative genius," I say.

"As I have witnessed firsthand." He lifts his glass. "To Catrina and her administrative acumen that will keep us all alive."

We tap glasses and drink just as the chips and guac arrive, this time delivered by the cook-in-training Dakota mentioned. "Sandwiches will be right up." She hurries away before I can tell her to hold the mayo.

"So, Lara Clarke, tell me more about the real you."

Ugh. This game. I hate this game. "Um, as you know, Archibald Clarke was my grandfather. I am on Thalia Island as part of his dying request that I protect his legacy. You know my dog, you know where I work … what else is there?"

He smiles through a sip of his half-finished beer. "I know the history of the Clarke family. That's why I'm here. I believe in your grandfather's vision." He pops a chip in his mouth, crunching loudly. "What I'm asking is, I want to know something about *you*, not the heiress, not the island's administrator or mayor or whatever your job is, not Humboldt's mom …"

"I inherited him. I'm not really his mom."

"I don't know … they say when someone has a pet, they start to look like each other after a while." He pinches one eye closed and tilts his head. "The resemblance is uncanny."

I kick him under the table.

"Ow." He takes another bite and then finishes his beer, signaling to the bar that we'd like two more. "He's a good dog. And he loves you, I can tell."

"*No*, he loves Finan," I say, instantly wishing I hadn't, hurrying to deflect. "Let's see … what about me … you know I don't like germs." I point to the wad of used Handi Wipes. "I have a weakness for expensive shoes."

He looks under the table. "Totally impractical for this environment, but OK."

"I like sappy romance novels that will tear out your heart and leave you sobbing alone in the bathtub with an emptied bottle of Pinot."

"Wow, that does not sound healthy."

"It is. Super healthy." I finish my beer as Dakota slides two more pints onto the tabletop and disappears again.

"What are you into? Your mom was a photographer. Obviously a world traveler, if she went to all those places to take such incredible pictures."

"She was a pilot too."

"Damn," he says, scraping guacamole from the pottery bowl. We've made quick work of it. "And that wanderlust didn't bite you?"

"I've traveled plenty. Went everywhere with Grandfather and Rupert," I say.

"And what about school? Sports? Cheerleading? President of the chess club?"

"Very funny."

"What? You look like you'd be good at chess. Or maybe poker."

"I am passable at poker," I say. "And I don't know ... I've tried lots of things. My grandfather made sure I was exposed to everything—I've had every imaginable lesson under the sun, from dance to music to horseback riding to archery. I even went to circus camp one year."

"As a clown, no doubt."

"*Obviously.*" I let him finish the chips, instead focusing on enhancing the warm glow slowing washing over me from the beer. "I've tried a million things—I just wasn't very good at any of them."

"So?"

"It helps to be good at something to want to keep doing it."

Dr. Stillson shrugs. "Maybe. Or you can just do it for the joy of the experience."

I take another drink. "Professional beer taster. I could see myself doing that."

"I think that is a real job."

"Then I'm going to look into it."

"You should try some of Mrs. Corwin's community builders," he says. "Pottery, painting, wildflower identification, tiny garden cultivation—I saw there's even a quilting class on the list."

I pretend to snore.

He smiles and shrugs. "I dare you to pick one thing. Try it for a week."

"And take a spot someone else might appreciate more?" This conversation is starting to feel a little too personal. These are things I talk about with Finan, not Dr. Stillson. And Finan doesn't pressure me into trying things I have no interest in doing.

"What's the ring?" He nods at where I'm twisting the thick band around my middle finger.

"My grandfather's."

"Aw, sweet."

"I think so," I say, examining the white gold and red-stone ring I am rarely without. "Makes him feel close."

Dakota breaks into the moment, hands full with our plated turkey sandwiches piled high with fresh greens she proudly explains are from vertical farm A, as well as homemade kettle chips from the same farm's potato crop. Everyone here gets so excited about our food being grown on the island. I'm just grateful we hired people with green thumbs or else I would starve to death—pretty sure Skip the Dishes doesn't deliver across the strait.

The food's arrival also truncates the conversation wherein Dr. Stillson is using whatever techniques he learned during the psychiatric portion of his medical training to unpack my deep inner self. I don't need to be analyzed by a guy who chews chips with his mouth open.

Also, I have no deep inner self.

What the hell, Lara ...

Who are you really?

Before the panic sets in, I slide off my chair. "How do you feel about Japanese whisky?" I ask, moving to the bar before he can answer.

TWELVE

TRAGIC KINGDOM

"Who wants more Gaga?" I yell into the mic. The crowd goes wild, everyone from Tommy's now migrated over to the Salamander. It's elbow to elbow with every over-nineteen member of Thalia Island's privileged community present and accounted for, the karaoke machine is smokin', and I can no longer feel my lips, which is exactly the way I like it.

I've gone through my limited repertoire, hardly caring if I can actually carry a tune this many shots in, but when someone hollers "Celebrity Skin" above the din, I decide to give the people what they want.

Courtney Love and I are one for an entire four minutes.

The crowd goes wild.

I pause long enough to finish the rest of a beer that somehow appeared on a tall stool on the stage—no idea if it's mine but I'm gonna drink it—and scan the crowd for faces I recognize. Dr. Stillson, or Liam, as he insisted I call him after I kept stumbling over the many consonants in his name (I blame the Hibiki, which is super good whisky, seriously), so now me and Liam are definitely on a first-name basis and I'm *pretty sure* Liam wants to see what color my panties are, but I am *not* that kind of girl. You can't just buy me a turkey sandwich and some beers and expect me to rub my boobs all over your face.

No, sir.

Anyway, as I was saying, I have no idea where he went. He was the one who said I should sing and now, where is he?

"OK, OK, OK, Thalia Island, as you know, I am so, so happy you guys are all here. Guys *and* gals and everything in between—yeah, yeah, I'm hip, not just a dumb millennial who only thinks about herself—OK, so anyway, I know these first couple months have been freaking *weird*, and like, we had that cult thing and that fucked-UP situation with that harpy Kelly Lockhart, but like, I just want you all to know that I think you are so great. You're, like, just awesome. I have all these new brothers and sisters, and it's so freaking cool." I pause and drink again, my throat so dry. I could really use some water.

"So, everybody knows that Big Dog got hurt today, and Dr. Stillson sewed him up and he's all better"—I pause while everyone applauds the doctor. "Ah! There he is! By the bar. Hey, Doc! Thanks for fixing my dog!" I wave like I'm a parade spectator, hoping to be seen by the May Queen. "Anyway, so I also want to thank Finan, beautiful, beautiful Finan, for scooping up my dumb dog and rushing him to the doctor and basically saving his life." More applause as everyone turns to Finan, leaning against the bar, not looking at all impressed.

"Awww, come on, Finny—why so serious?"

The crowd laughs.

"Do you people wanna hear a funny story about me and Finan?" A rolling roar and claps from the gathered souls. "So, like, you know my mom is dead, right? And yeah, you guys, the rumors about her working for the cartel or whatever, that's just tabloid crap, so don't believe everything you read on the Wicked Stepsister," I say. The crowd quiets for a sec. "Anyway, so, I'm like at the memorial service for my mom, and some idiot has put out a plate of pickles—pickles!— and my mom *hated* pickles, like, she would gag when she smelled 'em. And I was pissed because Rupert made me wear this stupid dress I hated and everyone was like, *Oh poor Lara her mom is dead and now she's alone*"—I pause for another drink, finishing the beer—"but I was, like, ten, and my mom was always gone so it didn't really make sense yet that she wasn't coming back, and so yeah, I see those effing pickles so I picked up the plate and I launch it—"

I mime the action, feeling the weight of the pickle plate in my hand, the power in my arm as I tossed it—

Except I lose my balance and I'm still wearing these McQueen wedges so I fall right off the short stage and somehow I've gotten tangled in the microphone cord so that's not helpful and when I land, my head bounces off the hardwood floor, which does *not* feel great and then there are people all around me.

"Lara, I think you've had enough." Len Emmerich takes the mic still clutched in my hand.

"You look like the tough Russian guy from *Rocky*," I say to him.

"Heyyyy, Lara, you OK?" Dr. Stillson—Liam—kneels next to my head as Len tries to disentangle the mic cord from my body.

"I hit my head. Really hard."

"You did. I heard it." His fingers probe my skull, and I close my eyes.

"Mmmm, I love it when people play with my hair."

"We should probably get you home, yeah?"

Eyes open again. "What? No! I gotta finish singing! We didn't even do anything from *Tragic Kingdom* yet and that is such a great album! Although seriously, why did Gwen marry that country singer dude? God, he is so squishy."

"All right, up you go," Liam says, helping me onto my butt.

I am so, so dizzy. "Hmmm, I think I want to lie down again." I try to, but another set of hands hoists me under the armpits and onto my feet.

"I'll take her home, Doc. If you can get Humboldt, I'll meet you at my truck."

"That's all right, Finan. I can drive her." Liam sounds a little pushy.

Uh-oh, are they gonna fight over me?

My head lolls on my shoulders and my ankles feel like they're held together by overstretched rubber bands. "Maybe I *should* wear

75

those ugly hiking boots, Finny. Then I won't have cold toes anymore."

"Stop calling me Finny," he growls. "Doc, I will meet you at my truck."

With that, Finan throws me over his shoulder, just like he did that day in the very muddy field when I ruined a perfectly gorgeous pair of Chloé Goldee boots. "Bye, everyone!" I push myself up against Finan's strong back, his muscles tensing under my hands with every step he takes through the parting crowd. "Sing some Gwen Stefani for me and don't forget to tip your waitress!"

The crowd claps and whoops as we leave, and the second we're outside in the cool night air, the roar in my ears is louder than the people inside the Salamander. "Put me down," I say, smacking Finan's ass.

He does not oblige.

I push myself up again over his shoulder, using what few stomach muscles I have—I really need to talk to Rupert about opening a gym or recruiting my old trainer—because being in this position makes my head throb too hard and the alcohol slosh in my stomach and I do not like that feeling *at all*. "Finan, put me *down*."

"If I put you down, you will fall again, and I am not taking your drunk ass over to Vancouver for an MRI because you split your head open acting like a drunken fool."

We're down the block when I see Liam coming out of the Salamander, throwing on his jacket. He jogs toward us just as Finan opens the dual-cab door of his big stinky truck and flops me onto the back seat.

"Geez, man, you don't gotta be so rough."

"Sit still. I'm going to get the dog." He slams the door and then locks the truck with his key fob. If I try to escape, the alarm will go off, and there is already too much noise pounding in my skull.

After approximately one million years, the side of the truck opens, and Finan and Liam have my giant pupper wrapped in a blankie, his ear bandaged up, a cone of shame around his neck. "Oh yeah, that's not gonna last."

"Sit up and let him rest his head on your lap. Can you manage that?" Finan asks.

"Don't have to be so mean," I say as Humboldt stumbles across the seat. His lips are a bit foamy and a prodigious line of drool has slimed the inside of his plastic cone but when he sees me, he whines and eagerly drops his upper half on my thighs. "Aww, buddy, did you miss me? You had a rough day, didn't ya ..."

Liam covers the dog with the rest of the blanket. "I'll call tomorrow and check on him. And you. Have a good night, Lara."

"Bye, Liam! Thanks for hanging out! That was so much—"

The door thuds.

"Fun," I finish. "You poor puppy ... we'll go home and you can have all the cookies and you can sleep on my bed and we will just stay away from those mean old raccoons."

Finan climbs in behind the wheel. He looks over his seat into the back. "You belted in?"

"Yes, *Dad*."

He pulls out of downtown, quiet the whole drive to our neighboring cabins. I'm spinning, my head bouncing against the truck wall if I close my eyes too long, my consciousness teetering on that precipice between feeling good and feeling like I might die. The sensation worsens when we hit our gravel driveway, bouncing all the way up the slight incline to the front of my cabin.

"Keys?" Finan reaches over his seat.

"Hmmm?" I wrestle my lids open.

"Keys to your place. I'll unlock it first, then take Humboldt in."

I hoist my purse at him. "In there somewhere." My head flops against the truck again. "I need water."

"You need a lot more than that," Finan mumbles as he searches through my bag. Then he's out, keys jingling, front door opened, and again at the truck. He opens my side and I almost fall out.

"What are you doing?" I snap.

"It will be easier to unload him from this angle. Can you stand?"

I fumble with my seat belt—it only takes a few tries to get it undone—and then slither out of the vehicle, determined to show him that I *can* walk upright. "See?"

He's ignoring me, instead helping Humboldt out and onto the ground.

"Poor Big Dog," I say, trailing them into my cabin. I shut the door behind us as Finan clicks on lights and leads Humboldt to the treat drawer. "Did you know that you two are my most favorite men ever?"

I slide onto my comfy sofa and reach down to take off my sandals but it's too hard so instead I scooch up and grab a pillow and shove it under my pounding head and pull the throw from the back and tuck it over my shoulders and yes, that's better. Way better, except it's so loud in here with so much silence.

"Lara." Someone nudges me.

"Hmmm ..." I can't open my eyes. Too hard.

"Take these—I can't leave it sitting here or Humboldt will eat 'em and we've had enough drama for one day." Finan pulls me to sitting, and not softly. "Open your eyes, please."

"Man, so bossy. That's why you're the boss, right, boss?" I smile, eyes cracked. I lift my left hand and rest it against his cheek. "God, you are so beautiful. Did you know that? Do you even know how beautiful you are? I miss you so much, Finan. I miss you so much." My eyes sting and I want him to say nice things back to me but instead he drops two Advil in my palm and then slides a glass of some sort of green juice into my other hand.

"Bottoms up."

I swallow the pills and finish the nasty juice. And then he removes the glass from my hand and I flop back down on the couch and he covers me with the blanket or maybe I cover myself, I don't know, but then the front door opens and closes and the only sound is Big Dog flopping onto the dog bed that has somehow appeared next to the couch in place of my coffee table ...

Good night, Lara.

THIRTEEN

FRIENDS WITHOUT BENEFITS

I think I broke my brain. Or maybe I just pickled it ... ah, the irony.

Rupert yells at me through the Lutris portal, undermining any progress the ibuprofen swallowed upon awakening might otherwise make. He's going on about "two strikes, Lara, this is two strikes," like I'm some stupid teenager who crashed the Range Rover into the fence. Again.

"Can you please lower your voice?" I hold the ice pack to the back of my neck.

"You are ridiculous, do you know that?"

My living room gets very quiet.

"I have trusted you to do the right thing in my absence. Instead, I wake to video and messages from Len Emmerich, detailing your exploits last evening. You do remember that a few short weeks ago, people were calling for your expulsion."

"Yes, and those people are *gone.*"

"Perhaps, but that doesn't mean everyone left behind thinks you're the cat's meow. You are responsible for the welcoming and assimilation of a whole new group in three days' time—and this is what they are coming to? An island of hedonism and debauchery?"

"It was KARAOKE, Rupert. I wasn't debauching anyone or anything."

"Tell that to their poor ears." Number Two sips from the teacup just off-screen. "This is your last chance to smarten up. Do you hear me?"

"Yes, whatever ..."

"I mean it, Lara. If you revisit the terms of your employment contract, you will note there is a conduct clause. Just like everyone else has to sign."

"I didn't kill anyone last night."

"I think Lady Gaga would beg to differ."

"Hilarious."

Another sip from his tea. "You are self-destructing. I don't understand it. Not one bit."

"That makes two of us," I mumble.

"What did you say?"

"*Nothing.* Is there anything else you need this morning beyond the scolding?"

Rupert exhales and leans back against his brocade chair. His hair is very thin and mostly grayish-white. I have to look away—the guilt is too much. He's fighting for his life, and I'm acting like an ass.

Again.

"I am a work in progress, just like everyone else."

"Then work faster." He sits forward, closer to the camera. I hate how pale he looks. "I thought you were on a steady course there for a moment. I thought you were ... exploring things with Finan."

"I was. And then he got mad about that stupid slideshow and bailed."

"He went to Vancouver to help his family, Lara."

"Maybe ..." I don't want to rehash all this with Rupert. "Liam Stillson thinks I should join some of Mrs. Corwin's clubs or whatever."

"Not a terrible idea."

"I'm not good at anything, though. Not like Mom was."

"I beg to differ," he says. "I think you are very skilled at self-pity."

I flip him off. He smirks. "Honestly, stop this absurdity. Stop tearing things apart. We do not have it in the operating budget to recruit a therapist to Thalia, though you can get appointments via the internet these days. Shall I make inquiries for you?"

"Save your money."

"Oh, I'm not paying for anything. It would come out of your salary, darling."

I've had years of therapy. Dealing with abandonment, dealing with mommy issues, dealing with lack-of-a-daddy issues, dealing with broken friendships, dealing with the pressures of public life, dealing with my alcohol abuse … And every time, I swear I will get better, I will fix things, I will stop acting out.

Voices float into the background on Rupert's end, and then a familiar face appears over his shoulder. Wes Singh bends and waves at the camera. "Hey, Lara," he says.

"Hi, Wes."

"Too bad you're not here. Brought some of my mom's cooking—tikka masala and *malai kofta* and fresh naan." He hoists a cloth bag by its handles.

"Too bad …" The idea of food, Indian or otherwise, makes my unsettled stomach curdle.

"Lara, I mustn't be rude. Please, think about what I've said. Two strikes." Rupert hikes an eyebrow and disconnects.

I drop my throbbing head onto my bent arms on the countertop, lifting it only when I hear a new sound behind me. "I told them you'd never leave that on," I say to Humboldt. I slide off the tall stool to take the cone away from him. He's chewed it into a dozen pieces already, and the length of gauze that was supposed to secure it to his broad head is tangled around his collar.

"You better not have swallowed any of this." I collect the chunks of mangled plastic.

I substitute the cone of shame with a chewy bone but only after he takes his antibiotics that somehow ended up in my fridge.

Somehow.

Finan.

Right. He brought us home last night.

Another flood of shame.

I need a shower.

~

W hen I shut off the water, the fragrance of my body wash is quickly overrun by that of fresh coffee. Pretty sure Humboldt hasn't learned how to use the French press (yet), so someone must be here.

Butterflies awaken, their wings coated with the Pepto Bismol splashing in my gut.

I hurry into my robe, my wet hair wrapped in a towel, bad breath erased with mouthwash. An examination in the mirror does not deliver a visage I'm proud of, but I also don't want whoever is here to leave.

Bracing for what's coming, I open the door and shuffle down the hall.

"I knocked, but you didn't answer. Came to make sure he had his antibiotics."

"Did I leave the door unlocked?"

"No. I took your keys last night. In case I needed to get in urgently."

"And so I wouldn't leave."

"Driving Rupert's Tesla into the strait probably wouldn't make him very happy."

I look toward the quiet Lutris screen, a snide comment locked and loaded about how Rupert has already slapped my hand this morning. I'm too tired to fire.

Finan stands from where he's crouched rubbing Humboldt's belly. "Coffee?" He moves to my kitchen island and pours two cups from the steeping press.

I'm nervous—I need to apologize, and I don't know where to start. I take the offered mug and lean against the oven behind me, forcing myself to make eye contact, even though I'm afraid of what I will see when I look at him.

"Finan ..." I pause and sip, careful not to burn my tongue, and then take a shuddering breath. "Thank you for bringing us home last night. I'm sorry for getting so drunk. I am aware my behavior was inappropriate, and I am truly sorry."

He nods once and moves to the fridge, takes out the creamer, and lightens his coffee without saying a word.

He then walks to the other side of the breakfast bar and slides onto one of the stools. "Have you checked your email this morning?"

"Did you hear what I said?"

"Yes."

"And?"

"And I don't know what you want me to say."

I set my coffee on the island. My post-drunk shakiness threatens to spill its contents. "I want you to accept my apology."

"OK. I accept your apology." He drinks and slides his mug onto the bar, his face unreadable.

I steady myself on the counter. "Um, OK ..." This is not going great. "What's in the email?"

"We're being summoned to provide statements for the civil action."

I nod once. "Yes, Rupert mentioned we might."

"Did he mention anything else?"

"Are we really moving on from last night—from yesterday? Because I sort of feel like that conversation isn't over."

Finan leans on bent arms. "Lara, I don't know what else you want me to say. I opened up to you on the boat, and you shut me down."

"But I didn't—I mean, I did, but I just didn't want you to blurt it out right then because you thought it might fix things."

"I honestly don't know what else to say to you. It seems like I say what I'm feeling, but you're not really listening."

"But I *am*. I hear what you're saying."

He shakes his head and then wraps his big hands around his cup again. "I don't understand why you do the things you do. We talked

83

about the town hall meeting, but last night … you had dinner with Liam Stillson. Then you got so wasted, you fell off the stage."

My cheeks superheat.

"Liam was going to drive you home, despite the fact that he'd been drinking too—then what? Were you going to invite him in? You are free to make whatever choices you feel are right for you, including who you invite into your bed—"

"Oh my god, did you think I was going to *sleep* with him?"

"I got the distinct impression that *he* thought you were."

"From what? Me doing a terrible cover of 'Tiny Dancer'?"

"No, because when I got to the pub, someone else was singing and you and Liam were all over each other on the dance floor."

Wait … we were?

I press my fingers against my closed eyes until I see stars. *I do not remember that part …*

Shit. Yes, I do.

Jesus, I kissed him. I remember now—his mouth tasted like stale guacamole.

"OK, OK, yes—" How can I fess up to this without digging myself a deeper hole?

"Lara, it's fine. I am not that guy who is going to tell you who you're allowed to press your body up against. But I *am* your friend, first and foremost, and it didn't look like you were making good decisions last night—and neither was our esteemed doctor." Finan finishes his coffee and moves to the sink, rinsing and setting his cup to dry. He turns, arms crossed over his broad chest. How I want to bury my face into him and make all my bad decisions float away. "Whatever is going on in your head, I want you to have the space to figure it out. I'm no shrink, but the stuff I see you doing, I was doing that shit after my dad died. Self-sabotage. It's a real thing."

I nod and look at my slippered feet. I hate that he's right. And I hate that I don't know how to get beyond this. I thought coming to Thalia, taking a big-girl job, playing the part of Grown-up No. 1 would fix all the broken bits.

Finan slides in front of me, our toes near touching. He lifts my

chin with a gentle finger. "Your grandfather said something to me once
—'There are some things you learn best in calm, and some in storm.'"

"Sounds like something he would say."

"Willa Cather said it originally, but it helped. With the storm. I
think you need to find some calm, Lara. I really do. Stop launching
yourself into the tempest." He leans in and kisses my forehead, and
I'm again dizzy from his nearness. It's all I can do to keep from
throwing my arms around him.

He steps back. "Until you find that, I want us to just be friends. I
don't want to ruin any potential future with you. And I think you need
to find yourself on steadier footing before you jump into anything
serious."

I don't want to agree with him. I want to strip off his clothes and
drag him into my bedroom and forget the rest of the world.

But it's clear—by the look on his face and the physical distance
he's now put between us—that this is not open for debate. Either we
are friends, or we're not.

I'm not ready to lose the chance to be more with Finan.

"OK," I whisper, sniffing back the threatening tears.

He bobs his head once and then moves toward the door, patting
his leg. "I'm going to take Humboldt out. You get dressed, and when
we come back in, maybe you can explain who that mysterious woman
is who keeps leaving presents on your porch."

FOURTEEN

DISCLOSURE

I n the spirit of friendship, of *camaraderie*, which, according to Finan, is where we are heading, we make more coffee, slide into my porch's Adirondack chairs, and I tell Finan everything.

Everything.

Even the parts Rupert told me to keep close. I share that Kelly has allegedly confessed to the murder of Derek Irving, that they found her phone on Cordelia Beach, that no one has any leads on where Ainsley/Iona currently is on the planet. I then tell him about Jacinta Ramirez, how she appeared in my cabin that night after the arrests were made, how she is living somewhere on Thalia, in a bunker built by my grandfather, and I haven't seen her since, other than the offerings she leaves outside my door.

"Do you think she's involved with Dea Vitae?" Finan fidgets with one of Humboldt's tennis balls while my dog watches on, begging him to throw it off the porch again.

"What? No. God, no. Yes, she was into *something* bad, but I don't know what exactly—she briefly mentioned something to do with her brothers in the Sinaloa Cartel. She's been hiding on Thalia for at least a year."

"A *year*?" I give him a moment to process—it's exactly how I felt when Number Two told me. "Where was she before?"

"No clue."

"How did she get here?"

"She said Rupert arranged it all, brought her into Canada. Her brothers are bad guys. They chopped off her right hand."

Finan's eyes widen. "Jesus. So ... the stuff about your mom is true?"

"I don't know yet. That night, our visit was brief, and she hasn't come back, at least not to talk. Apparently the bunker she's in has a surveillance system. She's been watching all this unfold the whole time."

Finan's head snaps toward me. "Does she have footage that could be used as evidence?"

"I asked Rupert. He said no. And no one can know about her or the bunker. He warned me not to tell Wes or mention it at all."

Humboldt trudges up the porch stairs, panting hard as he drops his slimy ball at his buddy's feet, but Finan is squinting toward the woods at the far end of our adjoining fields. "Did Rupert say anything else about her?"

"He said to let it rest. To let *her* rest. She's not a danger to us, Finan."

"Until her brothers find out where she is."

I hadn't thought of that. "She's got to be pushing sixty. And they already took her hand. What good would killing her do?"

Humboldt barks his impatience; Finan picks up his ball and lobs it into the field.

"At least he's feeling better," I say.

Finan's heavy boots shuffle against the deck and his chair creaks as he tosses the ball again and again for my seemingly tireless dog. An early July Saturday morning on Thalia Island, heading toward T-shirt warm this afternoon, for now partly cloudy with patches of blue sky squeezing through. The tree line along the property's perimeter teems with birds, the branches lush with beautiful, fresh green apparel happy to be bathing in the sun once again. The occasional breeze exchanges the scent of verdant growth and upturned dirt for a waft of the nearby ocean—with everything in bloom and growing like mad, I'm happy to report that summer here is gorgeous.

"We need to till these fields again. Should've planted them by now. They've gone fallow." Finan bobs his head toward our untended front gardens.

"Throw out some wildflower mix. Good for the bees. And add it to someone else's to-do list," I say. I dust my pant leg of Humboldt-introduced dirt. Though my coordinating sweatsuit *is* very cute, it's not appropriate for activities such as tilling dirt, nor is that a skill I'll ever be interested in learning. I'm happy to buy my very fresh produce from the Tipping Point that, by the way, I am supposed to be manning this afternoon.

"Speaking of to-do lists ..." Finan stands and dumps the rest of his coffee into the flower bed. "Gotta get out to the vertical farm. What's on your list today?"

I moan and lean my head back. "General store noon until four. New settlers are arriving next week. I should probably go into the office and deal with stuff."

Humboldt plods up the steps and flops onto his belly, finally tired. The now-dirtied bandage dangles from his ear. "He's going to need that dressing changed." Finan sets his empty coffee cup next to mine on the small repurposed crate side table.

"Finan ... how bad was it last night? Everyone saw me being ..."

He runs a hand over his beard. "They did. But most of them were either drunk or partaking of the local bud."

"Right."

"Make a plan, Lara. You need a plan." He waves and bounds off the porch. Big Dog pushes to sitting and watches Finan saunter down the gravel path toward his own cabin, though I doubt my slobbering mutt notices how beautifully that man wears his jeans.

Ugh. I miss weekends when I could stay in bed and Vera the housekeeper would leave food trays and I didn't have to worry about things like if the general store has enough toilet paper to get the island through until the next supply truck slides off the ferry. "Come on, mutt. Let's go pretend we're adults." I gather coffee cups, open the screen door for Humboldt, and slide inside, jumping and splashing coffee on my soft-rose sleeve at the voice in the kitchen.

"How do you like your eggs?"

FIFTEEN

NICE TATTOO

Jacinta stands at the island, a frying pan held up in her remaining hand. I lock the front door behind me, just in case.

"How did you get in?"

"Laundry room window."

"You fit through that?" *And how did I not* hear *it?*

Jacinta chuckles and slides the pan onto the cooktop. "I'm not sure if I should be insulted by that question."

"No, it's just that it's damn small."

"And I am *damn* clever." She winks. "Now—huevos rancheros. Where are all those tomatoes I brought?"

I smile sheepishly. "I ate them?"

"Gah, just like Cordi. Regular eggs it is, then. Scrambled or poached?"

I climb onto a bar stool, a million questions swirling through my head about why she's here, where she was before this, the story behind what happened to her hand, and of course, anything she can tell me about my mother and their time together.

Instead, however, I end up watching and listening while Jacinta cooks and directs the conversation. I'm afraid if I start with my own interrogation, she will disappear for another month.

She tells me about her childhood, how, as the oldest girl of eight kids, she was basically in the kitchen as soon as she could carry a pan without spilling it. Her stories detail a full life, about her mom and aunties and siblings and their animals and how they'd all run wild and free and how their father worked in Mexico City but would come home on the weekends with books and toys and sweets and how they were the first ones in their brand-new neighborhood to get a color TV and how her dad taught her to drive his Buick on the dusty road in front of their home, "which was a paradise all to itself, with big walls to keep strangers out and a pool and wildlife and our own gardens and sunsets like you've never seen."

"It sounds beautiful."

"It was."

"What did your father do?"

"He worked for the government. Accounting. Smart man."

"And your mom?"

"She was an artist. A painter. But this was the sixties and seventies. Her job was to have babies and thump us when we didn't study." She smiles widely as she slides a steaming plate of fresh eggs and toast in front of me. "I went to Universidad Nacional Autónoma de México. Wanted to be an artist, but I didn't have my mother's talent. My father begged me to study something practical—he said business, but I wanted to be outdoors, like I'd been my whole childhood—I didn't want it to end. We settled on geology. He knew he could get me a job. The government needed geologists."

"Wow … is that what you did, then?"

"For a little while." She smiles and shakes her head. "I was a few weeks from graduation, at school one night with friends to go to an art exhibit on campus. A young, rich Canadian woman had her photos in our gallery."

I pause, the bite of egg falling off my fork. "My mother?"

"Before she was your mother." Jacinta refills the electric kettle. "Parents have a whole life before they become parents."

"That's how you met?"

"Her photos of our native wildlife, especially the endangered species, were beautiful. I grew up very connected to our land, to the animals. I had to meet the photographer. But she wasn't there."

"She wasn't at her own exhibit?"

"I went every night for the whole three-week run."

"And?"

"And the last night, I waited, but she didn't show. I went back the next day when the campus gallery opened—it was the same day we were graduating, and my father couldn't figure out why I had to go to the school so early." She snickers as she fills a teacup with hot water. "I only met Cordelia when she was supervising the packing and loading of her pictures. She was trying to yell at these guys in Spanish, but they were laughing at her. I've never heard someone mangle a language like that."

Jacinta's giggle turns into a full-blown laughing fit as she tells me what my mother was *actually* saying versus what she was trying to communicate. "Ahhhh, yes, it took awhile, but she eventually learned to be gentler with Spanish." Her eyes soften as she cuts a fresh lemon into rounds; she then pulls a ginger root from a cloth bag she must've brought with her and shaves it over a freshly poured teacup of boiling water.

I nibble my eggs and watch her, smiling as I remember my mother talking animatedly in what I thought was fluent Spanish to the engineer in charge of the water reclamation pilot project at Clarke Manor. She said he helped her practice so she wouldn't lose it, though I doubt he loved having his busy days interrupted by his boss's wild daughter. Mom must've learned what she would whisper to me at night from the elegant but tough woman standing in my kitchen, again in black cargos and an off-white, long-sleeved top.

I want to know more. I want to know what happened after they met, where they went, if the stories about Cordelia Clarke flying drugs for the cartels to help remote villages are true.

My courage is hiding behind me, clutched to my pant leg like a skittish child. I should just ask—

"So, you had a late night." Jacinta slides the lemon-and-ginger tea in front of me. "You shouldn't drink coffee when you're hungover. Not good for you."

The moment passes. "How did you know?"

She lifts an eyebrow. "And where did your handsome neighbor go this morning?"

The warmth from talking about my mom, about their shared past, drains away. "We're just friends. He decided we should just be friends."

"And how do *you* feel about that?"

I take another full bite to avoid answering.

"Your mother liked the drink. Too much. It was the one thing we fought about." Jacinta carefully sets the skillet into the sink and washes her hand and stump, her eyes out the kitchen window focused on some distant thing only she can see.

"I don't mean to get so out of control."

She shuts off the water and dries her hands, turning to me. "Neither did Cordi."

"How do I fix this? I keep screwing up."

Jacinta moves to the counter directly across from me and leans on her arms, pulling her long, black-and-gray ponytail over her shoulder. "You let people love you. Believe you are worthy of their love. Find something you love more than the feeling you get when you're drunk."

I drop my fork and push my plate away. "You make it sound like I'm an alcoholic."

"Are you?"

I bury my face in my hands. "I don't know."

"Drink the tea. You're dehydrated."

I sip it. It's good. "I feel like I keep hitting rock bottom—how many bottoms are there in one person's life?"

"When you get to a spot where you're done looking for the bottom, that's when you know you're ready to try something different." Jacinta straightens and takes my plate. "There is no magical fix here, Lara. No pill, no book, no therapist, no knight in shining armor who will ride in and save the day. You have to do the work. You have to find a way to love yourself first."

This sounds like the psychobabble my last therapist fed me. It's why I stopped going to her. "What does that even *mean*?"

Jacinta scrapes the remnants of my meal into the green bag, a smirk on her face. "You even sound like her when you're angry." She shoves her sleeve back by pushing her left arm between her knees and then rinses my dishes.

My heart skips as I notice the tattoo on the inside of her right arm. "What's that?" I point.

She shuts off the water and moves to display her forearm. "Red beryl. One of the world's rarest gemstones."

I lean over to inspect the faded but hyperrealistic inking, my armpits dampening with fear. It's the same shape of the gemstone in the Dea Vitae symbol, the one painted inside the cresting wave.

"What does it mean?" I watch Jacinta's face for signs she's hiding something.

"It depends on your source." She runs a finger over the tattooed stone. "Some people think it will show you the real meaning of forgiveness. It's a good crystal to use for dealing with grief. Other spiritualists consider it a stone of love. I like that meaning best." Jacinta cups her hand over the tattoo and closes her eyes for a long beat. When she reopens them, she looks sad.

"In 1989 I supervised an exchange excavation in Utah with students from my alma mater. We spent two weeks in the Wah Wah Mountains with a group of American geology students, surveying the Utahan geological wonders. We visited an active mine, the Ruby Violet claim. This stone is found there, but very rarely. The first time I saw it, I fell in love."

"With a rock?"

"Blasphemer!" She laughs. "It's more than just a rock. Far rarer than a diamond. A miracle of nature—it takes exactly the right conditions and ingredients to make the red stone. Emeralds are in the same family. But the red beryl, or bixbite—there's just something about it … it stands on its own."

I look down at my grandfather's ring on my right middle finger—at the *red stone* in its belly—and tuck my hands in my lap. I wish I hadn't eaten those eggs.

"Do you remember the ring your mother wore? With the red gemstone?"

I don't remember my mother wearing jewelry very often. Except … "She wore a ring around her neck, on a chain."

"That was my first red beryl find. Tiny little things, very rare. I prefer the ones that can't be cut into gemstones. I like their wildness, their raw power." Her smile is melancholy.

I twirl Grandfather's ring around my finger under the counter's edge, out of view, hiding its gemstone against my palm. *No way this is red beryl. NO WAY Archibald had anything to do with this.*

Abruptly, Jacinta stands and pulls her sleeve down. "Any chance you're going into town today?"

I don't want to stop talking about the red beryl—I want to know why the hell she has the Dea Vitae gem tattooed on her skin. "Uh, yeah … I have to open the general store in an hour."

Jacinta wipes down all my counters and folds the kitchen towels over the oven's wide handle. For a minute, I blur my eyes and imagine it's my mother here cleaning and taking care of things.

"Can you bring me some items?"

I blink the image away and sip my hangover tea. "More toilet paper?"

Her cheek tugs. "Another package wouldn't go unappreciated," she says, rubbing the handless end of her right arm. She seems to do that a lot, like how Finan twists at his beard. "I need paper. Craft paper if you have it. The bigger, the better, but I'd even take some regular white copy paper and tape. Oh, and pencils. And maybe a sharpener?"

"I'll see what we have—I'll grab from town hall too. We have a big closet of office supplies."

"I would be grateful."

"Doing an art project?"

Jacinta's face widens into that warm, dimpled smile, the haunted shadows of a moment ago chased away. "You'll see."

SIXTEEN

MAIL CALL

As soon as I'm certain Jacinta has disappeared once again, I call Wes on the secure line. He's still at Rupert's, but I ask him to not put me on speaker—I want to talk to him only. That paranoid feeling is back.

What if Rupert and Jacinta are actually involved with Dea Vitae and this is just some elaborate cover-up? I stare at my grandfather's ring—this absolutely could be red beryl. I always figured it was a ruby. Never thought to ask. I always remember him wearing it, and the night he died, I slipped it on and since have only taken it off to bathe.

But for Archibald Clarke to have a possible connection to the gemstone on the Dea Vitae logo ... no, that's madness. No way.

"What do you know about red beryl?" I ask Wes.

"Uh, is it a wine?"

"It's a rare gemstone."

"Then nothing," Wes says. "What's up?"

"The Dea Vitae symbol—the one in the cave—the cresting wave with the red gemstone in its heart. Could that be a red beryl?"

"I didn't pay close attention to it. Just assumed it was a ruby or some New Age thing, like those Himalayan salt lamps my ex loves so much."

"It might be." I almost trip on my own feet—Wes doesn't know about Jacinta. Rupert warned me to keep her presence here a secret—I can't tell him about her tattoo! Shit. "I'm just curious if maybe it's this rare stone I saw on the internet. I was looking up gemstones that have to do with gods and goddesses."

"On a private browser, I hope?"

"Of course." I swallow the lie. "Anyway, I know it's weird, but the gem got me thinking that maybe it *means* something important to the cult people."

"Dunno." Wes is quiet for a minute. "Let me look into it."

"Thank you."

"And Lara? Please, stay out of trouble. Rupert needs to heal. Worrying about you isn't helping. Got it?"

I'm embarrassed again. "Yes, sir."

He disconnects.

I'm behind the Tipping Point checkout counter all of ten minutes before Liam Stillson saunters in wearing a big grin and brown corduroy pants. Really. Corduroy? He looks like that kid in my first grade reading group who loved peeing in the big palm plant the teacher kept in our classroom.

"How are you feeling today, Ms. Clarke?" he asks, playful smirk in place as he leans on the counter. His glasses are different—square today, and black. I think I like the tortoiseshell ones better.

"Tired. You?"

"Tired. But last night was the most fun I've had in ages," he says, "though I think I'm going to stay away from your Japanese whisky for a while."

Lightweight.

"How is Humboldt this morning?"

"Oh, he's good. Like normal. Except he chewed up his cone."

"I figured he might." A short line of customers appears all at once, as happens in stores. Liam grabs a hand basket and points, indicating he will be doing his own shopping.

The first three customers all have jokes about my stunning vocal performance at the Salamander, and instead of hiding behind my bad choices, I join in the jokes, *ha ha ha yes I am quite the entertainer be sure to make it to my next show*. It's all smiles and laughs until Mrs. Corwin slides two full baskets onto the conveyor, her thin, bloodred lips pursed, brow scrunched. I'm guessing this is her disappointed face.

"Hello, Mrs. Corwin." Customer service smile affixed, I pluck her items from the baskets, serenaded by the satisfying scanner beep as I get closer to finishing her order so she can take her disdain and her distracted husband right out the door.

"I haven't seen your name on any of the community builders yet, Lara," she says, folding her hands on the tiny shelf next to the debit machine.

"Yes, I'm still trying to figure out what looks the most fun." I scan a box of all-natural sheepskin condoms but keep my eyes on the screen. Alice Corwin is, like, seventy-one. I know I slept through most of my health classes, but I *think* she's past the point of being able to get pregnant, right?

"You need to pick at least two activities, preferably those that will show the island residents you are more than just a good time with a microphone."

The look she gives me—remember that scene from *Indiana Jones* when the Nazi dude's face melts? Mm-hmm. That's my face. The melting guy.

"I will check again this afternoon and look for a suitable activity to join, Mrs. Corwin," I say, loading the last of her groceries into her cloth bags.

"Two."

"I'm sorry?"

"Two activities." She taps her card and nudges Professor Corwin, his head again bent over his phone. He *hmmphs*, tucks his device into the pocket of his tweed blazer, and picks up the bags, following his wife out of the store.

When the line is dealt with, Liam reappears, his own basket now filled. "How long until you're not doing this anymore?"

"Soon, I hope. We have a handful of teenagers with the next batch of settlers. Hoping one of them wants a job."

He smiles. "No, I mean, when are you done here, *today*? Maybe we could get a late lunch or early dinner?"

Oh. Oh dear. Oh no. This cannot happen.

"Hmm, probably not today. I still have to go into the office after this. Going to be a late night."

"I can bring food out to your place?"

"Maybe a rain check?"

He moves to the card machine, head bobbing. "Sure. Next week sometime, then, maybe."

With his transaction finished, I tear the receipt and hand it over. "Thank you again for last night, Liam. It was fun. I just need to ... tone it down a little."

He nods. "Right. OK, cool. I get it." He eases his bags over his wrists. "Have a good rest of your weekend, Lara."

"I'll call Catrina about bringing Humboldt in for a recheck," I say just as he exits.

I'm an idiot.

The store is busy, which takes my mind off my continued gold-medal aptitude for bad choices. Even beefy Len Emmerich comes in to stock up for the week, his white-blond flat top and square jaw groomed as ever, and thankfully, the only dialogue exchanged involves him mentioning he's glad Finan made sure I got home all right. He can probably tell by the flames of humiliation licking my cheeks that I'm not interested in another lecture. As he pays, I quietly reassure him that I promise to behave. He winks and pulls a glass bottle of green juice from his purchases, handing it to me.

"Stay hydrated." And then he's out the door into the light summer shower from a few dark gray clouds that linger just long enough to dampen the sidewalks and young trees lining Main Street.

By three thirty, it's totally dead, my feet are aching, and I still have stuff I should be doing in prep for next week. I make an executive decision and close up early, pausing briefly at Tommy's for a muffin and coffee, grateful when no one stops me to revisit last evening's unrefined frivolity.

Town hall is quiet, and I'm so grateful. Beyond the lingering malaise from too much imbibing, I've had my fill of people. My cheeks ache from smiling. In the lobby, I say hello to my mother's photographs, a regular habit now every time I come into work. A moment to commune with her memory. I've ordered a half dozen more prints, a couple for here but the rest for my cabin. And I have it on the agenda for the next council meeting to talk about opening a proper gallery in one of the unoccupied storefronts. Artists live among us, and I think my mom would love it if they were able to share their work with their neighbors.

I slide my key into my mailbox, surprised to find envelopes inside. With so much of my life online, I rarely get physical mail, other than administrative stuff. We have an agreement with Canada Post that keeps junk mail off the island as we don't have the recycling capacity for useless flyers and ads. Every once in a while, I'll get letters from people telling me their sad stories and asking for money, but it seems the whole world has pretty much gone digital. Easier to email and ask for cash or yell at my family for whatever the writer is mad about than go to the post office and buy a stamp.

The click of my Loubi Bee sandals echoes through the silent lobby. In my office, I tap my computer awake and plop into my chair, thankful to be off my feet. I pull my phone from the pocket of my AllSaints biker jacket, checking for messages I missed during my store shift. That fluttery feeling surges when I see a text from Finan, but he's just offering to let Humboldt out and give him dinner if I'm not back by five.

Given that it's 4:15 p.m. and I haven't even opened my Lutris inbox, I text him back: *That would be great. TYVM. At the office until ?? Front door is unlocked.*

I send it, watching hopefully for the bouncing bubbles of a return message.

All I get is the generic thumbs-up. I hate that stupid thumb. It feels like a mean girl in the bathroom looking you up and down and snorting haughtily at your outfit and then pulling her posse out behind her like a line of obedient geese. An "I can't make time to talk to you right now" snub.

Whatever. Finan and I are friends. *Friends. Stop reading so much into it, Lara.* He's probably busy hammering or sawing or whatever it is he does out there that makes him so sweaty and delicious at the end of the day.

Stop, stop, stop.

I shall open the mail instead.

I grab my letter opener and separate the small stack. Almost all Thalia Island stuff—bills from suppliers, account statements, other correspondence I will scan and send to accounting. A letter at the bottom is for me, my name and address in practiced script. No return address, an American stamp.

I slice it open and pull free the folded paper. Upon flattening the page, I'm not sure what I'm looking at ... it's a low-quality, black-and-white picture of the number 700 in large metal numbers, printed on white copy paper. Imperfect print lines suggest it's come from a cheap printer.

"What the hell ..."

I flip it over, look inside the envelope, examine the postmark. I even smell the page for any clues. Nothing. It smells like paper and toner.

I rest it on my desk and stare at it. What does this mean? Was it mistakenly sent to me?

I look at the envelope again—it's my name and address, and both are definitely handwritten, though I don't recognize the scrawl.

A chill raises the hair on the back of my neck.

"Excuse me ..."

"Jesus!" My heart hammers as I take in the figure standing in the middle of my otherwise quiet office. "You can't sneak up on people like that!"

That girl, the one whose mom chastised me that day for saying *fuck* in front of her kids, is standing a few feet from my desk, her blond braids askew. She leans over slightly and points at her knees, both actively bleeding down her shins.

"You got any Band-Aids?"

SEVENTEEN

PRECOCIOUS LITTLE THING

By the time I have the kid—she reminds me that her name is Harmony—seated on the bathroom counter, my heart rate has slowed enough to remember that I do know where the first aid kit is and that since this small human is bleeding and 911 is not an option, I should probably do something to help her.

Except she's totally chill and not at all panicked by the rivers of blood staining her blond-hair-covered legs, and judging by the healed scars on her shins, she's either a daredevil or a klutz. She skillfully instructs me in the steps I am to take to clean and disinfect these latest bodily insults, extracting the necessary remedies, in order, from the well-stocked medical kit spread across her lap and countertop.

"How do you know so much about this?"

"I'm learning to skateboard. Before that, I was learning to roller blade. And then roller skate. And I like to go off jumps on my bike. Also I'm learning parkour but it's hard 'cause I'm still short and there aren't enough buildings here." She sucks in air through her teeth with the second spray of antiseptic. "That's not supposed to sting."

"Sorry." I dab at it with gauze. Once she deems both wounds sufficiently bathed of pathogens, Harmony expertly tears open a two-by-two adhesive bandage and smears it with antibiotic ointment.

"This will keep me from getting a staph infection." She hands me the huge Band-Aid and points to the first wound. "Did you know you can lose all your limbs if you get a staph infection?"

"How old are you?" I concentrate on applying the bandage without screwing up and thus necessitating a painful do-over. Or a staph infection.

"I'll be ten in three and a half weeks. But I want to be a doctor. So I read a lot about medical stuff."

"And your mom is OK with that?"

"My mom was going to be a nurse but then she got knocked up so now she takes care of me and my little sister while my dad finishes his PhD. That's why we moved here. So my dad can finish. He's gonna be a doctor. But not a doctor who fixes people. He's an organic chemist and he's working on the farms here, testing a pesticide he and his team developed. It's safe for humans and water sources but deadly for bugs."

I nod. This kid is way too smart for me.

"My little sister is kind of an asshole." She hands me the second bandage smeared with ointment.

I pinch my lips together, trying not to laugh. Finally, I manage, "Harmony, I don't think your mom wants you using that language."

"My dad says language is a tool, and we should be able to say what we want to express our feelings."

Again, me trying not to laugh. "And why do you think your little sister is an ..."

"An asshole? Because she is."

"OK, but what does she *do* to make you say that?"

"She's four and a half and she's dumb and she cries all the time about the stupidest things. Also she's still breastfeeding and as a future doctor, I think that's gross."

"Eww."

"Exactly. So, what classes are you taking at the community centre?" she pivots, picking through the first aid kit. "Can I have some of these tongue depressors?"

"Help yourself."

She takes a handful and then helps me zip up the bag. We've already removed her very stained socks and shoes, so she scoots around, feet in the sink basin, and we gingerly wash the dried blood from her shins. Once she's clean, we discover a few more cuts, so I watch as she dabs on more ointment with a sterile Q-Tip.

"You're really good at that," I say, putting the tube back into its spot in the kit. "Maybe Dr. Stillson should give you a job."

"Nah. I'm gonna grow up and work with little kids who have cancer."

"That ... is amazing, Harmony."

"Also, I saw Dr. Stillson kissing my mom, so I don't want to be a doctor like him."

I inhale with shock and choke on my own spit. Harmony reaches over and pats me hard on the back as I cough through it. She moves her damp legs out of the sink and fills a paper cup with water for me.

I sip and try to take a deep breath. "Sorry ... yes, thank you, I'm fine." I drink again. "Um, Harmony, you probably didn't see that."

"Just because I'm a kid doesn't mean I'm blind or stupid."

"No, no, of course not. Pretty sure you're the smartest person I've ever met."

She smiles, revealing those awkward adult teeth trying to squeeze in center stage. Definitely orthodontia in her future. But she probably already diagnosed that for herself. "Yeah, my mom thinks Dr. Stillson is hot. I read her text messages. She has a thumbprint phone so I programmed mine in one day when she wasn't paying attention, and now I can open her stuff. She texts my aunt in Toronto all the time, and I think my mom wants to have sex with Dr. Stillson. I think sex is disgusting, but if I have to do it to get a kid, I might. Or maybe I'll adopt an orphan. Aren't you an orphan?"

I cannot believe I'm having this conversation. "Sort of. But I think I'm too old for you to adopt."

"I don't want to be like Gillian and have a kid when I'm not done with school."

"Uh, OK, well, Harmony, I have work to do, so maybe you should get going. Won't your mother worry? It's almost dinnertime."

She hops off the counter, takes one look at her socks, and throws them in the garbage. She then slides her bare feet into her well-worn, bloodstained sneakers. "My mom thinks you're a drunken floozy who is only here because your grandpa was rich, but I like you, Lara. I think you're beautiful and you have nice clothes. And I really like your big dog. He's cute."

"Wow ... thank you?"

"Also, I looked up 'floozy' and I don't think that's you at all. You're not the one kissing doctors behind your husband's back," she says, finishing the laces on her left shoe. I again keep my laugh behind my puckered lips as I open the bathroom door and wait for Harmony to exit ahead of me.

"Before I go, can we pick out what classes we're going to take?" She walks down the hall, though instead of going to the main front door, she turns left into my office. I guess Harmony isn't leaving yet. "Can you bring up the schedule on the portal so we can choose together?"

I drop the first aid kit onto my small sofa and settle into my desk chair. Harmony sidles right up beside me. She smells like fresh grass and antiseptic and little-kid sweat. She picks up the weird letter sitting on the desk blotter, scans it, and then pushes it aside. "Click and go to the Lutris portal ..."

Harmony then walks me through all the community builders Mrs. Corwin has arranged, explaining why that class would be dumb (basket weaving) or boring (how to make kombucha) or not necessary (how to nurture a bountiful home garden) since her dad has a green thumb and a "special compost sauce" he's made for their plants so she already knows all about growing food.

By the time Harmony is ready to leave, we are registered for Beginning Pottery and Introduction to Acrylics. She lifts her hand for a high five. "What do you think you'll paint first?" she asks but answers herself. "I'm going to paint Humboldt."

She hops out from behind my desk and pats her pocket, bulging with her newly acquired tongue depressors. "Thanks for the medical supplies. I'll check in tomorrow and see if you've decided what you want to paint."

Before I can tell her that the office is closed tomorrow, she's out the door, my name floating through the hall. "Bye, Laraaaaa!"

I'm exhausted. She was here for ninety minutes, and I feel like I've run a marathon—plus I got absolutely nothing done, which means I *am* probably coming in to the office tomorrow. Yuck.

However, it *is* interesting to note that Harmony's judgy mother has a few sticky secrets of her own.

And that a certain town doctor maybe isn't all he appears to be under that polished exterior.

Who's the actual floozy around here?

EIGHTEEN

DADDY ISSUES

The subsequent few days are a blur, nothing but work, work, work. The arrival of our next batch of settlers on Tuesday and Wednesday goes off without a hitch, thank all the stars. And my new best friend Harmony has actually come in handy this week, despite her nonstop questions and the not-safe-for-work stories she shares about her mom that she definitely should not be privy to.

Given her affinity and talent for all things medical, she has taken over care of Humboldt's ear—at least as far as cleaning and rubbing antibiotic cream onto it. Big Dog likes this new kid, and he doesn't shake and whine like he does when Dr. Stillson gets too near. At the recheck appointment Monday morning? Ugh, what a baby. When he sees Harmony bounce into my office, his tail winds up and he flops his giant head onto her lap while she practices her technique.

It's been kind of awesome having her around. Conversation with the good doctor has gotten a little awkward since I turned down his dinner invitation *again*—you know, considering he's been sharing his mouth parts with Harmony's married mother.

It's Friday morning, and every muscle in my body hurts from helping move in settlers' furniture and boxes and offering hugs and handshakes. Last night was our first community-builder class—

Harmony did as promised and started her painting of Humboldt while the rest of us listened to a tutorial on why acrylics are best for new painters, the different brush sizes and their appropriate uses, how to set up our easels, and how to prime our canvases with gesso. That kid took her new palette and squeezed out the colors she wanted, picked a brush, and no kidding, by the time the hour wrapped, Humboldt's droopy face was taking shape on her ten-by-twelve canvas while mine sat covered with only a layer of eggshell.

And don't tell anyone—but I actually had a really nice time. Like, I'm looking forward to next Thursday. (However, I will quietly withdraw from the pottery class. I *cannot stand* having dirty hands, and according to the YouTube video I watched over lunch yesterday, pottery requires the artist to slap clay onto a wheel and then touch it. A lot. Gunk everywhere—on the skin, under the nails, all over the clothes. Hard pass.)

What I am *not* looking forward to is fifteen minutes from now when Dakota knocks on my door and drags me into the early morning for a run. We finally made time for that lunch date and have since fallen into an easy friendship—she's funny, warm, and kindhearted. Except when it comes to exercise, and then she's just sort of this crazed fiend who actually *enjoys* making sweat pour from her lanky, toned body. I warned her repeatedly over the past few days that I am out of shape, that I haven't jogged in easily a year, but she apparently received an email from Rupert about limiting my access to alcohol as a result of recent misdeeds, and she is now charged with making sure I stay out of trouble. He even used the words "Lara needs a friend" so I sound extra pathetic.

Thanks, Number Two.

I groan and roll out of my warm, cozy bed and shuffle into the bathroom. Eyes, face, teeth washed. Hair in a low ponytail. I squeeze my sore, PMS-ing boobs into my sports bra—all that bouncing should be fun for the girls today. Even Humboldt is confused about why I'm up with the sun. As I sit to pull on my socks and runners, he lifts his head from his pillow—now that he's taken over the unoccupied side of my queen-size bed—his eyes open just long enough to yawn and lick his chops.

"I'd make you come with us, but I'm afraid you'll get into another fight you can't win." I pat his hip and promise I'll be back soon. "At least I hope."

Right on time, Dakota is on my porch, already red-cheeked and bright-eyed. "Morning!"

"Are you always this happy at 7 a.m.?"

She smiles. "Got a water bottle?"

I hurry back in and grab it. When I return, Dakota is yelling hello at Finan who's climbing into his truck across the way.

"You sure you know what you've signed up for?" he hollers back to her. "Don't break your ass, Lara!" And then he's in his rig, laughing as he prepares to leave.

"Now *he* is a snack," Dakota says. "I don't know why you're not chewing on that regularly."

"High in cholesterol," I tease, wishing I could go back under my duvet but also grateful it's not raining or blistering hot already.

Dakota makes me stretch my already sore muscles, filling me in on where she usually runs and how we can modify today so I don't die.

Adequately stretched, I follow her lead down the driveway. Once we hit the road, it's like someone's turned Dakota's power switch on. She's careful to keep a steady pace for me, but she talks—the entire time. I guess she *has* been lonely.

I hear all about the swarm of new customers this week, how she's met the brewmaster couple who will eventually be opening their own brewery on the island—Thalia Island's own line of organic, craftsman beers!—and they're excited to pull some shifts at the Wandering Salamander to get to know their neighbors while also teaching her the fine art of all things craft beer. I try to ask questions in between but mostly, I'm focused on breathing and not barfing.

We make it into the downtown core but I ask to divert around the outer edge, even along the residential streets and past the community centre as I'd rather not have people see me like this. She laughs and obliges, regaling me with the story of how her beloved breakfast-and-lunch restaurant burned down, probably from a fire set by a homeless guy who'd been having a pissing match with the owner of a sushi restaurant a few doors down.

"I'm not mad at the guy—I mean, he just wanted a place to sleep and the owners down the way didn't want him on their back porch"— her voice bounces with every step—"but, like, to set the place on fire? And the buildings were old, right? All wood. They went up so fast."

"I ... am so sorry ... for your loss."

"I got the insurance money and could've reopened, but I talked to my moms, and then I talked to Uncle Rupert, and we all agreed I needed something new. A fresh start, you know? That's why when he suggested I come over here, I was, like, hell yeah."

"You call him ... Uncle Rupert? You get away ... with that?"

"Well, it would be weird to call him Dad."

I stop running, hands on my hips, gasping for breath. "I'm sorry— what did you just say?"

Dakota slows and jogs back the few steps to catch up. She's not even winded. "Rupert is my biological father."

My eyes about pop out of my head. "Are you messing with me?"

"You didn't know that?" Dakota jogs in place.

Oh my god, the more I stare at her, I can see it! "Uh, nooo."

"It's not like it's a secret or anything. He offered his swimmers so my moms could have me. Way before this was something people talked about in the light of day."

"How *old* are you?"

"Thirty-four this year."

I'm shaking my head. "I cannot *believe* he had a kid all these years and never told me."

"They didn't even tell me until I was thirteen. Ever since then, it's been Uncle Rupert. My moms are still together, although my mom, Julie, she lost her eyesight in an awful car accident when I was in high school. Drunk driver hit her. She was the primary breadwinner but couldn't work after that, so Rupert stepped in. To help. He's basically kept them in their house in East Vancouver all this time. He even paid for my university."

"Holy ... shit ..."

"Come on. We're ruining our split times. Race you to the end of the block!"

I let her run ahead. No way I'm going to win because I can't catch my breath in between laughs that Rupert is a *dad*. Stuck-up Rupert who always has opinions about my personal life but never let on about his.

Except by the sounds of it, he's a saint. Saint Rupert. He and Grandfather saved Finan and his family after Finan's dad got sick, and now I'm hearing that Mr. Prim and Proper, Mr. Biscuits and Tea himself is basically a gay Joan of Arc. He didn't save France in the Hundred Years' War, but he did save Finan's and Dakota's families.

I finally catch up and ask the Million-Dollar Question. "So, did they use a turkey baster?" I joke.

"Of course. How else do you do it?" Dakota winks and sprints ahead, smirking the whole way back to my cabin.

NINETEEN

TGIF

I crawl into work. No, like, literally. I have to forgo my usual Friday shoes (Alexander McQueen leather ankle-cuff stiletto sandals, in black) and wear my runners—much to the mirth of my fellow council members when I stumble stiff-legged into our ten o'clock meeting—because my calves are on fire. I've taken the max dose of Tylenol since ibuprofen has been burning my gut again, and per Dakota's instructions when she left my porch to jog back to her house, I am drinking a ton of water, so much that I have to urinate every ten minutes.

Not helpful considering I have much to do today—maybe I should see if the Tipping Point has any adult diapers.

First things first: I call Rupert and subject him to an inquisition regarding Dakota's bombshell revelation. "It's a surprise only to you, Lara," he says.

"Um, hello? Why wouldn't you tell me that?"

"Because it's not my story to tell. It's Dakota's. And she shared it, so now you know."

"Well, congratulations on being a dad," I tease.

"Uncle. I am an uncle."

"You're a saint, and you know it."

He waves a hand at the screen. As I got ready to come in after

Dakota left, I kept thinking about how Rupert does so much for other people—and I have been *such* a pain in the ass all these years. Even with the trouble I've caused, he still looks out for me.

"Rupert, I want you to know … I appreciate you."

He's mid sip from his tea so his perfectly manicured eyebrows do the talking for him.

"You're a really good person. I didn't know all this stuff about you —about how you helped Finan's family and how you helped make Dakota and then helped her and her moms, and still are all these years later. Every time I learn some new thing you've done, I feel even worse about being a jerk."

"Good. I'm glad you're finally seeing the light."

"Come on, Number Two. I'm trying to say something nice here."

He picks up a cell phone resting on the table screen right. "Must go. Have a productive day, behave yourself, and please, no food or alcohol poisoning at tonight's gala. Ta-ta, little cyclone." The Lutris screen goes dark.

"Fine," I say to myself. "Be that way."

"Be what way?" Finan's head pokes through my open office door. As soon as Humboldt hears him, he pulls himself off his too-small dog bed and wanders over.

"Oh my god, come in. I have so much to tell you!"

"I can't. Gotta go help finish setting up the bandstand. Meet you at Tommy's at one for a sandwich?"

"Can't. General store, training the new folks."

"Already?"

"They've been here a few days. And I am tired of wondering why Mrs. Corwin bought sheepskin condoms last weekend."

His eyes widen. "That's a story I haven't heard." He then looks down at Humboldt's repaired ear, spread flat against his palm. "You said Harmony has been taking care of this? It looks great."

"She's something else."

Finan kisses the top of Humboldt's head and then straightens. Again that urge to walk across the room and melt into him nearly overwhelms my good sense.

"So, I'll see you tonight?"

"Save me a dance," I tease, but not really.

"I'll check my card," he says, and then he's gone again. Humboldt plods back over and collapses onto his dog bed and sighs, his eyes sad.

"I know, buddy. I miss him too."

Harmony shows up at noon on the dot, plopping her backpack on the floor and then complaining with colorful vigor about the small school and how she hates this year-round schedule and how dumb the other kids are and how she thinks I should ask Gillian if she can work here at town hall and then she can do her classes on the internet so she can graduate from high school at twelve and get busy on medical school.

"You have to go to university first, don't you?"

"Duh, but I can do that too," she says. She's already settled in next to Humboldt, rubbing a different antibiotic cream from Dr. Stillson into his ear. My dog is so blissfully relaxed, he's bordering on unconscious.

The first aid kit sprawled next to them on my office floor has been decimated in the last week. Hoping the one I ordered to replace it arrives before anyone chops off a valued body part.

"Oh! I almost forgot!" She eases Humboldt's slumbering head off her tiny, denim shorts-clad lap, wipes her fingers on the Handi Wipe I offer, and then yanks open her backpack. "I went into the supply closet and got my painting out from class last night. The teacher let me work on it instead of planting bean sprouts like the other kids." She hoists the canvas she started during our community-builder class, holding the painted side against her chest.

"OK, close your eyes," she demands.

I smile and sit back in my chair. "Closed."

I hear her heavy skater shoes on the hardwood floor; as soon as she's next to me, it's that now-familiar scent of little-kid perspiration mixed with fresh paint. "OPEN!"

I do. She's spun her painting around, holding it proudly before her. "Oh my god, Harmony ..." I'm grinning so hard, my face hurts. Tears spring into my eyes, and I lower my voice. "This is really freaking good."

She beams. "I made it for you."

I look at her luminous face, shocked. "What? No! You can't give this to me. You have to keep it. It's incredible!"

"I want you to hang it by Humboldt's bed so he knows what he looks like. If he sees how handsome and brave he is, maybe he won't pick fights with raccoons."

I'm not sure I follow her logic, but given what I know about Harmony, there will be no refusing this gift. Gently, I take it, propping it between my hands on my desk. "Harmony, this is really, *really* amazing. It's now my very favorite thing in the whole world."

"Yeah, it's pretty good." She grins, staring at her handiwork. "I think I'm going to paint another Humboldt next week—I'll do one of him sitting next to that momma raccoon. Then maybe he'll see they can actually be friends."

"What a terrific idea," I say. My phone rings, and as I reach for it, Harmony slides back onto the floor next to Humboldt and pulls her backpack close. He knows what that means—lunch.

While I don't know much about kids, Harmony is definitely growing on me. Her company is nice, and it's great having her around to do little errands or to take Humboldt out for a walk. I'm able to take calls and answer resident questions and deal with emails all while she sits quietly on the floor with my dog's head in her lap, whatever book she's reading held steady in tiny hands that always seem to have painted nails in different states of chipping. She confided in me the other day that when her mom refused to let her wear nail polish "because it's toxic and vain," her dad invented Harmony her very own line of eco-friendly polishes that won't make her sick when she chews her nails, which she can't seem to stop doing. She also informed me that when the patents come in, her dad's going to sell his nail-polish formula for a bazillion dollars and then he's taking her to Paris to eat ratatouille, just like Remy the rat chef made in, and I quote, "the best animated feature of all time."

My young friend has very strong opinions and doesn't take anyone's crap, and I sort of love it. I need to be more like Harmony.

At one o'clock, the reminder alarm on my phone goes off. "I have to go to the general store and teach the new people how to do everything."

Harmony closes her bamboo bento box now cleaned of her lunch and stuffs all her things into her backpack. "I'm gonna go skateboard 'cause they have the street closed off. You guys should build a skate park here."

"I will bring that up to council next time we meet," I say. "You wanna earn some money?"

Her eyes light up. "Dog-sitting! Come on, Humboldt!"

He doesn't have to be asked twice. He patiently slides into the harness we ordered so he doesn't get away from Harmony, given the size of his body compared to hers. "Can I leave my junk in here?" she asks, tucking her skateboard under her arm. "If I lose another backpack, my mom'll kill me."

I nod. "I'll be down at the general store. Bring him to me when you're tired." I pull out my bottom desk drawer and hand her some compostable poop bags. "Just in case."

She stuffs them into her pocket and they disappear, just long enough for me to take a deep breath, sigh at my to-do list, and ease myself out of my chair to go pee. Again.

What I would give to be lying on a beach right now, letting the sun —and some hot masseuse with sea-green eyes and a one-syllable name—work out the knots in my sore legs.

Instead, my phone rings—someone calling from the general store, half a block from me. "Yeah, yeah, on my way …"

TWENTY

TEAM EFFORT

One nice thing about Thalia Island's community-based living is people actually behave like we're all in this together. The newest batch of residents settled in quickly and without drama, and pretty much everyone who isn't working elsewhere is downtown helping prepare for tonight's festivities. The cedar picnic tables and benches are up, the recycling and green waste bins are in place, the food tables have been arranged in a U with the grills at their apex, and an eclectic playlist of folk and rock music plays at a respectable volume from bandstand speakers that are just waiting for their chance to show us what they're made of.

Even Mother Nature has cooperated, granting us short-sleeve-worthy temps and blue skies that melt into purples and oranges the closer we get to kickoff.

The barbecues purchased for the first disastrous welcome-to-Thalia dinner are ablaze with the fruits of the island's labor, Tommy dressed in a brand-new apron Catrina bought for him that reads "May the Forks Be with You." Harmony laughed when she saw it—and then she laughed again when she had to explain it to me.

"What is wrong with you that you don't know about *Star Wars?*" She continued to laugh and point, so I made her pull on gloves and separate the silverware and then set up the dirty-dish bins. Joke's on me, though—that kid loves doing the stuff I hate, especially if there's money at the end of it. And I haven't seen Humboldt this happy in weeks ... not since Finan and I were hanging out.

The familiar pang aches in my chest.

Especially when I see the soft looks he's on the receiving end of over by the bandstand from the beautiful and very accomplished Lucy-Frank. A year ago, I would've stormed over and found a way to make a scene, to make her disappear in shame and never again come near the object of my affection. But I can't do that now—I'm allegedly an adult and I would never hear the end of it from pretty much everyone if I were to behave in such a way.

Plus ... I like Lucy-Frank. She's crazy talented and she's kind and brilliant and hilarious. I can see why Finan would be interested in her. Anyone with a modicum of sense would be.

I hate moments like this, when I have a clear picture of how little I've accomplished, of how much time and energy and money I've wasted running from what Grandfather and Rupert wanted me to become, living in the shadow of the myth that is Cordelia Clarke.

"What did that tablecloth ever do to you?"

I jump slightly, smiling when I see Catrina's understanding face looking up at me. I release the stranglehold on the fabric in my hand and nod toward Finan and Lucy-Frank. "She's beautiful and perfect and she has a career and a *purpose*."

Catrina takes the other end of the checkered tablecloth and helps me spread it without missing a beat. "She is beautiful and she has a career and a purpose—but she's not perfect. No one is."

"You know what I mean."

We move on to the next table. "The question is, is she perfect for Finan?" Catrina asks. "Have you talked to him? Since the boat ride?"

"Sort of." I don't share that Finan and I had an involved chat about the murder of Derek Irving and, of course, Jacinta, who no one else can know about, not even my beloved Catrina.

"I could insert a clever anecdote here about how I almost lost

Tommy to my college roommate, but I don't want to be cliché." She smooths the cloth over the rough end of the cedar picnic table.

"I like clichés."

"Suffice it to say that playing hard to get almost knocked me out of the race."

"How did you get back in?"

"By *talking*. By being honest. By being real and maybe even a little bare—emotionally, I mean. Leave your clothes on for that part." She giggles.

"Maybe ... but Finan knows pretty much everything about me already." We unfurl another cloth for the next table.

"But does he really?"

"The last time we talked, I apologized for that night at the pub ... he said we should just be friends and that I need a plan."

"And do you have one?"

I shrug. *Do I?*

"I don't know how to be 'just friends' with Finan Rowleigh."

She nods. "And smooching Liam Stillson probably doesn't help Finan think you want to be *more* than friends, hey?"

The urge to deflect, to turn the spotlight away from my mistakes, flares within and I blurt it out without thinking. "Speaking of Liam Stillson ..." Harmony catches my eye across the street, clearly done with her assigned jobs and now tossing a rope toy for Humboldt. She looks so happy and unbothered—and she's trusted me with the naughtiness her mother continues to engage in. I can't, and shouldn't, betray that trust. Especially since it's none of my business and won't be until Harmony shows signs that her mother's behavior is causing damage. "How are things going at the office?"

Catrina unfolds the second-to-last tablecloth. "Busy, as usual, although this new group of settlers hasn't been flooding us with appointments like the first group did."

"Probably because I haven't poisoned them yet."

"Ha," she says, smoothing the fabric. "Tonight we will be salmonella-free. Although if we don't get this shindig started soon, I might chew on the nearest human. I'm starving."

We finish the last table, turning to inspect our handiwork. Tommy signals with one of his oversized grill spatulas from across the street. "I'm being summoned. Shall I save you a seat at our table?"

"That would be great." I watch as Catrina hurries over to help her husband, smiling to myself as she cuddles in next to him for a quick kiss, listens to whatever he needs, and then disappears into the diner a few steps down the block. They seem so easy together, so comfortable—like one knows what the other is thinking without even saying it.

I thought Finan and I were getting to that place ...

Maybe I should do what Catrina says. Just *talk* to him. Lay myself bare emotionally.

I'm starting to forget why I'm even upset with him, why I've put this distance between us. As I watch him laugh and chat and move things around with Lucy-Frank's help, my jealousy inflicts physical pain. I want him to smile at *me* like that. I want him to offer *me* his hand for a high five.

"Lara!" Dakota waves and hollers from across the way. Finan hears her and his head swivels; he offers the smile that feels reserved for me before he resumes where he was with Lucy-Frank.

I walk toward my new friend as quick as I can given my continued muscular firestorm. She's grinning and shaking her head as I limp closer. "You really need to get off your ass more if you're that sore after a few kilometers."

"I warned you."

"And I will say, those runners really complete your outfit."

I smack the side of her arm playfully. I've had more than a few sideways glances today—everyone's used to seeing me in power heels, not turquoise Vessi sneakers. Don't care. At least I don't cry with every step. Also, my toes aren't frozen *and* if it rains, my feet are prepared.

"Shall we go get ready? Or do you want to sneak inside for a quick shot to loosen those muscles?" She nods toward the Wandering Salamander behind her.

"Uncle Rupert would be so disappointed if he knew you were

plying me with spirits after he forbade you from doing so."

"I'm not the one who has to climb three tiny stairs and give a speech tonight," she says. "Maybe you should hire a Sherpa to help you."

"And I see *you've* inherited Rupert's delightful sense of humor."

"Some nature can't be nurtured out." She winks and wiggles her butt.

I whistle for Harmony, now sitting with a panting Humboldt on the thin strip of grass adjacent to the town hall courtyard. They stand and jog toward us, Harmony's scabbed knees looking much better than they did a week ago.

"Are you leaving?" she asks, untwisting Humboldt's leash from her wrist.

"Just to change clothes. I'm going to take him home and feed him dinner."

"What are you wearing tonight? Are you wearing something fancy? I don't have anything fancy, so if you're gonna put on something nice, I gotta go home and change too—"

"Nothing fancy, Harmony. You look great."

She hands over the leash. "Also, just so you know, Humboldt peed on Mrs. Corwin's leg. She was standing there talking and I was fixing the silverware and I don't think he likes her but he lifted his leg and peed so yeah, she might be pissed at you about that later."

"Wow. OK. Thank you for that," I say.

"Also, you owe me twenty bucks now."

"Yes, boss. I'll bring you the cash upon my return."

"Cool. I borrowed my mom's credit card and ordered new anatomy flashcards so if I give her my money, she won't freak out again. 'K, gotta go get ready! Bye, Lara and whatever your name is!"

Harmony spins on her heel and sprints away, leaving the two of us openmouthed.

"What just happened?" Dakota asks.

"Harmony happened."

"Any chance you can run right now? Because Mrs. Corwin just saw you."

TWENTY-ONE

MAY I HAVE THIS DANCE?

Tonight's speech went far better than last time—my stomach didn't roil with an incoming gastric revolt, no one shit their pants in the front row, and everyone in attendance seemed happy and healthy and free of foodborne pathogens.

Thank the old gods and the new.

Nope, the only thing I had to contend with was dirty looks from Mrs. Corwin, who did not manage to catch up to us before we bolted and has, in fact, changed her clothes and is in yet another pair of sensible shoes. Oh, and making accidental eye contact with Finan at the front table, Lucy-Frank nursing a beer on his left side, leaning in to whisper this or that and earning his smile in return, which made me stutter and lose my place in my prepared note cards.

Attempted recovery came in the form of a joke about my lactic-acid-soaked brain thanks to a certain bar manager dragging me out for an early-morning jog. Thereafter, I used Dakota and Catrina as anchor points, avoiding further glances at Finan and Lucy-Frank, pausing my brief address only to return Harmony's enthusiastic hello as she stood on the bench at her table near the back. She changed into what looks like an Easter dress that might be two sizes too small, her hair in a haphazard side pony, but she's still rocking the skater shoes.

I wish I could be Harmony.

I welcome all the new folks and thank everyone for their help with setup, reminding everyone to check out the ice-cream sundae bar offered for the enjoyment of all, "including ice cream made from our three beautiful, seaweed-fed cows—keeps the methane under control," I joke, "and, of course, dairy-free options." I close with an invitation to visit the Wandering Salamander's mobile bar counter and dance the night away with Thalia Island's very own in-house DJ, Li'l Petey, actually an agritech who deejays when he's in Vancouver and was more than happy to spin for us, given I used up most of this quarter's entertainment budget on the band that never played at the last welcome party. Oops.

While Dakota and I dressed at my house earlier, I made a quiet promise that tonight I would remain free of the pollutants of idiocy, i.e., no booze. I need to work toward fixing what I've broken ... before it's too late.

With dinner finished and most of the tables stacked out of the way, residents and crew alike take to the "dance floor," the middle of the closed-off street, gathering in front of the bandstand where Li'l Petey is set up. Light strings zigzag above like extra stars. Solar-powered twinkly lights hug lampposts and flower boxes lining the sidewalks. Two outdoor, biomass-fueled radiant heaters have been wheeled in for those who might need them later, but it was 26°C (79°F) today, a respectable temperature for a coastal island. And when summer finally arrives in western Canada, we are all eager to indulge in short sleeves and flip-flops as long as possible, pushing our luck until it's time to put out the jack-o'-lanterns.

People laugh and mingle and hug and toast and kids run around sharing the scooters a few brought with them tonight. One of the younger crew guys is trying to teach our handful of teenagers how to ride his unicycle. And Harmony has a posse of small humans watching her every move, though I do note that her younger sister is again attached to their mom like a baby spider monkey.

That woman really does look like she could use a break. Her husband Zackery was here earlier to eat but has since disappeared ...

no wonder she lights up like a Christmas tree when Liam Stillson slides onto the picnic bench next to her. Just because Gillian is a mom of two doesn't mean she's not still a woman with needs. Then again, what do I know? I'm not a mom. Maybe once you squeeze live humans out of that part of your body, you no longer want anyone touching it ever again?

I smile behind my hand as I watch them, thinking of the illicitly eavesdropped text messages Harmony has paraphrased to me, despite my light scolding that she should *not* be reading her mother's private missives. And given what I unfortunately know, I'm thinking maybe Gillian really *does* want someone—ahem, Liam Stillson—touching that part of her body again. And soon.

"Oh, you're cooking up something. I know that look," Finan says, moving in beside me on the curb's edge.

"Where's your date?" I pretend administrator-level interest in the happy crowd before us.

He snorts. "You wanna dance?" He offers his hand.

"*Fine.*"

When our fingers touch, a shiver zips through me. Finan leads me onto the dance floor, and even though the song is fast, we're slow dancing, my left arm settled against his broad chest, hand curled around the back of his neck while he clutches my right hand over his heart. I feel it beating, though not as fast as mine.

Maybe because we're just friends?

I'm not used to being this much shorter than he is—I tried on heels tonight but my calves protested with flair—and it's hard to remain stoic, to not rest my cheek against him as he leads me wherever he wants to go.

"Any more news from our bunker friend?" he asks quietly.

I look around to make sure no one else is paying attention. "Nothing of import. How are things with Lucy-Frank?"

"She's fun. It's been cool getting to know her better."

"Good. That's good." I'm unable to hide the ice from my voice. I at once feel encased in it.

"Are you wanting to stay in town next week after the hearing?" he asks. I'd almost forgotten. We're supposed to be giving our recorded witness statements Wednesday.

"Are you?"

"I was thinking I might. Check in with my sister and the babies. Have dinner with my mom. I can crash there and then we can get an early start Thursday."

"Sure. Yes. I can just stay at a hotel." My whole being vibrates with disappointment. *What were you thinking, Lara? That he would want to shack up with you at the Fairmont?*

"Can't you stay with Rupert?"

"Probably shouldn't. He's still dealing with the treatment. Immunosuppressed. Plus the nursing staff have basically taken over his guest room."

"Right. That makes sense." We continue swaying as the song changes, neither of us making a move to stop or break off. "You could stay at my mom's. She has plenty of room."

"Oh. No, that's—I couldn't. I wouldn't want to be an imposition."

Finan chuckles. "Lara, my mom knows you. And Kira would love to see you, introduce you to the babies. Just stay over. You don't have the budget for one of your swanky hotels, anyway."

I look up at him, trying not to notice how his eyes sparkle under these stupid romantic lights.

"If it's not an inconvenience. I'm going to spend the afternoon with Rupert and probably Wes Singh, you know, to catch up, see what I can do to help."

He nods. "Totally. Makes sense."

"I could just get a taxi to your mom's after?"

"I'll come get you." He clamps my hand a little tighter against his chest. "Looks like there's a big storm brewing for end of next week, so I want to make sure we're home before that. Worried about high winds with the solar fields. Farm B's new foundation is about done, so that shouldn't be a worry ..."

This is the first I've heard of any storm. Plus, we're spoiled in British Columbia. Sure, we get walloped every decade or so with crazy snowfall or a vicious bite of wind, but comparatively, it's a walk in the park, so much so that the rest of Canada makes fun of us when we get a few inches of snow and everyone ends up with their cars hood first in the ditches. It's also why property values are through the roof—folks want to live in the most temperate region of this ginormous country.

It's also why when the weather people get super excited about pending storms, we all sort of just pat them on the head, smile politely, and go about our lives.

The song finally ends, and Finan releases me. "Thanks for the dance," he says, offering a wave as he floats away to melt into the crowd standing near the temporary bar. When Lucy-Frank slides up next to him and places a hand on his arm—a flirtatious, *possessive* hand —a new crack echoes through my chest, and the shoulder devil whispers in my ear that tonight would be a lot easier to get through with a little gin.

Except there is no such thing as "a little" when it comes to me and gin.

And I need to work on my plan. The plan that will bring Finan floating back to *me*.

"Laraaaaaa! Come on and boogie!" Benny and Amalie bounce and swing each other around, clearly making the most of baby Sativa being passed around Catrina and friends. I wave them off—I am a terrible dancer, despite all those years Rupert tried to make me otherwise via ass-breaking classes filled with stuck-up skinny girls.

But then Dakota is there, too, someone else minding the bar counter, and the three of them drag me into the center of the chaos, and we dance and twirl and jump until I forget that it's more than just my deconditioned legs that are hurting.

TWENTY-TWO

A TALE OF WOE

Saturday I spent a few hours at the office—thankfully not moving tables or cleaning up from the big Friday-night welcome fête—but after ribbing from both Catrina and Dakota, I swore I would stay home all day Sunday and *not* do anything related to actual work.

Since when did I become a workaholic?

It's sort of inevitable around here. Even Finan is rarely home, though I try to imagine he's out at the vertical farms or dealing with his crews instead of the darker thoughts I have about him naked and luxuriating in Lucy-Frank's bed.

I'm physically exhausted from the last week, and the soaking rain doesn't lift my mood much, especially after a spate of gorgeous skies and warm temperatures. But I can tell the vibrant poppies in my front flower beds (planted by someone long before my arrival) are very happy to have a sip, a moment's reprieve from the effusive brightness. I love how a summer shower explodes the color and life in the West Coast landscape.

I'm curled in my favorite overstuffed chair, laptop open, the curtains wide, occasionally watching the tree line and the distant field just in case Jacinta decides to reappear. She's again made herself scarce. I know she's still here—she collected the paper and pencils requested at our prior breakfast together, plus thoughtful gifts continue to materialize on my porch. Another small, handwoven basket cradling a clump of fresh basil, more tomatoes, a jam jar of the best strawberries I've ever tasted. She must have one hell of a green-house in that bunker.

Today, though … today I sort of feel like spending time with my mom.

I attach the thumb drive to my MacBook via the dongle ordered alongside the photo-quality laser printer, *technically* for the office but it's living here for now. The plan is to print out all these years of letters and notes and photos of Mom saved on the tiny drive. Especially the photo of a young Cordelia and Jacinta sitting in the open side of what I now know is my mother's beloved Cessna. I have a frame for a copy for Jacinta too.

I haven't felt ready to read my mother's correspondence—and my time has been occupied otherwise—but lately, I've been a bit more emotionally raw. Maybe because Rupert's still sick. Maybe it's Jacinta's stories about her life and the life she shared with my mom. Maybe it's because I turned thirty-one in May and am now officially *in* my thirties with nothing to show for it. Maybe it's because I could lose Finan's affections for good, like Catrina warned.

Or maybe it's just a rotten case of PMS and I will go back to being hard, mean, sarcastic Lara as soon as my period shows up. More than likely.

Big Dog sprawls next to my chair, flopping dramatically onto the area rug. I think he's happy to be home for once, to have a break from the constant energy that is Harmony Peck.

The goal for today is to print the letters before stopping to read every single one as doing that will spread this job into weeks of painful, heart-rending effort. I don't think that is a wise choice. Once it's all printed, I've got a three-ring binder and an old-school photo album waiting to organize and protect the fruits of today's labor.

I develop a system wherein I open a file, hit Print, and then close it again so I don't become entangled in the emotionality of seeing my mom's handwriting on my screen. It takes about four hours to get through the folder's contents, pausing only long enough for more coffee, bathroom breaks, and to replenish the printer's paper tray.

So far, so good. Holding it together.

I then move on to the photographs, taking care to separate her wildlife photos into their own distinct folder. I've opened so many of these already to order the massive prints now gracing town hall and soon to be in my cabin, but I never tire of looking at her work.

The farther I scroll through this packed folder, the more I find of Cordelia's life, both before and after she became a mom. I ignore the folder that contains the shots of me—the album I'm compiling will be about her, and about Jacinta wherever she shows up in the photos, as well as any unfamiliar friends I might ask Jacinta about when I see her next.

I open five photos at a time, scanning a little longer to make sure it is indeed Cordelia in the shot—it's sometimes easy to see why Grandfather teased that my mother cloned herself to get me. This new printer does a surprisingly good job, though I will make sure to get all these photos properly printed on archival paper next time I'm in the city.

Ahhhh, the city. How I miss you, darling.

And not *just you*, dear Vancouver with your clogged streets and bad drivers and hipsters and hobos, but your luxury living with access to food one doesn't have to make oneself. When Vera wasn't around to cook, prepared meals would be waiting in the fridge, or I'd send Olivia out to pick up food or groceries and then she'd cook. Or I'd just order takeout and some pimple-faced college kid would show up at my door, arms laden with my impending meal, and if he didn't stare at my boobs, I'd give him a decent tip. (Although when Connor and I were fighting, sometimes the tip would be bigger if the delivery kid *did* stare at my boobs. Yes, I understand that is problematic.) I should talk to council about starting our own Thalia Island brand of Skip the Dishes. Or maybe someone should be brought to the island to make sure I always have food. I'm even cool with keeping the boob-staring part out of the job description.

I consider calling Tommy's and driving into town to pick up dinner, but that means I'd have to tidy my appearance and smile at people. Gross.

Snack reluctantly assembled, I apply a deep-cleansing mask to my neglected complexion, a peace offering to my pores now that I am deprived of my regular visits to an aesthetician. I'm pouring boiling water over a tea bag when footsteps clunk against the porch.

Finan?

I scurry over and throw open the door. "Oh. It's you!"

Jacinta starts and flattens her hand against her chest. "This is a new look." She points at the greenish goo coating my face.

"You want to exfoliate? I have extra."

She waves me away as she steps inside; she looks relieved I've opened the door. As much as I'm peopled out, I'm guessing she may be the opposite. "Finan's truck is gone. Figured it'd be safe coming across the field before nightfall."

I'm surprised to note the sun is already behind the mountains, the cloud cover oppressive and threatening.

"You hungry? I just cut up some cheese for crackers."

"That's not dinner food," she says, pausing to remove her boots.

"I lack the gift for culinary arts."

Humboldt saunters over to grant Jacinta access to his belly. "His ear looks great."

"I have a child prodigy doctor-in-training to thank for that. Tea?" I ask, rounding the kitchen island.

"Orange pekoe, please."

As I'm preparing our mugs, Jacinta moves over to the coffee table where I've spread the printed photographs. "Look at all these," she says, her face warm with awe and what might be nostalgia. She kneels and takes them in, pausing longer on some. I want her to tell me the story behind every single shot.

"I'd forgotten a few of these memories ... Your mother always had her camera with her. Always. And this was in the days before digital cameras. She would have pockets bulging with film canisters and could make any closet into a darkroom."

I slide Jacinta's steeping tea onto a coaster. She points to a photo of the two of them, very young and fresh looking. "This was another art show she did in Mexico City, after I missed the first one." Jacinta smiles and laughs quietly. "We hit it off the moment we met."

"After she got done yelling at the gallery movers in mangled Spanish?"

She picks up the photo and really examines it. "God, look at those *tetas*. We were so perky." She giggles and slides the photo back onto the coffee table. "If you have a good camera, not a phone, take pictures of this body." She gestures up and down at me where I sit next to her on the couch. "You will never regret remembering what you looked like young, before gravity takes over."

She scans the photos and laughs once, pointing. "This trip! Ha! This was the Utah dig. *That* was a crazy trip. And, ah! India! We were looking for endangered Asiatic lions—"

"I have the shot of the lioness and her cubs hanging at town hall."

"That photo won her some big awards." Jacinta's proud grin is infectious. For the next hour, she walks me through their time together. When she knew she was in love with my mom, how that sort of love was very frowned upon back then, and even though Cordelia enjoyed the company of both men and women, she dedicated herself to Jacinta whenever they could be together. "AIDS was a new thing back in the 1980s, and it wasn't just happening to gay men. Everyone was scared, so we were careful, especially since we weren't living together all the time. Sometimes in Mexico City, sometimes in Vancouver. And my family is Catholic. Very traditional. My father would not have tolerated if he knew what I was."

"That must've been hard."

"It was. But we made it work." She holds up a photo of herself in khaki hiking clothes. "This was me when I was working for the government as a geologist. My father promised me a job, and he delivered. I was only there for a few years, but I loved it. Every second, even the bureaucracy when I spent more time shuffling paper than dirt."

"How come you didn't stay longer if you loved it so much?"

Jacinta sets the photo down. "Things got complicated. With my family." She grasps her steaming mug, her gaze fixed on the spot where her right hand should be. "My father made a bad choice. His children had to live with its consequences."

The living room is very quiet, other than Humboldt's snores. The light from the pendant lamps over the breakfast bar reflect in Jacinta's earth-brown eyes now that the sun is fully asleep and the room has dimmed. "My father had an affair with his secretary. She got pregnant. Rosario Garcia was her name—he was much older than she was. It was scandalous, but she would be an unwed mother, so she lost her job. Had to go back to her village, to her own family.

"Her father and brother showed up at our home one night. When my father refused to give them money, they killed him. Right in front of us. They also shot one of my aunts in the leg and said they were going to kill us all and take everything we had to pay for Rosario's honor, for her baby. As the oldest girl, I stepped in and told them that my two older brothers and I would bring them whatever they needed, for as long as they wanted, if they promised to spare us. They agreed."

She sips her tea and leans back into the couch. "Things settled down after that. My mother and my younger siblings had to leave our beautiful house—we couldn't afford it without my father's income. But I still had a good job, and my brothers were finishing university so they could eventually find good jobs too. We just needed some time to build up again, especially since we were giving the Garcias so much."

"Did they ever threaten you again?"

"A couple times, but we were able to calm them down. Eventually, things changed. We kept helping them. My brothers even went into business with Rosario's brother."

"Are you serious? After they killed your father?"

"What choice did they have? And money does strange things to people, especially when there is a lot of it."

Don't I know the truth of that.

"Why couldn't you go to the police?"

She laughs. "The police in Mexico are *very* different from the police in Canada, Lara Jo."

"This is … crazy. This whole story."

Jacinta sits up straight and puts her mug back on its coaster. "Can we cook and talk? Your growling stomach is very distracting."

Once again, I slide onto the bar stool, treated to the Jacinta Ramirez Cooking Show as she continues the story of her family, all while magically finding enough ingredients from my (embarrassingly) slim pickings to whip together a frittata. She interrupts herself only to point at a pad of paper to dictate a list of groceries for me to acquire for future meals. I do not argue with this plan.

She tells me about how her brothers eventually went from paying for their father's indiscretion to working for the Garcias. "They became enmeshed. Like cloth. They were making a lot of money, much more than they would have made if they'd finished school and gotten jobs in their chosen fields. They were living good lives, taking care of our mother and younger siblings and aunties."

I don't ask what their alternative employment involved; it's implied by the loss of levity in Jacinta's tone. "The village Rosario came from was very poor. With our money, her father and brother were able to start a new enterprise." She lifts a brow as she dices tomato. "The money helped the whole village—and my brothers and I couldn't resist our little half sister, even if we had lost our father to her family.

"But I saw an opportunity. My brothers and the Garcias were running their own operation, as part of a bigger network that would eventually belong to the drug lord known as El Chapo, but I knew, if I had the capital, I could help all those villages get what they needed. Lara, I'm talking basic sanitation—running water, electricity, paved roads. So many of these mountainous villages have little to no infrastructure. Clean water carried in buckets from the river, police who were easily bribed, citizens who idolize the cartels because they have all the money and power.

"When we first met the Garcias, they were driving two old trucks to deliver gas to their neighbors for about fifteen US dollars a week. You might see why they were desperate when Rosario, who was earning a very good wage ten hours away in Mexico City, came back pregnant and penniless."

"Yes, but to kill your father over it? Seems extreme."

"Life is extreme sometimes." Jacinta slides the uncooked frittata into the oven and then moves to tidy the dishes. I try to stop her but she again reminds me how pampered I am to have a dishwasher.

Apparently, after her epiphany about being able to do more to help these small villages, she called my mother. "We'd lost touch after the Utah dig—had a bit of a falling-out. We could never agree on a place to settle down together—and you know Cordelia. She wasn't one to settle down *ever*."

My smile has a sting to it. I do remember wishing the same thing, that she'd settle down, that she'd stay *home* with me. It was always so wonderful when Cordelia Clarke would blow open the front door and share presents and wild tales and gorgeous photographs, but I also knew, from very young, that her reappearance wasn't for good, and it wasn't for long.

"I knew your mother's taste for philanthropy was a little different from your grandfather's," Jacinta says, rinsing suds from the side of the sink. "I think she sometimes chose things to support just to get under his skin."

"I think you are absolutely correct." I sip my tea, but it's gone cold.

"I explained to her about the villages, how they needed our help. And there were women who wanted out, to get away from abusive relationships, to start somewhere new with their kids. Cordi packed her bags and flew down the next day."

"Wow. I had no idea." A sour breath of resentment blows through me. Where was I when Cordelia decided to drop everything to run and help Jacinta? How old was I? Did she miss me? How could she just up and *leave* me like that?

"Cordi arrived, and it was like we'd never been apart. When I took her into the mountains, to see the villages for herself, she was shocked. We used whatever resources we had, and of course, she had more than any of us." Jacinta turns off the water and moves to the counter opposite me. She reaches across with her single hand and rests it atop mine. "Your mother helped a lot of people, Lara. Especially women and children and her beloved creatures. I don't want you to *ever* forget the good she did for the world."

At the cost of me growing up motherless.

But I can't say that out loud, not when I see the tears in Jacinta's eyes, the sadness on her face. It makes me question if there is more to this story. If the hard part is yet to come.

Of course it is. I know how this story ends ... with Jacinta Ramirez in my kitchen making me dinner and my mother's bones forgotten in some faraway jungle.

And yet, I still want to know the details. How Cordelia died. *Why* she died. Jacinta was there. She has the answers I've wanted for twenty years, not trite, half-assed responses given to keep an orphan from asking too many questions.

I swallow hard and knot my hand into a fist under her grip. "What happened to her, Jacinta?" My voice is hoarse with pain.

Jacinta releases me and leans against the kitchen island. "Your grandfather was concerned that people down there would learn the truth of who she was, who her family was. She was a kidnap risk. He wanted her back in Canada—back with you—but she kept saying she would be home soon. She worried about you all the time, but she knew you were cared for here. I even urged her to go home, to be a mother. She put it off and put it off. 'Just one more village, Jac.' That's what she'd say.

"By this time, she was working on environmental projects with some of my government contacts. She was doing legitimate work alongside the things we were doing."

I'm not sure I want to know more about the things they were doing.

"It was an addiction for her, even after Archibald cut her off. Told her no more money until she came home to be a proper mother. But we still had people to help—we needed money. So, we used her plane to do some product transport. At first, it was just once or twice a month, but then demand increased and we realized if we could do more, we could actually scrape a little from the money being exchanged and continue to help the villages. It worked for a while …"

"Until it didn't."

She nods and sniffs, pulling a handkerchief from her pocket for her dripping nose. "Until it didn't." She sighs loudly. "Can you excuse me a minute?"

Jacinta moves quietly down the hall. The bathroom door closes and I hear her sobs from within. Not sure what to do to help. Guilt rests a hand on my shoulder—I started all this with the pictures spread everywhere—so I gather them in neat piles and slide everything into the binder on top of the printed letters. I then tuck the collection into the buffet-table drawer.

"Out of sight, out of mind," I whisper to Humboldt.

The toilet flushes and the tap turns on, so I grab the remote and click on the TV, scrolling to find something lighthearted and *not* having to do with our lost family.

Jacinta reemerges just as the oven timer dings. Her bright eyes are red and sad, her lashes still damp, her nose tip pink.

I'm dying to ask about the password for the locked folder … but I'm afraid of what's inside it, afraid it will hurt her more than she already is.

It's such an odd feeling to be around someone who knew so much about my mother, who loved her deeply. Certainly Grandfather suffered when Cordelia died, when he traveled to Mexico to try to find her … but we didn't talk about it. Cordelia was his only child, born late in his life to a woman who left because he never made time for love and she couldn't bear coming in last.

Cordelia made time for love, with Jacinta, and perhaps with whoever my father is and whoever came before, stories I'll never hear. She made time for love, and she died because of it.

My chest is so heavy.

The password can wait. Whatever is in that folder can wait.

I aim the remote at the TV hanging above the quiet fireplace and

ELIZA GORDON

sniff away my sadness, for Jacinta. "How do you feel about romantic comedies?"

"Got one that will teach you how to get your handsome neighbor back into your bed?"

I smile and keep clicking, grateful that Jacinta Ramirez has breathed life into a part of me I thought was dead forever.

TWENTY-THREE

WOULD YOU LIKE TO PLAY A GAME?

The afternoon and evening with Jacinta was equal parts heartbreaking and wonderful. After she disappeared into the trees, back to her mystery bunker, I resisted the urge to walk over to Finan's. His lights were on, and the low bass of his music danced across the space between our cabins. But I didn't know if he was alone. It's none of my business if he's entertaining someone, clothed or otherwise.

Monday morning, I woke up not feeling great, my heart and head encumbered with the weight of Jacinta's stories and the real tragedy of my mother's too-short life. It's why I've spent so many years not thinking about it. Doing whatever I could to *not* think about it. Having Jacinta on Thalia Island, watching her come alive as she relives their time together ... it's next-level emotion I'm not wholly prepared to manage, especially without Rupert—or a therapist.

Most of Monday was wrapped in a hangover-like fog, despite not a single drop of anything stronger than peppermint tea the whole day. I reached for my phone a half dozen times to call Number Two, but I knew he was scheduled for another treatment first thing, and he did not need me whining about my mommy issues. I did eventually talk to the home-care nurse Rupert refers to as Thumbelina, just to check on him after they got home. She said he was resting and would pass on my message for him to call. She sounds sweet. Even if she pesters him about peeing, it's clear he secretly likes her, or she'd have been replaced already.

But even today, everything is still jumbled and fresh, like a new abrasion waiting for its scab to form. My head is thick, my thawing heart leaden. Was it only Friday when I was so excited to share with Finan the gossip collected over the prior week, especially about Gillian Peck canoodling with Dr. Stillson? It feels ridiculous now, held against Rupert's illness, the real struggles Jacinta and her family faced, the serious danger my mother put herself in to help other people ...

My life and troubles and silly gossip are inconsequential.

As such, I don't have the first clue where to start to explain my current state to Finan. I already told him about Jacinta, against Rupert's wishes. And yet, this load seems too cumbersome to carry on my own, especially without turning to my usual salves.

I've managed to shuffle quietly through yesterday and this morning. Our newest population is an efficient, responsible group thus far —and I'm so grateful to not have the constant ache in my gut when the town hall's front door opens, not knowing if it's going to be someone coming to get in my face.

This sentiment is obvious in my colleagues' demeanor too. Amazing how much smoother everything is running without the Kelly Lockhart sideshow preempting the *real* work that needs doing. The farms are gorgeous and plentiful and bug-free so far; the rebuild of vertical farm B is, according to Finan and Joey and team, coming along ahead of schedule; and the second solar field is near completion after waiting months for necessary parts to arrive from the California manufacturer.

If I listen closely, I can almost hear Thalia Island singing her happiness. It's a welcome sound given our tumultuous introduction. I haven't checked my countdown clock in a week, which I consider progress.

Some concern was raised at this morning's meeting about a sizable weather system heading toward us from Hawaii, but it was agreed that people far smarter than I will continue to monitor and make adjustments as necessary, especially since we're protected by the much larger Vancouver Island on our western side—damaging winds always hit her harder. And who on the BC coast isn't used to our skies turning into waterfalls now and again? The more rain, the better—fills our massive rain barrels to safeguard what remains of this year's growing season. I will never complain about the rain here, especially considering the megadrought conditions scorching much of the western United States.

I also did not escape the post-meeting tongue-lashing from Mrs. Corwin about Humboldt's urinary mishap on her pant leg Friday afternoon, but when I offered to replace her ruined Naturalizer loafers and throw in some of her favorite eco-friendly Allbirds socks, she jotted down her shoe size, nodded curtly, and marched back to her domain.

"Happy Tuesday!" Harmony yells as she skateboards around the corner and into my office. "Hey, is that a new shirt? I like it."

"Aren't you supposed to be at school?" I ask, looking at the clock. Just after 2:00 p.m.

"I finished everything. And Ms. Williams gave me extra work that the high schoolers are doing, so I finished that too. She gets anxious when I wander around the classroom, so she let me go."

"Are you just showing off now?"

"It's not my fault I'm neurodiverse and brilliant." Harmony flashes a cheeky grin and scoots down next to a waiting Humboldt before his tail thumps a hole in the floor.

"He doesn't smile like that for anyone but you."

"Me and Finan. He loves Finan. Thinks he's his dad." She's not wrong. "Got any jobs for me today?"

"Did you pay your mom back for the anatomy flashcards?"

"Yeah. Oh, and my dad got me a suture kit. It's this silicone pad that feels like real skin, and it comes with little scissors and scalpels and forceps and nylon monofilament, so if Humboldt ever gets hurt again, I can fix him." Harmony lifts Humboldt's head, quickly inspects his repaired ear, and then smooches the top of his snout. He'd purr if he could.

"No idea what nylon monofilament is, but are you any good with spreadsheets?" I tease, my eyes blurred from the pile of numbers relating to quarterly operating expenses that I, of all people, am supposed to make sense of. Honestly, I only passed algebra because the instructor fudged my grade to keep me from returning for another semester of punishment (as in me punishing him. Come on, his hair plugs were terrible. Yes, I again am not proud of this chapter of my life). Maybe I should mention this to Catrina before our next council meeting. About the math part, not me taunting my algebra teacher over his follicular challenges.

"What's a spreadsheet?"

"The devil's work," I mutter. "You wanna sort the mail?" I point at the Canada Post pouch sitting just inside my door.

Harmony hops up and extends a hand for my weighty key chain, bouncing on tiptoes. I've never seen anyone get so excited about mail duty.

"The step stool is in the hall closet if you need it. Bring my keys back when you're done."

"Come on, Humboldt!"

What I would give for an ounce of Harmony's pep.

Two knocks rap on my open door. "Why are you green?" Catrina enters with a glass Snapwear dish that she sets on my desk blotter.

I lift a hand, as if taking an oath. "I wasn't drinking." I crack the container lid and inhale deeply—a still-warm, very aromatic fruit scone. "Got a lot on my mind. Maybe caught a bug from Harmony. Kids are covered in germs, aren't they?"

"She certainly likes you." Catrina angles herself over my desk to press the back of her fingers against my forehead, then my cheek. Apparently finding no cause for concern, she smiles and slides one of the bamboo chairs from the wall to face me. "You got a minute?" She sits and folds her hands in her lap.

"Oh dear. Usually people only ask that question when I'm in trouble."

She laughs softly. "Have you talked to Rupert today?"

"No." A chill licks my arms. "Why ..."

"I just got off the phone with his oncologist. They've admitted him to Vancouver General, for observation and fluids. Seems the treatment yesterday caused some trouble."

"Why am I just hearing about this?" I grab my phone to see if I've missed calls, texts, or emails. Nothing.

"His nurse called me first thing this morning, so I phoned his doctor. Rupert didn't want you worrying, so they asked me to let you know, in person, rather than over FaceTime or a text message."

"Is this serious?"

She scoots forward on her seat. "He's weak and not keeping food down, a bit dehydrated, and he had some chest pain. They've started him on a new drug called Rituxan, which has a list of side effects as long as my arm, but they're confident this is the right treatment for him."

"But is it killing the cancer? Why won't he just do chemo?"

"We're trying this first. It's a biological therapy versus a chemo-therapy."

"I don't know what that means. And I thought these doctors knew what they were doing!"

Catrina rises and moves around the desk. I sit frozen in my office chair, tears streaming down my face, and let her hug me. "What am I going to do if he dies, Catrina? He's all I have left."

How many more times am I going to ask this question?

I bury my face in my hands while Catrina shushes me softly, telling me he's going to be all right, that he will pull through this, but he's just hit a rough patch, and we need to do whatever we can to be posi-tive and ready to help.

"But I'm stuck *here*. I should be *there*, taking care of him."

"He has plenty of medical folks tending to his needs. You sitting in his townhouse watching him sleep isn't going to miraculously cure him." She pats my shoulder as she lets go and straightens.

Dakota! Does she know? Does Catrina know Rupert is her biological father? Dakota should know what's going on—or maybe she already does. Maybe her moms know and they've talked to her. I haven't seen her since the party Friday night ...

"You're going over for your witness statements this week, yes?"

I nod and blot my mascara river with tissue plucked from the box on my desk. "Tomorrow. Finan and I are going."

"Are you staying in town? Do you want to use our car?" She returns to her chair.

"I was going to get a hotel, but Finan said his mom wants me to come for dinner, so they invited me to sleep over."

"Eileen Rowleigh is the nicest woman," she says. "It'll be good to be around friends right now. And you get to see the new babies!"

Catrina seems far more excited about such a prospect than I. "I suppose I should take a gift."

She pulls out her phone and scrolls through, clearly looking for something. "The Johansson couple—she's a knitter. Gorgeous pieces. Spins her own yarn. They're our new shepherds—sheep, alpaca, some goats?"

"Right." I remember checking them in last week.

Catrina holds up her phone, opened to an Etsy page. "I'll message Brida on Lutris and see if she has a couple of baby blankets you could take over. Probably will want bamboo or organic cotton. Sturdier in the washer than wool."

"That would be great. Thanks, Catrina."

She swipes her phone dark and leans back in her seat. "I am worried about you, you know. My door is always open."

I nod, my throat too tight to talk.

"All done with the mail!" Harmony explodes back into my office, keys jangling from her belt loop. Humboldt gallops in behind her, a Greenie hanging from his sloppy jaw. Harmony herself has chocolate smeared across one cheek and the remnants of a giant cookie in her hand. "We got a snack. Found 'em in the kitchen."

"That's what they're there for," Catrina says. She rises and boops Harmony once on the nose before turning to me. "I'll message you about the blankets. Pop by the diner before you head to the marina—I'll put everything together in a nice basket."

"Thank you again. For everything."

Catrina waves and heads down the hall toward her own office.

"Were you crying?" Harmony unhooks and returns my key ring. Crumbs tumble from her lips with the bite in progress and bounce across my desk.

"My friend is sick. I'm worried about him."

Her eyes light up. "What kind of sick? Can I help?" Humboldt sits perpendicular to Harmony, watching the cookie in her hand like he's stalking prey.

"It's not the kind of sick we can help, kid."

"Cancer?"

"Mm-hmm."

She finally pops the last bite into her mouth; the disappointment registers in Humboldt's eyes as he sighs and returns to his bed to chew on his own treat.

"Don't be sad, Lara. As soon as I'm a doctor, I'll fix your friend."

"Thanks, Harmony."

My office phone rings, the display showing the caller's ID. "It's your mom."

"Don't answer it!"

"I have to. She'll just leave a message, or worse, come in here and get mad at me for teaching you swear words." The phone keeps ringing.

"I already know them all. *Fuck* is her favorite word."

I bite my lip to not laugh as the call goes to voicemail. "You should go or else she won't let you hang out here anymore."

Harmony exhales dramatically and plods over to her backpack. She drops onto the floor first and gives Humboldt a big kiss and whispers something into his ear. He shakes his head, sending spittle everywhere. Harmony's answering giggle always makes me smile, even against my will.

"Do I get paid for sorting the mail?" She climbs onto her skateboard.

"I'll add it to your weekly total."

She rolls toward the door, abruptly stopping at the threshold. "Oh, there were a couple letters for you but I put them in your mailbox since you were talking to Catrina. Byeeeee!" She pushes off and disappears, leaving chocolaty fingerprints on the doorjamb molding.

Since I am getting nowhere with this spreadsheet and the idea of food beyond Catrina's fruity scone or even coffee is too much effort, I shuffle out to the mailboxes. Four tries to find the right key.

I extract my mail, smile politely at another resident who's just come in to do the same, and slide into the kitchen to check the pantry for the illicit box of Diet Coke I hid within last week. I had a few cans tucked into a corner in my desk hutch, but *someone* took them.

Ah-ha! Still here. I slide a can out and wrap it in my mail so Mrs. Corwin, on the phone in her office, doesn't see me as I scurry past. Once I'm back in my own space, I open the can in my coat closet so the old bird doesn't hear the sound of imminent caffeinated, carbonated deliciousness.

"That crap will kill you!" echoes down the hallway.

I chuckle as I take the first sip. Also I am concerned that Mrs. Corwin might not be human. Who hears that well at her age? Guess she didn't spend her teens and twenties making out with randos on top of sedan-size subwoofers at Coachella.

I flop into my chair once again and pick through my new mail. Three letters from charities, two Thalia Island-related account statements, a reminder that I am due for a dental cleaning ...

And another envelope with my name and address beautifully calligraphed across its front.

Just like before with the one that contained the cheaply printed photograph of the number 700.

I look up to see if anyone's outside my office, which is ridiculous. This was *mailed* to me. No one would be watching.

My simmering nausea spikes. I'm hot and cold at the same time.

Maybe it's just a game? Or a weird chain letter? Some kind of joke? Maybe it's Connor Mayson trying to scare me, his brand of twisted repayment for me having a hand in the ruination of his career?

"You're being paranoid," I say. Letter opener wielded like a weapon, I slice the top of the envelope and pull out the contents.

Another low quality, black-and-white printed photograph—this time, it's my grandfather's gravestone in the sanctuary behind Clarke Manor.

TWENTY-FOUR

AN UNSETTLING DISCOVERY

A knock on the door. Seven thirty, on the dot.

"It's open!"

Humboldt's immediate whining and the ticking of his nails on the hardwood as he wiggles his butt is confirmation enough who's actually just let themselves into my house. "Is this your bag here?" Finan asks after a long minute of cooing at my dog.

"Yes, but my overnighter is on my bed. One sec." I'm finishing my makeup, trying to tie a scarf over my hair without undoing the last hour's worth of work—we really, *really* need a stylist on the island. Originally the plan was to take my namesake ferry over, but it's a Wednesday, and the *Lara II* doesn't run today, so Finan's boat it is— and that puts my coif in grave danger.

Finan leans against the bathroom door frame; our eyes meet in the mirror, but it's his smell that weakens my knees. Oh my god, so good … and he's in a suit, his starched white shirt unbuttoned at the neck, his beard groomed and undercut refreshed. I want to retrace the scar I gave him all those years ago. Seeing him dressed up takes my breath away.

I clear my throat, offer a tight smile, and continue with the mascara wand, though not without difficulty.

"You look like a movie star," he says, pointing at the scarf tied under my chin.

"I'll have to spend the trip in the cabin or risk looking like a kraken by the time we get downtown."

"I like it when your hair is messy." He winks and then straightens. "OK if I throw your overnighter in the truck?"

"Please."

He walks down the hall to my bedroom, and I have to brace myself on the vanity for a beat, eyes closed as I inhale the aroma he leaves in his wake. I *feel* his scent ... everywhere.

How the hell am I going to get through the next twenty-four hours?

We stop in town to drop Humboldt with Dakota. She was very upset after hearing about Rupert's hospital admission, so when I told her we'd be going to Vancouver for the meeting, she asked if she could look after Big Dog, "to keep me company," instead of us leaving him with Catrina. I gladly accepted. And Humboldt likes hanging out with Dakota at the Salamander—who wouldn't? He gets to nap all day while surrounded by people who slip him bites from their lunch plates.

I promise her I will give Rupert her love; she promises she won't fatten up my dog too much overnight.

The meeting in downtown Vancouver is slated to begin at 11:00 a.m. Crossing the strait will be a little slower than usual as that promised storm has sent scouts ahead. The rain is manageable, but the wind whitecapping the water, coupled with having to hide in the cabin for the hour-long crossing, makes for a nauseating start to what promises to be a stressful day.

The boat slows, and a quick glance out one of the cabin portholes reveals we're approaching the Horseshoe Bay marina. I button my trench coat to my neck and emerge from below as Finan expertly steers the *Lady C* into a moorage slip. Once we're tied up, he helps me onto the dock—not because I'm fragile but because I'm in patent leather, four-inch Louboutin heels, and an emergency room visit isn't on the schedule. He hands over our bags and then joins me off ship, following close behind as we head up the soaked ramp toward the parking lot.

Catrina and Tommy offered use of their car, but Finan had already rented one—a pearlescent Tesla, waiting for us in the lot. I'm grateful. Catrina's generosity is boundless, but their tiny compact is the opposite of comfort.

Traffic into downtown is not awesome. A wreck on the singular highway into the city, the TransCanada, means everything is slow-going. You'd think a city as big as Vancouver would have an advanced highway system along the lines of Los Angeles or even Toronto, but nope. Highway 1, baby. When she gets blocked, you wait.

Today, however, I am not complaining. Locked in a luxury car with the world's hottest man behind the wheel? It's a punishment I'm willing to endure.

Plus Finan off Thalia Island means I have uninterrupted private time to share everything that's been going on. We've made a few half-baked promises to meet for lunch at the diner or grab a beer after work, but said promises have gone unfulfilled. And whenever I see Finan walking across to Tommy's with Lucy-Frank or laughing with her at council meetings, my envy monster rears her ugly head, making me not want to tell Finan anything about anything ever again.

I'm an emotionally stunted five-year-old. And I *hate* that we're "just friends." It makes every exchange weird and awkward and I'm always waiting for the wrong thing to fall out of my mouth.

But there's no one in the car except us and the flashing red triangle on the car's navigation screen declaring that the accident ahead has not yet cleared. I'm so blissed out breathing the same air as Finan that I don't even care if we're late.

So I deliver the highlights in the saga of Jacinta and Cordelia with special emphasis on the red beryl, how it's on the Dea Vitae flag—and her tattoo—and possibly in Grandfather's ring I hold up as I talk. We parry theories back and forth about Jacinta's potential involvement, or even Archibald's or Rupert's, agreeing that it is a fantastical stretch that any of them would entangle themselves with something as insane as Dea Vitae. And Jacinta hasn't once mentioned anything remotely fishy that could be linked to some secret affiliation with a dangerous cult.

"Have you talked to Wes about this yet?" he asks.

"I can't. Rupert doesn't want anyone else knowing about Jacinta— not even you—but I did ask Wes if he's got any idea what's up with the stone on their logo. I planted the seed that it could be red beryl, that I'd been doing some research on my own." Finan's serious expression makes me nervous. "*Should* I tell Wes about Jacinta?"

"Maybe ..."

"But Rupert's been hiding her. For a long time. There's more to her story than she's shared, but it's obvious she isn't keen on being discovered."

"If she's a geologist, I suppose it could just be a weird coincidence. Maybe the gem on the Dea Vitae flag is something else entirely. Quartz or ruby or something."

"Could be. Jacinta said red beryl is rarer than diamonds, one of the rarest stones in the world. Why would this fringe group of cult freaks know about a super-rare gemstone that hardly anyone's heard of?"

He fidgets with his beard. I can practically see the wheels turning in his head.

"Oh! Also—I've been getting these *bizarre* letters. Handwritten envelope with no return address. Inside are these crappy black-and-white photos from a cheap printer. The first one, I thought maybe it was just a chain letter or unfunny joke from some weirdo. We get those sometimes."

"What was the photo of?"

"The number 700. Nothing else. But it looks like it could be an address?"

"And the second?"

"That one freaked me out—it's of Grandfather's grave in the sanctuary at Clarke Manor."

Finan looks over at me, eyes wide. "That is creepy."

"Right?"

"Do you have 'em with you?"

I throw a thumb over my shoulder. "In my work bag. I want to show Wes."

"Definitely. This doesn't sound random at all."

My purse buzzes; I pull out my phone. "It's the lawyers' office," I say, answering.

"Is this Lara Clarke?" The female voice on the other end sounds harried, some of her words overruled by the sound of passing sirens, as if the caller is outside. "This is Hailey Carson. Are you on your way to our offices?"

"Traffic—accident on the Upper Levels. We're on the Lions Gate Bridge now. Why?"

More sirens blare through the phone's speaker.

"They've evacuated our building. You can't come in—there's anthrax in the building."

I don't think I've heard her correctly. "I'm sorry—what did you say?"

"ANTHRAX!" she yells. "Someone mailed anthrax to our law offices, so we've been evacuated and the hazmat teams are herding us into tents down the block. Everything is canceled. We'll get back to you as soon as we can!"

She hangs up.

"Did she just say *anthrax*?"

My heart pounds so hard, I hardly hear Finan's voice as he merges onto the connector that will take us through Stanley Park and into downtown. Our eyes meet briefly before I happen to look at the car's display screen, at the directions to our destination. I tap on it, zooming in on the map.

"Holy shit …"

"What?"

"The address of the offices we're going to—700 West Georgia Street." I unbuckle my belt, earning the car's chiming reprimand of an unsecured passenger, and throw myself between the front seats to grab my work satchel. I dig through for the mysterious letters. My hands shake, my stomach again unsettled.

I sit and belt up again, sliding the first letter from its envelope.

I hold it up for Finan.

"Let's see if we can get down there," he says, speeding up and earning a few blared horns from the pokey cars in our way. We're a block from the high-rise when traffic halts, emergency lights up ahead from police and fire bouncing off neighboring behemoths in Vancouver's business core. A small crew of Vancouver PD officers direct people into the oncoming lane since the front of 700 West Georgia is undergoing an urgent blockade. Horns shriek, people yell—it's chaos.

We're one of the final cars to pass through as police drag the white A-frame barricades into place to close off the street behind us. I look at the front of our destination building as we ease past.

"Finan ..." I hold up the letter to the side of his view out my window. "Look at the address."

The photo is a match.

TWENTY-FIVE

THE SANCTUARY

W e forgo stopping in downtown and head to Clarke Manor. En route, I phone Wes Singh but since I forgot to bring the secure phone, our conversation is brief. He agrees to meet us at the estate within the hour.

When we arrive, a handful of cars are parked in front of the electric chargers in the small lot just off the wide gravel turnaround.

"Man, I forgot how big this place is."

"And Grandfather would want me to remind you that it has its own water reclamation and treatment system and is a hundred percent off grid, thanks to the solar and wind power infrastructure he pioneered —with your father's help."

Finan smiles as he pulls into an empty spot. The car, silent by design, is even more so now that we're parked outside the mansion, looking at each other, stunned by what we've just seen, worried about what is yet to come.

"Can I see the second letter?" Finan asks. I hand it to him. "Do you want Wes and I to go up there first? See if this is another clue?"

"It's definitely a clue. And whatever is here, I have to see it for myself."

Finan leans back in his seat. "It's weird to be here and know that none of you are inside anymore."

"It is." A quiet laugh slips out. "At the reading of Grandfather's will, when Rupert told me about the terms of my inheritance, I got so mad, I accused him of stealing Clarke Manor for himself. Even threatened to sue."

Finan smiles. It's a blanket around my shoulders.

"That's the day I stole Andromache."

"Ah, beautiful Andromache. She still doing OK without me checking on her every day?"

I nod, my heart squeezing a little at the reminder that Finan isn't in my cabin often enough to look after my stolen spider-plant child.

"What are they doing with this place, if Rupert hasn't claimed it to turn it into a den of iniquity?"

"The Clarke Foundation has moved in to start converting it into the Archibald Magnus Clarke I Centre for Environmental Protectionism. Or something. It's a long and very official-sounding title."

"Continuing his work, then."

"Aren't we all continuing his work?"

Finan's grin is proud. "We are."

I want to kiss him. Right now. More than anything. I want to climb across and smash my lips against his and make all the awkwardness of the last weeks melt away.

Before I can, an unmarked cruiser pulls up next to us. Wes waves as he throws it into park.

Finan reaches across the console and clasps my hand. Only then do I realize how stressed I am, his warmth over my freezing-cold fingers. "I'm here. OK?"

I bob my head a few times, fear choking my voice.

We climb out. Wes reaches toward Finan for a strong handshake, but I get a hug. "You doing all right? You look a bit pale." He taps under my chin.

"Life has been *a lot* lately." It's all I can manage.

"I know." He sighs and then extracts a pair of nitrile gloves from his black jacket. "Let me see these letters."

155

I've tucked them in the inside pocket of my lightweight trench coat. Upon handing them over, he moves to the Tesla's trunk and carefully removes the pages, examining their envelopes and then the actual letters.

"This photo is the actual address of the lawyers' offices on Georgia, where we were supposed to be giving our statements today," I explain. "I should've made the connection before."

He nods and slides the 700 and its envelope into a plastic evidence bag pulled from one of the pockets of his cargo pants. I want to make a joke about what else he's got in those magic pants, but a joke right now is clearly a stress response.

I remain quiet.

Wes opens the second letter. "This is here. At Archibald's grave?"

"Yes."

"Have you been up there yet?" he asks us both.

"No. We waited for you," I say. "I'm kinda freaked out. Didn't know if we'd need backup or something. If there's anthrax downtown, what the hell will we find up in the sanctuary?"

Wes examines the letter closely and then slides it into another bag.

"Oh my god, do you think there could be anthrax on the letters?" I hold my hands out in front of me, flipping them palm up, palm down, as if I would actually *see* evidence of the deadly bacteria on my skin.

"When did you first open the 700 letter?"

"Maybe ten days ago?"

"And you've not been sick. No cough, no skin lesions, nothing?"

"No. Nothing. I've been extra tired lately, but that's because of stress. Too much going on with Rupert and work and ..." I let the sentence fade without finishing it. Without adding anything about Jacinta—or Finan.

"I don't think we should go up there. Not without a team." Wes holds up the letters. "I'm going to take these."

"Of course."

He nods and then walks back to his trunk, opens it, and slides the letters into yet another evidence bag, this one paper. He pulls off the gloves and drops them in the bag too. "Here." He tosses me a tube of hand sanitizer. "For now."

I squeeze some into Finan's hand, the air immediately pungent with the sharp tang of the alcohol gel.

And then Wes is on the phone, seemingly calling everyone. He won't let us walk up to the sanctuary yet, and he goes inside the manor to talk to the Clarke Foundation director, telling her that everyone working within needs to evacuate outside to a staging area until the cavalry arrives.

Within just a few minutes, the turnaround and side lot are filled with Foundation people, confused about what the hell is going on, fanning themselves with their hands or random papers in the muggy, pre-storm air. I only know a few of these staffers and exchange polite smiles, but I stay with Finan near the cars per Wes's instruction that I not reveal what's underway. When the Foundation director again asks what's going on, Wes informs the group that there's been a security threat, the scene is now locked down, and everyone must stay off social media until the police have arrived and done a thorough scan of the premises.

He leaves out the part about how they're sending an entire hazmat squad to see if a bioweapon has been sent here too.

Three hours later, the fire department and enhanced hazmat teams finish what Wes explained is a "quick test" to check for the presence of contaminants. While the experts were inside, a lengthy white canopy was quickly erected outdoors to protect people from the sun, and every person present was asked to provide identification and contact information. By the time the hazmat-suited officers emerged, the Foundation staff were red-faced and irritated that they couldn't yet go back in to refill water bottles or use the bathroom.

The initial scan of the premises revealed no threat, so people were allowed to enter in groups of two to grab their things and leave. Without evidence of anthrax or other threat, no one needed transport to the hospital. The Foundation director was busy the whole time with Wes and the two hazmat captains running the show, discussing that this cursory sweep is just the first in a long checklist that has to be managed before it's back to business as usual. Wes also stepped out of their three-person briefing to call Len Emmerich over on Thalia and loop him in, to be on the lookout for anything unusual.

The attitude from Wes and his colleagues is clear: whoever is behind this knows what they're doing.

Once the last of the Foundation staff and standby ambulances have gone, Wes signals that it's time to go up to the sanctuary. It's ominous to walk along the wooded path with an entourage, some of whom are still in their scary biosafety suits. The day, this walk up to the small hill overlooking the mansion and lower property, is eerily familiar to the afternoon we buried my grandfather, though then, the sky spat her sorrow at us. Today she beats down with the hot rage like that brewing inside me.

Finan takes my hand. I let him.

As we approach the top of the incline, it's immediately obvious that all is not well in my grandfather's final resting place. Wes stops us.

"No. I want to see what they did."

He steps in next to me, an arm around my shoulders as I release Finan's hand and walk forward, officers flanking us.

Archibald's headstone is in pieces on the ground.

"How would they do this? It's fucking *granite*," I ask. "Don't we have security on the grounds? What about the cameras?"

It's not enough that the grave marker has been desecrated. The chunks of rock have been rearranged on top of my grandfather's resting place, on the healthy, compost-fed green grass that serves as blanket to the plain wooden coffin below holding his melting body, wrapped in a head-to-toe mushroom suit wherein the spores will eat his flesh and turn to nourishment for the surrounding flora.

The arrangement of the granite chunks reveals a picture painted onto the whole surface, like some sort of disjointed, macabre puzzle.

"Wes ... it's the cresting wave and snake tails. It's Dea Vitae."

TWENTY-SIX

THE BLUE ROOM

W e pull up to Finan's mother's house in North Vancouver, beyond exhausted. It's after eight o'clock, long past when we told her we'd be arriving, but after the discovery at the sanctuary, all hell broke loose. Another team was brought in to deal with what is now a crime scene. Rather than send us to the hospital—and risk news leaking about this latest brewing scandal—the regional hazmat team drew blood from Finan and me and Wes onsite. It will be sent to the provincial toxicology lab to test for anthrax, since we handled the letters that we now know are definitely tied to the attack downtown.

If our samples show evidence of anthrax bacteria, that's a whole different can of worms that involves antibiotics or perhaps even aggressive antitoxins delivered in an isolation unit in the hospital. The person drawing our blood explained everything—as the onsite quick-tests were negative for presence of anthrax, we aren't a contagion risk, but we should still change clothes and shower thoroughly before going out in public.

And while she explained protocol, my thoughts raced, cycling on one undeniable and immediate need: I must talk to Wes. Alone.

Definitely should tell him about Jacinta and her intense interest in red beryl, given today's developments. I can't hide her presence from him, despite Rupert's plea to the contrary. If she is somehow involved with Dea Vitae, I have to know so I can protect Thalia Island. So I can protect the people who are quickly becoming my family.

As such, Finan and I decide we'll spend tomorrow in the city and go back later than anticipated. That way I can meet Wes and then we can visit Number Two.

Just before we were cleared to leave Clarke Manor, Wes pulled me aside. "About Rupert … he's lost most of his hair, and what hasn't fallen out has gone white. And he's so thin, Lara. Even more so than usual. I wanted you to have tonight to prepare yourself." I hugged him goodbye and allowed Finan to entangle his fingers with mine as we walked back to the car. I stared out the window numb and quiet the whole trip to his mom's.

With the car off, he turns in his seat. "You OK?"

"No."

He reaches across and brushes my cheek with his thumb. I lean into it, grateful for his kindness, even if we're not technically *together* at the moment. He then squeezes my shoulder once and climbs out.

With a call ahead to his mom, Finan arranged for us to go in through the garage, into the basement bathroom to wash thoroughly and change into fresh clothing, just in case we *were* somehow exposed to anthrax. I follow him up the steep, stamped-concrete driveway to the double-car garage on the left, the side closest to the house open.

His mother awaits, standing in the arched wooden front doorway, an excited grin spread across her pretty face. The white-and-slate-blue house is three stories under a gabled roof, three wide windows spaced across the front topped with a white arched pediment. A well-mani-cured hedge sits under the windows, their bases decorated with fresh soil and healthy rose bushes in a rainbow of pinks, reds, and whites. It looks straight out of a storybook.

"I want this house," I mutter.

"My baby boy," Eileen Rowleigh says, arms outstretched, but then she drops them. "Let's get you two decontaminated and then, time for all the hugging."

We follow her through the garage, into the house, and down a wide, hardwood-floor hallway. She stops at the first door on the left and clicks on the light in an expansive bathroom with double sinks and a glassed-in shower.

"Fresh towels and a set of clothes for each of you on the counter. They should fit, Lara, though your legs are a lot longer than mine." She smiles. "Head upstairs when you're done. Oh, I've left a garbage bag, too, for you to seal your discarded clothes in. Just in case."

"Thanks, Mom."

"Your overnighters in the car?" she asks.

"I'll get them when we're done. Thanks for all this," Finan says.

Eileen pauses briefly at the open bathroom door. "It's so, so good to see you again, Lara. I can't wait to catch up."

She steps out, clicking the door closed behind her.

Finan and I lock eyes in the mirror, both of us chuckling under our breath. "Do you want me to wait in the garage or something while you shower first?" I ask.

"Not like we haven't showered together before."

"I know, but ..."

"You go first. I'll sit in here." He points to the toilet in its own small closet with a sliding pocket door. "Just don't use all the hot water."

Once we're bathed of potential deadly pathogens, we move upstairs to the main floor. Eileen shuffles toward us and wraps her arms around her son, again reminding me how sturdy he is, especially compared to his diminutive mom. When he lets go, she cups his cheek with one hand, tucking her gray-and-brown bob behind her ear with the other. I remember her face—from the memorial all those years ago, the horror when she saw the blood pouring down the side of her son's head.

"And Lara ... a hug for you too." She steps around Finan and pulls me into a tight, quick hug. She leans back, both hands on my shoulders as she examines my bare face and ponytailed, wet hair. "You are the spitting image of your mother."

"Thank you for all this." I gesture to the cozy sweatsuit she left for me in the bathroom. She was right—the legs on the pants are a bit short. "And thank you for inviting me to stay over."

She flaps a hand. "No way was I going to let you pay for a hotel, not when we have *plenty* of room here. Come on. You both look beat. Have you eaten anything? What a day you've had!"

Finan gestures for me to follow Eileen. The main floor is as charming as the exterior promised it would be—mahogany plank flooring throughout, a wide mahogany staircase to the left of the foyer trimmed with a wood-and-black wrought iron banister, eggshell walls offset by perpendicular walls in rich colors, LED pot lights warming each room, gilded mirrors and original paintings, mostly of landscapes, in spaces unoccupied by uniform wood bookshelves stuffed to bursting, and so many plants. No wonder Finan knows what to do with Andromache.

"Your home is breathtaking. I want it."

"We've been very happy here," Eileen says. "Finan, I brought your bags in." She points to our things tucked into an alcove—including the gift basket Catrina put together for Kira's newborns, which I grab—as we pass through to the kitchen. "I made a ton of food. And you have to meet the babies, Lara!"

The modern kitchen is open and bright, all white and marble and stainless appliances, a six-burner cooktop, wine fridge, and a bank of windows that looks out onto a lushly landscaped backyard, a shimmering turquoise rectangular lap pool lit from within. "OK, I definitely want to live here," I say again.

The kitchen melts into a giant family room with three black leather sofas, plush rugs underfoot, a live-edge coffee table that has been overtaken by two portable bassinets, one of which cradles a tiny, slumbering baby. The flat-screen TV set into the wall of mahogany bookshelves is on but muted, a dormant, glass-enclosed, natural gas fireplace center stage. The woman sitting on the couch is obviously

Kira, Finan's little sister. I haven't seen her in years, but the Rowleigh family dimples are unmissable.

"Kira, you remember Lara Clarke," Eileen says, her slippers scooting across the rug to check on the baby not in Kira's arms.

"Of course! Oh my god, so good to see you! We've been bugging Finan forever to bring you over," she says. "I'd get up but Ivy is still eating." She nods at the tiny, sock-covered feet sticking out from underneath the light blanket thrown over her shoulder. "This kid never stops. I will have zero boobs left when this is over."

"She's a little piggy, like her mom," Finan teases, leaning over to kiss his sister on the forehead. He kneels next to the coffee table, gazing lovingly at the baby boy snoozing in his bassinet. "I can't believe we were ever this small."

"*You* were never that small," Eileen teases. "Lara, I swear, when this one was born"—she nudges her son with her foot—"he was ready to play hockey. Ten pounds and then some!"

Finan's face is flushed, maybe from the hot shower, but this is what happy and relaxed looks like on him. It's nice to see him in his element.

"It's a miracle I said yes to any more kids after that," Eileen says.

"And aren't you glad you did?" Kira flutters her eyelashes.

"Except *you* were even bigger than your brother. So that was the end of that nonsense."

"Aww, she saved the best for last," Kira teases, sticking out her tongue at her brother.

Finan stands and grabs his mom, smooching her on the cheek while she bats at him. "Unhand me, you brute." She smacks him away, lamenting that he's too big to send to his room, then teasing him about his beard and how manly he looks these days.

I slide in next to Kira on the couch. "I brought you a basket of some things from the island. It's all organic, all natural. The blankets are handmade by a weaver named Brida—you can throw them in the wash and everything." I set the basket beside her, and she oohs her way through it. Three blocks of natural, handmade soaps, a glass bottle of all-natural lotion, some beeswax butt balm for the babies, two bottles of our first run of Thalia Island Lager, handmade paper you can recycle by planting in a pot and flowers will sprout from it, and a stack of Tommy's oversized chocolate-chip cookies in a reusable wrapper.

"This is incredible, Lara. Thank you!"

"Catrina put it all together."

Kira smiles. "That Catrina …"

"Right? She's amazing."

"Thank you again. I will use every single thing in here." She squeezes my wrist.

"All right, children, let's get this show on the road," Eileen announces from the kitchen, her hands covered in oven mitts.

Even though the aroma of the promised meal entices, I'm tired—and a little overwhelmed by the closeness and warmth of this family. Eileen is obviously thrilled to have both her children here, but I recognize the hint of sadness in her eyes, too, the one that misses the other half of her heart.

Speaking of, the family room's eastern wall is covered with photos, all in black frames with white mats. It's a gallery of the Rowleigh family, starting when Mr. and Mrs. Rowleigh were newlyweds, through Finan's and Kira's childhood—vacations, beach days, water fights, amusement parks, Finan sporting casts of various sizes and colors, team photos, Finan on a skateboard, surfboard, or snowboard, Kira on horseback, Kira skiing slalom races, both of them at their respective senior proms, graduation pictures, and up through Kira's wedding photos, Finan and his father in kilts bookending a gorgeous, laughing bride in a voluminous, off-white ball-style gown.

Finan moves in beside me and offers a few highlights of his life as a member of this family. "Don't forget to tell her about the bachelor party a month before my wedding where you and my fiancé and the rest of the wedding party were almost arrested because you are a terrible influence," Kira says as she slides past us into the kitchen.

The knot in my throat threatens to choke me. I don't want to be jealous of this man, of these people, of their stories and shared lives … but I am.

Behind us, Eileen sets out silverware and plates, piling one full for Kira who's bouncing a sleeping, post-snack Ivy on her shoulder. "I'll take the baby girl. You, eat, before Rowan wakes up. And you two, come! Food!" Eileen says.

I grab Finan's wrist and gesture for him to lean closer. "I'm exhausted. Would she be offended if I ate later?"

Finan shakes his head and places a hand on the small of my back, leading me toward the kitchen island. "Lara's going to crash for a bit. We can save her some, yeah?"

"Of course. Are you sure, sweetie? You need to eat."

"Thank you so much for everything, Mrs. Rowleigh, but I am wiped out."

"Absolutely. It's been a long day for you." She smiles softly. "Finan, set Lara up in the blue room. I've moved all the baby stuff aside."

"Oh. No, I don't want to take up space Kira needs."

"Ha. This house has six bedrooms upstairs. Plenty of space. Plus Kira's not sleeping over. She just wanted to see her dumb brother."

"Thank you. Sorry for skipping dinner."

"Don't mention it again."

I then follow Finan up the stairs, my weariness increasing with every step. I don't know how I will get down to the main floor again tonight.

He opens the door to the so-called blue room—immediately obvious why it's so named. Area rugs, bedding, the walls, and coordinating décor in every complementary shade of blue. Somehow, it works.

"My mom's favorite color," Finan says, hoisting my overnighter onto a padded bench abutting the foot of the four-poster, queen-size canopy bed.

"I haven't slept in a canopy bed since Europe," I say. "I will feel like royalty tonight."

"Oh, but you *are* royalty," he teases. "Bathroom is over there. No tub, but if you want a soak, we have a big jetted tub in the main bath down the hall."

"This is perfect." I perch on a wingback chair to take the pressure off my tired feet.

Finan leans against the adjacent antique dresser. "You wanna talk?"

"Not really."

"It's been a rotten day."

I nod, emotion burning my nose. "I feel sick. What they did to my grandfather's headstone …"

Finan slides a round ottoman over from against the wall and sits in front of me, taking my cold hands in his big warm ones. "We'll order a new marker. We can do it tomorrow."

I nod, unable to make eye contact or else I'll fall apart. "Archibald was such a good man. Why would someone do this? And *who* is doing this? What about surveillance? Clarke Manor has cameras everywhere."

"I don't know. Maybe it's an inside job."

"But *who*? One of the manor staff? Someone from the Foundation? Did someone disable the cameras and then climb the fences? With Kelly in jail—and they have no idea where Ainsley is—someone is coordinating this. It has to be one of their crazy followers, right? Wes said Dea Vitae has people all over BC now …"

"That would be my guess."

"And the anthrax attack—where would that even come from? If it *is* Ainsley, maybe she grew it or made it or however you get it, like what she did with the salmonella."

"I don't know, Lara. This is definitely not something I've ever experienced."

Of course not. Finan had a very normal upbringing, free of crazies and stalkers. The pictorial wall in their family room is evidence enough of that. "But why Archibald? Why Thalia? I feel like this is my fault, that I brought this upon us."

"No, no, no. This had to have been going on *long* before you were on the scene."

"I'm so confused, Finan. I don't know who to trust, who knows what, and who might not be on our side. What if Rupert is involved in all this shit, and he's been playing us the whole time?"

Finan rubs a hand over his beard, his eyes glazed with thought. "What would he have to gain from being involved with Dea Vitae? Rupert is an honorable man. He's not like Kelly or Hunter or Ainsley or any of those weirdos from the beach."

I look at him, searching his face. "I've even questioned you a time or two. If you might be involved."

He laughs. "The closest I've ever gotten to a cult is my undying love for the Vancouver Canucks, even if they can't win a Stanley Cup." He brushes a few strands of hair away from my cheek, but he won't let go of my eyes. "I've missed you, Lara. I miss you so much."

I almost crack one about Lucy-Frank but I don't have the energy for biting sarcasm. Because I've missed Finan too.

The air between us warms. Finan's soft, redwood-brown eyes flick to my mouth as he licks his lips, his hold on my hand tightening slightly.

"Finan, there are fresh towels for Lara in the armoire. I forgot to mention—"

He leans back and pivots to face his mom, now standing in my open door with an armful of folded towels. "Oh, sorry for interrupting," she says, backing out.

"You're not, Mrs. Rowleigh. Come in."

She does, but only a single step into the room. "Fin, I'll just put these in your bathroom, and I dished you up a plate, whenever you're ready. Have a good rest, Lara."

Finan squeezes my hand for a final time before standing. He offers a subtle wave as he closes the door behind him, leaving me alone in this room painted with all the colors of my sad heart.

TWENTY-SEVEN

GHOST FROM THE PAST

W es and I agree to meet at the same coffee shop as last time. I wasn't going to bring Finan along, not wanting to drag him into this any deeper, but when he showed up in my room this morning with a breakfast tray—bagel slathered in fresh butter, a yogurt-and-berry parfait, steaming coffee—I realized he's in this already.

Having him near makes me stronger. Makes me feel less alone, like there *is* one person left on the planet I can trust. And his mother is so kind, packing a picnic bag full of nonperishable snacks for our day, in case we get busy and don't have time to stop for lunch. Eileen Rowleigh is basically the nicest human on the planet. No wonder she and Catrina have become fast friends.

As Finan drives us along the Vancouver streets, I am bombarded with memories of my past life. Of nights spent partying with friends, invites to the biggest soirees from Canada's most high-profile celebs, of shopping trips that involved spending the kind of money Thalia Island uses for a month of basic supplies for her residents.

I almost ask Finan to detour past my old loft, but enough wounds are open and seeping on my heart right now. And I'm doing all right, aren't I? Other than Rupert being sick and the cult thing and the attempted murder of our lawyers and the desecration of my grandfather's grave and my dead mother's lover squatting in some mystery bunker and the overwhelming responsibility of making Thalia Island succeed and the all-consuming love I have for the man sitting next to me, even though I'm too chickenshit to tell him?

OK, so, *not* that great.

Finan parks down the block from the coffee place. Wes's gray cruiser is across the street. Of course, he's already here.

He waves when we enter, tucked in the same rear booth as last time, away from prying eyes and ears. I slide in, trying to rearrange the wind-warped mess of my hair; Finan takes drink orders and heads to the counter.

"How're you this morning?" Wes asks.

I shrug. "Have you talked to Rupert?"

"I did. Told him we'd be coming for a late lunch."

"Is he able to eat?"

"Some. My mom's been cooking for him, minus the spices—he can't handle it. But she's made it her personal mission to fatten him up on butter chicken and curd rice and every recipe that contains yogurt."

"What a punishment," I tease. "How 'bout you, Wes? You never tell me how *you* are."

He imitates the shrug I offered a few moments ago. I chuckle.

"You been staying out of trouble over there?" He hikes a bushy eyebrow.

"Seriously? You guys are like little girls with your gossip," I say. He laughs. "It was one night of careless karaoke. I didn't trash the general store, if that's what you're asking."

"I saw the video Emmerich sent over. You could have a singing career if this island thing doesn't work out."

I throw a sugar packet at him. "Number Two is an ass. I can't believe he showed you."

"Me and Rupert don't keep secrets from one another," he says, his face serious again.

It makes my heart pound—Wes may not have any secrets from

Rupert, but Rupert most certainly has a secret from Wes, and her name is Jacinta.

And I'm about to blow that right up.

Finan slides three mugs onto the table and sits next to me. He doesn't readjust when our legs touch; neither do I.

Wes thanks him and sips, his paws dwarfing the mug. "Your guys tracking this big storm headed our way?"

Finan nods. "Seemed at first like it was just going to be a lot of rain, but new models are suggesting a stronger wind pattern than we're used to for summer storms."

"Global warming is a hoax, though, right?" Wes says. Finan snorts.

"We should be fine. I've got the crews out securing anything that might be vulnerable. Vertical farm B is under construction, but I'm more worried about our newest solar field. Those panels were just installed. Might be some concern there."

As if on cue, a gust hits the window next to us, splattering it with the rain that settled in overnight, erasing yesterday's muggy breathlessness.

"Maybe you two should stay over another night," Wes says.

"It'll get worse before it gets better. And I need to be there overseeing my crews. This will be our first big wind test," Finan says.

"Hell of a trip across the strait." Wes looks outside at the young tree planted in its sidewalk cutout, the wind knocking its leaves and spindly branches like they're wrestling.

Finan's brow furrows. I didn't know he was worried about this. "You know how storms are here. The meteorologists work themselves into a tizzy and then it ends up being nothing," I say. "It'll happen this time too."

"Maybe." Finan relaxes his face when he looks at me. "Wanna put money on it?"

"You mean from my extravagant annual salary?" I tease. "I should save every penny for a pair of those hideous hiker boots you all love so much."

Finan nudges into me as Wes again scans the coffee shop, still quiet with only one other patron at a table on the opposite wall, bent over her laptop, earbuds stuffed into her head. "So. Lara—you asked me about the stone on the Dea Vitae flag."

I take a shuddering breath as Wes pulls out a black folder and sets it before him.

"It was an interesting question I hadn't considered before. Like I said, we just figured it was a ruby. I don't know if Rupert mentioned it, but Kelly Lockhart has gone full tilt in the crazy department, so much so that they've moved her onto a psych floor. But I questioned her about this stone, after you and I spoke. She said that it's red beryl, a stone that's in honor to that Babylonian goddess Tiamat—I told you about her before, Lara—who is at the heart of their belief structure. Apparently there's a lost collection of these sacred stones meant to serve as a conduit for Tiamat's return to Earth. It's their version of the Second Coming mythology."

I rest my head in my hands, elbows propped on the table. "I should not have eaten breakfast," I say. Finan flattens a warm hand against my back.

"In my searches, I did find tarot and crystal spiritualists who affiliated beryl stones—of all colors—to Tiamat, that these gemstones honor her. Allegedly, the red stones are the most powerful and offer people who possess them help with their difficulties. Or something."

I lean closer to Wes. "Is this somehow related to what they did to Derek Irving? To that poor raccoon?"

Wes looks around us again and then sighs. "*That* is not something I'm supposed to talk about, but red—and therefore blood—is symbolic to them. Sounds like the more zealous folks aren't shy about sacrificing living creatures to help the cause."

"But why did they choose Thalia Island?"

"Like I said before, Tiamat is the salt sea goddess. Followers believe she'll come to them first if they're near the ocean." Wes drinks and runs a hand over his long beard. "Apparently the orgies are part of it too."

"God, gross. Don't remind me." But I remember what Jacinta told me when she was explaining her tattoo, that some spiritualists believe red beryl is the stone of love—and that's the meaning she likes best. Oh god, my mother and Jacinta weren't involved in orgies, were they?

No. Of course not. They're not Dea Vitae followers. Jacinta is a geologist. End of correlation.

"And what about Ainsley? Or Iona—whatever her name is."

"Not a peep. She's on most-wanted lists around the world, Interpol has issued a Red Notice, but zilch so far." Wes slowly spins his cup on the varnished wood tabletop. "What I'm curious to know, though, Lara, is why you asked me about this stone in the first place."

I hear Rupert's voice in my head, from when we talked after Jacinta's first surprise appearance: *"Do not mention any of this to Wes. I have not disclosed Jacinta's presence to you because her situation is … complicated. I promise everything will become clearer, when it's safe for all parties involved to speak of it."*

Will I put Rupert at risk if I tell Wes about Jacinta? Will it endanger Wes? I already told Finan, despite Rupert's warning not to. Have I put Finan in danger?

Nausea curdles the breakfast sitting like a lump in my gut.

I cannot tell Wes about Jacinta yet. Not if it could put him, or Rupert, in jeopardy. I drop my hands into my lap, reaching over to squeeze Finan's leg under the table.

"It was pure curiosity," I lie. "I did a search for red crystals and gemstones that might look like the one on the Dea Vitae symbol. I didn't find anything about Tiamat—but the red beryl popped up, so I wondered if the stone in their flag might mean something more."

Wes watches my face for a second, and I'm afraid he'll see I'm lying through my teeth. "It was a good hunch." He opens the folder and slides out pages stapled together at the corner. "This stone is extremely rare, found only in a few spots in the US and very occasionally in Mexico. Also called bixbite after the mineralogist who discovered it in 1904. It's a close cousin to the emerald, the aquamarine. The color of the stone depends on the conditions where they grow. There are lots of offerings on eBay for rough stones, but gem-cut quality are few and far between …" He continues explaining physical information about the stone, and I try to hide that I already know most of this—because Jacinta told me.

"The Mesopotamians worshipped beryl as stones of magic, which is where Tiamat comes in." He flips the page of his stapled group and scans with a finger. His voice is so low, even if someone were recording us, they'd not be able to make out the audio later. "Dea Vitae was started by a wealthy Spanish guy named Casimiro Aguado, except we don't think that's his real surname since it literally means 'water,' and he was head over heels in love with this water goddess. Anyway, Cas reportedly had a vision from Tiamat—which is how most religious movements start—that he was to dig from the earth a group of red beryl stones that she would then bless. The next vision told him to collect followers who would help her come back and avenge her dead husband. According to Kelly Lockhart, when Tiamat returns, nonbelievers will be destroyed and Tiamat's disciples will inherit the world. And any help Dea Vitae followers offer in terms of ridding the planet of nonbelievers will increase their standing in Tiamat's eyes."

"Delightful," I say. "I knew my gut wasn't wrong about Kelly."

Wes smirks, sets the pages aside, and pulls out a glossy black-and-white photograph from the folder, flipping it around so Finan and I can see it. It's a little blurred, like it's been zoomed in to cut out the person whose slice of head brushes the side of the main subject's face.

My heart stutters with fear.

I've seen this man before.

"This is Casimiro Aguado—we think this shot is from the mid- to late 1980s."

Why is his face familiar?

"He created his cult and traveled the world recruiting people. He spent quite a while in the UK living under false identities, and then he just … disappeared. We don't know if he's in hiding or dead. Even Osama Bin Laden couldn't stay hidden forever, so now that international law enforcement is taking Dea Vitae seriously, Casimiro might resurface."

"Could Ainsley be with him?" Finan asks.

"We're looking at all angles," Wes says.

"We know she's involved, if she's actually the leader of the North American faction, so does it even matter if she's with him?" I add.

Wes shrugs. "It might, except Dea Vitae under Casimiro was a different beast. He seemed far more spiritual, more in love with his goddess and finding his magic rocks. Dea Vitae under Iona MacChruim has a healthy thirst for actual money and power—and no problems with violence. Tiamat is almost secondary."

"This is unreal." I scan the picture. "Casimiro looks so … normal."

Wes snickers. "So did Ted Bundy."

I shiver. "Can I take a photo of this? Just to have for my own files?"

Again, Wes examines my face as if looking for a place to lift the curtain on what I'm hiding.

"Trust me, Wes," I say quietly. "Please."

He moves his fingers off the photo's edge and bobs his head once. With my phone, I take two quick shots of Casimiro Aguado's face and then Wes tucks the eight-by-ten back into his black folder, stacking his hands on the table surface before glancing at his watch.

"You want to follow me over to Rupert's? Ammi Jaan will have food waiting for us." Wes drains his coffee. Though I don't match Finan's enthusiasm about imminent homemade Indian cuisine—my stomach is not right today—I'm excited to see Rupert, even in light of Wes's warning about his physical appearance.

I pull on my light jacket and we follow Wes out of the coffee shop, into the howl. Wes stops and surprises me with an impromptu hug, his heavy beard tickling the side of my face. "Don't let this one go. He loves you."

He steps back and pats my cheek once. "Meet you there?"

"Meet you there," I say. He winks and jogs across the street as Finan drapes an arm over my shoulders and hurries me to our car in the buffeting winds.

Once we're out of the pelting rain, he turns in his seat. "Wanna tell me what the look on your face was about when you asked to take a photo of that eight-by-ten?"

I sigh and close my eyes. "I think my mother knew Casimiro Aguado."

TWENTY-EIGHT

BLUSTER

Finan's expression does the talking.

"A few months ago, before I got to the island, Rupert gave me a thumb drive with photos and correspondence from my mother's life. I finally felt brave enough this past weekend to go through the letters and the pictures beyond her wildlife work."

"The canvases at town hall—those are from this thumb drive?"

I nod. "But there are others, including shots from Cordelia's life before me. I suppose some were after me too ... she was gone more than she was home. There's a folder on there with *just* photos of me, from my childhood. Some are from after her death, so I think Rupert must've put them together. Last Sunday I printed a bunch of the photos—I want to make a proper album. I don't know a lot about Cordelia Clarke, so I figured having a visual history of her life, combined with the notes and letters scanned and saved on the drive— that's an important history for me to have. To get to know the Cordelia everyone else knew."

Finan's hand is draped over the top of the steering wheel, his thumb drumming a silent beat against the black curve.

"One of the photos is of Jacinta and a bunch of people on some excavation—somewhere in Utah. And I swear Casimiro is one of the people in the shot." I pull the image up on my phone. "In fact, I'd bet my shoe collection that my mother took this very photograph."

"How did Wes get it?"

"No idea. Maybe the internet? Cops can get whatever they want, can't they?"

Finan takes my phone and studies the smiling, grainy face on the screen. "And you were going to tell Wes about Jacinta." He returns my phone; I click the screen dark.

"I was. And then I heard Rupert's voice in my head asking me not to. I'm worried it will put more people in danger, if Wes knows about her. I shouldn't have told you. Now you're roped into this."

"I'm in this no matter what," he says. "If you hadn't told me, I would've been angry."

"Just think how angry Wes is going to be when he does eventually find out about Jacinta, that I've been lying this whole time—that Rupert has been lying."

"He'll understand if you're doing it because you're worried about Rupert," Finan says. "But why don't you want him to know?"

"Because I don't want him to show up on Thalia with his team of stormtroopers again and crash into her bunker. It could get Rupert in deep shit too. I'm not saying another word about her to anyone until I have a clear understanding of how she's involved—because *clearly* she is, if she's in a photo with Casimiro Aguado from the 1980s."

"You think she's been lying to you about Dea Vitae?"

"I think she's been lying about *something*. I just don't quite know what yet."

I'd been hoping for a warm and fuzzy reunion with the man who has basically been my father for the last twenty years. But when we walked into the West End townhouse, the most striking thing was the smell. The fine fragrances Rupert usually pampers himself with have been replaced by pungent medicinal odors. And when we make it to the second floor where Rupert is ensconced in his overstuffed couch, a knitted blanket draped over his torso and legs, I thank all the gods Finan grabs me around the waist so I don't melt.

Wes was being generous when he described Rupert's condition.

He looks an inch away from death.

"Stop gawking and come in."

"Hey, Number Two," I say, trying to steady my voice. I slide into one of the wingback chairs facing the couch.

"Do not ask me how I'm feeling," he bites. "I'm not talking about medical issues with you today, unless it's specifically your medical issues because you look like hell."

"Oh, how I've missed that honesty," I bite back. "I look like hell because I am overwhelmed with worry about if you're ever going to give me my credit cards back. I've got my eye on some gorgeous Dior boots for fall, and it would be great if you'd stop being such a grinch."

Rupert smiles.

"Who wants chai?" Wes asks from the kitchen. Finan stands and offers to help.

I move from the wingback and slide onto the coffee table right in front of Rupert so my voice doesn't carry. "Wes showed me a photo of the guy who started Dea Vitae. The same photo was on Cordelia's thumb drive," I whisper. "I think she might have actually taken it—Jacinta's in it too."

"Did you mention her to Wes? Jacinta?"

"No. You asked me not to."

Rupert looks visibly relieved.

"*What* is going on? Is she—are you—involved in this cult somehow?"

His laugh catches me off guard. "Lara, I have done a great many ridiculous things in my life, but joining a cult based on some long-ago water goddess is not among them."

"Then why is the photo of this psycho on my mother's thumb drive? Did you know it was there?"

"I did not. I thought it was just another of Cordelia's photos from her many adventures."

"Then how is Jacinta involved? Why is she hiding on Thalia? She must've known this guy if she's in the photo with him—"

Before Rupert can answer, Wes rounds the corner with a tray of chai-filled cups, bringing with him the much more comforting aroma of cinnamon and cardamom. I resume my earlier spot in the soft chair, my heart racing with my burning need for answers.

And hopes of more one-on-one time with Rupert are dashed when Wes's mother Azrah shows up carrying cloth bags full of prepared meals. Thumbelina the nurse—who is actually *very* lovely—hovers when Rupert stands to move into the dining room. He swats her away, but when Wes steps in to offer an arm, Rupert takes it without a fuss.

I cannot believe how thin he is.

We take seats around his dining table as Wes's mother serves food. I try to help, but she insists I sit. Finan has yet to join us—I heard his phone ring and ever since, he's been pacing and talking in the bright, airy sitting room off the kitchen, his voice low and out of earshot.

I wait until Rupert and Wes have their plates, and for Azrah to sit with her own as well, and then I tear into the warm naan and cucumber yogurt and tikka masala "with low spice, for Rupert's belly."

As I'm reaching for a second round of the flat bread, Finan rejoins us.

"Finan, you really should feed her over there. This is almost embarrassing," Rupert quips.

I hike an eyebrow at him. "Seriously, Azrah, if you ever decide you want to move to Thalia and open a restaurant, I would do whatever you needed me to do. Dishes, sweep the floor, peel potatoes, if only I could eat like this every single day. You are a queen."

She laughs. "I always tell Vahar how lucky he is to have a mother who cooks like I do."

"I have the waistline to prove how lucky I am," Wes says, patting his not-quite-flat stomach.

"Vahar?" I ask, confused.

"My given name."

"Wesley was the name of the doctor who saved Vahar's life when he was a baby. We call him Wesley in honor of that man," Azrah chimes in, her face full of pride. She pokes her son hard in the biceps. "This one decided to come early. He was anxious to start living."

Wes looks embarrassed. "Ammi, stop."

Azrah regales us with wild tales of her son's childhood, how he was the smallest kid on the playground until fifth grade when he shot up and filled out. "He had a full beard before he started high school," she says, laughing. "And those boys who'd picked on him when they were little, they would run away when they saw my Vahar coming." Wes shakes his head at her, but it's clear he loves his mother very much. And it's nice to laugh and talk about someone else's life for a moment. A reprieve from the calamity stew we seem to be simmering in these days.

Finan's phone rings again, and he excuses himself just as Azrah scoops more rice onto Rupert's plate and insists he eat. But Rupert, brow creased, watches Finan leave. "Is he worried about that storm?" Rupert asks.

I look up from my plate. "Um, I don't know. Maybe? Should he be?" I'm sopping up the last of the sauce off my plate with the remnants of a samosa when Finan pops back into the room. I know that look. "What's wrong?"

"We should probably get going," he says, holding his phone before him. "That was Joey. Seems the first band of this storm system has arrived—the foundation at vertical farm B is underwater."

"Already?" I say, tapping my phone to check the time.

"We should go, Lara," Finan says, moving toward Rupert, hand outstretched. "It was so good to see you, Rupert." They shake, and then Finan stretches across to grasp Wes's hand as well. "Azrah, this food was a true delight. I look forward to coming back for more."

She jumps from her seat and disappears into the kitchen as I gulp down my lemon water and blot with a cloth napkin. "Do we have to go right this second?"

"Duty calls, little cyclone," Rupert says. "Come. Hug me and get out. I need a nap."

I do as instructed, hugging him tightly but gently, my worries flaring again when I *feel* how gaunt he is. As soon as I straighten, Wes is right there waiting. Such a contrast when he embraces me. "Take care of him," I whisper. "And call me with developments."

Wes lets go and bobs his head once.

As we're sliding into our shoes at the front door, Azrah hurries down the steps, her ornate purple *shalwar kameez* fluttering with her quick movements. "Take this," she says, hefting one of her cloth bags toward us, filled to near bursting with the food we didn't finish. "These boys have plenty." She leans close, her hand on my forearm as she lowers her voice. "I'm trying to get him to eat. He is too thin. The cancer is taking too much from him."

"I know ... thank you for taking care of him. I know he's a brat sometimes."

"I will always take care of Rupert. He is family." Azrah goes on tiptoes to kiss my cheek. "Safe travels. Be careful in the storm." She pats my arm once again and steps back, allowing Finan to help me into my jacket.

As soon as he opens the door, Azrah's words echo in my ears: "*Be careful in the storm.*"

The rain stabs our fleshy bits as we hurry down the block to the car, and I can't help but worry just which storm Azrah is referring to.

There are too many to count.

TWENTY-NINE

BY THE HAIR OF MY CHINNY-CHIN-CHIN

It takes us nearly two hours to get across the strait to the Thalia Island marina, and by the time we pull into our slip, both of us are as green as a new leaf from the insane waves and wind. I will be forever grateful to Finan for his expert navigation skills—or at least I will be when I'm no longer on the verge of throwing up naan and tikka masala.

Even getting the boat tied and our bodies up the dock to the parking lot is an exercise in brute muscular exertion. The wind and slicing rain—I've never felt this power before, not in British Columbia. Sure, there was that time I got stuck in a hurricane in the Caribbean, but if you insist on attending a music festival in the Bahamas in October, you already know you're rolling the dice.

Finan has to steady the truck's door for me to climb in or else I risk losing a limb from a gust slamming it closed. He runs around and jumps in on his side, his hair drenched from the short journey from boat to truck. I don't hazard a glance at myself in the visor mirror—I know I look like a drowned rat.

"That color of your skin really brings out your eyes," Finan teases. He digs through the console between us, pulling out a roll of peppermints.

I gladly take one. "Have you ever seen it like this?"

"Never." The wipers are flapping hard and fast but still can't keep up. "Maybe when I was a kid, but certainly not since."

"Maybe the rest of Canada will stop making fun of us for being such weather babies." Just as the sentence finishes, a loud crack echoes from the forest that flanks the parking lot, and a massive Douglas fir splits and falls, crashing seismically onto the open metal structure that shelters our canoes and rowboats. The corrugated roof crumples and the whole frame bends under the weight of the tree, crushing the contents within.

"Shit." Finan throws the truck into drive and floors it.

It's storm dark out, the headlights bouncing off the torrential sheets with every inch forward. The road from the marina into town is littered with debris, some of it big enough that Finan has to slow and drive around it or sustain damage to the tires or undercarriage. The truck itself is pelted with hail and branches and leaves; the young trees planted along the road are nearly bent in half under the wind's ferocity.

His phone rings again, this time routed through the speakers. "Hey, Joey ..."

"You're back on the island?" We can hardly hear him through the crackling speaker. "Benny and I are with a crew at farm B trying to pump the water out of the foundation. I've got people over at the solar fields. The new array is taking a beating." Joey's voice reverberates around the truck's interior as he yells to be heard over the wailing squall.

"OK, let me drop Lara off and set up a command center at town hall. I'll call you back in fifteen."

The line drops.

"Drop me off where? I'm not going anywhere. I need to help."

"Not dressed like that, you're not."

"So we run to the cabins, I change into work clothes, and then you put me somewhere to help."

Finan smiles. "You might have to wear those hiking boots."

"Ugh. If you *tell* anyone ..."

He chuckles just as a strong gust hits us and almost steals the steering wheel from his grip. His face again darkens to match the angry gray skies. "I think your fashion choices will be the least of our concerns."

"I think you're right."

~

An hour later, clothes changed and ready for battle, we slide into town hall. And yes, I'm wearing those ridiculous hiking boots —which are actually quite comfortable and my toes are nice and warm, for once.

Please don't tell Finan.

Whiteboards have been wheeled in from storage to keep track of crews and where every volunteer is stationed. We have electricity, thanks to generators powered by our on-island, wind- and solar-based energy supply, so Finan has his laptop out and is casting an intricate weather-tracking app on the huge flat-screen TV. The green-and-red, long-tailed blob that looks like it's eating Thalia Island? That would be our storm.

Or maybe it's Tiamat and she is, in fact, coming back to take what's hers. And me without my red beryl, unless of course Grandfather's red stone in the ring on my hand is indeed bixbite and in that case, I should prepare for the rapture.

Dr. Stillson and Catrina are in the building, setting up a triage center in case of injuries. Mrs. and Dr. Corwin are here making fresh coffee and manning phones and the Lutris portal and organizing the soaking-wet stream of residents who come into the building for help or shelter.

I'm not sure what to do, so I just wait for someone to bark an order at me. Until a bark is exactly what I hear, followed by ticking nails and footsteps behind. Humboldt waddles into the conference room, pausing inside the door to shake and splatter his love on whomever is nearest. Ignoring me, he bounds over to Finan, whining like he always does when he sees his buddy. "Dumb dog," I mutter.

"Heyyyy, you're back!" Dakota says, hurrying to my side of the table. I push up from my chair and she wraps me in a hug, her Arc'teryx coat bedazzled with fresh raindrops. "Was it seriously anthrax?"

"We don't know yet," I say, pulling a chair for her to sit beside me. "The investigators don't have much so far."

"That is *freaky*." She shimmies out of her coat and hangs it on the back of her wheeled seat. "How's Uncle Rupert?"

I don't want to lie, but ...

"Shit, that bad, huh?"

"He is *so* thin, Dakota. And his hair is mostly gone. What isn't is snow-white. It's crazy to see him like that."

She sniffs and nods once. "My mom said he looks pretty bad."

I wrap an arm around her shoulders and give her a second. It's weird to know someone who is as connected to Rupert as I am. I guess she is even more so since he's her biological father. I allegedly don't even have one of those.

She clears her throat and sits up straight. "I've closed the Salamander. No one's out right now anyway. This wind is nuts."

"Try being in a boat going cross-current," I say, sipping my ginger tea. "Even the hardiest sailor would be puking."

"What are we supposed to be doing right now? Everyone looks so busy." She scans the room. They *are* busy.

"I don't know. I'm waiting for Finan to tell me what he needs."

"Speaking of ..." She waggles her eyebrows. "An overnighter in the city with that fine specimen. Anything to share?"

"We were staying at his mom's. Not like we were going to get naked under her roof."

"Yeah, I can see how being adults doing consenting adult things might be weird." She smirks.

"*Inappropriate.* She was doing me a favor letting me stay there. I wasn't about to violate her son and then just leave the sheets for her to clean."

"Ew, well, when you put it that way ..."

"Hey, Dakota—" Finan, a phone against his ear, gestures to us. "You think you can come with me out to the solar array field? We've got five crew members out there, but they need our help. The wind is having its way on that side of the island."

"Absolutely. Wherever you need me." She stands and moves to the head of the table.

Humboldt finally sees me, tail wagging as he flops at my feet for a belly rub. I give him a quick scratch but then follow Dakota. "What about me? What can I do?"

"I need you here running things," Finan says. I look at his computer, the big screen tracking the storm, the ringing phone, the walkie-talkies buzzing in the background—

"No. I can't run all this. Seriously, I have no idea how to organize people to go where they're needed."

"Just listen to where the calls come in from, consult the white-board to find who's available—"

"Finan, *no*. Please." There's no way I can be responsible for all this. People will die. "I'll go with Dakota. She and I will deal with whatever the crew needs."

"Lara, I'm out of people to ask. I can't leave things unattended here," he says.

"Fine. Give me your keys. Dakota and I will do whatever you would be doing. I'm better at being told what to do in this situation—do not put me in charge of your command center."

Finan sighs mightily and scrubs a hand down his face. Seeing he's got no other choice, he digs into his front pocket for his key chain. "Benny's out there. Stop by the field garage at the end of Main Street and grab as much rope as you can find—they're in the big bins along the walls."

Dakota catches his keys in midair and bounds back to her seat to throw on her still-wet jacket.

Finan stops moving for a second and meets my eyes. "Be safe out there, Madam Mayor," he says, a worried glint in his eye.

"Phhht." I flap a hand at him. "What's a little wind after that delightful boat ride today?"

His smile is almost as good as a hug—almost—but we're not fixed yet. I can't lean in and steal a kiss. Not quite.

And then another phone rings, blowing the moment from under my feet as the storm batters the roof like it wants to come inside.

THIRTY

LOW BLOW

D akota beats me to Finan's truck. The heat blows from the vents as I climb in, a simple task made difficult by these damn gusts. She speeds toward the field garage at the opposite end of Main, just before the road leaves town behind to give way to the heart of Thalia Island. The wind knocks into the truck, but Dakota has a firm hand on the wheel. The wide driveway outside the three wood-and-metal buildings is covered in broken branches and bits of surrounding trees, but we manage to park close enough to the front door to get inside without too much stinging insult to our exposed skin.

Inside, we shake off and wipe wind-whipped hair off our foreheads and cheeks. "Have you ever been in here before?" she asks.

"Actually, no. Kind of terrible to admit, considering my job."

The automatic LED lights overhead are almost too bright, but given how dark it is outside, I'm glad for it. Dakota hurries over to a wall of plastic bins stacked on tall metal shelving, all marked. "I am grateful that whoever runs this place is neurotic."

We scan the bin tags. "Ropes!" I holler. Dakota helps me pull the oversized, Rubbermaid bin off its shelf—I'm thrilled she's as tall as I am. I pop open the lid. "Et voilà! Jackpot!"

Dakota hunts for something to carry the coils—the massive bin is too bulky to fit across the back seats of Finan's king-cab truck, and trying to lift it into the open truck bed ... yeah, not going to happen. We settle on a handful of expandable tote bags made from repurposed billboards, stuffing them to their limits with all the coils of sisal and hemp rope we can find.

I stand at the main door, first bag over my shoulder. "You ready?"

Dakota laughs. "'The storm is up, and all is on the hazard!'" she yells and then runs into the rain, throwing her bags and mine into the rear cab. I have no idea what she's talking about, but I follow her lead, repeating this same dance four more times until there's no space left in the truck. The garage locked up, we head out to the brand-new solar array field.

I squint through the racing wipers to try to spot Benny and his team in the maelstrom. "There! Over there!"

Dakota bounces us down the unpaved path that splits the field in half. Though it's usually easier to traverse thanks to a gravel coat, right now it's mud, water, and more detritus from the woods that flank both north and south along the open space. She leans on the horn a few times to be heard over the din, and the last blare grabs Benny's attention. He waves wildly and then hurries toward us nearly bent in half, weaving through the juddering solar panels, his arm raised to protect his face.

"Here goes nothing," I say, hopping from the truck and straight into an ankle-deep puddle of muddy water.

"Hey! You guys got ropes?" Benny shouts as he approaches.

"All the ropes we could find!" Dakota yells back. She opens the cab door and stands against it to keep it from slamming closed. A second crew member runs up behind Benny. His hood flies back—it's Geordie, the kid who delivers the mail. He grins widely. The two of them then haul ass to unload the bags of rope. Benny gives Geordie instructions on where to start and he's off like a shot, whistling at his fellow crew members.

"We need to tie the newer panels to one another and then to their anchors. They're bolted down, but they're not yet secured for this kind of wind. Each aisle has an anchor every twelve feet, so if you could help tie them together and then to their anchors, that would be awesome."

"We won't have enough rope!" I holler back.

"It's just a few new sections. Everything else is OK," he explains, voice straining to be heard. "If you two start in the northwestern corner, you can tell the new panels because they still have their protective film on the front. We're worried about the debris hitting and cracking them, but them flipping or blowing away is worse."

Dakota heaves a bag of ropes over her shoulder. "We'll figure it out!" she yells and then helps me situate a bag of my own. "Meet you back here when we're done?"

"Sounds great. Thanks, you guys!" Benny grabs the last two bags and hobbles east toward the others, just barely visible in the storm.

Hunched over, I follow Dakota to the northwestern corner where Benny asked us to start. I am beyond relieved when she pulls out the first rope and appears to know how to tie a purposeful knot.

"Girl Guides!" she hollers, grinning even as rain slaps her cheeks.

It takes a few panel frames to figure out the best way to go about this, but Dakota is smart as hell, so I just follow her lead, grabbing and unraveling ropes and watching her tie on and then affix to the embedded steel anchor points Benny mentioned.

We're at the second to the last row when a gust hits so hard, we both drop, arms interlocked, coiled like turtles in our shells, waiting for it to abate. The panels offer little protection, bouncing on their frames above our heads.

"You OK?" I ask.

"Yeah! You?"

"I think so!"

"Let's tie this last one on and then we gotta get back in the truck. Can't risk that last row!"

On our knees, we uncoil another rope and fasten it the best we can, given the fury trying to knock us on our asses. I'm at the last panel on the northwestern edge, second row, when I hear the distant whine of shearing metal, and then the wind slams into me like I've somehow wronged it, a punch right in the gut.

"LARA!" Dakota screams.

It takes a beat for me to realize what the burning is, why I suddenly feel a warm torrent soaking my lower abdomen and the front of my right leg.

I look down, not quite sure if what I'm seeing is real.

A long steel bar has skewered me. I reach around to my back—the bar is clean through, exiting painfully just above my right hip.

"Look, Dakota, I'm a human kebab." I laugh once, and then collapse.

THIRTY-ONE

THAT'S GONNA LEAVE A MARK

"Lara!" Dakota competes with the wind for my attention, her voice loud but still so far away. I'm on my left side, my face and head in the mud, the rain cold and stabbing, but the pain in my right half with every attempt at a breath …

"We need to get you out of the muck. Can you move at all?" Dakota yells, panic lacing her tone. I try to push up via my left arm, and scream. "Shit, shit, *shit*!" Dakota stands, the mud sucking at her boots as she scurries around me.

"Please don't leave," I say, only able to manage short gasps. So light-headed. And my midsection and right side are on *fire*. "Don't leave me here."

My eyes don't want to stay open but I register that Dakota is tearing off her jacket to drape over me. "Lara, I need to go for help. Do not *move*, do you hear me?"

I smile. My mouth tastes like blood. "Wait—don't go. Just drag me into the trees. Let's get out of the rain. Safer in the trees." The relentless wind means Dakota is in danger if we stay out here. Wherever my metal skewer came from, more could be awaiting their chance to fly.

"I shouldn't move you. I—I don't know what to do …" Dakota fumbles with her phone, cursing that the torrent makes the screen

191

unresponsive. I have to try to sit up again. If I can sit up, she can drag me under the nearby trees and we can get out of the deluge.

"Under my arms. Pull me under my arms," I say, but the force of exerting my voice to be heard is too much. I close my eyes again but not before placing my right hand on my abdomen, to feel if this is real or some nightmare I've fallen into.

I suck in through clenched teeth, dirt now mixing with blood on my tongue. "That's definitely real," I say, my hand on the cold piece of metal sticking out of my body.

"Lara, I cannot move you. The bar is angled downward. I don't know how to position you to not cause more damage," she yells.

"Listen to me," I say, reaching for Dakota to get closer to my face. "I will hold the bar if you can grab under my armpits and pull. I can use my left leg to push—"

"You are losing a lot of blood. I could make it worse if I move you!"

"My phone. Get my phone. Inside pocket. Gently ... then go over to the trees, out of the rain. Call for help. Call Finan."

Dakota digs into the warm zippered compartment of my coat for my phone, reassures me she will be right back, and dashes toward the tree line. Shivers are setting in now that I'm soaked to the skin. Just need to focus on short breaths that don't jar my upper body, that don't stretch the muscles in my side. Moving my right leg sends hot spikes of pain zapping through me, but the angle the leg is positioned in feels like it's pulling on the bar. I can't roll onto my back; the penetrating spear is definitely in the way of lying flat.

The longer I lie here, the less it hurts.

I rest my hand against the wound, now sticky with my blood. I wish it would stop raining. I'm so cold. I think my feet have fallen off. The inferno persists across my torso, though I can't tell where the bar ends and my body begins. The shivering intensifies the pain.

Dakota reappears, panting as she drops onto the ground beside me. "Lara, I'm going to slide your head onto my legs, get you out of the mud, OK?"

"Mm-hmm." I don't open my eyes as she lifts my thousand-pound head and slides herself underneath it. "That's nice." She's warmer than the ground. "Thank you."

"Finan's on his way. He's bringing Dr. Stillson and Catrina and everyone. We're going to get you some help."

"Thank you, Dakota," I whisper, and then close my eyes to focus on not shuddering against the ice and adrenaline racing for pole position through my heart.

～

"Heyyyyy, Lara, can you wake up for me?"

I know that voice. "Hi, Catrina," I say.

"Hello, darling girl. Dr. Stillson and I are going to have a look at what you've got going on, all right?"

"Lara, I'm here too," Finan says, wrapping my chilled, wet left hand in both of his warm, dry ones. The rain hasn't let up—I have no idea how long we've been sitting here—but I can feel Dakota quaking underneath my head.

I yelp when Dakota's coat snags on the bar. "Sorry, sorry," Dr. Stillson says.

Everyone is very quiet, only the wind yelling that something isn't right with this picture.

"We have to get her out of this mud," Dr. Stillson says. "The bar is all the way through, the wound open on both sides. It's probably impacted the small intestine at least." His and Catrina's voices melt into a hum in my ears as they figure out the best way to get me off the ground without making things worse. "No way a chopper can fly in this. Coast Guard can send search and rescue—call them first. We need to get her into the bed of a truck and then to the marina. Vancouver General and Royal Columbian have level 1 trauma centers —they're our best option," Liam yells above the wind.

Finan leans close to my face. "I'm going to get my truck. I will be right back. Stay awake, Lara. Do you hear me?"

I manage a smile. Hurts to talk.

When he releases my hand, it's so cold again.

"Lara, I'm going to give you a little something for the pain. Hold still for me," the good doctor says. He gently pulls the side of my waistband down and stabs my upper butt with a needle. A warm flood of something delicious courses through and takes the edge off the shivers, though it doesn't do a lot for the pain roaring through my right side.

"She's tachycardia," Catrina says, her fingers against the pulse in my neck. She rubs my forehead and cheeks free of muck while Liam thrusts his phone at Dakota and instructs her to call the Coast Guard.

"Lara, do you know your blood type?" Liam then asks loudly against my ear.

"O+."

"OK, good, good." Then there is more urgent discussion—I can't tell if they're yelling anymore because everything roars in my ears—but something about Catrina hurrying to the clinic to get blood from the fridge and to call ahead to Vancouver General and someone else standing nearby is on the phone with Cathy the ferry captain to get one of the smaller vessels ready in case the Coast Guard SAR team is too far away and Dr. Stillson must secure the rod in place to keep the bleeding under control and is there any way we can cut this down to prevent further injury upon moving and then more voices as a heavy canvas tarp is stretched out on the ground beside us ...

"Lara, can you hear me?" Dr. Stillson flattens a hand against my face. "We're going to slide you onto the tarp and get you into the truck now. This is going to hurt, but I need you to stay as still as you can and on your left side. Try not to scream—you're losing a lot of blood and your heart is beating very fast, so I need you to stay as calm as you can. Do you understand?"

"Can we get a drink after this?"

"Anything you want," he says.

"And karaoke. You have to sing this time."

"Promise." And then Dr. Stillson is barking orders at the crowd now gathered. I try to do what he says and not scream when they lift me, but I fail, howling until my throat gives and I fall into a dark, dreamless sleep.

THIRTY-TWO

TRAVAIL

I had an appendectomy when I was fifteen. My grandfather and Rupert sat next to my bed before they rolled me in, and they were there when I woke up. It was supposed to be day surgery, but my appendix was an overachiever and burst, so I got to spend a couple nights in the children's ward hooked up to IV antibiotics to kill the infection that spewed into my abdominal cavity and threatened to kiss my other organs. My grandfather later gave the hospital a generous endowment to say thanks for saving my life.

I remember very vivid dreams during that week, not what they were about but just that they were bright and stark and loud, and when I woke up, I was confused about reality versus what I'd dreamed.

This feels similar, except I don't remember the vivid dreams—I'm just not sure what's real and what's not.

Finan's warm hand brushing over my forehead is real.

The tubes and wires attached to my person seem pretty real.

The pain in my right side is different now—deeper, more wide-spread, but not burning like before—and my skewer is gone.

"Hi, you," Finan says. When he leans over and kisses between my eyebrows, even though he's wearing a paper surgical mask, I'm pretty sure he's real. "How are you feeling?"

"Thirsty," I say. "What did I miss?"

A nurse appears next to my bed and does nurse things, checking this and that and pushing buttons and I close my eyes again because my lids feel very, very heavy. Finan asks if I can have anything to drink, and she says no but that he can rinse my mouth with a sponge dipped in water and she'll get some balm for my chapped lips.

"Lara, are you in any pain right now?" the nurse asks.

"Mm-hmm."

"This little button"—the nurse places something in my right palm and positions my thumb over its end—"this is a pain pump. Press this, and more medication will release. Do you understand?"

"Mm-hmm." I press the button, followed by a flush of warmth. Feels like the water in the Caribbean. I want to go there …

"Where are we?" I ask.

"Vancouver General ICU," Finan answers. The nurse shuffles out of the room.

"Rupert?"

"He'll be back tonight, with Wes. Catrina and Dakota and Liam are in the waiting room."

"So I'm not dead?"

"No, you're not dead." Finan drops a warm hand onto my left arm, squeezing gently.

"How long will I be here?"

"A few more days. The metal bar impaled your small intestine. They fixed it, but they're concerned about something on the latest CT scan."

"I already had one surgery?" I ask, my words slurring in my brain. I wonder if they're slurring outside my mouth too. "Where's Humboldt?"

"He's with Harmony. You just worry about resting and healing."

"Good plan."

"I love you, Lara." Finan's voice floats into my head like a cluster of freshly blown bubbles.

Except I don't know if it's real, or just another vivid dream I won't be able to recall when I eventually tear my way out of this narcotic cocoon.

~

Twenty-four hours later, I'm a little more awake. As much as I love the feeling of floating naked in a bathwater-warm lagoon, it's disorienting. And the nurse encouraged me to go as long as I can between button hits. Finan hasn't left, or if he has, it's only been while I'm asleep.

The surgeon, an attractive woman who doesn't look much older than I am, comes in to inspect my surgical site and discuss my current status, explaining the surgery removed the damaged section of small intestine. The pelvis sustained blunt trauma injury along the right upper edge, now stabilized with bone cement and screws. I was lucky the rod missed my right ovary and the blood vessels that feed my right leg. But because I've spiked a persistent low-grade fever, they want to go back in laparoscopically and make sure the repair to the small intestine is intact. If everything looks good and there's no infection, and barring any unforeseen complications, I should be able to leave within a week.

"Unfortunately," she says, placing her gloved hands on the end of my bed, "you suffered a miscarriage due to the massive blood loss and the trauma to your abdomen. I am very sorry," she explains.

The book resting on Finan's knee slaps against the floor as he sits forward. "I'm sorry, what did you say?"

The surgeon looks at me, and then Finan, and then back to me, surprise registering in her eyes. "Lara, did you not know you were pregnant?"

What the ... "Uhhhh, no. That's not ..."

Finan is pale and wide-eyed. The doctor takes a steadying breath. "It was very early on, six to seven weeks by ultrasound. We've ensured there is no residual tissue in the uterus, and your hCG levels have steadily fallen since your initial admission. Given the nature of this injury and our hopeful successful repair, structurally you should not have any impediment to future conception. Again, I am so sorry."

She adds more about my prognosis and expected postsurgical and recovery pain levels and the likely need for physical therapy for the pelvis injury and then tells us to have her paged if I have any questions or new complaints. She smiles sympathetically and excuses herself.

Finan sits forward in the chair next to my bed, his hand wrapped around mine, careful not to knock loose the oximeter clamp on my index finger. "Did you know ...?"

I shake my head, eyes stinging and throat tight. "My periods have always been weird. And we used protection every time." I've been more tired lately, but I thought that was just a side effect of the recent carnage. And my boobs always hurt before my period eventually shows up. I was just waiting—and not realizing how long I'd actually *been* waiting. Other fish to fry and all that.

His eyes are bright with unshed tears. He then stands, pulls down his mask, and kisses me. "Jesus, Lara, I am so sorry."

"For what? This wasn't your fault."

He presses his forehead against mine. "For everything. I should've gone out to the solar field. I should've never let you go out in that storm. I'm so sorry for everything."

My head rests against my pillow again, the doctor's words cycling through my head like a bike in a velodrome. I was pregnant? And now I'm not?

"Are you going to be all right?" Finan asks, sniffing and replacing his mask over his mouth and nose.

What other choice do I have?

THIRTY-THREE

BEST WISHES

By my fifth day in the hospital, I'm well enough to be moved into a private room, which quickly fills with flowers and gifts from the residents and crew members of Thalia Island, employees from Clarke Innovations, a bursting bouquet of peonies from Eugenia ("From my yard, just for you!")—even little Harmony manages to get her latest painting of Humboldt (and the momma raccoon!) to me, thanks to Catrina. Catrina also warns me that separating Humboldt and Harmony when I do return to the island will probably require surgeons skilled in the separation of conjoined twins.

Eileen Rowleigh has brought homemade meals for everyone since the night we arrived—considering her son hasn't left my side other than to shower and change into the clothes she went out and bought for him. Lucky for me, I was cleared to start on clear broths as of last night, and she delivered—hands down the most delicious thing I've ever eaten. Actual food!

Number Two has spent as much time with me as his fragile state will allow, and Wes Singh hovers over him like a nervous mother—definitely more going on here than Rupert has shared. I'm so relieved that he has someone caring for him, especially as I am out of commission for the short term. As such, the time he is in my room is mostly spent on the phone talking to insurance adjusters about what happened out at the solar array field as well as grilling the doctors about what I will need to recover over the next few months so he can arrange to have it imported to the island.

If you don't have a dad, get yourself a Rupert. He's an excellent close second.

In a brief span while Finan is in the cafeteria with his mom, I tell Rupert and Wes about the miscarriage. Rather than a scolding, they take turns hugging me. I've never wanted kids—but learning I was pregnant with Finan's baby only to lose it has done something to my head. The nurse told me it would take a few weeks for the hormones to level out, and let's face it, miscarriage is sad. I'm grateful the people close are allowing me to process these feelings rather than chastising about responsibility and consequences.

And Finan ... he is definitely feeling something here. The whisper of "I love you" was, in fact, real. He's said it a few more times. We haven't talked much about me being pregnant, and we agreed that we have some stuff that needs untangling, but for now, I'm going to live in this protective shell he's built around us, relaxed and warmed by the bearded giant who sleeps in the vinyl chair next to my bed. He even offers to pay off nurses who try to shoo him out, leaving only when they insist so they can help me with dressing changes or bathrooming.

I never thought I'd get a round of applause for a bowel movement, but two of my nurses did just that. I'm pretty proud of myself, and grateful for the brains who invented that little red gelcap that helps everything slide right on out without painful straining. I feel like an Olympian.

I've resettled into bed on my own—and not loving that I have to use a cane on the left side because of the spear to my pelvic bone— enjoying a quiet moment without anyone here asking a million questions. The door opens and a gray-haired male nurse appears at the threshold, yet another bouquet in hand, except this one isn't flowers —it's fruits and vegetables, arranged and bound together with tulle in a wide-mouthed wicker basket.

"You're very popular," he says, looking around for a blank spot to set it. "Over here OK?"

"Wherever is fine. Thank you." I gently ease the coarse white blanket over my upper body. Mrs. Rowleigh brought me a beautiful quilt from her blue room, but it's too heavy against my healing wounds.

"This one has a present attached to it. Would you like me to bring it to you?"

"Sure. Thanks." I'm distracted by the stream of messages on my phone.

The nurse hands me the small, square white box tied with a raffia bow. "Does it have a card?" I ask. He reaches and plucks the small envelope from the plastic fork protruding from the bouquet. "Thank you."

"Do you need anything else?" he asks.

Looking away from my screen, I realize I've not seen this nurse before. He has a VGH ID badge on a lanyard around his neck, just like all the other nurses who've helped me, though I can't quite make out his name. Maybe he's new or has been off work since I've arrived on this floor. It's not like I know all the nurses who work here, even if it feels like it. "I'm good. Thanks again for bringing this in."

The man nods and exits, the door shushing closed behind him.

I untie the bow around the square box and lift the lid. Inside, displayed on a jeweler's card is a silver chain with a tiny pendant—a magenta-red, rough-cut stone cupped in a silver claw.

It's red beryl.

I drop it on my blanket like it's a viper.

With shaking hands, I open the small, florist-shop card, hoping that inside will be a note revealing this gift is *somehow* from Jacinta Ramirez.

"'Tiamat sends her wishes for a speedy recovery. Devotedly, Iona.'"

THIRTY-FOUR

ANOTHER DAY, ANOTHER CIRCUS

I ona MacChruim. Ainsley's true identity.

The door whooshes open and Finan saunters in, coffee in hand, followed closely by Rupert and Wes. I'm shuddering so hard, surges of pain rush through my belly and shorten my breath.

"Lara? What is it?" The pleasant smile on Finan's face melts, and he rushes to my bedside, spilling his fresh coffee as he slides it onto the side table.

"Wes ..." I point at my lap.

He steps next to the bed and stares down at the opened gift, twisting his head to read the card. "Don't. Touch. Anything." He yanks his phone from his black cargo pants and dials, moving to the windows, the view of West 12th Avenue partially obstructed by my bounty of get-well wishes. Finan helps Rupert into the big chair in the corner and then moves back to me.

"You all right?"

"Freaked out. Definitely freaked out."

He drops a hand on my shoulder, then cups my nape, his thumb rubbing gently. The room is quiet other than Wes's talking, all of us watching to see what comes next.

"Yeah ... OK, see you soon." He hangs up and moves into the bathroom, returning with a stack of paper towels. He helps himself to a pair of gloves from the box mounted on the wall, his jumbo hands struggling to fit into the purple latex. "You don't mind if I take this, do you?" he says, winking as he rewraps Iona's gift with the paper towels. "Did she send anything else?"

I point to the newest basket just as my hospital room door opens and Len Emmerich stomps in. "Hey, Lara," he says. "I was gone for, like, two minutes to pee. You just can't stay out of trouble, can you?" He flashes a smile before Wes asks him to go find the charge nurse.

"I need a big paper bag. Don't touch this," Wes says, pointing at the fruit-and-veg arrangement as he follows Len out of my room.

"Never a dull moment, little cyclone." Rupert shakes his head and pulls out his own phone.

Not even five minutes later, the room is filled with hospital security, three nurses, Len and Wes, and a couple of Vancouver PD officers. Wes grills the nurses about who has access to this floor, how gift deliveries are made; Len asks the two hospital security guards about the cameras monitoring the patient floors and where we can access the footage.

But before anyone leaves to go chase down Iona's latest dangled carrot, I'm asked to recount every moment prior to, during, and after this package was delivered.

"The guy who delivered it—male nurse, fifties, gray hair, maybe five ten, light green scrubs?"

"Did he talk to you?" Wes asks.

"Just asked me where I wanted him to put the basket and if I wanted the present attached. He asked if I needed anything else. I was reading through my messages on my phone and said no. Then he left."

The charge nurse crosses her arms over her chest. "We don't have any male nurses fitting that description on this floor."

"No doctors fitting that?" Wes asks the nurse.

"A doctor wouldn't deliver a gift. And the surgeons don't usually wear light green scrubs."

"This guy didn't have a white lab coat," I say, although that doesn't mean anything. Doctors probably take off their lab coats all the time.

"Lara, did you see his ID badge?" Wes asks.

"He had one on a lanyard just like everyone else, but I couldn't see his name. He was polite enough."

"Anything else remarkable about him?"

I shake my head no. He was just a guy who looked like a nurse.

Then the conversation picks up again and phones are pressed against ears as Len and the security guards leave to go to wherever the surveillance equipment lives. Wes is talking to his staff sergeant at the RCMP while the VPD guys glove up and lower the food basket into a huge paper sack provided by one of the nurses.

It's decided that I need to be sponge-bathed, dressed in a clean gown, and moved into another, more secure room until they're sure Ainsley—Iona—didn't lace her present with any of her clever biological masterpieces. Another enhanced hazmat team is en route to repeat the steps undertaken at Clarke Manor the other day when they suspected anthrax on the premises.

I ease into the wheelchair next to the bed. The nurse insists, afraid I'll trip en route to the new room since I've had very little practice with the cane. Finan reaches down and holds my hand as we are wheeled out and down the hall while a circus of law enforcement professionals swarm the floor. Visitors in other rooms are gathered and ushered into the hall as police look for anyone who might match the description of the "nurse" who delivered Iona's package.

I wait to speak until I'm in my new bed and the nurses have left Finan and me alone. "I don't understand why they're looking for the messenger. If he's Dea Vitae, it's not like he's going to stick around."

"Probably just need to cover all the bases. You know how they say that some criminals like to come back to the scene of their crime to watch the frenzy unfold."

"That supposed to make me feel better?"

Finan kisses the back of my hand clasped in his. "Len Emmerich has two gorillas outside your door. No one else is getting in here."

"What does she *want*, Finan? This can't just be about Thalia Island."

He shakes his head, his expression as confused as I feel.

"Instead of going home right after I'm discharged, do you think your mom would let us stay over a night or two?" I ask.

Finan hikes an eyebrow. "I'm sure she'd love it, but ... why, exactly?"

"I have an idea."

THIRTY-FIVE

A MOMENT'S PEACE

R upert doesn't make a fuss when I tell him we're returning to Thalia Monday instead of today. He actually seems relieved that, even though the doctors say I'm well enough to be discharged, I'll still be in town for forty-eight more hours, just in case I find new trouble to get into.

He makes a good point.

And Eileen Rowleigh is giddy we'll be staying with her. She even offers to make up the "very comfortable sofa bed" in the downstairs office so I don't have to navigate the stairs to the beloved blue room. I'm improving with the cane, but too far or too long upright and the aching kicks in. Rupert made it abundantly clear to my doctor that I have a history of alcohol dependency, so I was discharged with a handful of Tylenol No. 3 and instructions to take it easy for a month.

Leave it to Rupert to remind me why I still think he's a turd.

Once we're free of the constant interruptions and chaos of a busy metropolitan hospital ward—and the prying eyes of the Clarke Innovations security team outside my door twenty-four seven—Finan and I are very much in need of quiet and calm. We head directly to the Rowleigh home after I'm discharged, Mrs. Rowleigh again welcoming us with open arms. Finan helps me from the car, and his mom, who smells like a bakery, her cheek dusted with flour, is happy to show off that she's spent the entire morning throwing together all her baby boy's favorite treats.

I'm able to stay awake long enough for a cup of tea and half a berry scone, and then I excuse myself for a much-needed nap free of busy-body nurses or security guards.

It's the best sleep of my life. The entire day gone, wrapped in quiet, pain-free slumber, waking only because my bladder is threatening to ruin this lovely sofa bed.

Just after sunset, Mrs. Rowleigh shows me to the patio where she is enjoying a glass of wine while Finan mans the epic outdoor grill. The backyard is gorgeous, especially in the summer with the twinkly lights and garden sconces reflecting off the shimmering turquoise pool. Citronella burns in tiki torches standing sentry around the yard to scare off mosquitoes.

Though my guts are on the mend, I'm supposed to stay on a simple diet for a while longer. Color me grateful when Mrs. Rowleigh slides a plate of linguine tossed with olive oil and sautéed mushrooms, homemade bread, and probiotic-rich vanilla frozen yogurt for dessert. As much as I'd love to tear into the burgers Finan and his mom are enjoying, I don't want to end up back at the hospital.

Over dinner, I hear hilarious stories about Finan the energetic kid via his obviously proud mother. And his patio chair is never more than an arm's length from mine, his hand draped over my leg whenever he's not shoveling food or wine into his mouth. When I inevitably start to wilt from good food and charming company, Finan and Eileen insist I retire while they clean up. I don't argue.

A couple hours later, Finan slides into bed beside me, all pretense that we're just friends melted away. He smells freshly showered. "I'm jealous. I want a full-body shower," I say, inhaling deeply.

"I'll help you with that when we get home," he says, nuzzling against my ear. "Once Stillson gives you the all-clear, that is."

Gingerly, I turn onto my left side so we're facing one another, so I'm breathing his air and memorizing every detail of his face yet again.

ELIZA GORDON

Finan wraps his hand around mine where it lies on the bed between us. "Does your mom know ... about the miscarriage?"

He's quiet before he nods once. "I hope it's OK that I told her."

"I thought maybe you did. She was so nice to me."

Finan chuckles. "She's always nice to the people she likes."

"Maybe ..."

"It's been a rough week. She wants to take care of us, of you."

"I'm grateful."

"Do you want to talk about it?"

Instead of looking in Finan's eyes, I stare at our joined hands, my index finger tracing his veins and knuckles. "I'm not sure how I feel. Confused, I guess."

"About ..."

"Everything. I didn't know I was pregnant. I've actually never considered myself mother material. Too selfish. I can hardly take care of myself."

"You're great with Humboldt. And Andromache."

"When I remember not to overwater her."

"It's harder to overwater babies."

"Ha ha."

Finan smiles. "And Harmony. You're awesome with that kid."

"Harmony is a unique case. It's impossible not to like her. Plus she's smarter than everyone in the room. No wonder her mom looks exhausted all the time."

"We don't have to talk about having kids right now, Lara. We're still working on building an 'us.'"

"Yes ... but I'm still sad. I didn't want to be a mom, but I ... I love you ... and I'm not just saying that because of what we've been through in the last week or whatever, but because I *know* there's no one else in the whole world I want to spend my days and nights with. I'm not naive enough to think that this accident is the wake-up call I needed or that big epiphany people talk about with near-death experiences. But I also know that when that bar stapled me to the ground, the only person I wanted there with me was you."

Finan leans over and kisses me softly. When he pulls back, his eyes

208

sparkle. "I thought I was going to die when I saw you there." He kisses me again, longer this time. "I've never been so scared," he whispers against my lips. "The whole boat ride over. Thank all the gods you were out for that. The water was so rough, and every time the wind hit us, you would moan and I would yell. Catrina had to calm me down so I didn't go to the bridge and throttle the Coast Guard captain."

"Was Captain Cathy there? I vaguely remember seeing her ..."

"We had her on standby in case the Coast Guard's search and rescue crew wasn't able to help. You should've seen the look on her face when she saw you."

"Lara the human shish kebab."

"It was something else."

"Tell me you got pictures."

He barks a single laugh. "No, but Liam Stillson did. I think he was actually excited when he saw you and that metal rod."

"Weirdo."

"Just think if you'd slept with him ... he'd probably want you to dress up like his nurse or something."

I pull my hand free and smack his shoulder. "Ew."

Finan again envelops my hand with his, kissing my bent fingers as his smile slowly melts. "I'm sad too. That we lost a baby."

I nod, my throat aching with sudden emotion.

"But that doesn't mean we won't be able to talk about another one, if we decide that's what we want. Someday."

"Someday," I whisper.

Finan kisses me again, long and soft and warm. When his lips finally leave mine, he scoots so that my body is curved into his, safe and protected from things that go bump in the night.

THIRTY-SIX

THE MANOR

Finan and I wake early the next morning, coaxed into the kitchen by the aroma of coffee, more food, and the wails of new babies.

"My sister brings the twins on Saturday morning so my mom can babysit and Kira can take a hot bath and a nap."

"If we ever have kids, we're definitely moving to North Vancouver," I tease. Maybe making light of our recent loss will make it easier to understand. Eventually.

We take turns in the small bathroom getting ready for the day and then join his family for breakfast. Uncle Finan is immediately draped with a mewling Ivy who wants nothing more than to be danced around the room. It's so adorable, I don't even recognize myself, this soft, squishy Lara who swoons over hot men dancing with newborns.

Mrs. Rowleigh doesn't pry too heavily when asking what our plans are for the day, satisfied with my response that we're checking in on Rupert and handling some Thalia Island business before heading back on Monday. She doesn't need to know that we're going to Clarke Manor to snoop around and possibly uncover secrets being kept from the only Clarke remaining on the planet.

As far as I know, my grandfather's private study remains intact. The Clarke Foundation people are still settling in after their move from downtown as they work toward converting the property into a think tank for visiting environmental scientists and policy makers, but it's still Archibald's house. Even my room upstairs has been left untouched, though it's not much more than a guest room. I haven't lived at the manor in years. Rupert was supposed to oversee the liquidation of personal effects, but that endeavor was sideswiped by a monster truck full of cancer.

After breakfast—and a few attempts to get Kira's children to like me that didn't go *nearly* as well as it did with Uncle Finan—we politely excuse ourselves and head off toward the day's adventure.

As we pull into the lot out front of Clarke Manor, I'm glad to see no other cars here, other than one of the natural gas-powered trucks that belongs to the maintenance crew. That doesn't mean we're alone—there could be staff cars around back. I wipe my clammy palms on my pant legs, not sure why I'm nervous. This is still my family home, even if some kombucha enthusiasts have taken up office space in the grand dining room to save the whales.

"You ready?" Finan asks. I nod, and he hops out of his mom's car, walking around to my side to help me out.

"If anyone is here and asks what we're doing, I'm looking for my birth certificate."

"Got it."

"Also, I'd like a cane that doesn't make me look like a nursing home escapee."

"Maybe we can get the pole back that impaled you. Now *that* would be quite a cane."

I smack his shoulder as he closes the passenger side behind me.

The underarms of my shirt are already damp, and not just from the July heat, by the time I get the massive front door unlocked. Finan pushes it open and I follow him inside. "Hello?" I call.

No answer.

We walk through to the massive dining room that has been cleared of the long table Rupert and Grandfather and I spent countless meals around. The original art is off the walls, replaced by whiteboards and flat-screens and bookcases filled with thick binders whose spines sport the Clarke Foundation logo.

We wander through the downstairs, Finan close behind as I allow myself to feel my grandfather's absence in every room, something I've not done since his death. Even before that fateful day, I've hardly paid attention to what this house means to me, what it has meant to my family and our legacy, because I was too wrapped up in my own dramas.

I pause before a poster-size photo of Archibald and me, taken by my mother. We're laughing in it—I must've only been about five, and I can't even remember what was so funny. A new ache surges within. Being here, around his things, in the house he loved so much, it's an emotional torrent, a searing reminder he's not coming back. Not ever. Never again will Cordelia Clarke burst through those front doors like she's just discovered the lost Inca gold or proof of sentient life on Mars. Never again will I hear Archibald's hearty laughter floating from his sitting room where he and Rupert were entertaining guests.

"Lara?"

"I'm good." I nod and sniff. I'm *not* good, but we're here for a reason. "Let's go look in his office before someone shows up."

The door on Archibald Clarke's private study is controlled by a biometric lock that opens for only a handful of people, me included. I press my thumb on the tiny scanner. When it flashes green and the lock disengages, my heart flutters.

If I thought walking through Grandfather's house hurt, I'm about to get assailed by the mother of all memory tsunamis.

As if hearing my thoughts, Finan takes my hand and then pushes open the door.

My grandfather's ghost washes over me. I close my eyes and take deep, measured breaths, inhaling the traces of him left behind. Finan wraps his arm around my shoulders, allowing me to pause and steady myself. After a quiet minute, I reopen my eyes and look up at him.

"Let's start with his desk."

~

Two hours later, Finan and I are leaning over a roll of blueprints unfurled before us. "That's it. That's where the bunker is."

Finan points out the Thalia Island landmarks represented on the blue-and-white architectural drawings, though none of the current structures are present since these were obviously drawn up before the later plans that incorporated dwellings for residents and crew members, town hall, and the Main Street business strip.

"It's not where I thought it would be," Finan says. "These islands are all granite. How the hell did he blow a hole big enough for a bunker in the middle of the island?"

"No clue. But I look forward to knocking on Jacinta's door and asking her to explain everything she has so conveniently left out over our visits."

"Do you think she'll be freaked out that we found her?"

"I'll take her some toilet paper."

We're just rolling up the blueprints when we hear a car door slam. Finan and I look at each other, eyes wide, and then I remind him that I have every right to be here. Inside a hidden closet is a bank of screens attached to surveillance cameras that cover the entire property, but upon bumping open the mystery door, I'm unnerved to see the screens all dark, the system inactive.

Then again, why would it be on? No one's been here to monitor Clarke Manor for months, and it's filled with Foundation staff at least five days a week.

But if it *had* been on, they would've seen the bastards who desecrated the sanctuary. Not sure I understand Rupert's thinking on this.

"Should I go see who's here?" I ask.

"I'm coming with you."

"We could wait. Maybe they'll leave," I say.

"Or else whoever it is will start wondering whose car that is and call the police."

The decision is made for us when whoever is here bangs on the front doors, loudly enough that we can hear it all the way at the back of the manse.

"There's no one else to answer that?"

"We don't have house staff anymore. After Archie died, everyone was let go."

The banging gets more insistent.

"I'll go," Finan says.

"Ha! Not without me," I say, forgetting for a second about my stitched-up midsection, at least until it reminds me with my abrupt movement toward the study door. Finan takes my hand upon my yelp, hands over the cane, and we exit the study together, toward whoever is demanding entry.

Finan flips open the metal peek-through on the heavy, ornate door. "Can I help you?"

"Hi, oh, hi, good, I'm so glad you're still here. Can I please come in before someone sees me?" It's a male voice, but I can't see its owner.

"I'm sorry, the Foundation is closed on weekends. You'll need to return next week—"

"I'm not here on Foundation business. I need to speak to Lara Clarke. You're Finan Rowleigh, aren't you?"

Finan's shoulders stiffen and his grip on my hand tightens. "Who are you?"

"Right, yes, sorry. I'm an investigative journalist. I know everything about Dea Vitae. My name is Hale Watts."

THIRTY-SEVEN

HALE STORM

As soon as Hale is inside, I lock every bolt on the door.

"How the hell did you know we were here?"

Watts looks sheepish. "When I heard you were in Vancouver, I sort of waited for you to be discharged from the hospital, and then I followed you," he says, more question than statement.

"That's fucking creepy," Finan growls.

"I know, I know, but I swear, I'm only trying to help."

"Do you have ID? Anything that proves who you say you are?" I ask, at once wishing my cane was one of those that fired poison-tipped darts.

Finan's posture suggests he's ready to pound this guy into the ground if need be. Hale isn't small, but he's shorter than Finan by a good six inches. His more-salt-than-pepper hair is thin on top but well groomed, and his black, round-framed glasses fit his goateed face. He looks harmless, but then again, so did Ainsley.

His wallet extracted, Hale fumbles to pull out every piece of ID he has. "Press credentials are expired. Sort of lost my job."

"Something to do with a staffer?"

He snorts. "Yeah, right. I'm not that stupid."

I examine his ID—BC Services Card and driver's license, old ID card from the *Vancouver Sun* of a reporter younger than the one standing before me. "You could say you're Hale Watts. I've had people lie to me before about their identity. Recently, in fact." I hand him back his cards.

"Ainsley Kerr, I'm guessing?"

The only people who know her alias would be people close to the case. That's one thing about the RCMP in Canada—they are notoriously tight-lipped about ongoing investigations, not like the American police agencies who spew all the details to a relentless media the minute they get in front of a podium.

"Do you have someplace we can sit down? I don't know the details about what happened to you"—he nods at my cane—"but the look on your face suggests you're not very comfortable."

I glance at Finan, wishing he could read my thoughts. Instead, I nod behind us at the French doors that open to the dining room. "The Foundation has taken over this space. We can use the conference table."

"Great."

I lead, Finan bringing up the rear as we settle around the table, us on one side, Hale Watts on the other. He plunks his briefcase down in the chair next to him, scanning the room. "Cameras in here? Can anyone see in through these windows?" He gestures at the wall of paned glass overlooking the manor's front.

"The windows are treated so no one can see in. Surveillance is off at the moment."

"Anyone else on the premises?"

"Why? Are you worried about witnesses, Mr. Watts?" Finan asks, leaning forward on bent arms.

Hale Watts laughs nervously. "I'm not about to engage in a criminal act, Mr. Rowleigh. In my line of work, it pays to be paranoid."

"And what line is that?" I ask.

"I'm still working as an investigative reporter. Although most of the work I do now gets tossed aside as fringe journalism or tabloid sensationalism. People don't like hearing the truth these days."

He's not wrong.

"May I?" He points to his briefcase. "Papers. Just papers. No weapons or anything untoward, promise."

I nod. Hale Watts then slides his briefcase onto the tabletop, clacks open the locks, and extracts a beat-up file folder held together with rubber bands. He closes and slides the case aside. "This is just a slice of what I have on Dea Vitae. Didn't want to bring too much in case I got caught. I've been chasing them for a *long* time, and I'm sorry to admit it, but the activity on Thalia Island has rejuvenated my investigation. Very exciting," he says, pulling at the bands.

"I'm glad you think so," I say.

"I don't mean any offense. It's just when something this big comes along, it sort of infects you."

"So does salmonella and anthrax," I blurt. Finan squeezes my leg under the table.

"Wow, it's *true*, then." Hale's eyes look like they're going to pop out of his head as he pauses sifting through the pages. "I've tried to get Sergeant Singh to take my calls, but Mr. Bishop has threatened me with another restraining order."

"Another?"

"Oh, yes, Rupert Bishop and I go way back. And sorry to say that our interactions have not always been so ... cordial."

My spine stiffens. "Why would Rupert have a restraining order against you?"

Hale Watts stops moving and looks up at me, really scanning my face before folding his hands before him. "Cordelia. You look so much like her ..."

My heart thuds. "You knew my mother too?"

"I did. I adored your mother."

Finan drapes his arm over the side of my chair so I can take his hand. "Mr. Watts, please explain the purpose of your visit. Lara has been through enough in the last few months—we don't have time for cryptic bullshit."

Mr. Watts bobs his head once and returns to his folder. From it, he extracts a photo and slides it across the table.

It's the same photo from my mother's thumb drive, the stack I printed, the one Wes had zoomed in—with Casimiro Aguado. Hale stands and leans over the table, pointing with his index finger. "This guy here? That's me. Your mother took this photo on the dig in Utah where we found the stones."

THIRTY-EIGHT

A RED HEIST

"The stones?" I ask, wishing I had a gallon of water to pour down my throat.

"Red beryl."

I clamp on to Finan's hand. He nearly growls. "Keep talking."

Hale Watts settles back into his chair. "We were in the Wah Wah Mountains. This was August of '89. I was in Utah poking into some nasty business with the LDS Church, but then I met her—" Hale stands again and quickly points at another gorgeous young thing in the photo. "She was cute and fun, and she invited me to go along with her and her friends on some geology dig. I wasn't about to say *no*. I mean, look at me, and look at her."

So Hale Watts followed his penis into the Utahan mountains on a geological sexcapade?

"That's where I met Cordelia and Jacinta and this whole crew. About half of the folks were from Mexico, there on an exchange dig with some university out of Mexico City. The rest were American geology students, a few older rock hounds, and some hippies thrown in for the hell of it. Cas Aguado funded the whole thing."

"Aguado funded the excavation?"

"Yes."

This doesn't make sense. Jacinta said she was there chaperoning students from her former university. Why would Casimiro Aguado fund an excavation for a bunch of geology students?

Watts reads my face. "Um, so, Casimiro was always funding digs for whoever would go into the mines for him—it was kept on the down low because the mine owners didn't like the guy. He was slick as an eel, and monied to the hilt, but he also liked to party, and he wasn't stingy with his wallet. He attracted a lot of suckerfish, but he also had an undeniable charisma. It was easy and fun to be around Cas."

"And?" I ask, leaning forward myself, growing bored of Hale's reminiscing, antsy because I don't yet understand what this has to do with me, my mother, Jacinta, or Dea Vitae.

"We didn't know this until we'd been on the dig for about a week, but one night, everyone got stoned and/or drunk on whatever Cas had brought into the camp, and during this free-for-all, he sat around a campfire and revealed that he was a messiah of sorts. Said he had received visions from an ancient goddess named Tiamat, that he was paying for digs all over the place because she told him to collect these red beryl stones so she could return to Earth.

"We found a few tiny stones during our time in the mine, but Cas already had a considerable cache of red beryl with him. The night before this big party, he apparently had another of his peyote-soaked visions wherein Tiamat blessed these stones, which is why he was telling everyone about her imminent return."

"He was recruiting," I say.

"Indeed. At the time, Dea Vitae was in its infancy. He really believed in this Tiamat—believed she was going to come back and rid the world of evildoers, corporations and capitalists, people who weren't taking care of the oceans."

"He believed all that?" Finan asks.

"Devoutly."

"And how many people joined up?"

Hale Watts shakes his head. "I don't know. I stayed another week because I could smell something off, that tickle I get in my throat when I'm on to a story that could have legs. The girl I was with had already left, worried her Mormon parents would find out she was hanging around this guy."

"I would be worried, too, Mormon or not," I say. "What does Cordelia have to do with this?"

Hale sits straighter, flattening his hands on the table. "Well, that's the thing. Cordelia and her girlfriend, Jacinta, they were pretty disturbed by the stuff Casimiro was preaching to the students. They were supposed to be there watching over all these kids, and then the guy funding the whole trip turns out to be this total nutjob who gets everyone high or drunk and tries to convert them? That wasn't going to play well with the parents. So, Jacinta and Cordelia allowed the group to stay another two nights while they quietly arranged for everyone to leave, to get away from Casimiro before any real damage had been done."

"They left. Big deal." I slide the photo closer to me.

"It *was* a big deal. Because when they left, they took Casimiro's precious stones with them."

My blood freezes in my body. "*Who* took the stones?"

"Jacinta Ramirez. And your mother."

I'm already shaking my head no. Impossible. *Impossible.* Jacinta would've told me if she had the stones the Dea Vitae people—Kelly and Ainsley and the lot—were searching for.

"This doesn't make a damn bit of sense, Mr. Watts. I think you're full of shit, and I'd like you to leave now." I move to stand, grabbing at my cane. Hale Watts pushes up from his chair, his hands in front of him, pleading.

"I'm not lying, Ms. Clarke. I have nothing left to gain from any of this. I've already lost everything. My only loyalty now is to the truth."

"And what truth would that be? I've looked you up—I've read your blog. It's full of conspiracy theories and bizarro rants about everything from alien abductions to government cover-ups of money laundering in BC casinos."

"Can we please sit? You look like you need to sit," Hale says, gesturing at my chair, his brow wrinkled with what might be concern. I resume my seat, but only because standing sucks, jolts of pain blasting down my right hip and leg. "The alien stories—those are just to make a little coin. All crap, but it brings in good traffic to the site. However, the BC casinos are absolutely laundering money. That's not conspiracy—that's fact. One of the reasons I'm so paranoid is because the Asian organized crime network involved would very much like me to shut my mouth. I've even consulted with the investigating body on this, the Cullen Commission, though that's not to go any further than this room."

"The Cullen Commission? So the sparkly vampires are investigating this?"

Confusion knits Hale's brow. "I'm sorry ... vampires?"

"Never mind," I say.

Finan leans into me, whispering against my ear. "The money laundering story is legit. Commissioner Cullen is a real person."

"Oh." I take a deep breath. "Explain to me why my mother would abscond with Mr. Aguado's magic rocks."

Hale Watts shrugs. "Maybe they were worried he would open some portal and Tiamat would return."

"My mother was not crazy," I bite back.

He smiles. "I don't think they honestly believed any of Cas's horseshit. I'm just teasing, Lara."

"Maybe no jokes," Finan warns.

Hale clears his throat. "Sorry. I, uh, I think they took the stones because they were worried he was going to keep recruiting these young kids on all these excavations he was financing. Jacinta was worried it would end up in some sort of cult mass-suicide situation, like a Jonestown, which had only happened eleven years before. Horrific, that scene. Almost three hundred kids died there."

"So Jacinta *knew* Casimiro was a cultist?" I ask.

"He wasn't a cultist yet. Definitely on his way, though. So they took his red beryl, and of course, that sent him into a rage because the stones they took had allegedly been blessed by Tiamat herself during one of his alleged visions."

"Is that why Dea Vitae came to Thalia Island?"

Watts watches me, and I can see the gears working behind his eyes. "Do you know where Jacinta Ramirez is?"

I realize my gaffe too late but carry on otherwise. "Is Dea Vitae on Thalia Island because they think my *mother* is there? Or because they think the red beryl is there?"

Another pause before he answers. "Is it?"

I slap my hands on the table. "Of *course not*. How the hell would it be on an island that has only had people on it for a couple years, max, and especially since my mother has been dead for two decades?"

Mr. Watts sits back in his mesh chair, gently pulling at his goatee. "It's an interesting theory, though, right?"

"It's ridiculous. I can't even imagine where the stones would be, unless Cordelia buried them somewhere before she died."

"It's not without suspicion that your mother happened to go missing and was later presumed dead. What's to say it wasn't Dea Vitae exacting revenge?"

I want to yell at him that if that were the case, Jacinta would be dead too—but she's very much alive and living under a ceiling of granite on Thalia Island.

"Lara was ten years old when her mother passed," Finan interjects. "This interrogation has gone on long enough." This time, Finan stands and signals toward the door. Hale looks to me, as if I will provide some excuse for him to stay, but I'm with Finan. I'm tired, and these questions have just opened more holes with even more questions pouring out of them.

Mr. Watts sighs and gathers his file folder, rewrapping it with the rubber bands and sliding it into his weathered case. Finan moves to the dining room door, holding it open to make sure Hale Watts sees that he is definitely leaving.

"Lara, I didn't mean to upset you. I want to *help*. These Dea Vitae people are nasty business." He reaches into his wallet again and extracts a card, its edges worn, and pushes it across the table toward me. "Text me at this number and tell me how to reach you. I'll respond within twenty-four hours, if not sooner." He then moves toward Finan.

"Mr. Watts, do you think my island is still in danger?"

"Until Iona MacChruim is dead or in prison … yes."

"Why is she so dangerous?"

Hale turns to face me, incredulity washing over his face. "Because Casimiro Aguado is her father, and your mother was the last person to be seen with his treasure."

THIRTY-NINE

SPILL IT, NUMBER TWO

We watch to make sure Hale Watts leaves the premises before moving back into the dining room. "What the fuck, Finan?"

He's as pale as I feel, which speaks volumes considering I lost half my body's blood supply a week ago.

"We have to go back to Thalia. Time for Jacinta to start talking," I say.

He nods his agreement but paces along the bank of windows. "Why did Rupert have a restraining order out on this guy? Watts said he and Rupert go way back. There's something Rupert isn't telling us."

I laugh, but not because anything's funny. "There's a *lot* Rupert isn't telling us. Why would he keep all this from me?"

"I don't know. Maybe because you haven't been involved in business matters before Thalia Island?"

"But if Dea Vitae was actively looking for their magic rocks, wouldn't this shit have come up before now? Or did they see an opportunity with Thalia Island, and that's when they decided to make their move?"

Finan shakes his head, tugging at his beard. He stops and faces me. "We need to talk to Rupert."

"I don't have the secure phone or computer with me."

"Then call him and tell him we're coming over. Today. Right now."

Wes answers the door. "Hi, you two. Come on up. He's resting on the couch, but I told him you were on your way."

Finan helps me up the stairs, and though my pride wants to do this on my own, the whole right side of my body is grateful for the assistance.

"How you feeling, Lara?" Wes asks as we finally reach the top.

"Sore, but I'll live." I peek into the open doors of the sitting room. "Hey, any follow-up on the fruit bouquet and necklace from Iona?"

Wes shakes his head. "Clean of any biohazards, obviously. And no prints. Not anywhere. No trace of the guy who delivered it. She's good."

"She's a terrorist," I growl, and then look toward the sitting room. "I need to wake him up. You should come sit too. I have some questions."

"I can hear you," Rupert says from the couch. "Stop being dramatic and present yourselves so I don't have to contort my frail skeleton."

Finan and I move into the bright, air-conditioned room, the medicinal fragrance of our prior visit chased away by the flickering scented candle on the coffee table. The drapes are drawn just enough to let in some beautiful July sun but not so much as to bake us in our seats. Wes excuses himself briefly to make chai as I ease into one of Rupert's lavish wingback chairs.

"I see you've mastered the cane," Rupert says.

"If I have to use this for longer than another week, I want something more elegant. Maybe something with a dagger in the handle."

Rupert is still a mess—pale, thin, his hair haphazardly combed over in an attempt to hide how scant it's gotten, prominent purple bags under his eyes that he's tried to blot with light powder—but he looks awake and his sense of humor seems intact, an important sign with Number Two.

"Might as well cut to it since you and I both have limited windows of lucidity," I say, folding my hands in my lap. "We went to Clarke Manor today. I wanted to look in Grandfather's office for answers that no one else seems willing to share."

"And did you find any?"

"A few. Blueprints so I can find the bunker."

Rupert sits straighter and shakes his head. Ah. So he still hasn't told Wes about Jacinta Ramirez. That's between the two of them, but I need *answers* about Hale Watts.

"While we were there, we had a visitor." Something crashes in the kitchen, followed by Wes cursing under his breath. "Hale Watts popped by."

Rupert's mouth thins into an angry line. "He is a weasel of the lowest class, which is an insult to weasels."

"I don't care what kind of scavenger he is—he had some very interesting information for us, and I want to know if it's true. I need you to get your stories straight, Rupert, and explain to me why you had a restraining order against Hale Watts, how much you *really* know about Dea Vitae, and what the hell Cordelia had to do with Casimiro Aguado and his treasure chest of magic rocks. Did you know Aguado is allegedly Ainsley's daddy?"

Number Two sinks back into the cushions, eyes closed and chin angled toward the ceiling. Wes saunters in with a tray of hot teas, the room immediately perfumed. Once everyone has a cup, he moves to sit at the end of the couch, near Rupert's covered feet.

"Wes, I need to talk to Lara about some family matters. Can you give us a minute?" Rupert asks, though I can tell it pains him to request that Wes leave.

"Sure. I'll be in the den. Mariners are on. Finan, you want to join me?"

"I'd prefer him to stay," I intervene. "In case I need help with this stupid cane."

"Right." Wes nods once, stands, and closes the sitting room doors after him.

"Is he going to be offended that you kicked him out?" I ask Rupert.

227

"Wes is a grown man. He doesn't get offended by nonsense."

"Mm-hmm." I sip my tea. Rupert is definitely going to have some explaining to do after our departure, based on the furrow growing between his brows. "So. When you were in the hospital the first time back in May, I asked you about Dea Vitae, and you said, to my face, that you'd never heard of them. You acted as though all this cult stuff was brand-new information for you, even though it clearly *isn't* if you not only have Jacinta Ramirez hiding on Thalia but you had a restraining order against Hale Watts *and* the daughter of the leader of this cult was living among us, growing fancy carrots while on our *payroll*."

Rupert tugs at his blanket, folding the top and smoothing the fabric over his legs. "Yes. I did know what Dea Vitae was. That was a lie, one I told because the hospital was no venue for a conversation of this magnitude. However, I did *not* know they were on our island. That is the absolute truth. The whole scenario unwinding with Ainsley and Kelly Lockhart, that was just as horrifying and shocking to me as it was to everyone else. And who told you Ainsley, Iona, whatever she calls herself, was related to this fanatic?"

I watch his face for signs that he's lying, but I believed him before —I've never *not* believed him—so I don't even know what I'm looking for, to be honest.

"Hale told us. Today."

Rupert hmmphs.

"You don't believe him?"

"Much of what comes from that man's mouth is a vapid fiction."

"That remains to be seen. Some of the stuff he told us today is clearly true, or else you wouldn't be clutching the edge of your blanket like it's going to run away."

Rupert's hands relax, and he folds them against his stomach.

"It makes perfect sense that Iona is Casimiro's daughter—why else would she target our island?"

His head bobs in thought.

"And what about Jacinta?" I press. I'm not leaving here today without clarity.

Rupert looks over his shoulder once before answering, his voice lowered. "Jacinta Ramirez is on Thalia for a wholly different reason—she is hiding from her brothers."

"Is she, though?"

Number Two sighs heavily. "When your mother's plane went down, Cordelia perished, but Jacinta lived. The plane was full of valuable product that the local villagers helped themselves to, not realizing who they were stealing from. Jacinta was nursed back to health by these same people, but as soon as her brothers got wind that she was not only alive but that the people who saved her had stolen all their cargo, they went on a rampage.

"Jacinta was taken back to her family's compound—if you know enough about her story, you know her two brothers were working with the Garcias, prominent members of the Sinaloa Cartel—though her return wasn't a happy reunion. They had figured out that Cordelia and Jacinta had been stealing from them, little bites from the cash shipments to augment the monies they were already being paid to transport product across the border. They were then allegedly using this money for their pet projects in the Mexican countryside."

"Jacinta said they used the money for water, schools, medical clinics, women, and children."

"And there's no reason to suspect otherwise. You've seen her. She isn't someone with expensive taste. The two of them thought they were doing good, even while doing very, very bad things."

"Obviously Jacinta got away from her brothers."

"They cut off her hand as payment, which she later said was a mercy. She then bribed one of her relatives to smuggle her out of their house. She managed to get to Mexico City, but not before returning to the plane ..."

A solemn quiet settles over the room. "She went back for Mom?"

Rupert nods. "She wanted to bury her. But by the time she returned—Lara, are you certain you want to hear this?"

"Just say it, Rupert." My throat aches.

"Bones. All that was left. No one had moved Cordelia from the downed plane. The locals felt it was bad luck to touch her, that if they

229

did, she would haunt them. The plane had gone down in a jungle, so wildlife was prevalent in the area."

Wildlife. Beasts ate my dead mother. Delightful. I suppose there's a bittersweet irony there, given how much she loved animals.

Rupert slides the Kleenex box toward Finan, who then hands it to me.

"Jacinta gathered some of your mother's bones—small ones, ones she could keep with her to bury later—she also took her jewelry and a few of her teeth so your grandfather could be sure it was in fact his daughter when the time came."

I didn't know any of this. I thought Grandfather had looked for Cordelia but had never gotten a resolute answer about her demise. Why didn't Jacinta tell me? My tears turn hot with anger and resentment that all these people have kept such life-altering secrets about *my* life, *my* mother.

"And what about the red beryl stones? Were they in the plane too?"

Rupert shrugs and flattens his hand over his heart. "I swear on my mother's soul, may she rest in comfort, that I did not know anything about the red beryl or its significance to this cult. Jacinta Ramirez is on Thalia Island because she needed my help, and she was very important to your mother. Once she got into Mexico City, she made contact. I arranged for her to fly to Vancouver. When her brothers learned of her escape, she went into hiding. That is the whole truth about that portion of the story, God as my witness."

I wipe my nose and toss the wadded tissue onto the side table. "I can't believe you didn't tell me before."

"Lara, honestly, when have you and I had a meaningful conversation about *anything* in the last decade? You have been living in this world where all you cared about was yourself, your next party, your next shopping spree, your next trip. When Archibald died, everything changed. It was a shift that needed to happen, but with every seismic event, there are casualties. We are now just uncovering the rubble of what was Cordelia Clarke's life, and you are finally mature—and sober —enough to listen."

"How dare you."

"Don't, Lara. Don't posture. Not to me. Not here, not now. Take some responsibility. You've not been a member of this family for a very long time."

"But I am now! I'm here NOW!" I yell, bolting from my chair, not caring about the pain that rockets through me. "And I want the truth! Stop treating me like I'm some stupid brat who doesn't need to know all the hard stuff. I'm here *now*, and I demand you stop keeping me in the dark. You threw me to the wolves over there, Rupert. You handed me that giant key chain and that stupid dog, and then you *left* me to handle it all—"

"Yes, I am sorry my cancer diagnosis got in the way."

"Don't be a dick. You know exactly what you did, even without the cancer. You have been lying to me for years. And now you're lying to Wes, who I'm guessing is more than just your cop friend who makes a good cup of tea. Am I right, Rupert?"

He shrinks into himself again, his face tired, though our argument has infused his cheeks with a soft pink. At least I know he's still alive.

Finan stands and takes my hand. "You're shaking. Let's calm down and get what we came for, yes?" He cups the back of my hair. "Neither of you can handle this stress right now."

I slump back into the chair, angry that my side and back hurt, angry that I can't have anything stronger than a goddamned Tylenol, angry that Number Two has made decisions and kept secrets about my family over the two last decades and doesn't seem remorseful about having done so.

"Fine. If you didn't know anything about the cult or Casimiro and his stupid magic rocks, then why did you have a restraining order against Hale Watts?"

Rupert locks eyes with me, the hardness in his face melting as he fidgets with the edge of his blanket. He exhales slowly and then flattens his hands on his legs.

"Because he was in love with Cordelia. Obsessed with her. After she went missing, he kept showing up at the manor, insisting he could help Archibald find her, that he'd heard from people in his 'network' that she was still alive down in Mexico. Archibald listened to him, even sent him on a trip down there to look for her. But Watts is like a bloodhound—he gets on a scent and he starts asking too many questions, some of which should be left alone. He sniffed out Jacinta's involvement with the cartel and that she had escaped to Canada. I told him quite directly to fuck off via a long chain of restraining orders. He eventually fell away. I'd actually hoped he was dead."

"Well, he's not, and he still seems pretty obsessed with my mother."

Rupert twists so he's facing me straight on. "Be careful with Hale Watts, Lara. He's as loony as those Dea Vitae cultists. I wouldn't want you to become ensnared in any of his troubles, of which I'm sure there are many."

"That may be true, but according to him, Iona MacChruim is still a danger to all of us until she's somehow handled, or maybe until she recovers Dear Daddy's magic rocks. Cordelia and Jacinta took them, which means there's only one person left alive who knows where the hell they are now."

Rupert nods once. "You understand that it is not me."

"If you say so."

"I do."

"In that case, we will be returning to Thalia first thing tomorrow to pay a visit to Archibald's secret bunker."

FORTY

HOME AGAIN

Upon returning to the Rowleigh residence, I am so drained, I devour the light broth and fresh peach cobbler Mrs. Rowleigh made and disappear into our room. I need a few moments, just me and the quiet.

As I ease onto the sofa bed, my eyes close, burdened with the weight of the day.

Hale Watts is a weirdo, obsessed with my mother, but he was there when Dea Vitae was born, along with Jacinta and Cordelia.

Rupert lied to me about Dea Vitae but swears he didn't know they were on the island.

Rupert is also lying to Wes Singh about Jacinta Ramirez, though considering Wes's job, maybe that's a good thing. Wes probably wouldn't be able to look away from the whole messy snarl that is Jacinta's life.

Iona MacChruim is the daughter of the Casimiro Aguado, the charismatic cult leader from whom my mother stole a cache of sacred red beryl.

Iona obviously has it in for the Clarke family—she probably wants Daddy's pretty rocks back.

Which is why she and her minions infiltrated Thalia, why she poisoned the settlers and our lawyers, why her crazy followers destroyed my grandfather's grave marker—and why she sent me a warning while I was in the hospital.

But how did she know where I was? Did it make the news?

I consider getting up to ask Finan, but I can't. Too tired. And my phone is charging on the cabinet across the room, so even texting him isn't something I have the energy to do.

"Just go to sleep, Lara," I whisper to myself.

For once, I listen.

~

After a quick, early-morning visit by a home health nurse to check my healing wounds, I'm cleared to leave Vancouver and go back to Thalia Island. Good thing—even if she'd told me to stick around for another week, I wouldn't have listened.

I have things to do.

Finan arranged with Captain Cathy to meet us at Horseshoe Bay with one of the smaller electric vessels since there's no scheduled ferry today. After our goodbyes and promises to Eileen and Kira that we'll return soon for leisure and not because of some dire medical emergency, I spend the time during the Uber to the ferry terminal and then on the boat checking the hundreds of new emails and messages in Lutris that will require my attention once I'm back in the saddle. The nurse said I'm not to work more than fifteen hours a week for the next month; she gave Finan a dirty look when he snorted. Hell of a lot more than fifteen hours' worth of work sitting in my inbox.

We have new settlers arriving in two weeks. The damage from the storm isn't completely cleaned up and/or repaired, vertical farm B is still under reconstruction, and though I know Finan has been directing his crews the best he can via phone, Lutris, and video conferencing, he needs to be on the ground overseeing everything instead of making sure I can get to and from the toilet without tearing open my guts. We have to deal with the civil trial testimonies yet, now that our lawyers are back to work post-anthrax scare. And with Rupert still off the island, all of my regular duties, plus his, require attention.

I really miss that little button of floaty deliciousness I had at the hospital.

But as Thalia comes into view, a flutter trills in my chest. I'm actually *excited* to be returning to the island that keeps trying to kill me. A smile tugs at my lips.

"Wonder how you're going to get Humboldt away from Harmony," Finan says, kissing the side of my head. We haven't talked any more about the cold-shoulder period between us after my slideshow temper tantrum—or about the recent miscarriage—but I'm so happy that we're back to being Lara and Finan. It sucks it took a life-threatening injury to jolt us out of our snit, but I much prefer being on this side of Finan's warm smile than watching it from across the room.

Speaking of, will Lucy-Frank be pissed once she sees it's clear Finan and I are back together?

I think it's safe to assume we're an actual couple now, given our conversation that first night at his mom's about how we're building an "us," how we can talk about kids later, if that's something we decide *we* want. I consider asking Finan about Lucy-Frank ... and then realize I don't care. That's his business. I trust him to be a good man. And I'm done being *that girl* who allows her insecurities to ruin relationships.

Wow, maybe getting speared really did bring about an epiphany. I don't even recognize this calmer, gentler Lara.

Once we're docked, any worries about separating my dog from his ten-year-old BFF disappear. They're both at the marina with Catrina. Harmony holds a big poster over her head that says WELCOME HOME LARA, adorned with one of her renditions of Big Dog, who barks and bolts toward Finan as soon as we step foot on the dock. Thankfully, Finan gets in front of me as Humboldt whimpers and whines and wiggles his butt so hard, he almost falls into the strait.

"Oh my god, seriously, you are such a baby," I say, leaning over to pat his giant head, though he's too busy licking Finan's whole face to even notice I'm here. "Someone missed you."

"He missed you too," Finan says. "Come on. Let's get your mom onto solid ground. I would like to avoid another ambulance ride." He grabs the leash trailing behind Humboldt, and the dog practically drags Finan up the dock and into the lot. I give them a head start so as not to tip over into the water myself. Catrina is there to help me down the three short stairs.

"You look much better than the last time I saw you," she says, kissing my cheek. "Nice cane. Take my arm." I do, and she helps me up the incline toward her waiting car. Harmony sprints toward me, her sign flapping behind her.

"Lara! You're home! Oh my god, I missed you so much!" She opens her arms like she's about to hug me but then stops abruptly, just as I'm girding myself for a painful impact. "Catrina said you got *impaled*. When can I see it? Can I be in charge of your wounds? Do you still have stitches? Did you lose your intestines? Did you lose a lot of blood? Did you get any pictures? I could resew it for you if your stitches come loose. I've been practicing a whole bunch with my suture kit. Also I taught Humboldt some new tricks so when we get back to your office, I'll show 'em to you. Can I try your cane when we get to town hall?"

"Take a breath, kid." I poke her in the shoulder. "I missed you too."

She talks all the way to Catrina's car, filling me in on everything I've missed over the last ten days—she's done four more portraits of Humboldt; I missed painting class last week but it was boring "because we only painted ugly flowers" and someone brought disgusting brownies made of carob and whole wheat flour "and I couldn't even get through a whole bite and had to spit it in the garbage"; Mrs. Corwin gave her ten bucks to vacuum the council chambers but then made her take out all the garbages, too, and didn't even give her a tip; and Gillian Peck is still kissing Dr. Stillson and her dad found out so they had a big fight and "now my dad sleeps on the couch and fills the family room with farts."

"You've had a busy week."

"Ten days. You were gone for ten whole days."

"Right. Sorry."

Harmony throws open the back door of Catrina's car and launches herself inside, not seeming to mind that Finan is taking Humboldt with him. His truck is in the lot—brought down by one of his crew—and before we docked, Finan and I agreed he would head out to vertical farm B to check on the site while Catrina escorted me back to my cabin. Once he has Big Dog loaded, he waves and drives off.

"I'll bet he's glad to have a minute where he doesn't have to babysit," I say, easing into the front seat.

"Yes, he looks mighty distressed about 'babysitting,'" Catrina teases. "I take it things are mended?"

"On their way."

"What's mended? Does someone need stitches?" Harmony pushes between the front seats.

"Belt on, Harmony," Catrina says and starts the car, winking at me as she pulls out of the lot and toward town.

FORTY-ONE

REPOSE

O nce I'm back in my cabin, tucked into my couch with fresh tea, Tylenol, and lunch laid out on a TV tray (thank you, Catrina), my laptops and phones near, the only thing I *really* want to do is go find Jacinta's bunker. That is, after all, why Finan and I rushed back. To confront Jacinta. Find out what the hell she knows.

But I need Finan's navigational skills—knowing me, I'll get lost in the middle of the island and a cougar will have swum over in my absence and I will become its dinner.

Hey, stranger things have happened in the last few months. *Nothing* is impossible anymore.

Catrina coaxes Harmony out of my cabin with the promise of ice cream at the diner, although Harmony informs me she can get out here on her bike in ten minutes "if I pedal super hard," which she practiced while I was gone, so if I or Humboldt need anything, I should leave her a message on Lutris and she'll come right out. She props up my welcome-home poster against the fireplace, offers a fist bump, and bounces outside, a dervish of energy who leaves a Harmony-scented breeze in her wake.

I text Finan about his ETA at the cabins, to see if venturing into the woods is something we're tackling today. Though I'm anxious to talk to Jacinta, I'm not too disappointed when his reply mentions he's going to be awhile, that he'll bring an early dinner when he's done.

In the meantime, I will handle emails, answer the messages I can, respond to the well wishes from my fellow residents. I even draft a quick memo to let everyone know Finan and I are home and I'm recovering and looking forward to preparing the island for our newest settlers arriving the second week of August. The quiet of my cabin is interrupted only by the birds, crickets, and frogs that make Thalia their home. Catrina was kind enough to open all my windows before she left, allowing the July heat to flow through, tempered by our proximity to the ocean.

A couple hours later, my eyelids are heavy and my bladder is full. Carefully, I disengage from the pile of pillows and shuffle into the kitchen, moving to the window over the sink to say hello to my best girl. "Andromache, you look so pretty," I tell her, draping her lush, green-and-white blades over my fingers. "I'm sorry I was gone for so long. Looks like Auntie Catrina—or someone—took good care of you." I check her soil like Finan taught me, and then add a few teaspoons of water to her pot.

The sound of gravel under tires travels up the driveway through the open windows. Within a minute, the telltale bark informs me that my men have returned. I check the fridge, expecting it to be empty considering there wasn't much in there before I got hurt, but it's full of fresh food. A six-pack of craft beer and a bottle of white wine sit on the top shelf. Attached to the six-pack is a Post-it Note: "Welcome home, Lara! I missed you! xo, Dakota."

My front door swings open, and Humboldt plods in, tail wagging, another giant stick in his jaw. "Heyyyyy, buddy." I close the fridge and bend slightly to scratch his head—and grab a towel to wipe the slobber string hanging from his chin. Finan pauses at the door to remove his boots and nods toward the fridge.

"Catrina said she was going to restock for you."

"She did. Full of good stuff. Plus beer and wine from Dakota."

"See? You are loved," he says, closing the distance between us.

He wraps himself around me, smelling of the fields and summer sweat. I tip my head back just as he lowers his lips to mine. "Mmmm, you taste good," he purrs, kissing me again, longer this time, his hands sinking into my hair. "What did the doctor say about baths?"

Humboldt is licking something off my pant leg. I push back from Finan and look down at my dumb dog. "If you mean bath by bullmastiff tongue, no thank you."

Finan releases me, opens the fridge, and pulls out a beer. "No, I mean, can you take baths yet?"

"I can ... what did you have in mind?"

"Why don't you get naked and find out?"

A shiver runs through me. "You do know I can't handle your weight on me yet."

"I know." He winks. "Go get clean jammies. I'll meet you in the bathroom in ten."

Cane in hand, I amble into my bedroom, both turned on and nervous about the prospect of intimacy so soon after—well, everything—the accident, the subsequent surgeries, my still-healing pelvis, the miscarriage ...

I strip out of my clothes, realizing that Humboldt was licking my pant leg because I'd unknowingly spilled dressing from my sandwich. Now I have a grease stain *and* dog slobber. Nice.

I pause, wearing only underwear, in front of my full-length mirror, inspecting the damage from the metal rod for the first time straight on, now without the bandages. The sutures are intact, the surrounding area clean and only mildly pink, the pink of healing skin and not of inflamed or infected tissues the nurse assured me. The significant bruising in my midsection stretches around to my back and down my hip and butt cheek; it takes me a little by surprise, the purple mottling into shades of pink, green, and eventually yellow as it fades. The top of my left hand is still faintly bruised from the IV, and I've obviously lost some weight from not eating full meals over the last week and a half.

"You OK?" Finan leans against the door frame into my room. I close my robe over myself.

"Just having a look at the damage."

He walks in and offers his arm. "Come on. I'll wash your hair."

In the time I was undressing, Finan managed to clean and fill the tub, light candles, and pour two glasses of wine. He stops me beside the tub and tugs on the belt to my robe.

"It's not going to gross you out, right? To see the injury site? Not exactly looking awesome naked right now."

"Ha," he says, brushing his lips across mine. "You always look awesome naked." He pushes the robe off my shoulders and it puddles onto the floor. He unhooks my bra; my skin breaks out in goose bumps as it, too, drops, followed by my panties. "I'm helping you in. No more accidents."

He's moved a stool next to the tub, so I sit on it, the cool metal nice under my bare ass, and Finan swings my legs over the tub's edge and into the water. Perfect temperature. Counteracts the summer heat but not too cold to bring on a chill. I ease in, the water wrapping me in a protective pod.

"Are you not getting in?" I ask.

"Probably best I don't. I'm grimy from the field, and I don't want to introduce germs to your incisions." Finan moves the stool to the end of the claw-foot tub. "Lean back and relax." He hands me a glass of wine. "Sip first. Then I'll take it. You need to relax all the way."

I do as instructed, the beautifully cold wine rushing down my throat and splashing in my stomach. He takes the glass and sets it on the floor before repositioning behind me.

"Where is Humboldt?"

"Eating dinner. He's fine. Just *relax*."

I lean against the curve in the tub, my head back as Finan untangles my hair from its messy bun and finger-combs it. I feel like I should say something, that I should fill the quietude with conversation. Instead I let the water do the talking, the birds outside adding their pair of pennies. The lit candles around the sink and on the toilet tank dance under invisible puffs of air, competing with the midafternoon sun to see who will give off the most enchanting light.

Once my head is thoroughly soaked, Finan squeezes shampoo into his palms and again buries his fingers in my hair, bestowing upon my scalp a massage that rivals an orgasm. I moan—I can't help it. He chuckles.

He leaves no follicle untouched before moving to my ears, my jawline, gently kneading the back of my neck, around the front to my collarbones, and then up to the TM joint in front of my ears. He then rinses the shampoo, followed by application of conditioner that he massages into every strand before tilting my head back. He's grabbed my favorite moisturizer and massages my eyebrows, around my eyes, across my forehead, down my cheeks, under my chin, and again along the jawline and ears.

By the time he's rinsing off the conditioner, I have all the structure of an overcooked noodle. The water has grown cool, but I am on fire under his touch.

"How in the world will I ever pay you back for this?" I say, barely above a whisper. He leans over, kissing me upside down.

"I'll take an IOU." He stands and moves to the side of the tub, reaching down under my arms to help me out. I'm weak from relaxation, but pain twinges in my side with the effort of standing. "You OK?"

I step out of the tub, dripping onto the bath mat, and take the towel he's holding out for me. Rather than wrap myself in it, I drop it on the floor and reach for the hem of his shirt.

"Lara, we can't. Doctor said no sex for a bit."

"The doctor said no *intercourse*. He didn't say anything about me making sure you're clean from head to toe."

Finan's laugh bounces off the ceiling as he helps me undress him. Both of us naked, we move to the shower. I can't stretch to wash his hair, so he obliges by lowering to his knees, wrapping his huge hands around my hips. He flattens his cheek against my abdomen, his eyes closed for a moment, as if he's thinking what I'm too afraid to say out loud—about what we lost, even though we didn't even know we had it.

He then gently kisses around my belly button while I scrub his scalp and knead my thumbs into his neck. It's not nearly as thorough or romantic as what he's just done for me, but when he stands to rinse the shampoo under the waterfall shower head, I wrap my left arm around his waist, my face against his broad, wet chest, and take him in my right hand.

"Lara, oh my god," he groans. As I work him into a frenzy, he pushes me back just enough to cup my head in his right hand, kissing me fiercely, moaning against my mouth as he gets closer. "I love you, I love you, I love you," he says against me, his whole body shuddering as he pulls me against him, both arms wrapped around my body, his breaths like he's just run a race, his heart pounding under my ear pressed to his chest.

"I love you so much," he says, kissing against my wet hair again. "Please heal quickly so I can repay you in kind."

"I look forward to that," I whisper against his smiling lips.

FORTY-TWO

EMPTY SPACES

"You ready?"

"Ready as I'll ever be," I say as Finan finishes tying my laces.

"I like your boots." He lowers my foot from his lap to the floor.

"Shut it, Rowleigh. Or no more happy-ending showers for you."

"Whatever you say, my lady." Finan stands and bows before me. He then pulls out his phone, bringing up the hand-drawn map he made off the blueprints we found in Grandfather's study. It's just light enough outside for us to see where we're going but hopefully keep us out of view of other folks who might be up and at 'em early, passing by on the road.

Before falling asleep wrapped in each other's arms last night, we debated whether taking Humboldt was a good idea, if he'd give us away or cause more trouble out in the woods. But the alternative—leaving him alone in here while we're out hiking around and thus risk him anxiety-eating my couch—was less appealing.

"Come on, Big Dog." I snap on his reflective harness. "He needs to stop nibbling from plates at the Salamander, or I'm gonna have to custom order his next vest."

"This beast is all muscle, aren't ya, bud." Finan opens my front door and the dog bounds out ahead of us. We've each got a backpack with water, our phones, a first aid kit, portable snacks, a bear whistle, and a flashlight, just in case. Thalia Island is not a big place—it's not like we could get lost forever, but the woods are still densely packed, and if a cougar *did* happen to make it across to our island, we don't want it practicing its stealth on us.

According to the blueprint and Finan's mapping skills, the bunker is in the heart of the forested area that borders the plot of land where our cabins sit, about a kilometer and a half in. Walking there shouldn't take more than thirty minutes, probably slower given my hindered gait, but pinpointing the entrance will be the tricky bit. I'm sure it lacks a sign that says HERE I AM, THE SECRET BUNKER, with a giant neon arrow pointing at its subterranean entryway.

The sun makes quick work of burning away the summer-morning coolness, and dry wild grasses crunch underfoot as we cross the untended field that stretches between my cabin and the tree line. The grass between the cabins has browned and stopped requiring weekly mows, at least until the rain starts again.

"You doing all right?" Finan asks as we approach the forest.

"You don't have to ask me every ten minutes." I'm not going to tell him that my hip is already on fire, that the ibuprofen is slow to work, and Tylenol doesn't do anything useful anymore. We're on a mission. I can handle some pain.

Humboldt leads the way, snout to the ground, stopping to bark at crows or dig at a downed, rotten stump in search of whatever has scampered underneath. We follow him out of the bright sun into the protective canopy of forest, an instant relief to my already sweaty skin. The wind kicks up now and again and the trees talk to us, creaking and swaying, hollers of birds in their branches, chittering squirrels fighting over turf. The carpet of pine needles and mosses and damp, rich soil spices the air. Verdant ferns have seized the space between trees, their new fronds curling toward the breaks in the ceiling for a single kiss from the blazing sun.

As expected, our excursion is slow going, and after forty minutes of quiet, Finan halts. "I don't know what we should be looking for. I'm going to guess a hatch of some sort—the blueprints did not indicate a traditional entry into the space but rather one that looked something like the doorway into a submarine."

"In through the top."

"Right."

"If we keep going north, we'll end up at the edge of town. It has to be around here somewhere, unless I've misread everything."

"The island isn't big enough to not be able to find the bunker," I say. "Let's walk in a square from this point—you go that way, I'll go this way, heads down, assuming the door is in the ground. What—forty paces along and then turn, and then we can close in on diagonals?"

"Excellent plan, my lady." Finan winks and continues north along his side of the square. I turn and slowly walk in a westerly direction, head down, scanning the ground for anything that looks different from the surroundings. I count my forty paces and turn north again for another forty, then pivot so I'm walking in a southeasterly diagonal. Finan is ahead of me on his own diagonal when Humboldt breaks the sanctuary with a series of excited barks.

He barks and jumps and barks again, digging like his life depends on it. It's probably something that smells like food. Humboldt may not technically be a hound dog, but don't tell him that.

I spin and walk toward him, mostly to make sure he's not about to get sprayed by a skunk or remove his head from the soil with a critter clamped onto his snout. I've had enough vet bills for this year, thanks.

Oh god—what if he's found *more* bones?

Carefully, I approach. "What are you freaking out about?" Sure enough, he's dug a giant hole, his face and legs covered in moist earth, jowls frothed and sloppy, a smile spread across his derpy face. I take another step, and my cane hits something that doesn't sound like dirt. I tap it again. "Good boy, Humboldt," I say, rubbing his back, relieved there are no bones clamped between his teeth. "Hey, Finan! I think we found it!"

Finan jogs over while I unzip my backpack and pull out the waxed pouch with Humboldt's treats. "Here ya go, my boy." Big Dog, clearly pleased with himself, gingerly takes the Greenie bone and plops into the hole he's just dug.

"He's going to need a bath," Finan says.

"Lucky you."

I tap my cane again so Finan can hear the hollow thud underneath. He kneels and swipes at the ground. Sure enough, an army-green hatch has been covered from the outside with dirt and debris.

"That doesn't make sense. How would she cover it from the inside?" I ask.

Finan sighs. "Probably means she's not here."

"No ... no, shit, no."

"Only one way to find out." Finan continues wiping away the hatch until he finds the rusty green pull tucked under a metal flap. He lifts it and yanks on the handle, and the hatch opens to the world, revealing a descending ladder. "I'll go first."

"I don't need you to be the hero."

He snorts. "I just want to be there to soften your landing when you fall off that ladder."

"So gallant."

"A true knight does his best to serve his queen."

"Glad to see I've been elevated to my proper status." I pinch his arm as he positions himself on the top rung and lowers into the ground. I watch as he goes, counting his steps. Ten feet in. "How's it look?" I ask.

"Clean. Empty. Come on down."

I lean over and dangle my cane so he can catch it. "Humboldt, you stay." He looks up at me, blinks once, and then returns to his snack.

I'm careful climbing onto the metal ladder, easing my sore body slowly, glad Finan went first as he makes sure I don't lose my balance on that still-weak right side. I step onto a rubberized black floor, the bunker pretty much as I'd imagined, except bigger.

"How did he blast through all this granite?" Finan asks, touching the rock wall just behind the ladder. The black flooring extends throughout the whole place. The northern end of the bunker has a ten-by-ten room with a wall of closed-circuit TVs, all currently dark.

Finan puts his hand along the side of the bank of screens. "They're cold."

A Tesla Powerwall, mounted on the western side, is still on. "Obviously they've made recent upgrades," I say, checking the battery's stats. "It has to be connected somewhere to solar or wind."

"Having a gas generator down here would be dangerous. Exhaust fumes, plus it's noisy," Finan adds, shaking his head. "Your grandfather was a true visionary. He was dreaming up this Jetsons-level technology when Elon Musk was still playing with blocks."

The bunker is a rectangle. The surveillance room doubles as an office, metal shelves of books along the opposite walls. Scanning their spines, these were clearly brought in decades ago—everything from survival tips to botany textbooks to *Advances in Hydroponics* published in the 1970s. Another shelf holds a set of newer publications—Jacinta must've brought those in, either on her own or via Rupert. There's even a book on army-style medical procedures and first aid for animal bites. I guess that might be necessary for someone hiding in the literal belly of a remote Canadian island?

We move out of the surveillance room/office and head back toward the entrance, discovering a set of sliding doors that hide shelves full of canned goods, all of it still good. "Obviously Rupert did a restock for her," I say, resentment tingeing my words. A second set of sliding doors opens to a kitchenette, complete with a water purification system built into the wall that feeds into a wide stainless steel sink. A modern water cooler with a plastic, water-filled jug sits on the end of the counter, though I'm guessing she was using the bunker's system to filter and refill her potable water.

We're fortunate to have clean, glacier-fed water in this province, plus we don't get any sort of water delivery to the island, and certainly not in big plastic jugs. The kitchenette holds a double-burner stove and a small fridge, which, when opened, is clean and empty but still cold. A heat and humidifier system is bolted to the wall just outside the kitchenette, and it, too, is cool to the touch.

The opposite end of the rectangle holds two rooms, a big one that branches left, aglow with purple-hued greenhouse lighting, chock full of soil tables, giant, round terra-cotta pots, and metal shelving absolutely bursting with fresh food. I pluck a ripe strawberry from one of the terra-cotta pots and pop it into my mouth. "Damn. She really did grow all the stuff she brought me." I hand a bright red berry to Finan.

The second room off the greenhouse is tiny and has a made-up twin bed on a metal frame in the middle against the western wall, another metal shelving unit with books and personal hygiene supplies, a flat-screen TV and DVD player on an otherwise empty dresser, a small vanity and sink with an age-stained mirror hanging over it, and an old wooden nightstand with a bedside lamp sporting an embroidered shade that gives the room a warm, yellow glow.

"Where the hell did she go?" I ask Finan, lowering myself to the bed. "This doesn't make sense. If she's in danger, why would she disappear without saying anything to me?"

Finan scans the shelves, wiping his fingertips across the surface. "No dust. She hasn't been gone long," he says. "Do you think she would've gotten in touch with Rupert?"

"I don't know. I'll call him when we get back. See which version of the truth he's willing to share."

Finan moves to the opposite side of the bed and opens the cupboard under the sink. Finding nothing, he crouches before the nightstand and opens the narrow drawer. "Lara ..."

Carefully, I turn. He's holding out a silver-framed picture. I take it, my breath stuttering for a beat. Finan slides onto the bed next to me; its metal springs groan under the added weight. "Is that you?" he asks softly.

I smile as I regard the framed photo. "Mm-hmm. My mom and me. And Jacinta. I don't even remember this. I didn't know I'd met her before."

"You're little here. You wouldn't have remembered her."

"I guess ..."

Finan stands again and looks through all the dresser drawers. He then pulls every book off the shelf, flipping pages, shaking each one to see if anything falls loose.

Nothing.

It's as if she wasn't even here.

"I feel like I imagined the whole thing," I say, pulling off my backpack so I can take this photo with me. No use leaving it here. Who knows if Jacinta is ever coming back?

"You didn't. I saw her too." After he's gone through every obvious storage place, Finan drops to the floor and feels around, as if looking for another hidden door. He lies flat and checks under the bed, and then stands, picking up the pillow, its case pressed and neat. He pats down the tawny blanket, picks up the lamp, takes the mirror off the wall and looks behind it, even contorts himself into the small sink vanity.

"You watch a lot of spy movies, don't you," I tease.

"Just trying to think where I would hide something if I had something to hide."

"That's the kicker, though, right? What would she have to hide, other than herself?"

Finan dusts off, head shaking. "Maybe we should go. Give Rupert a call. If she's gone, that can't be good."

I nod and then reach over to turn off the nightstand lamp. If she's not here, she won't need it.

We opt to leave the greenhouse lights on—if nothing else, we will come out every few days and harvest the food she's grown. Total waste not to. Finan and I agree, too, that we're going to fire up that surveillance system—see what we can see on this island of ours. Maybe we'll pick up Jacinta hiding somewhere else.

Finan offers his hand, and I take it, pulling myself off the creaky bed.

"Don't worry. We'll figure this out," he says, leaning over and kissing my cheek. I'm suddenly so tired—I'd been expecting a confrontation, hoping for some revelations ... instead I found an empty bunker and no sign of the one person who has the answers I need for a resolution.

Nothing but frustration.

FORTY-THREE

JRCCLC070792

By the time we're back at my cabin, it's after eleven, our skin and clothes soaked with our efforts under the baking sun. Humboldt bites at the water coming out of the garden hose before lapping it from his silver bowl almost as fast as it fills. Finan and I take turns at the kitchen sink, splashing our faces and pouring refreshment down our parched throats.

He opens my fridge and pulls out two bottles of green juice, handing me one. "You gonna call Rupert?"

I limp into my bedroom and pull the secure phone and laptop from my armoire. The phone is against my ear when I rejoin Finan in the living room.

"Hey, Number Two. You busy?"

"Just getting some chemicals shoved into my veins by an angel in a lab coat. Is it important?"

"It is." I hear beeping in the background, followed by someone talking to Rupert about putting the phone away. "Can you call me when you've got a minute?" I hoist my backpack onto one of the stools at the breakfast bar and pull out the photo of my mom and Jacinta and me.

"I'm here for another three hours. I'll phone tonight, yes? I'm not allowed to chat in the treatment room."

I sigh. "I hope it goes well."

He laughs dramatically. "Please stay out of trouble until dinner." He hangs up.

Finan slides my juice bottle across the island toward me. "If I go to work, you'll be all right?" I take the juice and limp over to the couch, setting the picture frame on the coffee table so I can really look at it.

"Yes. I have stuff to do too."

"You want a ride in?"

"No, you go ahead. You've spent enough time playing nursemaid." I actually don't know if I can drive yet. Haven't tried it.

Finan finishes his drink and rinses the bottle, setting it upside down in the drying rack. He then moves to me on the couch and takes my face in both his hands. "Maybe I like playing your nursemaid, my queen."

We kiss, his lips cold and wet from his juice. I want to grab him and drag him into my bed and lock all the doors and flush all the phones down the toilet.

Humboldt barks from the porch, immediately followed by whimpers and the ticking nails that indicate he's on his feet and very excited to see whoever is here.

Jacinta?

"Hi, Lara! Told you I could get out here by myself!" Harmony pounds on the wooden screen door, opens it, and lets the dog in before bounding in herself.

Not Jacinta.

"You two have fun," Finan says, kissing the tip of my nose before standing. "You make sure Lara doesn't trip with that cane, yeah?"

"I totally will. And if she falls, I can stitch her up. I've been practicing!"

"I know she's in excellent hands," Finan says, rumpling Harmony's hair as he walks past. "See you for dinner?"

"Only if you're cooking!" I holler after him, cut off by the screen door banging closed.

Harmony plops onto the couch next to me. "So, what are we doing today?"

I laugh. "Nothing that will require you to administer stitches."

"You're no fun."

"I've heard that before."

Harmony leans forward and scoops the framed photo off the table before scooching in closer to me. "Who's that?"

"My mom and me and her girlfriend."

"You're so little!" she says, giggling. "Look how cute you were. I was a cute kid too. Not like my dumb sister."

"You're still a cute kid, and your little sister is adorable too."

"She's an asshole. I already told you that."

"Oh my goodness, Harmony, that mouth of yours is going to get you in trouble."

"You sound like Gillian." She runs her fingers over the embossed edge of the silver frame. "Your mom was really pretty. She's dead, right?"

"She is."

"Do you miss her?"

"I do. A lot." Unexpected emotion burns my sinuses.

"Was she a good mom?"

"I think so. She was gone a lot. She flew airplanes and took photos—"

"The photos at town hall, right?"

"Yes. Those were hers."

"She was a good photographer."

"She was."

"How did she die?" Harmony sets the photo on the coffee table before leaning back and wrapping one of her sticky hands around my upper arm.

"Her airplane went down."

"She died in a *plane crash*?"

"She did."

"Oh my god, that is super sad." Harmony pats my arm twice and then sits forward again, snatching the photo from the table. "I think I've seen this lady before. Does she live on Thalia?"

My heart stutters. "You think you've seen *this* lady?" I reach over Harmony's hand and point directly at Jacinta in the photograph.

"Mm-hmm. She looks familiar. When I was riding my bike out here last week, practicing to see how fast I could get to your cabin."

"Where did you see her?"

"In your field."

"You couldn't have seen this lady, Harmony."

"Did she die in the plane crash too? Holy crap, do we have ghosts here?" She pulls the frame closer to her face, examining Jacinta in the photo. "No, no way. She wasn't a ghost. I saw *this lady*. She had the same long, black hair."

"Lots of people have long, black hair."

Harmony is already shaking her head no. "I'm a pretty smart young woman, Lara. I know what I saw."

I try not to laugh. I love Harmony's confidence, how at ten, she's already referring to herself as a young woman. "You are the smartest person I know, Harmony."

"You told me that before. Are all your friends dummies?" she asks, handing me back the photo. "Anyway, got anything to drink? Then can we go to town hall? I want to do the mail, and now that you're home, I can earn some money again. Mrs. Corwin is too cheap to work for."

"There's some Diet Coke in the back of my fridge, but don't tell your mom I gave it to you."

Harmony flies off the couch and into the kitchen, hooting her excitement the whole way. I set the frame on the table again, staring at it, wondering if in fact Harmony *did* see Jacinta in the field out front before she disappeared to wherever she is now.

"Drink that at the breakfast bar so Humboldt doesn't knock it over. I'm going to get ready, and then we'll head downtown, 'K?"

Harmony gives me a thumbs-up and slides onto one of the stools. Diet Coke is a big no-no around here—all chemicals and caffeine—but it's also delicious, and it's not going to kill Harmony to have *something* a normal kid living on the mainland would get.

I grab clean clothes and slide into the bathroom and take a quick sponge bath. Fresh deodorant, some light makeup, moisturizer everywhere—I forgot sunscreen this morning and I now have a pink neck and pink arms and cheeks from our sojourn into the woods—and fix my hair so it looks presentable.

"Humboldt, look out!" echoes from the living room, followed by the sound of breaking glass. "Hey, Lara! I need a broom!"

I tuck in my blouse, grab my cane, and hobble into the living room. Harmony is hunched near the fireplace hearth, pushing Humboldt back. "His tail knocked over your picture. I'm so sorry. The glass broke but I don't want him to get cut."

"Humboldt, come," I say, patting my leg and moving into the kitchen. As soon as he hears the treat drawer open, he saunters over. "I'll clean up the glass, Harmony. Don't want you cutting yourself. Bad enough I gave you pop."

"I'll do it! You can't use a broom with your cane," Harmony says. I point to the cupboard where it's stored, following her over with a paper bag for the shards. "You should vacuum, though. My mom always does that so we don't get little pieces in our feet."

"I will. Tonight. We'll take Dumb Dog with us."

"Don't call him that," Harmony says, sweeping the glass into the dustpan. "He can hear you."

She slides the now-glassless silver rectangle onto the coffee table. She then hands me the photo, liberated from its frame. "Sorry he did that," she says.

"Not your fault. His tail is a whip." I look again at the photo, somehow more alive without its glass. I flip it over, hoping someone thought ahead enough to write the date it was taken. In ballpoint pen at the lower corner, it reads: "JRCCLC070792."

Our initials, followed by July 7, 1992? I would have just turned two years old here, which looks about right.

Harmony slurps out the last drops from her pop can. "OK, ready to go!" She hops into the kitchen and drops the can in the recycling bin. "Can we put my bike in your car?" she asks.

I set the photo on the fireplace mantel, grab my key chain, both phones, and the secure laptop, throw my work satchel over my shoulder, and limp after my dog and his favorite, freshly caffeinated ten-year-old.

FORTY-FOUR

CARROT CAKE

I square Harmony away with the mail and a handful of other chores and errands since, as she's reminded me at least a dozen times, "School is out for three weeks, so I can do whatever I want!" This includes resuming babysitting duties for Big Dog because she'd rather be *anywhere* but at home with her mother and little sister, and "my dad says that being out in nature is a healthy coping mechanism." I have to remind *myself* at least a dozen times a day that Harmony is a decade old and not some ageless celestial being from another solar system.

I ease into my office chair, which holds a fancy new seat cushion to better support my healing parts, thanks to Catrina. She popped her head in just after our arrival to let me know I have an afternoon appointment with Liam Stillson so he can check my stitches and the bruising.

Grateful for the follow-up support; not excited about Dr. Stillson groping my half-naked person.

Dakota floats into my office just after Catrina leaves, an iced latte and still-warm raspberry scone in hand followed by gentle hugs and the promise that she will be acting as my interim physical therapist "on the request of Uncle Rupert." She fills me in on the gossip I missed while off the island, including the breaking news I'd already heard from Harmony that Gillian Peck and Dr. Stillson have been found out, and Zackery Peck has made inquiries to town council about the possibility of moving into one of the tiny houses or maybe even crew lodgings for the time being.

"Our very own soap opera," Dakota says.

"As if my exploits weren't enough drama already."

"You gotta admit, though—sorta nice to have the heat off you for a second."

I nod. She's right. If everyone is busy gossiping about who Dr. Stillson is kissing, they'll be less likely to pick apart my every move. And yes, the onslaught of gifts and flowers during my hospital stay was pretty awesome. Almost like a real family, *real* friends. All I had to do was take a shaft of metal to the abdomen to find that!

"You OK, Lara?" she asks.

We make eye contact, and I speak before thinking. "I had a miscarriage. We were pregnant."

"Oh ... shit."

"Yeah."

"Are you all right?"

"I guess? I never thought of myself as the mom type, being that I am basically the most selfish person on the planet."

"Maybe *old* Lara was, but not you now. Not this Lara."

I shrug and sniff. "It's probably just the hormones leveling out. Doctor said it would take a little while."

"What did Finan say?" she asks quietly. "I mean, assuming it was Finan's ..."

"Of course, it was. There hasn't been anyone else since I've been here."

She nods. "Right. Sorry. Dummy me."

I take a deep breath. "He was as shocked as I was. The doctor told us when Finan was in the room—she must've assumed that we knew. Makes sense, though. He was with me every second I wasn't in surgery."

"Awww, that is so romantic." A dreamy look washes over Dakota's sun-kissed face. "Does he want kids?"

"He does. His sister Kira has newborn twins. You should see him with them. It's enough to get any woman's ovaries screaming."

"Do you think this is something you guys will revisit in the future?" Dakota's gentle demeanor makes it easy to talk to her; she isn't prying or nosy. She's not cataloging my secrets to run off to WickedStepsister and spill the beans. She seems concerned, like she really cares about what happens to me and Finan.

It's nice.

"He said we should probably work on an 'us' before we talk about having kids. Not that he wouldn't have welcomed this one ..."

Dakota moves around the desk, wrapping herself around me in a tight but soft hug. When she pushes back, her eyes sparkle with unshed tears. "If there is anything I can do, let me know. You've been through so much in such a short time. I know how much it sucks to go through hard shit and not have anyone to talk to. I'm here, if you ever need me."

I squeeze her wrists in thanks. "You're like all the best parts of Rupert, without the pompous attitude."

She laughs. "I can be pompous when I need to be."

"I doubt that."

She returns to her chair, replacing it against the wall. "I gotta head back to get ready for dinner. Baseball on the big screen tonight, and Len Emmerich and his guys always fill the place."

"Len's back? He's here on the island?"

"Yeah, they came home last night. He hasn't checked in with you yet?"

I shake my head. "He didn't expect us back until this morning. I didn't change my itinerary with him."

"Don't go rogue, Lara. After everything, let the security guys do their job." She knocks twice on my desk.

"I'll send him a quick note in Lutris."

"And starting tomorrow, we'll be going for daily walks around the community centre just after lunch, rain or shine, so make sure you eat. No high heels!" she sings as she heads toward the door. "Call or text if you need anything. Consider me the annoying big sister who won't leave you alone!" She winks and disappears down the hall.

An annoying big sister. I chuckle. I still cannot believe she's Rupert's kid. *So* weird.

And I do miss my high heels. Nothing but Vessi sneakers for the last two weeks and those dreadful hiking boots when absolutely necessary. Thank goodness there're no paparazzi over here. The shame!

I open Lutris and message Len Emmerich to let him know we returned yesterday. I fully expect an admonition as soon as he's within shouting distance of town hall. In the chaos of everything since Iona's surprise package at the hospital, I forgot that I'm now supposed to check in with Len before going anywhere. Oops.

Then again, if I'd told him about our unscheduled visit to Clarke Manor, we wouldn't have met Hale Watts, and there's definitely more to that story.

My inbox pings with Len's return message: *"Rupert informed me yesterday. Please let me know when you leave the island or otherwise engage in behaviors that could bring peril to yourself or others. Len."*

"*I owe you a beer,*" I reply. Wait for thirty seconds.

"*A pitcher should cover it. LE.*"

I'm glad he has a sense of humor under all that muscle.

As I stare at his name on the screen, I can't help but think about Jacinta's presence on the island—there's no way Rupert would've told Len Emmerich if he didn't even tell Wes. But Harmony swears she saw "that lady" in the field out front of our cabins.

Did Rupert give Jacinta a heads-up about Hale Watts's little visit? Is that why she disappeared?

I grab my purse from the big bottom drawer of my desk and pull out my mother's thumb drive. While it's registering on my desktop, I stand slowly and close my office door, just in case. Harmony is out with Humboldt, plus I gave her extra money to buy herself something from the diner. I should still have a little uninterrupted time.

I double-click the drive to open its Finder window, and just for the hell of it, I do a global search for Hale Watts.

Five documents contain his name.

Five.

I double-click on the first one. It's in the Excel spreadsheet, and in Spanish. Open up Google Translate, again wishing I spoke more Spanish than just how to ask for another beer.

Pago, método de pago. Payment and method of payment.

They paid Hale Watts money? For *what*?

The line item doesn't offer any further information about what the payments might have been for. Neither do the subsequent four listings for payments ranging from $25,000 to $100,000 USD.

What is going on here?

Rupert said Watts told my grandfather he had proof Cordelia was alive in Mexico and that Archibald sent Watts in search of her. I can understand money changing hands there. But why would there be payments in a spreadsheet Jacinta clearly had a hand in managing, considering it's in Spanish?

My brain feels like a tangled mess of Christmas lights and only every other bulb works, so even if I can straighten it, I still have to figure out which of these bloody bulbs is the one shorting out the rest of the string.

I flop my head onto bent arms atop my desk.

I *could* send Hale Watts a text on that number he gave me, give him a private email address to get in touch, see if he has anything he's willing to share. But how would I approach that? He cannot know that Jacinta is—was?—on Thalia Island. I don't even know what my questions are at this point, other than why did Jacinta give you tens of thousands of dollars you conveniently didn't mention at our visit the other day?

I *really* need to speak with Rupert.

My phone lights up with a notification, so I open my work email, already full again despite my efforts to weed out the chaff over the last few days. This newest missive: another request from Mr. Peck about finding alternate accommodations or else he might have to take a leave and go back to the mainland. Yikes. I can't have him leave in the middle of his research, so I'll need to address this today.

Below his email is a string of new invoices for the contractor out on vertical farm B awaiting my approval so they can go to accounting. And a handful of messages from settlers scheduled to arrive in the next wave.

Nestled in the middle of this unread pile is an email via our website's Contact page, from a Bugs Bunny. I'm about to delete it—we get a ton of spam from hateful trolls—but the message reads, "Found this carrot. I know how much you like carrots. They make excellent cake. -HW," followed by a link. I know better than to click on dodgy links sent via email, but HW ... that has to be Hale Watts, right?

I cannot open this now. I have to use the secure laptop, in case this *is* some sort of virus. Killing the Thalia Island internet service would not please Jeremiah the Lovely IT Guy, or my fellow residents. And I just got them back to liking me.

I jump as Mrs. Corwin raps her knuckles on the glass wall of my office. I close the email program and reach around to yank out the thumb drive. An error message pops up on my screen, and I quickly minimize the Excel window. "Come in," I holler, dropping the drive into my bag, safe and sound.

"Hello, Lara. I am so glad to see you've made such a swift recovery," Mrs. Corwin says, sashaying into my office, her open padfolio nested in her skinny arm. "In preparation for tomorrow's council meeting, I thought you and I could have a sit-down about some of the items we need handled prior to the arrival of our newest settlers. Only two weeks to go!"

Before I can muster a response, Mrs. Corwin drags over a chair and launches into a to-do list that threatens to topple and bury me underneath it.

At 3:30 p.m., Lutris dings with a message, and I'm so grateful for the interruption, I almost cry. Mrs. Corwin has been talking for two hours, and although we've gotten through a number of important points on her epic list, her inability—or reticence—to

listen to my suggestions and instead bulldoze through with her solutions to our current registry of issues has me fighting to keep my eyelids open.

"Ah, that's Catrina! I have an appointment with Dr. Stillson. He's taking over my postsurgical care," I say, wincing dramatically as I stand.

"Oh, yes, of course. Off you go. We can finish this when you get back."

"I'm not supposed to work full days yet, so I'll probably go home after my appointment. Can we tackle your remaining items tomorrow morning with everyone else?"

Mrs. Corwin nods. I know she likes talking to me one-on-one because I'm less apt to argue and thus she gets her own way. But she gets stuff done, I'll give her that. As annoying and condescending as Mrs. Corwin can be, she is a million times easier to work with than Kelly Lockhart ever was.

Harmony rounds the corner on her skateboard, almost colliding with our senior authoress. "What did I tell you about skating in town hall?"

"Sorry, ma'am," Harmony says, jumping off her board and pulling Humboldt's leash closer so he doesn't slobber on the old biddy.

"I know you two have some sort of arrangement here"—she gestures between Harmony and me—"but this is still a place of business. Skateboarding indoors is inappropriate."

"Yes, ma'am," we say in unison. We wait until she's out of my office before giggling behind our hands.

"Are you leaving early?" Harmony asks, climbing onto her board again.

"I have to go for a checkup real quick."

"I thought you were gonna let me do it!"

I laugh. "Harmony, I need someone who's finished medical school to look at my surgery sites."

"Can I come with?"

"Oh my god, you are incorrigible," I say, throwing my work satchel over my shoulder. "As long as you *promise* not to say anything about him and your mom. I do not want to get involved in any of that, and you shouldn't either."

Harmony offers a pinkie finger for a promise. I wrap my own pinkie around it, trying not to cringe at how sticky she is.

"Come on, then. To the doctor we go."

FORTY-FIVE

MORE SECRETS?

My first mistake: allowing Harmony to come into the exam room with me.

Second mistake: Believing her pinkie promise that she wouldn't say anything to Dr. Stillson about him kissing her mom. I don't think I've ever seen a human male turn that shade of embarrassed.

In her defense, though, Dr. Stillson smooching a married woman—Harmony's *mother*—is causing trouble for my young sidekick. I guess she has a right to ask about it, however inappropriate that she's involved in her mother's sordid affairs (literally), especially since she seems to know more than she should given her penchant for snooping through text messages not meant for her precocious eyeballs. And it's very clear, judging by the latest email, that Daddy Peck really wants out of this situation.

Dr. Stillson does his best to deflect by distracting Harmony with the stethoscope, my surgical sites, and detailed explanations about how to assess wound healing, how bruises are formed, how the body absorbs the bruising gradually, which is why the skin is a rainbow of colors, how to check for postoperative complications, and how to listen for active bowel sounds to make sure the intestines are healing after the injury and surgical repair.

After listening to my guts for an eternity and asking about poop, she deems me healthy enough to continue on with my life.

Humboldt, on the other hand, is very uninterested in what my bowels sound like and won't stop whining and pawing at the door. "He probably has PTSD from when the raccoon got him," Harmony says, returning Stillson's stethoscope. "I'll take him outside until you're done, now that I know you're gonna live."

"Thank you, Dr. Peck," I say.

"Before you go ..." Dr. Stillson moves to the wall of cupboards and opens a drawer, pulling out a second stethoscope. "You can have this one."

Harmony's eyes bulge with awe. "Are you *serious*?"

"Every young doctor needs one."

She looks like she's about to hug him but instead she throws out a sticky hand. "Thank you, Dr. Stillson. I look forward to working with you." He indulges her handshake, smiling as she skips out of the exam room, a very relieved Humboldt in tow.

Once the door is closed again, Stillson turns and leans against the counter. "Do you have any other questions or concerns for me, now that our young charge is out of the room?"

"You gotta stop messing around with her mom. At least until Zackery Peck is out of the house."

Dr. Stillson exhales so hard, his shoulders droop. "I don't even know how it happened."

"Harmony has been reading her mom's texts for a while now."

He flushes anew. "I am the worst human ever."

"Not sure about the worst, but maybe stop canoodling with the married mom of two until she's separated?"

"Please ... don't tell anyone."

"It's not my mouth you have to worry about," I say, nodding toward the door. "Pretty sure everyone already knows."

"I'll fix this." He scrubs a hand down his face and then crosses his arms over his chest. "Thanks for your discretion."

"What are friends for?" I tease.

"How are you feeling otherwise?"

"Sore."

"Bowel movements regular?" He helps me lie back once again so he can listen to my guts this time.

"As I told Dr. Peck, yes, I am pooping."

"And no straining?"

"The Colace keeps everything nice and regular."

He palpates my abdomen, checking the healing wounds but then also over my uterus. "It's back to normal size. I'm really sorry about your miscarriage." He takes my hand and uses his other arm to help me sit up again.

"It's all right. I didn't even know I was pregnant, so it was a bit of a shock. For both of us."

He nods. "Do you want to talk about going on an oral contraceptive or perhaps another form of birth control? I could have Catrina do the pelvic exam, if you're more comfortable with that."

"I'll wait for now. Talk to Finan. I'm not a fan of the Pill."

"Lots of options these days. Let me know what you decide," he says. "As far as mobility, keep using the cane for now. And you should abstain from any, uh, load-bearing activity for at least another few weeks. Give the repaired pelvis bone time to heal fully." He helps me off the table.

"So, no sex is what you're saying."

"Just not missionary style." He blushes again. "You shouldn't have, uh, another person's body weight on you. Not quite yet."

"Roger that."

"And call me immediately with any pain, swelling, fever, or if anything changes."

"Promise." He looks almost as relieved as Humboldt did upon opening the exam room door. A flood of cool air flows in. "And Liam, thank you again. For being there that night, saving my life and all."

He smiles. "What are friends for?"

~

Harmony and Humboldt are lounging in the long grasses next to the doctor's office, absorbing that late afternoon sun like a couple of solar panels. As we walk back to town hall, and my waiting car, my bag vibrates under my arm, but I can't answer whoever is calling until Harmony is done talking about the rhythm of Humboldt's heart that she's spent the last thirty minutes listening to with her new stethoscope.

We stop next to Rupert's Tesla, which I've pretty much claimed, and I open all the windows to cool it down as well as the back door for Humboldt to jump in. "I'm going to head home, kid. Did you put today's hours on your time sheet?"

"Gonna do that now!" she says, dropping her skateboard. "Do you think Mrs. Corwin will let me listen to her heart?"

"Does Mrs. Corwin have a heart?"

Harmony giggles. "See you tomorrow, Lara. And don't forget to come up with an idea for Thursday paint night—you can't miss it this week!"

She glides away as I slide in behind the wheel, crank the AC, and roll up the windows. Humboldt is collapsed, stretched across the entire back seat. "She wore you out too?" He doesn't even lift his head in response but rather sighs heavily, a long drool string running off the seat and onto the floor.

I open my satchel and dig out the burner cell phone. Three missed calls, all from Rupert. At least he phoned me back.

I pull out of my spot and call him. Yes, distracted driving is illegal in British Columbia but I'm basically the mayor *and* the queen here, and I cannot wait another second to talk to Number Two.

"Lara," he answers.

"I was at my appointment with Stillson."

"Everything in order?"

"Looks like it."

"And you've spoken to Dakota?"

"She came by earlier. Said you've asked her to handle my physical therapy?"

"I've asked her to make sure you're up and walking. I'm sure you'd like to be rid of that cane sooner rather than later."

"Unless you're planning to get me the one with the dagger. Did you see the link I sent?"

"Very funny." He coughs. At least it sounds dry. "Don't fret. It's allergies. Wes's mother thought it would be darling to bring us a kitten she found in the alley behind her building but didn't realize I'm allergic."

"Can't Wes keep it at his place?"

Rupert is quiet. "He's here most of the time these days."

"Ah. So what are you going to do about the kitten?"

"Catrina said she'd collect her on their next trip over."

"Awww, that Catrina. She's pretty great," I say, slowing as I approach our driveway. I love how fast this car is.

"So, your call sounded urgent."

"Indeed," I say, rolling along the gravel drive. "Finan and I took a little walk this morning."

Rupert is again quiet as I pull to a stop in front of my cabin.

"Where is Jacinta, Rupert?"

He sighs. "She's safe. That's all you need to know."

"Is it? Because my little friend Harmony, the kid who wants to be a doctor when she grows up, the kid who misses NOTHING that happens over here? She says she saw Jacinta in the field in front of our cabins last week."

"How would she know who Jacinta is?"

"In the bunker, the only personal effect left behind was a framed picture of me and Mom and Jacinta when I was a baby. I brought it home. Harmony saw it, asked questions about my dead mother, and then pointed to Jacinta and said she saw 'that lady' last week."

"She's a child. Easy to explain away."

"Not *this* child, Rupert. This child has an IQ that would diminish Einstein."

More silence. "Did she tell anyone?"

"Who would she tell? To anyone else, it would be just some lady walking in the fields."

"Unless she doesn't see this lady elsewhere on the island and decides to ask about her."

"I suppose," I say. I hadn't thought of that. "Right now she's a bit preoccupied with her mother's theatrics. Gillian Peck and Dr. Stillson are sleeping together, and the kid knows."

"Ah, so that's why Mrs. Corwin emailed me about a tiny house for Zackery Peck."

"He emailed me again today, asking. It sounds like things are getting desperate."

He sighs again, louder this time. "I thought living on Thalia Island meant we were free of such petty suburban dramas."

"What did you expect when you put all these millennials in a fishbowl? Like Jeff Goldblum says in *Jurassic Park*, 'Uh, life finds a way.'"

"Ian Malcolm."

"I'm sorry?"

"Jeff Goldblum doesn't say that. Dr. Ian Malcolm says that," Rupert replies.

"Oh, forgive me, *nerd*." Humboldt farts in the back seat; I lower my window so I don't die. "Rupert, why did she leave? Why didn't Jacinta at least say goodbye? Will I ever see her again?"

He lowers his voice; it sounds like he's very close to the phone's mic. Guessing he's not alone. "She is safe. That's all I can tell you right now. Please, don't go looking for her. It will only trigger more red flags."

"Does Len Emmerich know that Jacinta was on the island?"

"No."

"And you don't want him knowing?"

"Absolutely not."

It's my turn to sigh. "Too many unanswered questions here, Rupert," I say, leaning my head against the car's frame. I consider telling him about the payments to Hale Watts in Jacinta's spreadsheet, but until I have a more comprehensive understanding of the bigger picture, I'll share this discovery only with Finan.

"Please be diligent about reporting your itinerary to Len Emmerich. He and his team are on the island for a reason."

"We're still in jeopardy, Rupert. Watts said so. Until Iona is picked up, she's not done with this place. Or with me."

"That is why Len Emmerich is your new best friend."

"Ha."

"I'm gravely serious about this, Lara. You are not to leave the island without informing Len. If you and Finan decide to take a boat ride, you will give Len forewarning so he can arrange to have someone accompany you."

"How romantic," I say, though my heart's not in it. Knowing Iona is out there waiting for a slip-up, something to give her an in, is enough to keep me onside with Rupert's requests.

"I need to go. Thumbelina is here."

"Tell her I said hello."

"Don't encourage her," he says, and then disconnects.

FORTY-SIX

DIG DEEPER

I give Humboldt an early dinner and set myself up on the couch with both laptops and phones. Finan's last text said he'd be out at vertical farm B until at least six and then he'd handle dinner, if I can wait that long. Definitely can wait—gives me more time to pull out my internet shovel and set to digging.

I log into a VPN, open an incognito browser, and bring up my work email, rereading the correspondence I strongly suspect is from Hale Watts: *"Found this carrot. I know how much you like carrots. They make excellent cake."*

Did I make a joke about Ainsley and her famous carrots to Hale?

I'm on a secure connection, so if this link is a virus, I have no idea what havoc it will wreak, but at least I won't take down Lutris and the rest of the island with me.

And I have to know what "carrot" he's dangling.

Click.

The screen opens to a plain gray desktop, the URL a series of numbers—an IP address? In the middle is a singular file folder labeled *"Daucus carota* subsp. *sativus."*

It's the only file. I hold my breath and double-click to open it.

Inside is a list of PDFs with titles that start with numbers and therefore don't make sense at first glance. It's obviously someone else's filing system, and I will have to decipher it to figure out what lies within. But the longer I scan, the clearer it becomes. The file numbers are in date order, reaching back to the 1990s. I click the first one.

It's a transcribed conversation ... between Archibald M. Clarke I and one Casimiro Aguado. At the top of the PDF is a black box with a gray arrow embedded in the page. I click on it.

It's audio. My grandfather's voice fills my living room. Head-to-toe chills consume me.

"Holy shit."

I listen for about a minute to the back-and-forth between Archibald and this man whose accent isn't always consistent. The conversation starts out friendly enough but doesn't take long to "get down to business," as Casimiro says.

I press stop. Then scan and open the next file and the next and the next. Not all have embedded recordings, but they are *all* conversations between other parties and my grandfather, *all* of them relating to Cordelia's involvement in unsavory activities—and the threats being made to keep her secrets quiet.

My heart pounds painfully as I open the files that were made after her death.

More of the same.

Casimiro Aguado wants his cache of red beryl back. Archibald Clarke has no idea what he's talking about but offers to buy him some new rocks if it will end this ridiculous intrusion. "I want *my* treasure. My stones have been blessed by Her Royal Eminence, Tiamat of Babylon, and your daughter and her lover stole them."

So then the blackmail stage is set, Casimiro extorting my grandfather for *huge* sums to keep Cordelia's involvement with the Sinaloa Cartel quiet—to keep the Garcia and Ramirez brothers out of my grandfather's very prosperous yard, so to speak—unless Cordelia gives up the red beryl.

"What the fuck? How did you even get these?" I ask the invisible Hale Watts in my living room. These conversations must be from wiretaps or maybe even video surveillance, then transcribed into written documents by someone my grandfather trusted. Who made these files? Would Rupert have typed up these conversations? I cannot imagine him trusting anyone else with information this sensitive.

Shit, this means Hale Watts knows *everything*.

Everything except where Jacinta Ramirez is right this second.

Nervous sweat coats my underarms and upper lip and the back of my neck.

As I scan through, it's clear Casimiro Aguado had uncovered the truth about Cordelia and Jacinta and their philanthropic activities in Mexico, and if he's bullshitting, he's a convincing liar. My grandfather attempts to reason with him throughout the conversations, reminding him that he, too, could uncover Casimiro's growing fascination with the cult lifestyle, how international financial regulators would be very interested in Aguado's money laundering and other illegal schemes, to which he repeatedly answered that he has "friends in high places. No one will touch me."

The last "carrot" in the file is dated 2016, and it isn't Casimiro in this conversation—it's a woman with an unremarkable accent who refuses to identify herself by name but promises that the Aguado family, and Dea Vitae, isn't done with the Clarkes. My grandfather again reminds the Aguado representative that "for the *last time*, I have no idea what these silly stones are or where my late daughter may have concealed them. This has become tiresome."

Could this unidentified female be Iona? If the FBI and Interpol information is correct, she's four years younger than I am, so in 2016, she would've been twenty-two. Old enough to hide her Scottish roots laced in her speech patterns? The threatening parry on this page sounds very similar to the prior transcripts with Aguado, maybe even sharper.

Very well could be Iona, which would make this my first possible lead that connects the two of them.

Except the other person in the exchange who could confirm all this —Archibald M. Clarke—is dead.

If Rupert transcribed these calls, he would recognize her voice, wouldn't he?

And yet Iona still ended up on our island as sweet grad student Ainsley Kerr. She fooled us all. *How?*

One by one, I download and print all the PDFs, just in case this website disappears, which is likely—Hale Watts doesn't seem a total moron. But I am still flummoxed about how and where he acquired these super-secret conversations. Is he a hacker too?

Once everything is downloaded and saved and printed for backup, I close the website and open another private browser to search for Casimiro Aguado. Based on the cursory examination of the transcribed dialogues, he is not as kind and philanthropic as Hale Watts made him sound. In fact, sounds like Aguado was a sizable sleazebag who profited handsomely off my grandfather's fear of exposure.

And for what? Kelly Lockhart blew that can wide open at her little town hall symposium wherein she laid bare my mother's past. Did Iona put her up to that, even after all the money paid to keep them quiet?

Looks like Aguado didn't bother to hire scrubbers to clean him off the web, which makes sense, given the nature of the articles that come up—this guy is a class A narcissist. Photos of him posing with groups of people in exotic locations, some clearly at geological sites while others involve Speedos and bikinis and showcase the aqua waters of paradise stretching into the background. He's handsome in that eccentric way—nose a little too big and eyes a little too far apart, sort of like pre-gray Richard Gere if Richard Gere were a Spanish billionaire draped in nubile, buxom adorers.

The articles online talk mostly about his money, his love of geology, his ventures wherein he gave a lot of dough to geology and archaeology projects globally, including a meaty donation to the University of Babylon in Hillah, Iraq, nestled in the heart of ancient Mesopotamia.

Tiamat is his chosen Babylonian goddess. Is that why he gave an Iraqi university such a hefty endowment, or did he discover her there while on a geological adventure in the ruins of early civilization?

A few pages into the search results, the first articles about Aguado's parareligious activities surface. If it's this easy to find stuff about him online, no wonder Wes Singh knows so much—except for the bits about him extorting Archibald Clarke. Did Rupert keep that from Wes too?

Looks like Casimiro definitely wanted to launch his own church, but when he failed via mainstream efforts, he veered a little too far into Crazy Town and decided to "start a family, one that honors the return of our beloved salt sea goddess, Tiamat of Babylon."

Yes, I'm all for religious freedoms, but come on, that's cuckoo pants.

The next article is in Arabic, a photo of a crowd of Iraqi, university-age students in front of a rough brick temple in the middle of a desert landscape, the group surrounding Casimiro standing before a lusciously sculpted, sand-colored figure of a woman I presume is Tiamat—is this where it all started?

The next article is a scanned clip from an Edinburgh newspaper, but there's no visible date, other than the date of upload. Looks like the '80s or early '90s, judging by the hairstyles. My heart accelerates again. More photos of Casimiro in front of another elegant sculpture—this one bronze—and more young students. It's obvious he would have had plenty of opportunity to be around willing, starry-eyed students, plenty of chances to make a baby Iona.

Is her mother somewhere in this photo of fresh-faced, apple-cheeked young adults?

Interestingly, none of these articles directly refer to Aguado's "family" by the cult's name, Dea Vitae. Looking that up specifically brings the same articles I've already seen, plus the new ones from the recent developments here on Thalia and elsewhere in Canada, the local media outlets offering photos of news conferences and task force briefings in their dance to share as little information as possible with the public. Safe to say, however, Dea Vitae is no longer in the shadows.

The last article with any useful crumbs is from 2015 and talks about Casimiro's sudden disappearance from public life. Some conjecture exists about a possible devastating diagnosis that pulled him behind the curtain, but then he just fades into the sunset with mentions only in tribute to the charitable gifts bestowed around the world.

That timing would align with the transcribed conversation with the unnamed woman in 2016.

Speaking of, I want to look up Iona next, so I click on one more hit with Casimiro Aguado's name in it—an article from a Spanish newspaper in Madrid. The browser offers to translate it for me, again quietly reminding me of my linguistic shortcomings. It's about Aguado's significant estate and the fight over who gets it.

Is he definitely dead, then?

I scan ... according to this, there is an ongoing legal battle among blood relatives and Dea Vitae "family members" to control his financial empire as he is no longer capable of doing so.

Not dead, then. Maybe Alzheimer's or something equally degenerative and incapacitating?

I search for Iona MacChruim. A half hour into the rabbit hole of scanning every article that mentions her name, I cannot find any connection between Iona and Casimiro beyond the potential link from Watts's "carrots"—no Scottish-sounding names come up in the coverage of the cat fight over Aguado's hoard. Plenty of most-wanted posters and articles about the recent trouble Iona's caused, including a lengthy piece in the *Vancouver Sun* about how she's the head of this scary cult taking the Pacific Northwest by storm. The article contains *so* much of the same information as what Hale Watts gave us, the writer *must* know Hale, must have consulted him as the anonymous source.

Hale Watts can't get any respect in the journalism community anymore, so he's tapped a former colleague to bash the pans together on his behalf? Smart.

My back and leg are aching—the latest round of analgesics has worn off—so I carefully pull myself to standing, stretch, and wander into the kitchen to swallow a few more ibuprofen, sticking my finger in Andromache's pot to make sure she's not thirsty too. Upon looking out the kitchen window, across to Finan's quiet cabin, a pang of sadness buffets into me.

My grandfather was being blackmailed because of my mother's terrible life choices.

We had a miscarriage.

Jacinta is gone.

It's this last thing that hits me harder than expected. I swipe the tears off my cheek, questioning why I'm so sad about her disappearing. Maybe because it feels like losing my mom all over again? Jacinta was my strongest tie to Cordelia. Yes, Rupert knew my mother, but not like Jacinta did. By the sounds of things, they were each other's soul mate. And the few times Jacinta was here in my cabin, making me a delicious meal and telling stories in her melodic voice, her long ponytail swishing and her smile wide and bright as she moved about the space ...

I'm so sad she's left, and that she did so without telling me she was going.

I want to know more about her, more about her time with my mother.

Cane in hand, I amble to the sideboard and retrieve the album with my mother's correspondence, printed out but quickly tucked away after upsetting Jacinta on her last visit. I don't know specifically what I'm looking for, so I grab the thumb drive from my purse again, just in case.

Perhaps I will find more of Hale Watts—or Casimiro Aguado—hiding in the ivy-covered lattice of the tragic story of Cordelia Clarke and Jacinta Ramirez.

FORTY-SEVEN

EXTORTION IS THE NEW BLACK

F inan walks in just after seven, a cloth takeout bag from Tommy's in hand and a fresh bottle of wine under his arm. When he sees my puffy eyes and tear-stained face, he puts everything down, moves the laptops, and melts into the couch beside me. "What's going on, L?"

I cry harder now that he's here, everything a tidal wave. The little voice in the back of my head reminds me these are leftover hormones, which makes it worse, a reminder that what was there two weeks ago is no longer.

Finan lets go and looks at the album and loose pages on my lap and spread out to my left. Humboldt has squeezed between my legs and the coffee table, his droopy eyes worried as he whimpers and flaps his tail against the floor.

"What's all this?" Finan picks up the top page. "Ah." He scans the letter from Cordelia, this one about her adventures in Kenya, photographing orphaned elephants and their keepers at the Sheldrick Wildlife Trust. He smiles at the crudely drawn baby elephant at the bottom of the page. "She sure loved the creatures."

I nod and reach to scrub Humboldt's broad head.

"Why are you looking through all this right now, if it just makes you sad? Haven't you had enough trauma lately?" He places the letter back onto the stack and rests his warm, wide hand against my nape, his thumb caressing below my ear.

"Hale Watts."

Finan's hand pauses, squeezing my neck for a beat. "What about him?" he growls.

"No, no, it's fine. I mean, it's *not* fine. He sent me a link to a site with a bunch of transcribed conversations, including raw audio, wherein Casimiro Aguado was blackmailing my grandfather to keep quiet about Cordelia's involvement with the cartel, so that's some real bullshit, but I was just looking through these to see if Mom ever mentioned Hale or Casimiro directly. Hale said he knew Cordelia and Jacinta, so I'm still looking to see if she ever mentioned either of them in her letters."

"And nothing so far?"

I shake my head. "It would make sense to not mention Aguado. Who knows if Cordelia knew about the blackmail before she died. And of course, after she died, no way to know if Jacinta was aware of what was going on because she's vanished, and I can't ask her."

"You talked to Rupert?"

"Yes. He won't tell me where Jacinta is. Only that she's safe."

"Did you tell him about this new info from Watts?"

"No. I opened the link after I talked to Rupert. I don't know if I should tell him, though. Not yet."

Finan pulls his hand away and leans forward, elbows on bent knees, hand rubbing at his beard the way he does when thinking. "You think Rupert told Jacinta we'd spoken to Hale?"

"Maybe. Even though I don't know what the point of that would be. Unless Jacinta is afraid of him somehow?"

"You saw how he looked when he asked if we knew where she was. Almost ... *hungry*."

I wipe my face on the sleeve of my shirt and gently lean forward to grab my laptop. I click open the thumb drive again—and show Finan the spreadsheets listing the cash payments to Hale Watts.

His eyes grow dark as he scans. "Why the hell would they have paid him so much?"

"I don't know. Was he doing some work for them, maybe as an investigative journalist? Rupert said Archibald sent Watts to Mexico to look for Cordelia after her plane went down—he'd convinced my grandfather Cordelia was still alive."

"But those payments wouldn't be included here. That was Archibald's business, not Jacinta's." Finan looks at the spreadsheet again. "When did Cordelia die?"

"August 2000."

"Two of these payments are dated before her death—and three are after, the last one in 2005 for $75,000. That is a shit ton of money for some"—he air-quotes—"'investigative journalism.'"

I hadn't thought to note when the payments were made. "Do you remember if Rupert mentioned what year Jacinta made it into Canada?"

"I don't think he did."

"But it would make sense—if they were paying Hale Watts before Cordelia died, maybe it was for work he was doing for them, but the payments *after*, what if those were to keep him quiet about something? Those payments are the biggest, and the closest together," I say.

"Quiet about something—like where Jacinta was."

"Do you think Hale Watts was blackmailing Jacinta, after she escaped from her brothers?"

Finan sighs heavily. "I think it's a big possibility. Would explain why Rupert won't tell us, or Wes or anyone, for that matter, where she is."

Oh my god, that makes perfect sense. Now I feel terrible that I was prepared to tear Jacinta into strips about her deceit. She's just trying to stay alive, to stay away from the hounds out there who want to sink their teeth into her flesh.

"Why would the brothers care if Jacinta was still alive? Don't you think they would give up after all these years, to leave her alone?"

Finan shrugs and then slides my laptop back onto the coffee table. "Family is weird. Some people have a harder time letting go of things,

I guess. And everything I've heard about the cartel system—no one escapes. At least not alive."

"So basically everyone was blackmailing everyone else here. What a great group of people my mother managed to collect."

The corner of Finan's lips tug, as if to smile, but his face is sad. Humboldt barks once, making me flinch painfully. "He needs dinner." Finan stands but helps me up first.

"Too much activity today. I feel like an old woman. Everything creaks and hurts."

"Getting impaled will do that to a person," he says, kissing me softly. "Come on. Let's put food in your growling belly. Then a bath, then bed. Enough of this for tonight."

I glance at the ominous pile of unanswered questions spread all over the couch and coffee table.

"I wish she hadn't left. If she'd just waited, she could've explained things."

Finan pets the back of my head. "I know. Maybe she'll be back, talk to you then."

"I hope she's safe," I say, voice cracking.

Gently, he pulls me against him. "If Rupert is involved, you know she is."

A panicked thought stabs through me like a bolt of lightning. "Oh my god, what if he dies? What will happen to her then?"

Finan wraps his big hands around my cheeks and makes me look at him. "You are overtired. Seriously, let's take this one clue at a time. Don't start thinking about what-ifs."

I nod against his curiously soft palms. "OK. You're right."

"Food. Wine. Bath. Sleep. That is what you are to worry about for the rest of this evening." He kisses me.

But even as I tick off everything on that list, just as the lightweight cotton sheet drapes over my shoulders and the man of my dreams eases into his own rest beside me, my mind isn't ready to turn out the lights just yet, instead poring over the conversations and transcribed notes and articles. The inside of my head looks like the oversized bulletin board of a slightly off-kilter investigator—pictures and notes and pieces of evidence, all linked together with thumbtacks and red yarn—the crime underneath begging to be solved, screaming at the onlooker: "I'M RIGHT HERE. THE ANSWER IS RIGHT HERE, YOU DUMMY."

The last thing I remember before falling asleep is the weight of Finan's hand on my shoulder and the feeling of calm that washes over me.

One clue at a time.

FORTY-EIGHT

PUZZLE IT OUT

Dakota is taking her job as my physical therapist a little too seriously. She shows up at town hall at noon on the dot, every weekday, without fail, and forces me out of my cute sandals and into sneakers and then makes me stretch, followed by a walk around the neighborhood, rain or shine, of which we have both, considering it's late July in British Columbia. Our summers are absolutely hotter than they were when I was a kid, but Dakota says global warming is not an excuse for me to not exercise, so she makes sure I stay hydrated and consume my share of Thalia's bounteous summer fruits.

After the overwhelming Monday—finding the bunker, discovering Jacinta's disappearance, and reading through Hale Watts's garden of terrible, wormy carrots—it's as though the old gods and the new said, "OK, guys, foot off the gas. Let's give Lara a second to breathe." I couldn't be more grateful.

At night, Finan and I spend hours going over the conversations and transcripts, listening and scanning for any new information that might eventually be of use to Wes and his investigators—because we will definitely have to turn all this over at some point if we want to stop Dea Vitae from multiplying. Iona MacChruim is still on the lam, but that doesn't mean she's not near.

Every time I think of her, I shudder. Knowing what these people are capable of, the threats Casimiro exchanged with my grandfather, the horrors of what the cartel might actually do to Jacinta if they get hold of her again …

It makes for uncomfortable bedtime reading that births distressing nightmares.

But Dakota's daytime efforts to fix my broken body are working. I was able to ditch the cane after the first week, and I've been testing my pain tolerance around the house while wearing my beloved high heels. Finan approves of this—short shorts, Louboutins, a vacuum cleaner in hand. Thankfully, the physical therapy has also meant that I'm able to tolerate *other* activities involving skin and bone. And my bearded hunk of man meat is enjoying the process of christening various parts of our cabins where his body weight on top of me isn't required.

Definitely getting my groove back.

Proven to everyone during the party on Monday, August 9, when we welcome our newest settlers. Food, dancing, the official debut of our Thalia Island Wandering Salamander microbrews, enough ice cream that even Harmony put a hand up after her third helping. That kid continues to amaze me, weathering her parents' marital storm like a seasoned mariner. Her dad moved into his own tiny house last week, and Harmony followed him, despite her mother's shrieks heard island-wide that she had to stay with Gillian. After a sit-down with Mrs. Corwin, Catrina, and Tommy, Gillian and Zackery Peck agreed that getting lawyers involved at this point would require them leaving Thalia Island and going back to Vancouver, so why not let Harmony choose where she wants to live?

It worked.

And Harmony has been floating ever since she moved her stethoscope, suture kit, and medical books into the tiny six-by-six nook that is *all hers*. "Don't have to listen to my asshole little sister scream about wanting the boob anymore. This is the life," she said, stretching on her bunk as she showed me around their new place.

She's otherwise stitched to my side during the workweek, trading off Humboldt duty with Finan, who's been busy with the vertical farm B rebuild, the first stage of which is slated for completion by September 1. On the weekends, Harmony pedals her little heart out and pops up on my porch, asking if she can bake cookies in my kitchen or if Humboldt needs a bath or if Finan has any new work injuries that need tending. "Staphylococcus is no laughing matter, Mr. Rowleigh," she chides as she bathes his cuts in ointment and wraps them in Band-Aids he'll discard as soon as she's back on her bike.

It's nice when she's around. Neither of us says it, but it's a glimpse … of maybe. Someday.

As Finan and I lie tangled in my bedsheets, the evening's libations still on our breaths, our bodies sweaty and spent, I make a joke that if we did ever have a kid, there's no guarantee they'd be like Harmony.

"Is that a bad thing?" Finan teases. I nudge his ribs and roll onto my side to kiss his nipple and drape my right leg across him. "Nah, she's incredible."

"She is. I'd just be afraid we'd get a dummy. I wasn't good in school."

"You're far from dumb, Lara, and you know it."

"Still …"

"We would have an awesome kid. Look how well you've done with Humboldt." He snickers.

"Oh, good. So I'd be able to teach my kid to sit, stay, and not eat the couch."

"It's a start."

I pinch his side. He flinches and rolls so he's over the top of me, his legs scissored, trapping me beneath him. "Speaking of starts," he says, his voice husky, "I can't seem to stop now that you're healed."

"Who's asking you to stop?" I pull him into me, devouring his lips and opening myself to him so we can pick up where we left off.

"I need a shower," I say, the sun teasing the horizon, painting the early sky in soft oranges and pinks. Finan groans and rolls over, his hair a mess, the musk of our entanglement heavy on his skin. But before his body can respond to my imminent departure, Humboldt bounds onto the bed, his long chewy bone clenched in his slobbery jaw.

"OK, OK, we're up," Finan says, pushing the dog off the bed. He stands and stretches, giving me a million-dollar view of the perfection that is Finan Rowleigh's body. "Are you checking me out?" He smirks.

"Always."

He pauses at the tufted armchair in the corner to slide into sweats and his T-shirt, lifting the gauzy curtain to look outside. "Red sky at night, sailor's delight. Red sky in the morning, sailor take warning."

"Is the sky red?"

"Pink."

"Is that your professional meteorological opinion, sir?"

"Definitely," he says. "I'll start coffee. Meet you in the shower?"

"Mmm, aye-aye, captain."

I ease out of bed and give my body a chance to adjust, relishing that the soreness I've awoken with comes from a wholly different, more enjoyable source than this summer's prior mishaps. I slog into the bathroom, melting under the shower head as the waterfall cascades over my hair and shoulders and down my body. Finan steps in just as I'm lathering up.

"Is your stomach ever not growling?" he teases.

"I was just thinking about that frittata Jacinta made during one of her visits. I wish she'd left me the recipe."

"I could manage one of those."

"Yeah?" I ask, eyes closed and head back as he scrubs shampoo into my scalp.

"Has Harmony mentioned her again? After she saw Jacinta in the field?" he asks.

"No. Hoping she just forgot. And then she felt so bad after the picture frame broke."

"She broke it?"

"Humboldt's tail broke it."

"Ah. Time to rinse," he says, grabbing the flexible shower hose and holding it over my soapy hair.

I'm about to remark on how heavenly this is, how I will definitely find a way to repay him for his personalized salon services, when a line pops into my head:

JRCCLC070792

The number on the back of the photograph of me and Mom and Jacinta.

"Oh my god."

"What?"

"I have to get out. Hurry. Rinse me off."

"Lara, what's going on?"

Once I'm rinsed, I flee from the shower, throw on my plush robe, wrap my wet hair in a towel, and scurry into the living room. MacBook open, I plug in the thumb drive and open the Finder.

Double-click on the password-protected file labeled "JR."

When the password box comes up, I type "JRCCLC070792."

The file opens. I'm trembling.

"Finan!" I yell.

The shower shuts off. Finan, dripping on the hardwood, stands at the kitchen threshold in nothing but a bath sheet. "Are you all right?"

"The password. The file opened."

He quickly dries off, wraps the huge towel around his waist, and tiptoes over. "What file?"

"On the thumb drive Rupert gave me—there's a password-protected file labeled *JR*. I've been trying to open it for months. The back of the photo in that frame we took from the bunker had 'JRC-CLC070792' written on it. It's our initials plus the date the photo was taken."

"And that's the password?"

I grin, as if I've just unlocked the secrets of the universe.

Except the opened folder doesn't hold much. I double-click on the first item and it fills the screen. Numbers, and half of that Carl Sagan quote: *Survival is the exception.*

"Great. Another puzzle." My grin fades.

"Wait—no—those are coordinates." Finan leans closer to the screen. "Yeah, those are latitude and longitude."

"To *what?*"

"Grab the secure laptop."

I hustle into my room and pull the boxy computer from its hiding place in my armoire, setting it on the breakfast bar. As soon as it's awake, Finan opens a browser and asks me to read the series of numbers. A map pops up; he scrolls and zooms in.

"Is that ... Mt. Magnus?" I ask. He scrubs a hand down his face, through his beard, eyes wide as he stares at the map on the screen.

I yank my grandfather's ring off my middle finger.

Survival is the exception. On the plaque at Mt. Magnus.

Extinction is the rule. On the inside of his ring.

He knew. Archibald knew where she put the stones, and so does Jacinta.

"Finan ... the red beryl ... it's *here.*"

FORTY-NINE

SNAKE IN THE WEEDS

"What do you mean ..." Finan pales.

"I mean, it's *here*." I show him the inside of Grandfather's ring. "The first half of this quote is on the plaque at Mt. Magnus. This, plus the coordinates ... they're clues, Finan."

He doesn't say anything.

"But when would she have had time to bury it? Did they do it together, before my mother died, or was it something Jacinta did later on her own? I thought no one was on the island until a few years ago."

"Obviously Jacinta has been here longer than we originally suspected," he says.

"Unless Archibald—or even Rupert—did it."

"Possible, but unlikely." Humboldt scratches at the closed screen door. Finan rises to let him in. "I'll make coffee. You get dressed," he says.

"Do you think I should call Rupert? Ask him if he knows ..."

Finan's already shaking his head. "Let's wait."

"The stones are up there, Finan. They have to be."

He leans against the counter while the kettle simmers, all muscles and smooth skin. "Maybe. But Mt. Magnus is a big place. It's not like we can use a metal detector or infrared to scan for it."

"And we can't use a hound dog because all our dog does is drool." Humboldt, planted next to his treat drawer, quirks his head at me, as if he knows I'm making fun of him.

"He found the bunker, didn't he?"

I smirk. "Yes, he did. But I don't happen to have any fresh red beryl on me to give him a lead." I look down at my grandfather's ring on my finger. I still don't know if this stone is beryl or ruby or something else entirely. I'm too afraid to find out. "What about the plaque, though? What if it's hidden in that stump?"

Finan gnaws at his lip. "Maybe."

"That would fit the clues with the Carl Sagan quote cut in half, on the ring and on the plaque."

"Or else it's a red herring simply because Archibald loved that quote."

The kettle boils. I watch Finan as he scoops freshly ground coffee into the French press. "If you keep ogling me like that, I'm going to have to file a complaint."

"You can file it in my panties."

His laugh startles the dog. "Put some clothes on while this steeps. Otherwise, we'll be late for work. Again."

"Work? I'm not going into the office yet. I'm going up the mountain. To look."

"Where?"

"I'll start with the plaque. Do you have a crowbar in your truck?"

"Pause—you can't go up there alone. You know the rules. Also, we have meetings this morning. Can we agree to go about business as usual so we don't call attention to ourselves, and then at lunch, we can head up and look around?"

"Finan, seriously? This is way more important than listening to Mrs. Corwin nag me about skipping the pottery class I signed up for."

He moves across the kitchen and leans on the counter, resting his hand against my cheek. "Please, Lara, I want to keep you safe. Can you let me do that?"

I hate how sensible he is sometimes. But he's right. If we don't make an appearance at the meeting, alarm bells will go off, and Len

Emmerich and his muscled militia will throw a hissy fit when I *do* finally show up.

Plus it's kinda sweet that this half-wrapped snack cares about me.

"Fiiiiiine," I moan dramatically, sliding off my stool, stopping just long enough to kiss Finan and grab his tight butt through the towel.

In the bathroom, I moisturize my skin and pull product through my hair. I left it wrapped in the towel too long, and now I don't have time to dry and curl it, so topknot it is. As I pull on a fitted sundress and pluck my favorite Hermès sandals from the closet, I already know concentrating this morning is going to be impossible. The council meeting first thing is to tie up loose ends with the new settlers; the widespread storm damage still isn't fully managed; and we have to talk to the contractor about the repairs still needed out at the solar array field.

And that's just before lunch. Beyond that, Finan and I have been summoned to appear in Vancouver next week for the rescheduled testimony in the ongoing civil action with Kelly Lockhart; and Rupert is supposed to be going in for his last immunotherapy session this Thursday.

Too much going on. Too many spinning plates.

And *none* of it feels nearly as important as going up to Mt. Magnus with a crowbar and a prayer to uncover whatever Jacinta has hidden for me somewhere around 48° and 123°.

"Lara …" Finan's head pokes around the door to my room. "Come here for a sec?" He's pulled on fresh clothes from his overnight bag in the bathroom. Too bad. I liked him naked.

"What is that look on your face?" I didn't hear Lutris shriek, none of our phones went off, no one banged on the front door with a giant rock, Humboldt hasn't been outside long enough to tangle with any wildlife, and as far as I know, no incoming nuclear attack has rained from the sky so far today. "You're making me nervous."

"Just … come here."

I slide on my second sandal, take one last look in the mirror, and follow Finan out.

The secure laptop is still open on the counter. He moves in front of it and then positions so I can see the screen.

"What am I looking at ..." I don't have to finish the sentence. I recognize this site. It's Hale Watts's blog. He's written a new piece, and its headline screams at me in angry, bold letters:

"DAUGHTER OF ARCHIBALD CLARKE I HEAVILY INVOLVED WITH SINALOA CARTEL; LOVER AND ACCOMPLICE IS HIDING IN BRITISH COLUMBIA."

Finan's hand weighs heavily on my shoulder but my fists are knotted so hard, my arms shake.

"Hale Watts is a dead man."

FIFTY

RED SKY IN THE MORNING

I call Rupert on our way into downtown. "Hale Watts outed my mother—and Jacinta—on his blog."

I have to repeat it for him twice.

"For fuck's sake," Rupert says, followed by a heavy exhale. "Did you tell him *anything* about Jacinta? Anything at all, Lara—*think!* This is a matter of life and death."

"NO! I swear. Finan was there with me when Watts found us at Clarke Manor. *I swear*, we did not say a thing about her. Whatever information he's used for this article definitely has not come from me, Rupert. I promise."

I can hear his teeth grind through the phone. "That man is a stain."

"I'm so sorry."

"Her brothers will come looking. Dea Vitae is going to be on us like flies on fresh offal. And now I have to tell Wes everything. I cannot protect Jacinta if I don't." He's quiet for a moment. "Where are you now?"

"Heading into work. I figured out the password to that JR file on the thumb drive."

"And?"

"And ... the file contains what look like coordinates, in addition to half of Grandfather's favorite Carl Sagan quote."

"Coordinates to what?"

"Mt. Magnus. We think the red beryl is up there, Rupert."

He sighs again. "Jesus, come take me now."

"We've got meetings this morning, but after, we'll go up and look—"

"Absolutely not. Stay off the mountain until I talk to Wes. We will need to have a secure meeting—you, me, Finan, Wes, and Len Emmerich. Everything has now escalated, especially with that pitiful troll posting his vicious vomit all over his blog. Only a matter of time before the press gets wind of this."

As if on queue, his other cell phone rings in the background. "Speak of the devil ..."

A chill has wrapped itself around my whole body, despite the warm summer air flowing in from the open truck window.

"I'll be in touch. Keep the secure phone near." Rupert disconnects.

"He said to wait?" Finan asks as he slows and pulls into a diagonal Main Street spot down the way from town hall.

"Yes. We're going to have a secure meeting with Wes and Len first, and he wants us to stay away from Mt. Magnus."

Finan bobs his head as he turns off the truck and unhooks his belt. He leans over and drapes his manly paw over my clammy hand. "I love you. Everything will be OK."

"Promise?"

"Pinkie promise," he says.

It's an absolutely fair estimation to say that 10 percent of my brain is on Mrs. Corwin and her unending agenda and 90 percent on WTF is going on with Hale Watts, Jacinta Ramirez, Mt. Magnus, and Dea Vitae.

How could all this carnage come from a pile of red rocks? They're not even worth much in terms of money—couldn't Casimiro Aguado just buy another box of pretty magic stones and then have a dream orgy with his water queen and leave my family out of it?

Oh, Mom, why did you always have to thrust a spear into the wasps' nest?

The meeting finally adjourned, Finan and I pause long enough in the break room to make more coffee. Our late nights have been fun, but the bags under our eyes give us away. I tease him that tonight, before we get naked, we will do masks. Rehydrate our skin. Reclaim our youthful glow.

He kisses me, almost too deliciously, before heading out, freshly refilled Thalia Island travel mug in hand. "We should do salmon tonight. Tommy's guy is coming by today," he says on his way out the door.

"You cook, I'll eat!"

Despite the tempest roiling around everything else, I am, in this moment, incredibly grateful for the safe harbor that is Finan Rowleigh.

Harmony is a little late today—her last day of this three-week break before school restarts tomorrow—arriving at lunch with a bundle of fresh wildflowers in hand and a long-winded story about how she got to spend the morning with her dad in his lab and that he's ordering her a new bike since she's outgrown her current one and how she's decided that at Thursday's paint night, she's going to do a portrait of me with Humboldt instead of just Humboldt this time, so I should wear a color that makes my eyes "pop." Her words.

"What jobs do you have for me today?"

I send her to Dakota first—she needs help rolling cutlery, refilling condiment bottles, and unpacking the new Wandering Salamander coasters that arrived yesterday. Then to Catrina at the café to wash produce for salads and peel potatoes for hash browns. The mail bag arrives while Harmony is out, awaiting her return, which happens just after three, her sweaty body skateboarding around the corner and into my office.

"Mail call!" She drops a letter on my desk.

"Thank you," I say, my attention on the invoices displayed across my screen. Mrs. Corwin alleges that the lighting contractor on farm B has billed us twice for the same LED system, so I'm trying to find the invoices to show her she's wrong, that the systems we were billed for are, in fact, separate.

"Can you finish the mail from Canada Post?" I ask, pointing in the general direction of the mail bag.

"Where's Big Dog?"

"Out with Finan." I then mumble under my breath about Mrs. Corwin not knowing how to read invoices. "Give me a sec, Harmony."

She props her skateboard against the couch—new protocol after a near miss when I was still using the cane, which resulted in a stern talking-to from Dakota about how we can't leave the board where Lara can trip on it—and grabs the Canada Post bag. She says something to me about needing a new time card but then hops out my door and into the lobby.

I hit Print on the invoices in question and flop back into my chair, sipping from my tepid coffee. The secure phone sits quiet on my desk. I pick it up and scroll to make sure I didn't miss anything from Rupert.

Not a peep.

The letter Harmony dropped on my desk leans against my bamboo pencil cup emblazoned with the Thalia Island logo. "Mail call," she'd said. That's weird … she hadn't unloaded the mail yet.

I pick up the envelope and turn it over. My name is written across the front.

The familiar handwriting thrusts my stomach into my feet.

I extract my letter opener and slice open the seam, withdrawing the single sheet of paper from within.

It's another grainy photograph.

But this one is of Finan.

"What the … HARMONY!" I'm up and out of my chair, running to the door. We collide in the hall. "Harmony, where did you get this letter? **Where did it come from?**" I hold it in front of her.

297

"A lady. I was skateboarding back from the diner. She stopped and asked if I would bring it to you."

I drop to my knees. "Harmony, this is very important." I'm trying to keep my voice calm, but my hands clenched around her arms are sending the wrong message. I relax my grip. "I need you to tell me *everything* about this woman. What did she look like? Exactly where did she give you this letter?"

Harmony nods, her eyes dampening with the threat of tears. "Am I in trouble?"

"Oh, god, no, sweetie," I say. "I just really need your help."

She nods again and drags the end of her blond ponytail around to her lips. I stand, pull out my phone, and call Len Emmerich. He's down the street in their offices. I tell him what's going on.

"On my way," he says.

"Meet us outside." With the letter and envelope, I drape a hand over Harmony's shoulder and steer her out of town hall. As we walk, I call Finan, begging him to pick up.

It goes to voicemail.

I call again, and again, and again.

Voicemail every time.

I text him: *Please call me as soon as you get this. I love you.*

Eyes glued to the screen, I wait for the three response bubbles to dance, to tell me he's OK and he's received my text and he's responding to assuage my paranoid, spiraling thoughts.

Len hurries down the sidewalk within a minute, accompanied by two of his guys. Harmony tells us everything she can remember about the messenger—a lady shorter than I am, long, black hair in a pony-tail, big sunglasses, a baseball hat, dark pants—and shows us exactly where the lady gave her the envelope. As soon as she says "long, black hair," my heart pounds so loud, it overwhelms my ears.

It couldn't have been Jacinta. She's not involved in this—she's not even *here*, at least according to Rupert. Plus, she would never do anything to hurt Finan. *Would she?*

Len takes the photo and envelope from me, slides it into yet another evidence bag, and then sends his guys to pull every camera angle from the last ten hours.

"Have you been able to reach Finan?" Len asks as he calls him himself and puts his phone against his ear. I watch, shaking with anxiety as Finan's familiar voicemail message echoes out of Len's phone speaker. "Check Lutris," he tells me. Of course! I hadn't thought of that.

I open the app and look for Finan's beaver avatar. "He's at the marina!" I say.

"You have a car downtown?"

"No, Finan drove us in."

"I'll be right back." Len pauses and puts his hands on my upper arms. "Lara, he's probably just working down at the dock. Either way, call Catrina. Send Harmony to Dr. Stillson. We need to do a quick-test to make sure there are no biohazards on the letter." He turns to Harmony, who now really does have tears streaming down her face. He kneels before her. "Don't be afraid. We just need to make sure you're not hurt."

"Did that letter have something on it that will make me and Lara sick?"

Len shakes his head, his voice soft. "We just want to find the lady who gave this to you. And since you didn't know who she was, that seems a little weird since we all know everyone else here, yeah?"

She nods her head and wipes her nose on her shoulder. "We're not gonna die, right?"

"Nooooo, of course not."

I dial Catrina. "I need you to come to town hall. Another letter has shown up. Can you take Harmony over to Liam? She and I are the only ones who've touched it so far ... yes, I'm with Len right now." My voice breaks as I see Catrina, still on the phone with me, bounding out of the diner across the street, eyes wide with concern. I disconnect and slide my phone back into my pocket.

Len sprints down the block to grab his vehicle, the bagged letter in his grip, just as Catrina skips toward us. "Hey, Harmony, let's go bug the doc about some more supplies for your medical bag, shall we?" Harmony nods and clamps onto Catrina's open palm.

I kneel and wrap her in a hug before they walk away. "I love you like my own kid, Harmony. I promise you didn't do anything wrong. Do you hear me? You and me, we're fighters. We're gonna be fine."

"And what about Finan? And Big Dog?"

"I'm sure this is all just a mix-up. Finan and Big Dog will be back by dinner, and we will all laugh at how silly we look, getting worked up over a dumb letter from some weird lady. It's probably just a practical joke."

But I can see by the look on Harmony's face that she doesn't believe me for a second. She knows this isn't a joke. She was one of the people who got sick with the salmonella poisoning; she was in town hall when I showed the slideshow of Kelly Lockhart murdering that raccoon; she knows we have more security here than before and that there are cameras hidden everywhere, even if the rest of the settlers aren't supposed to know about that.

Harmony is young, but she's also brilliant.

She lets go of Catrina's hand and wraps both her arms around my neck, about knocking me over. "You're my best friend, Lara. You and Big Dog. Please make sure everything is OK," she says, a fresh sob rocking through her.

I hold up my pinkie. She eases back and wraps hers around it, shaking on our deal.

"I'll see you in a bit," I say.

"I can finish the mail when I get back."

"Don't worry about that for now." I wave just as Len screeches to a halt along the curb. I hold up a hand to tell him to wait for a second and then skip-hop back into my office to grab the secure phone.

Once I'm in Len's truck, he flies out of downtown and to the marina, tearing into the lot in record time.

"That's his truck!" I say, yanking off my belt and opening the door almost before Len throws his rig into park.

"Lara, wait. Don't touch anything!" Len hollers after me, but I'm already flying toward Finan's vehicle.

The engine is still on.

"Lara!" Len jogs up behind me. He has now pulled on nitrile gloves and tries to move me away from the door handle, but I fight him off and open the truck, anyway.

"Len ... is that ... blood?"

The steering wheel, the seat, the floor mat.

And Finan's phone, the screen freshly cracked, on the console. I tap it and see all the missed calls and text messages piled on the spider-webbed screen.

I scream until the gods above beg me to stop.

~

END BOOK TWO

~ Book Three coming December 14, 2021! ~

Don't despair ... their happy ending is near.

Planet Lara

SANCTUARY

Book Three, **DECEMBER 14, 2021!**

S·G·A
BOOKS

COVER REVEAL
THIS FALL!

JOIN THE RAFT!

I f you want to be the first to hear about the **PREORDER** for the third book in the **Planet Lara trilogy**, *Planet Lara: Sanctuary*, join the Raft*. Publication date for Book Three is December 14, 2021. And there are more Eliza Gordon books coming in 2022!

Two ways to join the Raft: Join my private readers' group on Facebook, or sign up for my newsletter!

Welcome aboard!

In the wild, sea otters hold hands so they aren't separated in the tides. These groups of floating otters are called "rafts."

ACKNOWLEDGMENTS

Books are not written alone. It takes a team of superheroes to get this sh*t done. Here are my fellow word warriors:

Stacey Kondla, my fabulous agent, I'm so happy our paths crossed. I cannot wait for all three *Planet Lara* audiobooks from Dreamscape Media, thanks to you! Woohoo! Cheers to many more deals together, my friend. It's fun. Let's do it again and again times infinity.

Toni Freitas, my co-editor, and insanely intelligent environmental consultant, just ... wow. You already saved my book, so I'm pretty sure you're going to save the world too. Thank you for sharing your brain with me and picking up stuff I totally didn't even think about. People with your intellect and passion give me hope for what otherwise feels like a very bleak future. Keep up the good fight.

Katie Drenth, my secret weapon, the world's most incredible beta reader, book blogger, and author cheerleader. Your keen eye, terrific editorial insight, and endless excitement for all things Eliza Gordon are priceless. Seriously—you are outstanding.

Katrin Bartas and **Deb Hardy**, my little sweeties, thank you for always being my Very First Readers, for listening to me freak out, and for talking me off the ledge on the regular. I am so, so grateful Hollie Porter and Jayne Dandy made us friends.

Leslie Wibberley, accomplished author (and retired physiotherapist) who I met years ago at the gym where we bonded over our love of writing and books. Your friendship—along with Best-Hugs Bonnie, Katherine, Ronda, Kirsten, Margarita, Ami, Christine, Farida, and the whole Golden Ears gang—has changed the course of my life over the last six years. Thank you for making sure Lara had her cane in the proper hand, for catching my medical errors, and for always cheering me on so I don't give up. Your opinion means much to me!

Brandee Bublé for the continued love and crazy enthusiasm for the Eliza Gordon books. I am very much looking forward to *your* next book project, sister!

Jane Omelaniec, my best and longest-running friend, you know the drill. Thank you for sticking around and for not believing I'm a black hole.

Stephania Schwartz, writer and editor extraordinaire, for keeping me sane and on track through this last year of utter mayhem. Kiss Archer for me.

Bailey McGinn of Bailey Designs Books, *je t'adore*, and cannot wait to see your latest work in progress. It's going to be a five-star design, I'm sure! Give them 1000 kisses from Auntie Eliza/Jenn wayyyy over here in your gorgeous homeland.

Dr. Arvin Gee, assistant professor of surgery and trauma/critical care surgeon at Oregon Health Sciences University, who generously provided the details of what happens to Lara in that ONE CHAPTER. Told you guys it was gonna get juicy. And thank you to my brave, brilliant cousin **Ann Moffitt Whitson** for introducing us!

Staff Sergeant Tyner Gillies of the Royal Canadian Mounted Police (RCMP), fellow scribe and adopted little brother, who patiently explained to this expat how the RCMP works and how it is, in fact, different from American police agencies. Thanks for your time and for understanding that when I ask questions about DNA, body decomposition, forensics, and bioweapons, it's cool. It's for a "book." *insert maniacal laughter*

(As with all the expert advice collected for my books, any screw-ups are 100 percent mine.)

Carmen Jones of Tomes and Tales Books, Gifts & Tea, for ALWAYS selling my books (both Jenn Sommersby and Eliza Gordon titles), and for your enduring friendship. I cannot believe our babies will be graduating soon. Let's be friends forever, OK? Also, I can't wait to go book shopping and wine drinking in Victoria with you, so let me know.

Tamara Gorin of Western Sky Books for stocking *Planet Lara* in your store. I look forward to post-pandemic, bookish shenanigans!

(Locals, check out **Tomes and Tales**, **Western Sky Books**, and **Totally Bookish** (out in Mission—tell Ami that Eliza/Jenn sent you!) for all your book and gift needs. SUPPORT OUR LOCAL INDIE BOOKSTORES!)

My beta team—Katie, Katrin, Toni, Deb, Leslie, Miranda, Melena, Jeanine, and Valérie—seriously, without you guys, my books would suck. Your feedback and insight always improves my stories. Always. I'm fortunate to know some very clever humans.

My ARC team and Raftmates, the readers who post their reviews, share my books with friends, post teasers and graphics on social media, and lift me up when things feel too hard: Amber J., LJ, Katie (yes, again!), Stephanie B., Dr. Marsha, Dr. Kira, Vicki and Miss A, London Sarah, Louise V., Tammy, Anima-Christi, and all the Rafties in our FB group! Thank you for being part of Elizaland, even if *Planet Lara* isn't your favorite. It's been fun to stretch my wings—I hope you stick around for more fun to come!

Frontline and healthcare workers around the world … *thank you* for your continued service, even in the face of intolerable ignorance and soul-crushing exhaustion. Thank you to all the scientists whose big brains and endless dedication to humanity meant that I could gratefully become a proud member of House Moderna. COVID, you can fuck off now, thanks.

And last but never least, GareBear for twenty-one years of managing my madness and for the Howling Cat (my very favorite place in the whole wild world) where I can escape to write without one of the three tuxedo children begging for cookies or one of the three human children showing me yet another hilarious TikTok or YouTube video. And as far as kids go, my wee hobbits, Yaunna, Brennie, and KennyG, you know you're amazing. I tell you a hundred times a day, and I will tell you a hundred times more tomorrow. Also: Too many cherries or plums = you will have to poop a lot (especially if you go to soccer practice right after). Never forget!

Until December, my friends! Be safe out there and take care of one another.

ABOUT THE AUTHOR

A native of Portland, Oregon, Eliza Gordon (a.k.a. Jennifer Sommersby) has always lived along the West Coast. Since 2002, home has been a suburb of Vancouver, British Columbia. When not lost in a writing project, Eliza is a copy/line editor, mom, wife, bibliophile, Superman freak, and the humble servant to three pampered tuxedo cats (@tuxietrionurojo on Instagram!).

Eliza writes women's fiction and romantic comedies; Jennifer Sommersby writes young adult fiction. Her debut YA title, *Sleight*, was published in 2018 by HarperCollins Canada, Sky Pony (US), and Prószynski i S-ka (Poland). *Fish Out of Water*, a riff on *The Little Mermaid*, in conjunction with the wildly popular YouTube film production company, YAP TV, released in 2019. The sequel to *Sleight*, titled *Scheme* in the US (Sky Pony) and *The Undoing* in Canada (HarperCollins), released spring 2020. Eliza/Jenn are represented by Stacey Kondla at The Rights Factory.

WELCOME TO PLANET LARA, BOOK ONE

"There are ... stipulations on your inheritance, Ms. Clarke."

Lara J. Clarke is used to getting her own way. Motherless at ten and raised by her oft-absent eco-warrior/philanthropist grandfather, she lives the high life afforded by her seemingly bottomless trust fund.

That is, until Grandfather Archibald sheds his mortal coil in a very public manner, and Lara's privileged life is set adrift—and headed for a collision course with the gorgeous, private Thalia Island off the coast of British Columbia. According to the will, Lara will step into the role of Project Administrator, wherein she has one year to fulfill her late grandfather's dream of a self-sustaining, eco-friendly, family-centered utopia.

The stakes are real: fail, and lose access to the family fortune—forever.

Convinced Thalia Island will be an extension of the heiress lifestyle she's long led, Lara is surprised to find her new coworkers—and neighbors—aren't as pliable as the underlings of her former life. Even with the hunky lead engineer Finan Rowleigh showing her the ropes, Lara quickly learns just how unprepared she is to trade her Louboutins for Timberlands.

When a series of calamities reveals a sinister element undermining the security of the island and her residents, Lara and Finan must reach beyond their job descriptions to protect Archibald's precious utopia from those who would do her harm.

And while keeping her late grandfather's flame alight, Lara finds her own flame burning hot for a charming, kind man who wants nothing from her but her heart.

All three PLANET LARA books are coming SOON to AUDIOBOOK from Dreamscape Media!

MUST LOVE OTTERS, REVELATION COVE
BOOK ONE

Hollie Porter is the chairwoman of Generation Disillusioned. At twenty-five, she's saddled with a job she hates, a boyfriend who's all wrong for her, and a vexing inability to say no. She's already near her breaking point, so when one caller too many kicks the bucket during Hollie's 911 shift, she cashes in the Sweetheart's Spa & Stay gift certificate from her dad and heads to Revelation Cove, British Columbia.

One caveat: she's going solo.

Hollie hopes to find her beloved otters in the wilds of the Great White North, but instead she's providing comic relief for staff and guests alike. Even Concierge Ryan, a former NHL star with bad knees and broken dreams, can't stop her from stumbling from one (mis)adventure to another. Just when Hollie starts to think that a change of venue doesn't mean a change of circumstances, the island works its charm and she dares to believe rejuvenation is just around the bend.

But then an uninvited guest crashes the party, forcing her to step out of the discomfort zone where she dwells and save the day ... and maybe even herself in the process.

Available now for your choice of e-reader or in paperback. Audio available from Dreamscape Media!

HOLLIE PORTER BUILDS A RAFT, REVELATION COVE BOOK TWO

raft (noun): when two or more otters rest together, often holding hands, so they don't drift apart

Hollie Porter has put her old gig as a 911 operator and sad single girl in an attic-bound box, right where it belongs. She's rebounded nicely from her run-in with Chloe the Cougar in the wilds of British Columbia, and this new life alongside concierge-in-shining-armor Ryan Fielding? Way more fun. After relocating to Ryan's posh resort at Revelation Cove, Hollie embarks on an all-new adventure as the Cove's wildlife experience educator, teaching guests and their kids about otters and orca and cougars, oh my!

When darling Ryan gets down on one NHL-damaged knee and pops the question of a lifetime, Hollie realizes this is where the real adventure begins. It's all cake tasting, flower choosing, and dress fittings until a long-lost family member shows up at the Cove and threatens to hijack her shiny new life, forcing Hollie to redefine what family means to her. What is she willing to sacrifice to have one of her very own?

As Ryan's words echo in her head—"Our raft, our rules"—Hollie has to face facts: a raft isn't always tied together with blood and genetics. Sometimes it's secured by love and loyalty ... with occasional help from the clever creatures that call Revelation Cove home.

Available now for your choice of e-reader or in paperback.
Audiobook available from Dreamscape Media!

LOVE JUST CLICKS, REVELATION COVE
BOOK THREE (STANDALONE)

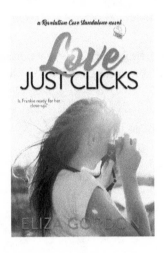

A new cover for 2021!

Frankie Hawes is happy to shrink into the background and play personal assistant to her superstar-photographer father and prodigy older brother. But when bad luck and bad timing collide, Frankie has to dust off her photography skills and head north to shoot the Meyer-Nelson wedding at the picturesque Revelation Cove in British Columbia.

It's one thing to take Instagram pics of neighborhood dogs, but unless an Alaskan malamute wanders into the bridal portraits, Frankie fears the worst. Enter wedding guest Sam McKenzie, childhood friend turned handsome bachelor, who brings with him the tricks he learned hanging around the Hawes family, including how to manage the abrasive bridezilla who happens to be an old bully from their shared past.

Reuniting with Sam helps Frankie see that her black-and-white existence on the sidelines has the potential to snap into high resolution—if only she'd allow it. As feelings grow between the pair and Frankie juggles the business during a family emergency, she realizes that maybe it's time for her to pull focus in her own life.

Love Just Clicks is a standalone romantic comedy, set in the Revelation Cove universe and featuring a few of your favorite characters from *Must Love Otters* and *Hollie Porter Builds a Raft*.

Available now for your choice of e-reader or in paperback. Audiobook available from Dreamscape Media!

I LOVE YOU, LUKE PIEWALKER

For fans of *Star Wars*, cosplay & geek culture, and delicious pastries!

If you find yourself talking to Jayne Dandy, limit the conversation to ducky collectibles and *Star Wars*. Best not to mention men, dating, or S-E-X. Jayne's fine with the way things are—writer of obituaries and garage sale ads by day, secret scribe of adventures in distant galaxies by night. But a crippling fear of intimacy has kept her love life on ice, and hiding behind her laptop isn't going to melt it anytime soon.

When her therapist recommends she write erotica as a form of exposure therapy, Jayne is hesitant—until she's unexpectedly downsized at work. Since rent and cat food won't pay for themselves, Jayne adopts an intergalactic pseudonym and secretly publishes her sexy stories to make ends meet. To help out, her adorable, longtime friend Luke, co-owner of the popular Portland food truck Luke Piewalker's, hires her to sling turnovers at his side.

Right on schedule, sparks ignite.

As Jayne's secret career soars, she has to juggle the unforeseen demands of her alter ego alongside her newfound feelings for Luke, threatening a tailspin that will either make her face down her neuroses or trigger a meltdown of Death Star proportions.

Formerly called *Neurotica*—same fun story with an updated look!

Available now for your choice of e-reader or in paperback.
Audiobook available from Blackstone Audio!

DEAR DWAYNE, WITH LOVE, FROM LAKE UNION PUBLISHING

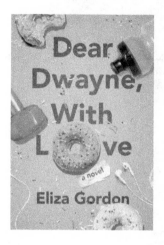

Dream big. Movie-star big.

Wannabe actress Dani Steele's résumé resembles a cautionary tale on how *not* to be famous. She's pushing thirty and stuck in a dead-end insurance job, and her relationship status is holding at uncommitted. With unbearably perfect sisters and a mother who won't let her forget it, Dani has two go-tos for consolation: maple scones and a blog in which she pours her heart out to her celebrity idol. He's the man her father never was, no boyfriend will ever be —and not so impossible a dream as one might think.

When Dani learns that he's planning a fund-raising event where the winning amateur athlete gets a walk-on in his new film, she decides to trade pastries and self-doubt for running shoes and a sexy British trainer with adorable knees.

But when Dani's plot takes an unexpected twist, she realizes that her happy ending might have to be improvised—and that proving herself to her idol isn't half as important as proving something to herself.

Available for Kindle and in paperback, as well as via Kindle Unlimited, Audible, and audio CD.

This is a work of fiction. While Dwayne Johnson p/k/a The Rock is a real person, events relating to him in the book are a product of the author's imagination. Mr. Johnson is not affiliated with this book, and has not endorsed it or participated in any manner in connection with this book.

Find the Eliza Gordon library at the following retailers, available in e-book, print, and audiobook*.

Links via elizagordon.com!

Amazon globally

Angus & Robertson

Apple Books

Barnes & Noble

Biblioteca

Bol.de

Chapters/Indigo

Google Play

Ingram

Kobo

Mondadori

Overdrive

Scribd

Thalia.de

24 Symbols

and more!

S·G·A
BOOKS

*Audio from Dreamscape Media, Blackstone Audio, and Lake Union/Amazon Publishing, *Planet Lara* audiobooks coming soon from Dreamscape Media!

Piracy hurts authors.

"FACT: $300 million [USD] is annually lost in author income due to pirated book sales."

~ https://bookriot.com/piracy-in-publishing/

And that's just the number for the United States!

<u>Very few</u> authors are wealthy. Most of us have day jobs. And yet, we all turn to books, music, TV, and movies to get us through.

Pretty please, with sugar on top,

Support authors.
Buy our books so we can write more for you!
Then give yourself a high five for being awesome.

Thank you!

S·G·A
BOOKS

9 781989 908068